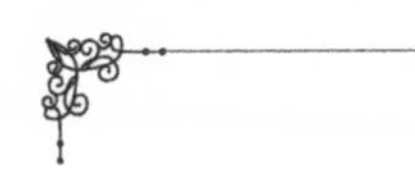

THE SPIRITED MRS. PRINGLE

Jillianne Hamilton is an author and history enthusiast. Her debut novel, *Molly Miranda: Thief for Hire*, was shortlisted for the 2016 Prince Edward Island Book Award. She lives in Charlottetown on Canada's beautiful east coast.

OTHER BOOKS BY THE AUTHOR

The Lazy Historian's Guide to the Wives of Henry VIII
Molly Miranda: Thief for Hire
Molly Miranda: Thick as Thieves
Molly Miranda: Honor Among Thieves

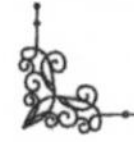

The Spirited Mrs. Pringle
By Jillianne Hamilton

www.Jilly.ca
www.LazyHistorian.com

ISBN: 978-1-7752560-4-5

Published in 2021 by Jillianne Hamilton and Tomfoolery Press.

Book and cover design by Jillianne Hamilton.

THE SPIRITED
MRS. PRINGLE
JILLIANNE
HAMILTON

TFP

ONE

Cora

Saturday, June 30, 1888

Perhaps I only imagined Mr. Rigby, or maybe he was a ghost all along. Either way, he has apparently disappeared.

I sipped my drink, my eyes darting to the door every time it opened. Beside me, Polly Foster was having her first glass of champagne.

"Papa would not approve," she repeated between timid sips. "He says women should not drink, that it leads to sin."

"Oh?" I tore my gaze from the door for a moment to look down at petite Polly. "And does he usually say this while enjoying a whiskey?"

Polly blinked up at me. "How did you know?"

"A lucky guess, my dear." I glanced away, disappointed to see some other gentleman let himself in.

I cursed myself silently for becoming obsessed with Mr. Rigby. From my seat at the theater, I had spent the entire time trying to casually scan the audience in search of his beautiful face.

The crowd swelled at intermission thanks to the horde of fallen women who purchased cheap tickets, making my hunt even more challenging.

My friend Mrs. Viola Lockhart, an acquaintance of Mr. Tom Lindsey, had kindly provided an invite to Mr. Lindsey's post-play gathering. Mr. Rigby said he would attend as well. So there I stood by the fireplace, desperately watching the door and waiting, my champagne glass already running dry.

It was most pathetic.

As I looked around the crowded house I wondered if there was a person in London *not* invited to Mr. Lindsey's home that night.

Viola spotted us and joined Polly and I by the fireplace, her husband, Dr. Lockhart, trailing after her.

"Dr. Lockhart, Mrs. Lockhart, you both look well tonight." Polly glanced down at her glass and back up to Dr. Lockhart. "Please do not tell my father I had champagne. Better still, if he asks, you did not even see me here tonight."

Dr. Lockhart grinned. "If Dr. Foster asks, I will tell him you were helping the sick, feeding the poor, and praying for all of our wretched souls."

Polly nodded enthusiastically, not realizing he was joking. "Yes, he will like that, thank you."

While Viola and Polly were engrossed in their gossip, Dr. Lockhart turned his attention to me, his easy smile spreading wide as he surveyed me from head to toe.

"You look well this evening." He paused. "You are always at the height of fashion. Do not tell Viola I said this, but she is a bit jealous of your exceptional taste." His eyes roamed over my curves a little too freely, despite his wife standing nearby.

Draped in layers of peacock blue and green silk, ruffles and ribbons, my dress that night *was* made just for the occasion, the colors chosen to complement my flaming red hair, milk white skin, and emerald eyes. But I certainly had not put the effort in for Hugh Lockhart, the imbecile.

"I will not tell her you said that," I replied.

Dr. Lockhart excused himself to speak to one of his chums and Polly and Viola sidled up to me. The door opened, and I quickly glanced at it. Viola caught my eye.

She pursed her lips at me. "Cora, who are you waiting for?"

"Nobody," I said quickly. "A friend."

Viola's eyes flickered with mischief. "Polly, I want to introduce you to some friends. They will just adore you."

Polly nodded at me and followed Viola obediently, looking back at me over her shoulder. Poor thing, like a lamb in a den of wolves.

The door opened and closed several times, but my Mr. Rigby had still not arrived. I cursed him for making me wait like this.

Mr. Lindsey, his cheeks red with drink, spotted me, beamed, and joined me at the fireplace.

"Good evening," he said with a bow. I feared his seams may give way under the action. "My mantle has never looked more stunning than it does with you standing near."

I smiled weakly. I had met Mr. Lindsey a few times before and excessive flattery seemed to seep from of his mouth at every opportunity.

"Your home is lovely," I replied. "You have exquisite taste."

His portly face widened as he smiled. "Thank you, my dear. It is so important to show your good taste in all things whenever possible." His gaze flitted across my chest. "I always make time for pretty things."

I fought the urge to wrinkle my nose. "Of course."

Mr. Lindsey sipped from his glass, clasping it within stubby fingers. "Did you enjoy the play this evening?"

"Oh, yes. It was a delight. I assume you had a hand in that?"

Mr. Lindsey, a theatrical investor of some renown within my social circle, gave a single nod. "I expect to see a healthy return from that production."

There was a flurry of activity when the door opened and Fannie Dixon, the play's lead actress, stepped inside. One of the most famous women in London, she was one of the few actresses in Britain that had managed to keep her stage career going for more than a decade and had the unique ability to perform dramatic parts as well as comedies.

An actress who can make someone cry and laugh—now that is true talent.

Mr. Lindsey, easily one of the tallest men in the room, raised his hand and waved her over to us. Despite the throng of guests trying to get close to her and their autograph books shoved in her direction, she flashed her perfect smile at them and squeezed her way through the crowd.

Miss Dixon, resplendent in a gown of rich red fabric, gave Mr. Lindsey a quick kiss on the cheek. "Mr. Lindsey, your small gatherings are never quite as small as you say they will be."

"They're all here to see you, my dear," he said. "How could I refuse your adoring fans?"

Adoring fans. I let the phrase roll around in my mind. *What would that be like?*

During this short exchange I watched from the corner of my eye as several attendees craned their necks to get another look at her, as if she might disappear at any moment before they were able to get their cursed autographs. Polly stared agog at me and then back at Miss Dixon from her perch on the staircase.

Miss Dixon smiled wide at me. "I just love your dress; it is stunning." She tilted her head slightly. "Do I know you from somewhere? Are you an actress?"

I introduced myself, pretending to act much calmer than I felt. "No, not an actress." *If only.* "Just a theatrical enthusiast," I clarified.

We *had* met briefly once before, right after she starred in a production of *The Taming of the Shrew*. Her dynamic portrayal of Kate had made me an instant admirer and I had joined the crowd in the lobby to get her autograph.

I was not about to tell *her* that though.

She smiled graciously. "Did you enjoy the play this evening?"

"It was fantastic," I said, possibly a little too quickly. "You were perfect in that role."

"Well, she certainly should be," Mr. Lindsey butt in. "It was written *for* her."

Holden Booker, one of the lead actors from the play, arrived and the autograph seekers bubbled up with excitement again, swarming the foyer and hallway.

Miss Dixon gave us a polite nod. "I should go before they swamp Holden, poor thing. Please excuse me."

As she waded back into the din, Mr. Lindsey's smile returned to me. "Oh, I suppose I should try to keep the guests in line before they devour the cast. Shall we speak again later?"

Before I could respond, he clutched my hand roughly and lifted it to his moist lips, kissing the top of it.

"Of course, Mr. Lindsey." I gave a quick nod, pulled my hand away, and watched as he waded through the crowd once more.

"Buffoon."

My heart jumped at the sound of his smooth, deep voice. I wanted to spin around and throw myself upon him, but I persuaded myself to maintain a coy distance, especially in front of so many people. Instead, I looked over my shoulder and up at him, my previous annoyance at his delay evaporating immediately.

"How do you know our gracious host, Mr. Rigby?"

His icy blue eyes sparkled as he looked at me and an air of amusement played on his full lips. I wanted nothing more than to taste those lips and touch my face to his cheek, letting his black whiskers tickle my skin.

"I am trying to persuade Mr. Lindsey to invest in my play," he said.

Turning fully to face him, I stepped closer.

"It is not yet finished, but I am confident in the bones of the story," he continued. "I'm still looking for the perfect ending." He folded his hands in front of his solid frame, leaning his back against the wall.

"I'm intrigued."

This wasn't the first I had heard of Everett Rigby's passion for playwriting. It was one of the first things he had told me about himself when we met during a play intermission a month before.

Mr. Rigby straightened his posture, slipped his hand under mine, and lifted my gloved fingers to his lips, letting his kiss linger for a moment.

"I am so happy to see you," he said quietly, leaning in closer to me.

He lowered my hand but only so he could entwine his fingers with mine, using the fullness of my skirts to hide our intimacy.

I gave a quick glance around to see if anyone was watching our inappropriate behavior. One couple I did not recognize hovered nearby, studying us curiously. Well, they were watching Everett at the very least, probably for one of three reasons: he was the only man of Indian descent at the party; he was incredibly handsome; or, perhaps, a combination of both.

I smiled sweetly at Mr. Rigby, my heart hammering in my chest and my breath short. "As am I."

Even though we had only met a few times, I had a fondness for Mr. Rigby I had never felt before. Our conversations were stimulating. and he made my pulse race with every touch. I risked my reputation by exchanging amorous notes with him. His letters were like a spectacular poetic salve for my spirit, a heavenly delicacy for my hungry heart.

Mr. Rigby gave my hand a squeeze. "Care to take a walk with me in the garden?"

I nodded and followed him through the house to the back door. No other party guests had discovered the private oasis, protected by vine-covered stone walls and a veil of darkness, the air thick with the exquisite perfume of peonies. The streetlights and the full moon illuminated the enchanting little green space, home to well-groomed flora and a koi pond. This little refuge was just dark enough to keep our identities hidden if anyone happened to look out a window or down from a balcony.

A marble statue of a goddess—Aphrodite, perhaps—watched over the garden, encouraging us in our tryst.

Mr. Rigby took me to the far end of the garden, still clasping my hand in his.

He looked at me for a long while and then lowered his eyes. "I feel as if I want to tell you so many things, but now that you are here the words escape me."

I positioned myself in front of him, my palms sliding up his chest to rest on his firm shoulders. "Let us not waste this moment with words, Mr. Rigby."

He kissed me then, sweetly and gently, and his soft lips teased mine with their tenderness. My heart unfolded like a shy rose in my chest, its petals unfurling as the warm summer sun hits them for the very first time.

He kissed me like a delicate thing, as if I might break. I melted into him, encouragingly, and shivers ran through me as his arms enveloped my waist, drawing me into him. He instantly became hungrier for me, his kiss speaking all of the words he could not find. I gripped his shoulders as his tongue met mine, lost entirely in our secret moment in shadow. We stumbled clumsily against the stone wall behind us as Mr. Rigby buried his face into my hair, trailing kisses down my jawline and neck. My breaths grew ragged, my chest heaved, and I held on tighter to him to combat the sudden lightheadedness.

How does he make me feel like this?

I pulled my lips from his and searched his eyes, wondering if he wanted me as much as I wanted him. I would have given anything to disappear into the night with him, find some secret place, and give him my everything. My body ached for his intimate touch.

Just then I heard the intoxicated giggling of another pair of lovers as they tripped down into the garden. This was soon followed by the familiar sounds of lips smacking against lips. They obviously had not seen us, but it was by luck alone.

Next time, we might not be so fortunate. My reputation is at stake.

I cupped Mr. Rigby's face in my hands and gave him a quick kiss.

"I must return to my friends before they grow worried

and send a search party," I whispered beside his ear, giving his earlobe a quick peck, followed by another on his cheek.

I adjusted my skirts and tucked a few stray curls back into place as Mr. Rigby cleared his throat and straightened his waistcoat and jacket. I smoothed some of his dark hair back into place. He smiled shyly at this gesture and took my hands again.

"When will I see you again?"

The pleading in his eyes made me want to weep.

"We will arrange something," I said. "I promise."

Instead of returning to the house with me, Mr. Rigby pulled himself onto the wall's upper ledge.

"Last chance to run away with me tonight." He stretched his hand out to me and arched an eyebrow up.

What if I just left with him? What if I just gave in?

If my heart had the final say, I would have let him pull me over the wall with him and we would have fled into the darkness of London, the glow of the oil lamps lighting the way to our new life together.

My head, in the end, won out.

"I cannot." My throat constricted around the words.

Mr. Rigby's face softened. "I know." He gave me a final wink and disappeared behind the garden wall.

I sighed and made my way back inside to rejoin Polly and Viola. For the short while I remained at the party everything was a slow blur of faces, laughter, liquor, and small talk.

"Are you feeling alright?" Polly's enormous and constantly concerned eyes blinked at me. "You have gone dreadfully quiet."

"I must have caught a chill when I was admiring Mr. Lindsey's garden," I said. "Perhaps I should retire for the night."

In the hansom cab home, I touched my fingers to my lips, willing Mr. Rigby's kiss to stay there as long as possible, or, at least, until his lips could wake my slumbering heart once again.

Marshall lowered his book—a tome on lung diseases, no doubt—just below his eye line as I passed the front parlor on my way upstairs. I had not expected him to be home when I arrived back. I intended to act as if I had not seen him, but he immediately thwarted that plan.

"It is late, Cora." His mouth remained hidden behind his book, but his cold, angry, and unblinking eyes bore into me.

"Yes. Apologies," I said quickly. "I completely lost track of time."

He sighed loudly and closed the book in his lap, resting his folded hands on top. "Why do you continue to believe this type of behavior is acceptable?"

I blinked at him, my mind chasing after the most believable lie. "Polly and Viola and I—"

"Were at a party, I know. Hugh mentioned it this morning." He waved his hand at me, his voice descending into a low grumble. "You lied to me about where you were going tonight and now you come home drunk—"

"I am *not* drunk," I said, my voice clipped. "When I asked if you minded if I went out tonight, you said no—"

Marshall rose, his book sliding off his lap and onto the floor. He stepped directly in front of me, towering over me—one of his favorite intimidation tactics that I had seen many, many times. "Do not dare raise your voice at me, Cora. I spent the evening here alone—"

I burst out laughing before he could finish. "Yes, I am certain you missed my company *terribly*," I blurted in between cackles. "Had I been home, we would have sat in silence while you read, or you would have excused yourself for the evening and left to…" I trailed off and gave him a look. "Well, whatever it is that you do in the evenings."

I had no proof he kept a mistress. Given his disinterest in physical intimacy, his lack of attentiveness, and his frequent disappearances, I wagered a mistress in a flat somewhere was likely a solid guess. That, and the unique aroma that clung to his clothes when he returned from those particular late-night escapades.

Marshall pressed hard on the spot between his brows,

rubbing it with two fingers; a telling sign of one of his oncoming headaches. He snatched his book off the floor and returned to his easy chair, flipping through the book's pages to find his place.

I started up the stairs.

"I looked at a flat in Covent Garden today," he said casually.

My hand stilled on the polished wooden railing. "What do you mean?"

He is buying a love nest for his mistress.

"I believe it is time for us to consider alternative living arrangements, Cora." He turned the page of his book, not bothering to look up at me.

I stared at him. "I do not understand."

"You are a hindrance to my happiness."

"A hindrance?" Angry thoughts and words batted around in my head at a dizzying speed. I stepped back down to the landing at the bottom of the stairs and slowly approached him. "What are you—"

"Our dispositions are too dissimilar and we do not complement one another. We never have." His gaze fell to my abdomen for a fraction of a moment before landing at the bit of carpet at my feet. "It is quite clear we are incapable of having children. Thus, there is no need for us to share a house any longer."

The skin on the back of my neck grew hot. "You want to evict me from our home because we cannot have children?"

"Evict is not the word I would use—"

"Do you not see how cruel that is—"

"Forgive me," he said. "I misspoke. *You* cannot have children, but I have proven myself capable."

Marshall was right; I suppose that was what made the remark especially cold. His first wife, the ghost he was still very much in love with, had died in childbirth with their son. It was clear to both of us our childlessness was my fault and mine alone. *I* was the broken one.

His tone continued to be humdrum and that made my

blood boil even more. "I believe we should live separately and find contentment that way." He paused. "Or we could consider divorce."

"We will do no such thing, Marshall," I snapped. "Divorce would ruin the both of us, not just me. Do you really think your patients would continue to call upon you if you went through with it?"

"My patients are not your concern," he spat, his volume raising. "Separating, one way or another, is the only sensible solution to our unfortunate situation."

I folded my arms across my chest. "Perhaps you should lock me in the attic or send me to a nunnery."

His eyes hardened and he rose from his chair again. "You are behaving like a child, as usual. I expected you to find the idea appealing or at least acceptable—"

"Really? You thought I would find abandonment *acceptable*?"

"Paying for you to live elsewhere is not abandonment." His jaw clenched around the sentence like it was a tough piece of meat between his teeth. "I would have thought you would rather write letters to your lover in the privacy of your own home, rather than under my roof." He stormed passed me, his shoes heavy on the staircase steps.

A wave of nausea pummeled my stomach, knocking the breath from my lungs. The sound of his bedroom door slamming upstairs was but a faint whisper, nearly smothered by the roaring in my ears.

TWO

Cora

Sunday, July 1, 1888

"Did you meet anyone interesting last night?" Viola asked Polly the next day as we sat at a table in our favorite tea room. "Preferably someone your father would never approve of."

I stifled a giggle behind my teacup.

Polly contemplated. "Well, I suppose that one fellow was quite nice. What was his name again? Andrew something?"

"Andrew Powell," Viola said with a flick of her dainty hand. "He is penniless, dear. Last year his father gambled away everything the family had." She rhymed off a short history of Mr. Powell's financial trouble. "Please do not look at me like that, Polly. I *do* feel bad for the man, but these things can not be helped."

"You *did* ask for someone her father would not approve of," I gently reminded Viola with a smile.

Viola looked back at Polly. "Who else did you meet last night?"

"Oh! I met Fannie Dixon, the actress," she exclaimed. "She is so beautiful and charming. I was so nervous to speak to her—"

"I meant eligible gentlemen, Polly." Viola threw me a glance and I immediately felt for poor Polly.

The three of us all enjoyed theater but Polly and I both followed the lives of actors and actresses, reading gossip periodicals religiously. Viola was quite content to attend plays while also having a low opinion of the performers on stage. Viola's husband and my husband were both doctors for London's social elite and Polly's father was one of the most respected doctors in the city, so becoming friends with both of them and bonding over our shared interest in theater brought at least a little sunshine into my life.

"Oh." Polly blushed, her fair skin around her jawline and ears turning pink. "Papa would never allow me to consider anyone that would attend a party like that. He would never let me leave the house again if he knew I was even there."

Viola sighed, giving up on our young and inexperienced friend. "What of your night, Cora? Did your mystery friend ever arrive?"

I felt my skin flush, my heart giving a little flutter at the memory of the previous evening. I couldn't stop thinking about his soft lips or how his arms felt as they wound around me. Every time I thought of our kiss, I thought my heart may burst.

"Yes," I said quietly. "He did."

Viola smiled knowingly behind her teacup while Polly blinked her immense eyes. "What friend?"

"My friend is just, um, just a friend from my childhood," I finally said after a moment's hesitation. I finished off my tea, trying to avoid Polly's curious gaze.

Polly, satisfied with that answer, turned the conversation swiftly back to Fannie Dixon but I wasn't listening, instead wandering back into the blissful thrill of the exchange in the garden.

Although Viola knew no details of my dalliance, I believe she suspected my wandering eye. She likely thought it was a playful distraction with a few meaningful looks and perhaps a love letter or two exchanged and nothing more. She had no idea that I was falling in love with Everett Rigby.

The love letters.

Marshall did not try to speak to me again the night before and I stayed in my room that morning until I knew for certain that he had left for the day. I was not ready to discuss my correspondence with Mr. Rigby *or* the idea of Marshall and I living separately.

My stomach churned as I thought about what Marshall might do. He had never raised a hand to me before but perhaps my behavior had finally gone too far. A cold shiver tickled my shoulders.

Something Polly said, in the midst of her prattling, caught my attention.

"I was so surprised to see Elaine at Maidenhill that I nearly fell off my chair," she said, gesticulating with her petite hand. "I couldn't believe my eyes—"

I cut in before she could continue on with her dull story. "Have either of you been asked for a reference from Maidenhill, about me?"

They glanced at one another.

"No, sorry," Viola said, avoiding my gaze.

Polly smiled. "I am sure your invitation will come any day, Cora."

How can that little simpleton look encouraging and *pitying at the same time?*

"Of course," I said quietly.

The Maidenhill Club had been snubbing me for over a year by not permitting me to join because, well, I was not sure.

I learned of the club from Viola and Polly—both of them members—shortly after becoming Mrs. Pringle and waited anxiously for my invitation. Many wives of doctors within our social circle were members so I fully expected an invitation. After several months of waiting, I wrote them to request membership, hoping they would appreciate my ambition and then offer me an apology as well as a place at their club. Being a member of the club meant that I was an important part of our social circle. I thought perhaps I could befriend a few of the other members, using my various charms and graces, and by doing so, increase Marshall's reputation as well. His own lack of charm and wit was certainly not going to win him any new patients.

After a year and a half of marriage, I had received neither a club invitation nor an apology.

I had the right friends and had married the right sort of gentleman, and yet they continued to ignore my application. A clear refusal of membership was at least a reply of some kind. The lack of any response whatsoever was abominably rude.

Unfortunately, it also made me want to be a member of their stupid club even more.

I suspected my membership was withheld because my late father was unknown within London society and, perhaps, because I had not been educated in London. Apparently growing up just outside London meant I was some kind of cad and undeserving of their respect.

Viola added casually, avoiding meeting my eyes as she spoke, "You could perhaps write to The Cottingham Society and see if they are accepting new members."

Polly's eyes widened slightly at the suggestion. My jaw clicked audibly as it clenched.

The Cottingham Society was a social club for middle class women who could not afford the membership fees of Maidenhill and did not have the same social connections as Viola, Polly, and I. Cottingham was a favorite haunt for scholars, writers, and suffragists. Working women.

The comment was most certainly meant as a casual insult.

"What a silly suggestion, Viola." I let out a little laugh. "What on earth would make you say such a thing? I do not know any members of that club and I have no idea what I would have in common with those ladies."

Viola sipped her tea. "It was just a suggestion."

Polly, bobbing up and down slightly, held her nearly empty

teacup out in front of her. "I've finished my tea. Do mine first."

I held her cup in my palm and moved my arm in a circular motion to swish the contents of the cup around before inspecting the inside of it carefully. The remnants of the tea speckled the bottom of the white porcelain in various shapes and I rotated it in search of symbols.

"I think you are to travel soon," I said, angling the cup further away from me so Polly could see. I pointed at the two prominent dark brown shapes along one edge. "See, that means travel."

Polly blinked at me, snatching the cup away so she could look at it closer. "Cora, that is incredible! I hadn't told you I am traveling to Brighton to visit my aunt next month."

"You did not have to tell me," I said, a satisfied smugness in my voice. "The tea did it for you." I turned to Viola. "And you?"

With a quick eye roll, she passed her cup to me and I repeated the circular motions before studying how the tea formed inside. The tea leaves had collected into three solid perpendicular lines at the bottom of the cup.

"Hmm," I said. "A change is coming."

Viola raised a skeptical eyebrow. "Is that so?"

I pointed. "These three lines mean something in your life is about to change—"

"What kind of change?" Polly's wide-eyed stare was earnest enough to make me feel for the poor, naïve girl.

I slid the cup onto its saucer on the table. "I cannot say for certain."

Viola pointed to my cup. "What about yours?" She snatched it up before I could and moved her wrist back and forth before peering inside. "Oh, yes," she said, using a dramatic tone, "mmm, yes. This eye symbol means you will see something silly in a cup and make it seem like it has meaning or says something about the future. How *fascinating*."

I laughed and plucked the cup away, studying the tea myself. "Viola, you have many gifts but reading tea is not one of them." I slid the cup onto the table with its saucer, a slightly worried feeling creeping up on me.

The "eyeball" symbol Viola had seen usually means a new beginning. I could not guess what that meant for me. Not that she did the circular motions properly anyway. Still. It made me uneasy.

"Excuse me, miss," a middle-aged woman from a nearby table said. "We could not help but notice you telling fortunes." Her companion smiled eagerly. "Would you mind…?" She raised her cup.

I flashed them a wide, toothy grin. "Of course!"

I had only been home for a few minutes when a visitor knocked at the door. I heard Louise open it, surprise in her voice.

"Oh, good afternoon constable," she said, catching my attention from the nearby parlor. "How can I help you, sir?"

I rose from the little desk and joined Louise in the foyer. The police constable looked very grave, his eyebrows pinched together, his mouth a straight line across his face.

"Good afternoon, ma'am. I'm Constable Fletcher of Scotland Yard. Are you Mrs. Pringle, the wife of Dr. Marshall Pringle?"

"I am." I raised an eyebrow at him. "Please, do come in." Louise closed the door behind him.

"Thank you, ma'am." The constable removed his helmet, tucking it under his arm and following me into the parlor. "I think you ought to sit down, Mrs. Pringle."

I stared at the stout man for a moment. There was only one reason a constable from Scotland Yard would visit my house and make such a suggestion.

My stomach dropped, and my mouth suddenly felt quite dry.

"What has happened?" I did not sit. There was no point.

Constable Fletcher winced. He swallowed before he spoke. "Dr. Pringle has died, ma'am."

I looked at Louise. Her lower lip trembled. An unexpected ache formed in my throat.

"I see," I said, my voice catching on the words. "How did it happen?"

His mistress. She has gone and murdered him.

"The incident is still under investigation, but the coroner believes he had a heart attack late last night, likely due to an overindulgence of—" he lowered his voice, "—opium."

"Opium," I repeated louder, combined with a startled laugh. "My husband doesn't use opium!"

The constable averted his gaze to the left suddenly, his lips tightening a little.

I squared my shoulders. "My husband, a highly respected physician, specializing in diseases of the *lungs*, does not use opium. He doesn't even smoke."

I was met with pitying looks.

"Did not," I corrected myself.

"I know this must be a shock for you—"

"Of course it is, you half-wit! I am saying there must be some mistake because my husband..." I trailed off as I caught Louise wincing. I sighed at her. "Did he?"

She lowered her eyes. "Yes, ma'am. I think it is why he suffered from headaches so often."

So it was not a mistress after all that kept him out so late.

I slowly returned my gaze to Constable Fletcher. "My apologies." I finally decided to sit as this information settled in my mind. "Was he at an—" I closed my eyes, disgusted the words were leaving my mouth, "—opium den when it happened?"

"He had just left the establishment, ma'am. Right outside their door, I believe."

"I am sure that will do wonders for the reputation of their business," I said quietly. "Did someone identify him? Are you quite sure it is Dr. Pringle you found?"

"Yes, ma'am," he said. "The owner of the establishment knew him on sight."

I was surprised to feel a tear sliding down my cheek. I had not even noticed it forming before it fell.

Constable Fletcher and I spoke for a few more minutes. As soon as he left and Louise had closed the door behind him, she let out a quiet sob before clamping her mouth closed again, desperate to hide her grief from me, the freshly baked widow who had only shed a single tear.

"I can fend for myself for a while if you require some time," I said on my way upstairs.

"Would you like—"

"Louise."

She gave a quick curtsy and disappeared. Her grief was genuine, I realized, having served in his house for over ten years. I took no issue with a servant displaying grief. I just wished I felt half as sad as she looked.

I continued up the stairs, stopping to peer into the bedroom Marshall and I had occasionally shared. I stepped inside and slowly approached the bed where our failed attempts at conceiving had taken place. I slid onto what was sometimes my side of the bed, the pillow still firm as if it were brand new.

He had been a good doctor, I had to admit. He dressed well and was the tall, dark, and handsome type that I had read about in novels as a young woman. When he came to our home in Molesey to see if anything could be done about my father's consumption, Marshall seemed like he actually cared as he gave Aunt Charlotte and I the unfortunate news.

I immediately saw the next year of my life laid out before me: Charlotte and I taking turns nursing my father as he wasted away. I couldn't take it.

I recalled the moment when I made the decision that would alter the trajectory of my life.

"Thank you for your kindness, doctor," I said as Marshall packed up his medical bag and slid his arms into his coat. "I just wish my father had let us summon a specialist sooner."

He had been round a few times at that point, trying various treatments and then seeing if any of them took.

"Please forgive me for not being able to do anything for him," he said, his voice low and serious. "I am very sorry for it. The most we can do now is make him comfortable." He slowly moved his eyes up my neck and looked

at me for a long moment just then, very much like the time our eyes had met over the table when he stayed for dinner the month before.

"It is not your fault," I said softly. "However, I know of something that would perhaps help heal my broken heart."

Marshall's brows knit together, and he set his shoulders back a bit.

"I would very much like to write to you." I feigned shyness and lowered my eyes. "You likely think me a very forward young woman to wish such a thing."

"Yes, Miss Green, it is forward." He studied me for a moment. "But I will gladly write to you."

When we married two months later, I was happy to be a bride but just as relieved to escape my father's bedside.

I rolled over on my side, half expecting to see the shape of Marshall on the bed beside me, his wakeful spirit angry to catch me back in this room after I failed him time and time again.

"I cannot disappoint you anymore," I said out loud, but quietly, a sob stifling my words, "and you can no longer disappoint me."

THREE

Amelia

Wednesday, July 4, 1888

"My beloved, you look divine." Simon, for the second time that day, kissed my cheek. "Wedding dresses suit you."

I smirked. "Oh? Perhaps I shall wear one more often."

He stuck his chin out defiantly. "The lady jests at the sanctimony of marriage. I will not stand for such disrespect."

I tightened my lips, my chest quivering with laughter. Not that my chest could do much quivering anyway, what with the tightness of my corset under layers of ivory lace and silk and faux flowers and who knows what else. I would have married in my best sensible dress if Mama had not insisted on me being the height of fashion on my wedding day. My torso felt so confined while the skirt was extra voluminous, creating an extreme hourglass.

I absolutely cannot wait to get this dress off and go to sleep after this day is done.

"But I am quite serious when I say, wife, that you look

beautiful today." Simon's eyes were warm and genuine.

"And you, husband, have obviously been dipping into your flask," I teased.

Looking around the garden where our family, friends, and other guests mingled, I noticed many of them were strangers to me. Business associates of our families, no doubt.

I found myself watching pretty little Beth Baxter. Nobody knew quite what to say to the girl, so she stood off to the side by herself, alone with her punch. Nineteen at the most, she kept tugging at a bit of draped fabric on her gown, smoothing it out incessantly. I watched the tiny young woman glancing around nervously and then fussing with the fabric around her middle a bit more. She must have felt me watching her—our eyes met and we both gave an uncomfortable smile and an awkward little wave from our places across the green.

I gave Simon a little nudge with my elbow and leaned closer to him.

"I think your new stepmother might be expecting."

Simon frowned. "Expecting *what*?"

"The crown jewels to be delivered to her at any second." I gave him a look. "A baby, obviously."

He ran a hand through his thick blond waves. "Surely not. She and Papa married only a few weeks ago."

"Yes, well, perhaps the marriage came after the—"

"Do *not* finish that sentence, Amelia, I beg you."

I hid my giggles behind my gloved hand. "Yes, sweetheart, as you wish. Oh, dear. She's coming over."

Simon scoffed under his breath before plastering a wide smile across his fine face. He opened his mouth to speak but Beth beat him to it.

"Amelia, you are such a vision of beauty and you could not have picked a finer day for a wedding," she exclaimed, clutching my hand. "I am so jealous. It poured down rain on my wedding day."

"Did it? I thought it only snowed in Canada," Simon teased.

"Not in June, silly," Beth said before wincing slightly. "Well, not usually anyway."

Her Canadian accent seemed so alien to my ears. Despite having lived in London my entire life and hearing all types of accents on a regular basis, Beth's accent was one I did not come across often.

"So kind of you to come all this way for our wedding," I chimed in. "I hope the voyage was not *too* dreadful."

Beth, a fair-skinned, fair-haired wisp of a woman, smiled nervously, folding her doll-like hands together in front of her. "It felt quite long. I have never been so happy to walk on solid ground."

I imagined the poor girl, dealing with seasickness and morning sickness simultaneously.

"I hope you and Joseph are able to stay in London a while before returning to Canada," I added. "Seems a shame to travel all this way only to stay a short time."

A slightly sad expression flashed over her face, her large blue eyes looking away from mine. "I believe I am to stay here while he goes back to Canada."

Simon and I exchanged worried glances.

"Surely not," he said. "A newly married couple should not live separately for such a long span of time."

"He is always so busy with the business," Beth said in her mousey voice. She had a look about her that made me think she might cry at any moment. I wondered if that was permanent. "He mentioned that he would like me to live with…" Her eyes darted to the mass of people in the garden. "Oh no. I have forgotten. I have met so many people today and I cannot remember which are Baxters and which are Spencers."

I laughed. "There is essentially no difference between the Baxters and the Spencers. We are all basically one family, so not to worry."

It was true. Since combining skill sets as young men, Joseph Baxter and George Spencer built their business together, first on Britain's railroad, then in America before moving to Canada.

Back home in London their children grew up and were educated together. The Baxter-Spencers had already seen two separate marriages take place within the family. My wedding to Simon was the third of its kind, continuing the family tradition of strengthening the bond between the two clans.

God help us all if Joseph and my father ever had a quarrel and decided to break their partnership. It would make for entirely uncomfortable family gatherings.

Simon's father taking a Canadian bride surprised us all. We always knew he would remarry eventually but choosing a woman young enough to be his daughter gave us all a bit of a shock. However, her obvious fidgeting with the front of her dress clarified a few things.

"I believe Joseph said he wished me to stay with…" Beth pursed her lips as she struggled to remember "Ida? Eva?"

"Ivy?" I suggested.

Beth looked relieved. "Yes, that's the one."

I nodded and pointed to the elegant woman in blue. "That is Ivy Spencer, my mother. She would certainly be a gracious hostess to you, as long as you do not have a mind of your own."

Beth blinked at me, wide-eyed. Simon cleared his throat, warning me.

"I am only joking. It will be fine."

From across the garden, Joseph beckoned his young bride. She made her apologies and returned to his side.

I heaved a sighed. "That lonely young woman is going to be visiting us often, isn't she?"

"Almost certainly."

"Perfect." I looked up at him. "Do you have any—"

Simon handed me the little silver flask before I could even finish the question.

I was exhausted by the time Simon and I arrived at our new home that afternoon. A little smaller than the house I had grown up in but more than enough room for the two of us, Simon had moved in a few weeks before the wedding to get it set up just right for us. He took it upon himself to pick the decor as I never cared for choosing such things and simply did not have the knack for it.

Simon gestured to a young woman in an apron and cap soon after we crossed the threshold. "This is Matilda, the housekeeper."

In the midst of the day's excitement, I had forgotten about having a new housekeeper. A new husband, a new last name, a new home, and now a different housekeeper than the one I had grown up knowing. Fatigue washed over me and all I could manage was a weak, weary smile.

"Lovely to meet you."

"Good afternoon, ma'am," she said in a charming Scottish accent.

Simon beamed, clasping my hands in his. "I have a surprise for you." He led me to a door behind the front staircase and stood beside it. He nodded at it. "Open it."

I turned the polished doorknob and pushed the door in and inhaled sharply.

"Oh, Simon!" I grabbed his hand and kissed the top of his knuckles, squeezing his fingers tight within mine. "It is wonderful!"

I stepped into the little room so carefully, as if heavy steps could shatter the dream I might be in. It was a private study, one wall lined with bookcases right up to the ceiling and one wall lined with windows. A desk, grand but not ostentatiously so, stood proudly in the middle of the room, a sparkling black typewriter placed in the center. I gasped when I saw it.

"Oh, Simon, no. You shouldn't have. It's too much!" I delicately ran my fingers over the white glossy keys, practically salivating at the thought of breaking in that divine hardware.

Simon flopped down on the sofa that lined the third wall, stretching out and propping his feet up on the round sofa arm. I had a feeling he picked out the sofa mostly for his own use as he had a habit of falling asleep while waiting for me to finish writing.

I shook my head at him, feeling as if I might cry—not a

common occurrence. "We can certainly not afford all this."

"I called in some favors and traded a few things but yes, dear, we will be living on bread and water for a year because I knew you would like it." He gestured to the desk. "Sit down, will you? I want to see my queen at her throne."

I slid my finger along the shiny desktop as I moved around it, pulling my skirts in closer to myself so I could actually fit in the chair at its place of honor behind the desk. I grinned at Simon. I did indeed feel incredibly powerful.

"Not bad," I said.

Simon laughed.

"Really, Simon. You know me. You know you didn't have to do this for me—"

"Oh, I know. But I wanted to." He lowered his eyes, his face turning serious for a moment. "You did such a kindness for me today." He hopped up from his lounging spot and leaned over the desk, cupping my face in his hands. "Your friendship means the world to me. Your sacrifice—"

"It was not a sacrifice, Simon, I told you—"

"I know, I know." He sighed and propped his pointed elbows on the desktop. "I fear you will meet someone and want to marry them, and I will be in the way and you will resent me for it."

"Despite this ridiculous dress, a marriage—a real one—is not for me. I have no desire to be with anyone in that way. Marrying you was no sacrifice. Today saved us both from familial expectations that neither of us could ever meet. How many people are fortunate enough to get to marry their dearest friend?"

Simon sniffled and wiped a tear from his eye. "Not many, I suppose."

"Exactly."

He stood up straight and adjusted his waistcoat, smiling weakly at me. He beamed suddenly. "Heavens! I just remembered we were given some very good wine as a wedding gift. Why on earth are we not drinking it at this very moment?"

"Can I please change out of this dress first? I may genuinely pass out if I need to wear it for another moment."

I followed Simon out of the study, but he paused to gesture back to the typewriter. "Oh, Amelia," he said, "you had better get to writing today because this room isn't going to pay for itself."

FOUR

Cora

Friday, July 6, 1888

Mr. Rigby sipped his tea, peering at me over his cup. "How was the funeral?"

That was genuinely the last thing I wanted to think or speak of. It had all been so taxing and, well, somber. The previous few days had been a blur of preparations and sympathy cards. Consolatory notes flooded in from friends, minor acquaintances, and people I did not even know. It shocked me how saddened many of his regular patients were to hear of Marshall's death. Perhaps he was kinder to them than he had been to his own wife.

"I suppose all went as planned," I said. "I am just grateful his horrible family is in Liverpool and could not attend."

"Did any members of your family attend?"

"I have no family left on this side of the Atlantic."

Since the weather was fine, Everett and I took tea in the garden behind my home, a small but lovely little spot. Nothing like Mr. Lindsey's extravagant garden, of course, with its fountain and seclusion. I had already spotted Louise spying on us from the windows that overlooked our little salon for two.

Apparently, she had not believed me when I told her Mr. Rigby, a man of Indian descent, was a cousin of mine.

"I forgot to tell you about the last conversation I shared with my husband," I said, lifting my teacup. "Our final moments together were unfortunately unpleasant. We quarreled and then…" I winced. "Well, he somehow knew you and I write to one another."

Mr. Rigby's eyebrows went up. "Oh."

I sipped. "I guess it does not matter now. I mean, it's not like you two knew one another anyway."

"Indeed." His brows knit together. "Was he terribly angry?"

"Not particularly. I genuinely think he just wished to shock me into silence." I paused. "In that, at least, he was successful." Setting my tea down, I caught sight of my black sleeve and frowned at it. "Expecting widows to dress in black is cruel. Losing one's husband is difficult as it is without having them dress in a color that does not suit them."

"I never understood that custom," Mr. Rigby said, leaning back in his chair a little. "The length of the mourning period is absurd as well."

I barely knew *Marshall for two years and now I am expected to grieve the loss of him for two years. While wearing black. Ridiculous.*

"If I am to marry again, I shall need to do it while I am still young. I agree, two years will not do."

He paused. "How long *would* you wait?" He lowered his eyes for a moment before looking back up to me. "If there were, say, someone who loved you and wanted to marry you, would you still wait?"

My heart quickened. I knew what he meant. I just had not expected his directness. Instead of finding his haste improper, it thrilled me.

I lowered my gaze again. "I do not know." Tilting my chin up slightly, I regained some composure. "I suppose it depends if I received an offer tempting enough to risk damaging my reputation."

My comment was rewarded with a deliciously mischievous smile.

Mr. Rigby continued. "What would make the offer impossible to decline?"

You. Ask me. Ask me now. Do it, you fool. Just ask me and I will marry you today. We will leave London and go to America where no one will know us, and it will not matter that I went from wife to widow to wife in a week.

"Hard to say." I rested my hand beside my teacup and ran a fingertip over the etched flower design on the porcelain. "It would have to be a man of exceptional character." I brushed my pinky against his for a moment before picking up my tea again. "Why, do you know of anyone?"

Mr. Rigby's eyes lingered on my lips. When he eventually pulled his gaze north to my eyes, his jaw tightened. "Did you love your husband?"

"I beg your pardon." I sat up straighter.

"It is a simple question."

"It is a very inappropriate question."

"As opposed to the rest of this entire conversation?"

I glared at him. "Please do not make me say it."

Mr. Rigby hesitated and nodded, his lips a tight straight line. "Drink your tea if it was a marriage of convenience."

I sipped.

He seemed satisfied with this. I watched as he considered, and I thought for a moment that he might actually propose just then. Instead, he stood up and faced the garden wall. He sighed and lowered his head.

"Cora, I—"

"Mrs. Pringle," Louise said, appearing in the doorway nearby, "that police constable is back. He's got Mr. Jennings with him. I told them you were unavailable, but he said it's important he speaks with you immediately."

Louise shot Mr. Rigby with a vile look.

"Mr. Jennings?" I repeated. "How very odd."

Mr. Rigby folded his hands in front of himself. "I have an appointment shortly I must attend to anyway."

"Louise, please take Constable Fletcher and Mr. Jennings to the parlor. I will join them presently." I stood, sliding my teacup onto the small table.

After Louise disappeared back into the house, I stood in front of Mr. Rigby. "I wish you did not have to go." I slipped my hand into his, giving his fingers a gentle squeeze. "Our visits are never long enough."

He smiled shyly and lifted my hand to his lips, laying a tender kiss upon it. "Until next time, my darling."

I saw him to the door before joining the constable and Mr. Jennings. Mr. Jennings, a stout balding man with tiny round spectacles, had been Marshall's lawyer for many years. I could not comprehend why he was in my parlor, why the constable was back, or why they had come to see me together.

"That was my cousin who travelled to London for the funeral," I said as I sat on the chaise, even though neither of them had asked who I was with.

Mr. Jennings nodded solemnly. "My condolences, Mrs. Pringle. Such a tragedy to lose a husband so young, especially a man so brilliant. I hope you are taking care during this difficult time."

"Thank you," I said.

"I remember when my sister lost her husband," he continued. "He was a younger man, too. She was devastated for months. Rarely left her bed some days. Took to weeping in the middle of conversations completely unrelated to him. We all worried—"

"Mrs. Pringle, there are a few developments into the investigation into your husband's death," Constable Fletcher said, kindly interrupting Mr. Jennings.

"Investigation?" I looked at Mr. Jennings and then back to him. "I was told it was a simple heart attack."

"It was," the police constable said. "But we believe it was brought on by physical and emotional, uh, stress."

"What do you mean?"

"As you know, Mrs. Pringle," Mr. Jennings said, "there was a delay in getting your husband's will prepared for reading. A few numbers didn't add up just right. It would appear that Dr. Pringle was, well, in a bit of a tight financial situation."

"That is not possible." I gestured dismissively with my gloved hand, shooing the outrageous statement away.

Constable Fletcher gave a half nod. "It's true, ma'am. It would appear he required funds and went to … an unwholesome crowd for a loan."

My mouth dropped open slightly and just hung there for a moment, my eyebrows raised high.

"He was overdue on a loan payment and someone was sent to give him a bit of a scare," Fletcher continued. "The man who threatened your husband outside of the opium den has been apprehended after a witness came forward to identify him—"

"This is the most preposterous thing I have ever heard in my life," I said with a laugh. "How could Marshall ever be desperate for money? His clients were all socialites—"

"You would be shocked at how many socialites are deep in debt themselves, my dear," Mr. Jennings said, his eyes looking tired. "Addictions to gambling and excess tend to drain accounts. It would seem your husband was a very good doctor but took far too many IOUs and I am afraid it got the man into some trouble. I imagine he had a lot of expenses to cover and simply not enough income to cover them."

"Like what?" I exclaimed. "The doctor and I lived within our means."

The two men frowned at me simultaneously.

"Dr. Pringle did tell me you were an admirer of the finer things," Mr. Jennings said, nearly mumbling.

"Oh, so it's *my* fault Dr. Pringle was literally scared to death? Perhaps if he was a better businessman or-or-or perhaps if he wasn't spending so much money on opium every night," I snapped. "Don't you *dare* suggest such a horrible thing to a *widow*, especially when it sounds like it was nobody's fault but his own." I spoke the words before I could stop myself. I quivered my lip a little and dabbed at the corner of my eye for added effect, squeezing out a tear on cue.

Mr. Jennings' eyes fell to his lap. "My apologies, Mrs. Pringle. I meant no offense."

"The gentleman your husband owed money to," the constable went on, "he's known to Scotland Yard. He's a shady fellow but always has his men do his dirty work for him. It would appear our hands are tied when it comes to the money owed to him. The deal was solid."

"I understand," I said bravely, adding a faint crack to my words. "I will pawn some of the jewels Dr. Pringle gave me and it will all be taken care of."

Constable Fletcher and Mr. Jennings exchanged looks.

"Mrs. Pringle," Mr. Jennings said, still not meeting my gaze, "I'm afraid it's a bit more dire than that."

He has destroyed me. This is all his fault. Even in death, he has achieved his goal of making me miserable.

"We can offset most of the debt by selling all of the furniture with the house," Mr. Jennings had said minutes after breaking the news, reading casually off a list. "Your housekeeper and cook will have to go I'm afraid. Do you know if your husband ever kept a safe of some kind? Or maybe he had investments I might not know about?"

"I-I-I don't know—"

"I recommend you do an inventory of your jewelry, gowns, and other valuables you can part with and get an estimate of their value," he continued. "Do you have any relatives who could repay some of the debt?"

I just blinked at him, my throat aching. "No." I closed my eyes to stop the room from spinning.

"Do you have any family you can stay with once the house is sold?"

Tears ran down my cheeks and slipped off my chin. "You

know I do not, Mr. Jennings." I broke into a sob I had been trying to suffocate. "What shall I do?"

Mr. Jennings, a man of numbers and business, was only married to his work and had no idea how to deal with a bankrupt widow. He looked at me, horrified, and gave my hand two quick pats.

"There, there," he mumbled. "Don't you have an aunt? Perhaps she could take you in."

I glared at him, wiping at my face. "No. She died."

"Ah." Mr. Jennings returned to his list.

Aunt Charlotte was—as far as I knew—still very much alive. The only mother figure I had ever known had left for America shortly after my father died and not a letter had passed between us. An uncomfortable tension was very much still thriving when we said our goodbyes. Aunt Charlotte and America were my last resort.

"What about Dr. Pringle's family in Liverpool?" He handed me his handkerchief.

I bristled. "They despise me."

I had once found a letter from Marshall's snobbish sister in which she referred to me as a "common tuft-hunter," suggesting a venereal disease had caused my barrenness. So, no, I would not be seeking the Pringles out for shelter.

Mr. Jennings gave it another try. "Do you have any friends here who would take you in?"

Polly was the first friend to come to mind but I doubted her father—the miserly old grump—would ever agree to support me. I considered asking Viola for help but quickly remembered the way her husband Dr. Lockhart looked at me at every occasion we met. It seemed unkind of me to invite myself into their home and put unnecessary stress on their marriage.

"Unlikely."

Mr. Jennings paused for a long while. He closed his eyes, removed his spectacles and rubbed his forehead. "It seems to me Liverpool may be your best option."

"What if … I remarried?"

Mr. Jennings cocked his head. "Remarried? Mrs. Pringle, your husband is not yet cold in his grave."

"My situation is dire." I clutched the handkerchief tighter. "A woman has few options in this world. If a kind man would take me into his heart and home and under his protection, why shouldn't I accept his offer?"

"*Accept his offer?* Has someone proposed to you? So soon?"

I hesitated. "It was hypothetical."

Mr. Jennings' mouth twisted into a deep, tight frown as one eyebrow went up. "I'm afraid your situation is anything but hypothetical. I recommend that you write to Dr. Pringle's family and explain your circumstances." He slid his spectacles back on. "Maybe leave the bit about the opium den and the brutes out of your letter."

"Mrs. Pringle?"

Snapping out of my trance, I dropped my spoon into my soup, sending warm broth sloshing over the sides of the bowl. I was not even sure how long I had been staring in deep thought.

"My apologies, ma'am, I didn't mean to startle you," Louise said. "Are you quite well, ma'am?"

Not at all.

"I am fine. Please do not be concerned." I sat back in my seat. "I am afraid I have no appetite this evening."

"Shall I get Cook to prepare something else, ma'am?"

I winced. *Cook. Louise. They will need to be told tomorrow morning.*

"No. Thank you, Louise." I slid my chair out and wandered out of the dining room. "I believe I am just tired."

Louise found me in my bedroom a few minutes later, struggling to untie the ribbons of my corset.

"Ma'am, let me help you—"

"No," I snapped, backing away. "I need to … I wanted to see if I could do it myself."

"Of course, ma'am." She gave a short nod and left me to it,

her pinched expression dripping with concerned confusion.

Louise and Cook will be gossiping about how their mistress has gone mad at the loss of her husband. No, not her husband. Just all of his money.

I stared at my reflection in my dressing table mirror, my chest heaving, every single word Mr. Jennings had said running rampant through my mind. Snatching my comb off the table, I turned away from the mirror and looked at my back in the mirror. Maneuvering my wrist just so, I slipped the comb into the loop of my corset ribbon and pulled it free. I loosened the rest of the ribbons the same way before I was able to wriggle out of it.

I let it fall to the floor and smiled, triumphant.

I will figure this out. I have to.

Dearest Cora,

I was surprised to hear from you so soon after the funeral. I am sorry I did not get a chance to speak with you for longer at the service. Dr. Pringle was a great man and cherished within London's medical community. Papa was simply devastated to hear of his passing. I am beside myself with concern for your unfortunate financial situation. Our prayers and thoughts are with you in this time of horrendous loss.

You must know that despite our deepest desire to assist you, we are unable to invite you to stay with us at present. Papa says our home is full as it is and we simply cannot make room. Although I am not quite sure what he means since we have three unused guest bedrooms. However, he says he expects you will be back in a better position in no time at all. He is so clever about these things you know.

My sincerest apologies, Cora. You know I would have you live with us in a minute if it were up to me. If there is anything else I can do, please do not hesitate to let me know. I am sure I can be of some use in another way.

Would you like to come for tea next week? We can discuss further any time you like and are available.

Your loving friend,
Polly

Dear Cora,

Unfortunately we are unable to offer you a home at this time. Hugh's vile sister and her three repellent children stay with us so often that we cannot give up the guest room.

Please forgive me for not being able to attend the funeral as I was ill. Hugh says the service was well done.

Sincerely,
Viola

FIVE

Amelia

Thursday, July 12, 1888

How do two people so different end up seemingly happily married?

This question came to mind nearly every time I found myself in the company of Mrs. Esther Granville. Having no brothers to carry on the family printing business, Esther had managed her father's pride and joy—a newspaper, pamphlet and catalogue printing operation on Fleet Street—since his death ten years before and it had thrived under her direction.

She was an extraordinary woman, a brilliant businesswoman, and I admired her immensely. Well, mostly. My esteem for her diminished slightly when I recalled that she settled for the curmudgeonly editor at *The Gazette Weekly*, my boss. The two had a fondness for words and one another and that had been enough to sustain their marriage. Although Mr. Granville's views were more conservative than Esther's, his admiration for his wife's ambition and business savvy never faltered.

I imagined my marriage to Simon would likely be similar,

except we would not, obviously, have children together.

"A woman *can* have children *and* a career outside the home. It's not only possible but I believe it is the future," Esther said, speaking passionately to the audience in the room, some of them watching more attentively than others. "We must petition the government to create some kind of social program that allows women to work outside of the home while also being mothers. Having reliable childcare is a *must* if women and men are ever to reach parity in this world." Esther's wide, serious eyes softened and she gave a slight nod. "Thank you."

The room of women, all of us members of The League for the Advancement and Enrichment of Women, applauded, myself clapping more enthusiastically than many. A few of the ladies in the row in front of me exchanged looks with one another, their eyebrows cocked.

I knew that look; I had seen it before from many of the L.A.E.W. ladies. Esther and I had both been criticized several times for having ideas too progressive for even these women.

If you cannot suggest ideas for radical change at a women's suffrage society, where *can* you?

Just imagine the look on their faces if Esther had brought up her opinions on birth control.

After Esther spoke, Mrs. Kent rose to address the room. "Good evening, ladies. I know this is an unorthodox request but I was wondering if we might take up a collection for a friend of mine. She used to be a member of this very society. Do any of you remember Mrs. Morton?"

Several women nodded.

"Well, as many of you may know, she lost her husband last year and has since fallen on hard times. She is moving in with her son soon but could use a little bit of charity until then."

Mrs. Carrigan, the club's founder and president, nodded in approval. "Mrs. Morton is such a kind woman and would do all she could for any of us. I am sure we can gather something together."

We broke for refreshments and Esther sidled up to me while

I was surveying the sandwiches.

"Mrs. Morton made a bad financial decision and now we are expected to pay for it instead of giving to people who actually could use our charity," she grumbled. "Why give to the homeless or the sick when you can give money to Mrs. Morton?" She frowned and moved along to the pastries on the long buffet table.

I eyed her. "What did she do?"

Esther pulled me aside so the other ladies could not hear our gossip. "Are you familiar with spirit photography? When a photographer uses tricks to make it look as if a ghost is in the picture with the person posing?"

"Oh, lord."

Esther continued. "The woman became obsessed with these pictures because she felt like it was the only way to be close to her husband again. The photographer took advantage of her trust completely and charged her a ridiculous price for several of these photographs. When her son found out and told her this photographer was a charlatan, that it was all tricks, well, the snake had already left London before her son could confront him." She shook her head. "She was humiliated, and her son is furious with her, the poor fellow."

"What on earth?" I immediately felt my insides burning and the skin over my knuckles went taut. "He took advantage of a vulnerable widow. He used her grief to his advantage. That is despicable."

Before I could think on it any longer, Mrs. Carrigan smiled wide at me and joined us, not sensing we were having a private discussion.

"When do you return to work, Mrs. Blushing Bride?" She sipped her tea.

"Oh. I started working again the Monday after the wedding." I smiled weakly and felt myself tense. I knew what came next.

She widened her eyes at me, truly shocked. "Mrs. Baxter, you didn't! No honeymoon on the continent before returning to the newspaper? What a shame." Her eyes glinted with mischief. "Oh, well. Perhaps you are trying to get as many stories written as you can before you and Mr. Baxter start a family."

I swallowed and clamped my lips together. "Mm," is all I said, adding a slight nod for effect.

Mrs. Sheldon, a woman in her forties and not one of the club members I usually spoke to, scampered over. "Mrs. Baxter, dear, let me know if you need any baby blankets or clothes. My sister makes the most darling baby blankets."

Next, Mrs. Dalton floated over. "Oh! We should have a baby shower here for Mrs. Baxter! Wouldn't that be lovely?"

"Of course," Mrs. Carrigan added. "That sounds like a delightful idea!"

Perhaps if I concentrate hard enough, I can make myself disappear and they will just keep talking and not notice I am missing at all.

Esther glanced at me, likely sensing my discomfort.

"Speaking of children," she said, "what can we do to further this idea of speaking to someone in Parliament about the childcare idea? Do we know anyone who we could talk to?"

I slipped out of the huddle and returned to the buffet table. I picked a carrot from a vegetable platter and crunched lazily. When I married Simon, I knew that would change how people saw me but I had hoped it would not begin so soon after the wedding. I had gone from daughter to wife and then immediately to will-be-a-mother-soon.

Eventually, I figured, they would assume Simon and I could not have children and that would be that. They need not know that I did not want children and that I certainly did not want anything to do with how children come about.

From what I could overhear from my spot by the wall, their conversation had turned back to babies. So-and-so's daughter was expecting. So-and-so's sister had just given birth to her third. So-and-so's niece was expecting for the first time and was so excited to be a mother, et cetera, et cetera.

Esther joined me again, a weary smile on her lips. "Are

you alright?"

"Oh, I am fine." I sighed. "Just something new I have to get used to, I suppose."

"Our bodies are never truly our own, even in the eyes of these forward-thinking women." Esther plucked a sandwich plate from the table. "Mr. Granville said something about you only being at the newspaper for a few more months."

I sighed again, feeling my forehead pinch. "Really? He is looking to replace me already?"

"Not because he *wants* to, dear. He just expects he will *have* to," she said. "I cannot come out and tell him that will not be an issue, now, can I?"

Esther was far more involved in her husband's business than most wives, in part because Mr. Granville had a very high regard for his wife's opinion and partly because she was the publisher of the newspaper. She was also a major reason Mr. Granville hired me in the first place. I owed her everything for that.

SIX

Cora

Saturday, July 14, 1888

Why is it that bad news always travels so much faster than good?

This is the thought that entered my mind as Tom Lindsey sat in my parlor, a mere week after I had learned of my husband's death and, more significantly, my insolvency.

Mr. Lindsey kept sighing and shaking his head, his oversized moustache quivering each time. "It's just such a shame, Mrs. Pringle. As you know, I'm a businessman. If I'd known your husband was having difficulties, I would have done my best to assist him. I hope you know that."

Louise brought tea in for us and silently left the room. She and Cook had already found new positions in houses nearby and were scheduled to begin in a few days.

"Of course. I appreciate the thought, Mr. Lindsey."

A lot of good that does me now, Mr. Lindsey.

He pulled a flask from inside his jacket pocket and poured a bit of its contents into his teacup. He raised his eyebrows at me, raising the flask. "Care for some extra flavoring in your tea? You seem like you could use a drink."

"No, thank you. I'm fine."

In truth, I wanted to grab the flask and pour the remaining liquor down my throat. I had finished off the rest of the wine we had in the house. Melancholy strolls around my house were not complete without a glass of wine in hand. After all, wine pairs well with tears and an uncertain future.

He pocketed the flask and gave his tea a quick swirl with the spoon. "If you are in a hurry to sell, I can purchase the house from you today and resell it for you."

"That won't be necessary," I said. "Mr. Jennings knew of a family in the market for a house in this area. The papers were signed yesterday."

The last of the wine disappeared shortly after that.

"Ah, very good." He winced. "The furniture too?"

I picked up my tea. "Yes."

Thank you for reminding me.

Mr. Lindsey reached into his coat again. I assumed for his flask again but instead, he retrieved a flat, square box. He lifted the lid, revealing an exquisite necklace. Sparkling garnet stones surrounded by circles of diamonds lined the intricately woven chain, the largest gem dropping down in the middle. My eyes bulged, darting from one perfect cut to another. It was magnificent, like something royalty might wear.

"Do you like it?"

Tearing my eyes away from the glittering beauty, I looked up at Mr. Lindsey. "Pardon me?"

Mr. Lindsey chuckled. "'Tis a gift, my dear."

I slid my cup and saucer on the nearby table before I dropped it from my trembling fingers. "Mr. Lindsey, I'm afraid I do not understand."

That was a lie. I understood just fine. I just hoped my understanding of the situation was incorrect.

"Mrs. Pringle, I know this seems sudden, but I have admired

you for so long," he said without even the slightest hint of hesitation or nervousness. "You can expect many more fine things like these if you were to become Mrs. Lindsey."

I swallowed, my throat becoming dry. "Oh."

"You could even stay in your home until we are wed. I can take care of you." He slid the box onto the table, next to our teacups.

"Mr. Lindsey, I—"

"I apologize if my proposal seems quick, given your husband's recent passing. I was afraid if you moved out of London due to your financial difficulties that I would miss my chance."

My eyes slowly lowered to the necklace. The clarity of the diamonds was truly impressive, each one hugging an expertly cut red stone. I desperately wanted to try it on, even for just a moment, but I was aware of what kind of message that would send.

Why not at least consider the proposal?

I would certainly be one of the wealthiest women in my social circle and have the finest gowns and jewels in any room I entered. The Maidenhill Club would wish they had accepted me while they had the chance. We would have a summer house in the country, perfect for getaways. Our house in London would be enormous, full of friends whenever we threw fabulous parties and the garden would…

The garden.

My mind flashed back to that night in Mr. Lindsey's garden. Recalling the way Mr. Rigby had kissed me among the shadows, my lips tingled, and my heart raced. His beautiful face pressed to mine, his arms tight around me. Mr. Rigby had referenced marriage when we had met last, although I had not seen him since. Perhaps he had heard of my financial situation and was frightened off by it. Mr. Lindsey certainly had more money than Mr. Rigby, but Mr. Rigby was the man who held my heart.

I had already married one man I did not love. I could not do it again.

Lowering my eyes, I turned away. "I am afraid it is too soon for me to make such a significant decision."

Mr. Lindsey quickly moved from the chair to the sofa beside

me, taking my hands. "You sweet girl. We can be engaged in secret until your mourning period is over. I admit, I am not a patient man but I will wait if I need to." His sausage fingers clamped onto my hands so tightly it nearly hurt.

"I am sorry," I said firmly. "It is not the right time for such talk."

"Of course," he said, placing one palm on my cheek. "You are a lady. I understand."

Suddenly, Mr. Lindsey's wet mouth was on mine and his arms were around me, pulling me closer to him. His breath smelled of fish and liquor. I had tried to be kind and this is where it got me: a sloppy kiss and fishy breath. I pushed on his chest, trying to free myself from his repulsive assault. As soon as his arms had loosened, I brought my hand back and slapped him across the face, sending him back in his seat, my palm stinging from the impact.

I quickly rose, my chest heaving, my chin still wet with his spit. "You need to leave this instant."

Mr. Lindsey quickly lowered his eyes and nodded, finally looking slightly embarrassed by his actions. "My apologies, Mrs. Pringle. I was overcome by my love for you. We will discuss this again at a later date—"

"No, we will absolutely not discuss it ever again," I spat.

His nostrils flared. "I see." He stood, grabbed the necklace box from the table, stuffed it into his jacket pocket, and headed for the front door. He stopped suddenly and faced me again. "I took you for a wise woman who would recognize a good opportunity. Isn't that why you married dull Dr. Pringle in the first place?"

"Dr. Pringle was twice the man you will ever be," I said quietly. "I asked you to leave."

And Mr. Rigby is ten times the man Dr. Pringle was.

Louise appeared with Mr. Lindsey's hat and he snatched it away from her. He looked back at me, the open door in his hand. "Enjoy being penniless with the props boy."

"What do you mean by *that*?"

He slammed the door behind him, leaving me standing there in a daze.

What props boy? Who is he speaking of?

After Mr. Lindsey's visit, I shut myself away in my bedroom, frazzled and sapped of energy. I lay in bed and stared at the ceiling, my mind racing.

Was he … speaking of Mr. Rigby? How could Mr. Rigby be a props boy? It does not make sense. He wears fine clothes and speaks like a gentleman and comes from a good family. Perhaps Mr. Lindsey just said that to confuse me.

A very particular nagging feeling tugged at my thoughts and would not let me be. I had to get it straightened out as soon as possible. I wrote a letter to Mr. Rigby and invited him over for tea the following morning. As I wrote his mailing address on the envelope, I considered where my letters were going when we corresponded.

Is it even a real address? If it is not, how are my letters getting to him?

Holding the envelope between my fingers, I ran my thumb over the edge of it, my eyes fixed on the address I had written out so many times in the last several weeks. I pondered what Mr. Lindsey could have possibly meant by his comment.

I shook my head.

This is ridiculous. Of course, it is a real address and he certainly lives there. Mr. Lindsey is mistaking Mr. Rigby for someone else. He has to be.

I gave my letter to Louise to give to a messenger and, feeling frightfully uneasy, I told her to go find that address.

"You want me to go to Skylark Road? To Mr. Rigby's house, ma'am?"

I hesitated. "Yes. I would like to know … what the outside of his house is like." I straightened my posture. "Do not knock on the door, do not try to see Mr. Rigby and, if he is around, please do not let him see you either. If something seems … amiss, please do ask around about Mr. Rigby."

She blinked at me with large, round eyes. "Yes, ma'am."

Now I am no longer the penniless mistress of the house, now I am the completely mad and *penniless mistress of the house.*

When Mr. Rigby arrived for tea the following morning, I was waiting for him in the garden. The sky was gray, the air warm. Beyond the garden wall horse hooves trotted, and a mother encouraged her children to keep their clothes tidy.

I held my elbows, wrapping my arms around myself. Facing away from the house, I heard Louise bring Mr. Rigby out to the garden.

"Shall I bring tea, Mrs. Pringle?" she asked.

"No," I said without looking at either of them. "That won't be necessary."

Once I heard Louise return to the inside of the house, I felt Mr. Rigby approach. He stopped a few feet behind me.

"Is something wrong?"

A rush of emotion rose in me like bubbles in a bottle of champagne. I managed to keep the cork in for the time being.

"I keep thinking about the last time we sat together in this garden," I said quietly, still unable to face him. "If you had asked me to marry you, I would have accepted. I would have run away with you. I would have done anything. But everything is chaos now."

"What do you mean, my darling?"

"Please—" I snapped, "—do not call me such things." I slowly turned around to face him. I had intended to keep my eyes free of tears for this conversation but, alas, that plan was made in vain. I swiped at a stray tear as I finally met his gaze for the first time in several days. "Mr. Rigby, where do you live?"

His left eyebrow raised. "Skylark Road."

I closed my eyes at the words and my lips tightened.

"No," I breathed. "I have been sending letters to you at Skylark Road for weeks but that is not your home." I slowly opened my eyes, my vision blurry in both from tears. "Tell me the truth. Where do you live?"

Mr. Rigby ran a hand through his thick dark hair, his face looking pained. He took a seat and let out a long breath, considering his answer.

He squared his shoulders and finally looked back at me. "I rent a room on the South Bank, just on the other side of Waterloo Bridge."

"You are friends with the Skylark Road tailor because you know him through the theater so he agreed to accept mail there on your behalf," I said firmly, feeling a bit more confident.

Mr. Rigby stared directly ahead at the garden wall. "Yes."

"You work at the Princess Royal Theatre … with props."

He gave a tiny nod.

"You wanted to trick me and manipulate me." My skin prickled, and my jaw clenched. "And humiliate me."

He jerked his head towards me and raised himself from his chair quickly. "No. That was not my intention at all."

"What possible motive did you have for lying to me about your family?" I hissed.

"You wouldn't have looked at me for a single moment if I had told you the truth," he snapped back. "I made up a story about my family because I didn't want to…" He hesitated. "… lose you." He continued, his speech quickening. "I wasn't trying to trick you when we met, I was trying to charm some investors and get them interested in my play. I really *am* a playwright, that part is true. That's why I was at the theater during intermission on the night we met. I was trying to speak to Mr. Lindsey. But then I met you." He paused, giving me a moment to remember that fateful night, before clamping his eyes shut again. "I knew as soon as I told you, I would never see you again."

I folded my arms across my chest again. "Did you think I wouldn't eventually discover the truth? That-that-that you don't come from a good family?"

"That I don't come from money," he snapped. "That is obviously what you mean, you might as well just say it."

"You say that like it doesn't matter. Of *course* it matters."

He opened his sad eyes. "I thought if I managed to get a few investors interested in my play first you would be impressed enough to be with me." A tiny, self-pitying smile blossomed on his lips. "A stupid plan; I realize that now."

"Everything is ruined," I exclaimed in a tear-choked creak, looking away from him. "*I* am ruined, Mr. Rigby. I will have to accept Mr. Lindsey's proposal."

"Tom Lindsey proposed?" he burst. "You can't marry that beast!"

"I have no choice." I seethed, a tear escaping down my cheek. "I must remarry or leave London. Dr. Pringle lost all our money and I have no one I can turn to."

Mr. Rigby, quiet for a moment, took my hand but I pulled away. He winced, obviously hurt.

"Where would you go if you left London?"

"Perhaps America," I said. "The house is already sold so I must make my decision soon."

"So far away." Mr. Rigby's shoulders slumped slightly.

I glared at him. "The distance is no matter to *you*. I don't even know why I am telling you this."

Who else in this whole bloody country is going to show you sympathy?

"Please," he said in a near whisper, "don't marry Mr. Lindsey. I beg of you. He will be disloyal and unkind to you." He paused. "You don't … *want* to marry him, do you?"

"Of course I do not," I snapped. "America, Mr. Lindsey, or … destitution." My voice broke on the word and my chest gave a little heave as a sob escaped my lips.

If Mr. Rigby had wrapped his arms around me at that moment while I wept, I would not have pushed him away. My body longed for some kind of consolation and comfort. He did not move though, his pride likely still stinging. I had no reason to want him to touch me. He was a liar.

"I don't expect you to accept but I would curse myself for not suggesting it," he said quietly. "Marry me."

I stared at him, my blood boiling. "What would possibly make you think I would consider *you*? The only thing I know about you is that you are a penniless liar. You are a stranger to me." My chest heaved again, this time with rage. "And you're a playwright. What a perfect ambition for you, Mr. Rigby. You are impeccable at making up stories, aren't you?"

I said it to hurt him as he had hurt me, but Mr. Rigby barely moved.

"No, I could not keep you in the manner to which you are accustomed." He raised his eyes to meet mine. "If you truly hated and distrusted me, you would not have allowed me to return to you. I choose to have hope that you still love me at least a little. I would make it my life's mission to endeavor to make you happy."

"How dare you be so forward. I am a mourning widow."

"You did not love him," he said firmly. He looked away, sadness in his eyes. "My humble home is open to you if you require more time to decide what you will do or where you will go, if you require a place to stay." He plucked a piece of paper from his pocket, jotted his address, and left it on the table. "I must go attend to my duties as a lowly working man now. Goodbye, Mrs. Pringle." He gave me a quick nod and disappeared from the garden.

I slowly moved my hand to the edge of the table. Placing a fingertip on the scrap of paper, I slid it closer to myself. His handwriting was neat, each letter tall and well-formed. I crushed the paper in a tight fist, satisfied by the sound of crumpling.

What if Mr. Rigby is the only ally you can count on? Do not throw his friendship away if it means your survival.

I hesitantly unclenched my fingers and put the note back on the table, running my finger over the hard creases, smoothing it out, before slipping it into my pocket.

My chest tightening, I fled to my bedroom, meaning to throw myself upon the duvet in a dramatic fashion and flood my pillow with tears. Instead, I found Louise folding my things neatly into a chest.

She quickly rose and nodded. "Can I bring you some tea—"

My lip quivered as I stared down into the trunk. "What is to become of me?"

SEVEN

Cora

Monday, July 16, 1888

I received a reply from Marshall's family in Liverpool; just as expected, they would not have me, likely believing I was at fault for our debts and that I should live with the consequences. I did not have time to wait for a reply all the way from America. I had to be out of my beloved home within a few days.

Taking a deep breath, I began my letter to Mr. Lindsey, accepting his proposal. With my pen ready to form the first word, I took a deep breath to steady my quivering hand.

You must accept. It is the only way.

My fingers remained reluctant to move, leaving a dot of ink on the paper where the tip of my pen stalled. As the ink sank into the fibers of the page and spread into a perfect dark circle, my chest tightened and my eyes stung. I wiped the tears from my eyes and forced my pen to the paper again, pushing my hand in an unnatural direction.

Dear Mr. Lindsey,

I

I put my pen down and raised from the desk, stomping my foot and squeezing my fists. I paced. I stared at the ceiling. I cursed myself for being so cowardly.

The nights of loneliness I endured with Marshall and the months of miserable unhappiness wrapped around my ribs like a rope, squeezing the breath from my lungs. I placed a flat hand on my chest and sat back down, fighting the sudden weakness in my limbs.

Louise peered around the corner of what was once Marshall's office. "Ma'am, are you alright? You look quite unwell. Shall I fetch a doctor?"

It was her last full day in my employ. The following day she would help me prepare for the final time before taking up her new position in someone else's household.

"No, Louise, thank you. I am fine."

I despised the piteous look she had plastered on her face since the moment I told her of my pathetic circumstances.

Her sweet smile had become a tight, straight line and her brows were knitted together in concern.

Well, at least I will not be seeing that irritating expression for much longer.

"Can I at least bring you some tea, ma'am?"

I nodded silently. After she left, I slid the page from the desk and slowly tore the thing into four pieces. Then, each of those scraps was torn in half and then dropped into the bottom drawer of the desk.

If Louise deserves happiness, why do I deserve a lesser fate?

America. I will go to America.

Just after lunch the following day, I sat silently in a hansom cab as it made its way to my temporary home. I silently prayed my trunks were tied down securely as we jostled about on busy London streets and across Waterloo Bridge.

An additional trunk occupied the seat across from me inside

the cab while the seat beside me was occupied by a stack of three hat boxes. Choosing which of my hats and dresses and keepsakes to bring with me and which to sell had been one of the most trying experiences of my life as I had an emotional attachment to many of the pretty things I had in my collection. Remembering what I wore to what event and who had complimented me was a special talent of mine.

The condition of the buildings gradually declined as we traveled closer to our destination. Having never seen that area of London before, I had been assured that it was a reasonable neighborhood, a mixture of merchants and working-class residents. Additionally, I had been told that there were many regions of London far worse off.

As the number of poorly-clothed urchins increased, the more regretful of my decision I became.

I heard the driver halt his horses as we arrived in front of a pub. Assuming there was an issue with the horses, I stayed put and waited until we continued on our way.

"We're 'ere, miss," he shouted, hopping down so he could unload my trunks.

I peered my head out. "Are you quite sure this is Guildford Row?"

"I know my way aroun' London, miss," he said, dropping one of my trunks roughly to the ground.

I winced at the sound it made as it hit the muddy street.

A line of tall, narrow buildings with rough gray brick exteriors loomed over me, each story jutting further out than the level beneath it. As I slid from the hansom, the putrid scent of human waste combined with the aroma of various nearby food stalls, both smells staging a violent assault on my senses.

My hat boxes piled high in my arms, I rushed to be near to my trunk before some filthy vagrant could take off with my things. The driver slid the second trunk down and it landed on the first one with a loud thud.

"Careful with the lady's things, good sir!"

I barely recognized the man. He wove his way through the

thick line of food vendors and curious onlookers. His voice was different—friendly, but not as refined as the voice I had come to know—and instead of a fine top hat, he wore a bowler with a few lightly scuffed edges. His wool jacket and tan waistcoat were respectable but looked like they had seen several years of use and mending.

But those eyes. I could never mistake those eyes.

Mr. Rigby, once standing at my side, smiled weakly at me. I had never felt so relieved to see a familiar face than at that moment.

"Good morning, Mrs. Pringle," he said, touching the brim of his hat.

A stout woman in her late forties trailed after him, her curly gray hair escaping from the front of her white cap. She glanced at Mr. Rigby, as if for verification. A boy, probably thirteen or fourteen, followed behind her. The thin, scrappy young man had the same uncontrolled curls and the same straight, slender nose and I quickly realized that he must be her son.

The final chest was removed from the inside of the cab and Mr. Rigby's eyes grew wide as he surveyed the pile of trunks in the street. As I paid the driver, Mr. Rigby scratched the back of his neck, his eyes darting from trunk to trunk, hatbox to hatbox.

"Mr. Rigby," I said with a polite nod. "I hope you are well."

His dumbfounded expression melted to one of sincere warmth. "I am, thank you. I trust—"

"We should start with the biggest trunk first," the wiry boy yelled over the street cacophony. "You take one end and I'll take the other?"

"Yes, right," he hollered back, looking a little annoyed to be interrupted. "Mrs. Pringle, this is my friend Mrs. Harris and her son, Frank."

Mrs. Harris smiled wide. "Lovely to meet you at last, dear. I hope you and I will be good friends."

Before I could reply, Mrs. Harris had whipped around to yell at her son. "Frank, you be careful with this nice lady's belongings, do you hear me? If you so much as put a scratch on 'er things,

I'll have your guts for garters!"

Frank and Mr. Rigby continued carrying the trunk into the crowd, disappearing behind a man carrying two barrels on his shoulders. Mrs. Harris turned back to me, her face angelic and her cheeks pink.

"Now, you and I will just sit here with your things until they get back." Something caught her eye behind me. "Hey! The hell are *you* gawkin' at, toad? Get outta 'ere, this ain't none o' your concern. Be gone!"

She turned back to me and smiled sweetly once more. "I live righ' across the hall from Mr. Rigby. He's a right proper gen'leman, that one."

I took a seat on the top of a two-trunk stack, my arms wrapped tightly around a hatbox. I smiled, not knowing what to say.

"I hope you don't mind me saying so, miss, but you don't look a thing like Mr. Rigby."

"Oh, well, yes," I said. "He was adopted, after all." I swallowed. Even though I had just met the woman, I already felt guilty about lying to Mrs. Harris.

"Oh, yeah, right. That's right." She nodded.

To make our living arrangement appear proper, Mr. Rigby and I had agreed to pose as sister and brother during the course of my visit. I could not afford to stay at a hotel or rent accommodations *and* pay for the crossing to America on my own so staying with Mr. Rigby was my best option. My only option, really.

It likely still seemed a bit odd, the two of us, but I figured once I was in America with Aunt Charlotte, my reputation in England wouldn't matter one bit. I knew I could start over completely in North Carolina, make a fresh beginning as a different woman if I so desired. It was certainly the right course of action.

I leaned closer to Mrs. Harris so I wouldn't have to yell over the street noise. "Where exactly did they take the trunk?"

She pointed up to an open window on the top floor of the

building next to the pub. "That's Mr. Rigby's flat, just there. I expec' you'll be quite comfortable there, my dear."

I nodded, gripping my hatbox tighter.

"Is it just you and your son?"

"No, no. Mr. Harris is there too, and my daughter Penelope as well." Mrs. Harris' eyes turned a bit sad, her gaze far away. "I expect she will be leaving us soon though."

"Oh," I said. "Is she ill?" I had heard many stories from Marshall about the poorer areas of London being full of sickness and disease. I wondered how many children Mrs. Harris had lost to such tragedy.

"What?" She wrinkled her nose. "No, child, she's gettin' married soon."

"Oh!" I laughed, surprised. "That is wonderful!"

"Her beau 'as a bakery on the nex' stree' over." She smiled proudly and then let out a long sigh. "That'll just leave Frank at home. Mr. Harris and I raised six little ones there. It's not fancy like I expect you're used to, but suits us well enough." Her eyes darted to something behind me. "Oy! You! Eyes off the goods, lad! I'll have your hide before you can e'en blink!"

Mr. Rigby and Frank returned to us just then to take the other trunks up. As I followed Mrs. Harris up the stairs, I was relieved to be getting out of the street but suddenly very aware that Mr. Rigby and I would be left alone very soon, just the two of us.

After much huffing, puffing, and complaining about how many trunks I had, my things were finally all slid into Mr. Rigby's flat and Frank and Mrs. Harris left us to get settled.

"It's small but it's home," he said with a flourish as he pushed the door open for me, not meeting my gaze as he did so.

Still clutching my hatbox by the ribbon handle like it might fly away, I slowly advanced into the flat. The room was a bit dark, only lit by the front window and two small gas lamps. Two wooden chairs were positioned at a small table and, nearby, teacups hung from hooks mounted on a darkened fireplace. A threadbare rug lay upon the floor—I had to imagine the rough wooden floors were in bad shape if the rug hiding them was the more appealing option between the two. A small desk in the corner was piled high with books, a messy stack of papers beside it. I imagined Mr. Rigby toiling away at his desk until the wee hours of the morning, the bottom of his palm stained with ink, trying to get his play just right.

I heard a 'swoosh' as my bustle bumped the coat rack by the door. This place wasn't even big enough to accommodate my skirts properly. I slid my hatbox onto the table and continued the grand tour.

Mr. Rigby maneuvered around me and opened the door on the far side of the room. "The bedroom is all yours while you're here."

I silently gave the tiny room a once-over and gave a quick nod. I was grateful the bedroom shared the fireplace as I never slept well when I had a chill. I went back to the main room, giving it another quick scan. My eyes landed on the shabby easy chair by the window—I guessed Mr. Rigby would be sleeping there while I was his guest.

"Right," I announced. "It needs a woman's touch, certainly, but it will do for the time being," I unpinned my hat from its perch on my curls.

I gulped silently, realizing I had never lived in a house without a kitchen or dining room before. The first time I had lived without any servants at all. The first time I had lived alone with a man who was not my husband.

The first time I had ever needed to risk my reputation as a lady in order to survive.

Mr. Rigby smiled weakly. "Are you certain you'll be fine here while I go to work? I'm sure Mrs. Harris would love your company if you wanted to spend the rest of the day with her."

No, no, no. Don't you dare leave me alone here in this horrible slum.

"Of course." I smiled.

He nodded and headed for the door. "I'll likely not see you until the morning as I won't be home until late. Mrs. Harris will bring you a plate of whatever she has for supper." He bit the corner of his lip. "Are you sure you'll be alright?"

"Yes, Mr. Rigby," I lied.

His mouth tightened. "Since you're my sister for the time being, you should call me Everett."

"Oh. Right. Everett. Of course."

He gave me a polite nod and left. I locked the door behind him before going to the front window to watch him walk away from the building, disappearing around the corner.

I went to Everett's bedroom and gently set my hat on the wooden chest at the end of the bed. Taking a seat, I gathered a fistful of the blanket and raised it to my face, gingerly inhaling its aroma. As expected, it smelled like Everett; somehow like a sweet pastry from a coniferous woodland. I pulled more of the blanket to my chest and hugged the bundle tightly.

And then I cried until my stomach ached.

By necessity, Mrs. Harris and I became acquainted with one another very quickly. She brought me supper and, later on in the evening, gave me some pointers on how to dress and undress by myself. I had expected to have to contort myself into unnatural shapes in order to lace up a corset and tie my various skirts into place. but Mrs. Harris talked me through the process. I could tell my inexperience tried her patience though.

I frowned at myself in the mirror.

All that effort for black and dreary mourning wear. What a waste.

Around nine o'clock the following morning, Mrs. Harris invited me over for tea, assuming I would not mind the company. She assumed right.

Yawning into my palm for the third time, I lazily stirred my tea.

"Sleepin' in a new place is always difficult, innit, dear," she commented in a hushed tone. "You'll be righ' as rain in a few days, just you wait."

"I hope so."

"So, what was Mr. Rigby like as a young lad?"

I was far too sleep deprived to think of anything creative.

I paused. "Mostly the same."

Mrs. Harris seemed content with that answer and she gave an understanding nod. "Good man, your brother. He's a hard worker. Very clever, too."

I nodded and sipped my tea. "Clever. Yes, I suppose he is clever."

Possibly too clever.

As soon as I put my hand down, Mrs. Harris clasped my hand, giving it a gentle squeeze.

"You must miss your husband terribly. I dread the day God takes my Horace from me." She put her hand—rough and raw from years of hard work—to her heart, closing her eyes and tipping her head up to the ceiling. "He's as healthy as a horse thankfully. I can be grateful for that. Mr. Rigby said your man had a heart attack or—"

"Some bullies scared him to death and made his heart explode," I said bluntly with a small shrug. I did not know if that was exactly true, technically, but my flair for the dramatic sometimes caused me to exaggerate in order to entertain or, at the very least, shock into a stunned silence.

After I departed Mrs. Harris' flat, I watched out the front window while Everett slept. Most of the performances at the theater took place in the evening so his hours varied from mine. Despite the sadness the view from the window caused me, it was a better spectacle than inside; Everett continued to snore, his mouth open, his hand down along the side of the chair with his fingertips brushing the floor.

It was then that I realized life in this flat would be very dull. I would have to find entertainment somehow.

Perhaps I could write to Polly and get her to invite me over for lunch. I could never invite her here, that was out of the question.

When Everett finally woke, it was like he had been startled from a bad dream. He bolted upright, inhaled sharply, blinked, looked around, stared at me for a moment and then, realizing why I was there, sunk back into his chair.

"Good morning," he said finally. "You should have woken me. I could have made us some tea."

A pang of regret struck me.

I should have made tea for him.

I knew how to make tea. I used to make tea for Papa, Charlotte, and I all the time. I was not entirely useless.

"Was I snoring?"

"Yes."

He frowned. "My apologies."

He rose, gave a quick stretch, and reached for two tin boxes on a shelf. Within minutes, we were sitting together at his breakfast table, eating scones with jam, as if that was something we did together every single morning.

We sat in silence, save for the sound of our chewing and the quiet bubbling of the kettle on the fireplace.

I patted a crumb away from my lip with a fingertip as we had no napkins. I snickered quietly, my eyes fixed on the empty tin box between us. Everett raised an eyebrow at me but stayed mum. I snickered again and then my snickering turned into silent giggling. I put my hand over my mouth, my shoulders quaking as I tried to hold in my laughter. I did not work.

Everett just blinked at me.

I shook my head as my riotous laughter, interspersed with deep breaths, gradually subsided.

"Are you … quite alright?"

Slowly turning to him, tears still stinging my eyes, I let out another chuckle. "Honestly? No. I am not quite alright."

He winced.

"I slept in a stranger's bed last night," I said. "Well, that is not actually the case. I laid in a stranger's bed and stared at the ceiling last night. I went from living in a lovely house on a lovely street in a lovely part of town and now I am, well, *here*. My wretched husband left me destitute and homeless. I was quite in love with a man who does not exist. I am here because I am desperate and had nowhere else to go which is truly pathetic and sad." I took a breath. "Mr. Rigby. Everett. This whole situation is absurd and terribly uncomfortable. I have no reason to trust you." I raised my hands and dropped them lazily to my sides. "And yet, here I am, sitting at your table, eating scones with jam."

Everett slowly sat back in his chair, his arms folded across his chest. "You're not sure you can trust me. You're just deciding this now?" He raised an eyebrow. "I wish I would have known that before I lugged three enormous trunks up here, let you sleep in my bed, and shared my scones and jam with you." A mischievous smile crept onto his lips.

"You think this is amusing, do you?"

"A bit."

I clenched my jaw. "I assure you it is *not* amusing to me—"

"No one forced you to come here," he said in a cavalier tone. "You had enough money to rent a little room somewhere and you could have lived there comfortably until you heard from your aunt. Instead, you chose to take me up on my offer to stay here, despite discovering I misrepresented myself."

He was wrong. I did not actually have enough money to pay for both a room and the crossing to America, but I didn't want him to know how little money I had left.

"I could not live alone," I said, my words clipped. "It is not safe for a lady."

"Ah, but according to you, *I* might not be safe either. Perhaps I seem a safer option than a rented room." He placed the back of his hand to his forehead. "You flatter me."

I could feel the edges of my nostrils flaring as I stared at him across the table. I struggled to find something to say. "How did you learn your manner of speaking?"

"The theater."

"And where did you get your clothes?"

"Pardon?"

"The clothes you wore when we met before. Where did you get them?"

His smugness faded a little, but he tried to keep his

confident expression intact. "I borrowed them from the theater costume room."

"A liar and a thief. The two go hand in hand, I suppose," I said, tipping my nose and chin slightly up.

He seemed unmoved by my cruelty. "Are you always so brazen to people trying to help you?"

"Only when I am trying to learn what they are getting out of the situation."

He looked at me for a moment and then closed his eyes. His mouth spread into a grin in one corner. "I see now." Faced with my look of frustration, he continued. "You don't understand why someone would go out of their way to do something kind for another person without getting something back in return."

"You are a man," I said. "I do not expect you could ever understand."

Everett thought for a moment before rising from his chair. He fished for something in a drawer before returning to the table. He slid a smooth, well-crafted pocket knife across the table. I picked it up and unfolded the blade, checking the sharpness of its edge. I looked back at him.

"I know what it's like to feel unsafe. It's a hellish thing." He nodded to the knife. "You have my permission to cut my throat if I lay a hand on you, Mrs. Pringle."

Strangely enough, that did make me feel much better. I folded the knife back up and slipped it into one of the pockets of my gown, tucked in safe but always within easy reach.

"Not Mrs. Pringle," I reminded him. "Cora."

EIGHT

Amelia

Thursday, August 9, 1888

"I would like to write a story about Martha Tabram," I announced, marching into the office of Mr. Thaddeus Granville. "I want it."

Mr. Turner, the senior reporter at our paper, plucked the cigarette from his thin lips.

"I was about to go write something up right now," he said, letting the smoke pour out of his mouth.

Mr. Granville shook his head at me. "The details of her murder are too ghastly. Apologies, Mrs. Baxter, the answer is no."

"I have obviously already read all the details," I said, crossing my arms over my chest, "and I did not faint *or* swoon. Not even once." I smirked.

My boss frowned at me, deep creases forming in his forehead. "I cannot have a lady from a respectable family like yours waltzing into the East End to interview, uh," Mr. Granville struggled to find a phrase that wouldn't offend my delicate, feminine sensibilities, "women of ill repute." His shoulders slumped.

"Your father would have my head."

"I am no longer my father's property, remember?" A familiar tightness gripped my jaw. "I assure you, Mr. Baxter would be enthusiastically encouraging of such a venture."

"My answer is still no."

"Not even if I use my pen name?"

"No."

"What if Mr. Turner accompanies me to Whitechapel to make sure I am not in danger?"

"I don't have time for that," Mr. Turner added on his way out of Mr. Granville's office, apparently done listening to me beg for my chance.

"I am *sure* Mr. Turner would do a fine job with the story. I have no doubt of that. Perhaps we can do two pieces! *I* wanted to do more of a heartfelt look at her life, perhaps speak to her friends or family so the poor woman is more than just a corpse, but a *person*. If I could just—"

"Mrs. Baxter," Mr. Granville said, his voice louder and more rigid "I believe you owe me five hundred words on that local voting thing, or should I give that to Mr. Turner as well?"

"Local Government Act," I mumbled. "It is almost finished."

"Good girl." He plucked up a newspaper from his messy desk and disappeared behind its wide open pages.

I scowled at his newsprint shield, hoping it might just spontaneously combust in his hands. Alas, it did not, so I shuffled out of the room, closed his office door behind me, and returned to my desk.

Mr. Turner glanced at me as he hammered on his typewriter like it owed him money. "I promise I will be nice to her in my story."

I snatched the newspaper from my desk and reread the story of Martha Tabram, what scant details were available. The poor woman was found in Whitechapel two days prior, her body a chaotic collection of thirty-nine stab wounds.

What monster could do such a thing?

"Does this … even make sense to you? What possibly could

be the motive for such an act?"

Mr. Turner raised an eyebrow. "What, are you a detective now?"

"Are you truly not curious?"

"If I try to rationalize the horrors and cruelties in this world, I go mad." He scratched his neck. "What is another word for 'examination'?"

"'Investigation'? 'Inquiry'?"

Mr. Turner nodded and continued typing.

"Why did you become a reporter, Mr. Turner?"

"Because my wife and children get rather cross when I don't feed and clothe them."

I picked up my cup from my desk and grimaced as I sipped the cold tea. "I begged for this job because I wanted to write for a newspaper that published stories that *really* matter; stories that change peoples' lives and make the world a better place to live in."

"And because no other newspaper in London wanted their own Nellie Bly," Mr. Turner added cheekily.

"Well, yes, that too."

NINE

Cora

Thursday, August 9, 1888

Over the next week, my suspicions of Everett Rigby waned but I continued to carry my knife close at hand. After a while I put it away and forgot I had even wanted it. I reminded myself that just because he had deceived me did not immediately make him some kind of villain.

The days began to bleed together with absolutely no distinguishable difference between any of them; I prepared tea for Everett while he slept in his chair nearby, we ate a late breakfast together, he would leave for work, I would desperately look for things to do around the flat, Mrs. Harris would bring my supper, and then I would go to bed, not seeing Everett until the next morning. Sometimes I woke up when he returned home, sometimes I did not. I began to sleep a little easier, gradually becoming more accustomed to the hollers of merchants selling their wares, street performers, the occasional tussle between drunkards at night, and the amalgam of other sounds I was not used to.

When Everett was not home, I people-watched out the window, I read and reread my novel, napped, stared at the ceiling, and, on occasion, looked through Everett's belongings. I never found anything interesting except for dozens of unfinished play drafts. Everett brought me a new novel days after I had arrived, and I had finished it in an afternoon. I was so desperate for entertainment I even considered cleaning or doing mending.

Between breakfast and Everett leaving for the day, he and I would play cards. On one particular day, he told me about a new play starting at the theater soon.

I sighed. "I wish I could go see it."

"Who said you can't?" He shuffled the cards and dealt them again. "One of the fellows at the ticket booth is a friend of mine. I can—"

"And risk running into an acquaintance? No, thank you." I eyed the collection of cards in front of me. "It's almost two o'clock. Won't you be late?"

"Today is my day off." He smiled wide and set the stack of cards down between us.

"Really? Can we go do something?"

"You just said you don't want to risk seeing an acquaintance."

"None of my acquaintances will be in this part of London," I clarified.

The corners of Everett's eyes pinched. "You want to do something around *here*?"

"Why not?" I knew my clothes would likely make me stand out a bit but that had never bothered me before. Besides, if anyone got too close, I had my knife. "What do your people do for entertainment?"

His eyebrows lifted. "*My* people?"

"You know what I mean."

He thought for a moment. "Usually on my days off I run errands, maybe see some chums and the like." Everett paused. "For a while, until quite recently, all my free time was spent trying to impress a lady." He smiled weakly.

I lowered my eyes and busied myself by sliding my cards back in the deck. "What else do you do?"

He rubbed the back of his neck. "Well, there's the zoo, music halls, the circus … or we could find a bookshop and get you a couple more novels and magazines to read?"

"Oh! Can we go to a music hall? That sounds—"

"I'd really rather not." He frowned. "Why don't I take you to the zoo this afternoon? It'll be jolly—"

"Do you not care for music halls?"

He opened his mouth and then hesitated. "They're … fine. I just have—"

There was a knock at the door. Everett and I exchanged glances before he raised from his chair to answer it. A messenger boy handed him a note and Everett, peering back at me, unfolded it. I could see the outline of his jaw shift as he clenched.

"They need me at the theater right away," he said, glaring at the note. He gave the boy a coin. "Tell them I'll be there shortly. That's a good lad." The boy nodded and disappeared down the hall. Everett looked back at me. "I'm afraid the zoo must wait."

"That is unfortunate," I said, not bothering to mention that I had no interest in going to the zoo anyway. "Is something the matter at the theater?"

Everett rushed around the flat, collecting a few things. "One of the backstage lads got sacked. My guess is the director walked in on him and the director's wife."

Everett made a quick exit, leaving me alone. Again.

That evening after supper, Mrs. Harris arrived to collect her plate as usual. The meal had been bland, its horrid texture at least offering some kind of culinary interest. Despite the lack of flavor, I thanked her profusely for the food.

"My pleasure, Mrs. Pringle," she said, before bumping her hip on the edge of the table, nearly dropping the plate. "Oops. Pardon me." The gloss of her eyes and the pink cheeks gave her away.

"Mrs. Harris, are you … having a pleasant evening?"

Simpering, she looked half amused, half embarrassed. "Indeed I am. I like a bit o' gin sometimes. But, then, who doesn't?" She thought for a moment. "Why don't you come over and 'ave a drink with me? You must be terrible lonely here all by yourself."

She barely had the words out of her mouth before I was up out of my chair and following her across the hall.

Not used to the strength of gin, it did not take me long to feel its effects. Soon, Mrs. Harris and I were chatting and laughing comfortably like old friends, my cheeks hot. All the stresses of being a delicate and demure lady melted away with every drop that crossed my lips.

"I'm so sorry 'bout your husband, my dear," Mrs. Harris said, raising a glass. "Let's drink to his memory."

That's a waste of good gin, Mrs. Harris.

"No, let's not."

I hadn't meant to say that out loud. Mrs. Harris blinked at me, her eyes like saucers.

"No," I began again. "Let us drink to something a little cheerier, shall we?"

"Let us drink to your brother then. A finer man there was never."

I raised my glass. "To Mr. Rigby."

Oh. I shouldn't have called him Mr. Rigby, that might sound strange to her. Oh dear.

Mrs. Harris did not notice. She looked quite peaceful, two hands cradling her glass as we sat by the fire. The empty gin bottle sat on the kitchen table. I made a plan to ask Everett to pick up a bottle for me. I wondered if he and I should have a drink together. Perhaps it would make things less tense between us.

"Good man," Mrs. Harris said again, inspecting her glass. "Good taste in gin too for a teetotaler."

"I didn't know that," I said with an arched brow. "Wait, did he recommend the gin or give it to you?"

Her mischievous smile returned once more. "He's keepin'

me in gin while you're stayin' with 'im. Bringin' you meals," she glanced at me, "keeping an eye on you."

I let myself slide further down in my armchair, turning my eyes to the fireplace. "Of course he is. He must think I am a child."

"Don't tell 'im I told you, miss, and don't be too hard on 'im. He's a good lad."

Except when he lies.

I raised from my chair, a bit unsteadily, and frowned at the empty bottle on the table. "I suppose this means I should retire for the night."

Mrs. Harris, peering at me from around the edge of her chair, gave a little shrug. "There's a pub downstairs."

"I've never had beer before," I admitted to Mrs. Harris as we sat across from one another at our snug pub booth. "I don't think I like the taste very much at all."

Mrs. Harris, certainly more sober than I, smirked at the empty glasses on the table between us. "You sure about that, love?"

I bit the corner of my lip and struggled to smother my giggles, my nose making terrible snorting sounds instead.

"Miss How-Do-You-Do can't hold her liquor. I bloody knew it," Mrs. Harris said. "Well, your highness, unless you got a few coins tucked in there somewhere, we may need to call it a night."

Slowly turning my head to scan the other pub customers, a plan began to form. I had noticed several customers watching me since I arrived, taking note of my gown. I certainly did not fit in well with the working-class crowd this pub catered to. But, perhaps, that could work to my advantage.

Leaning forward, closer to Mrs. Harris, I whispered, "Follow my lead."

I grabbed Mrs. Harris' hand and announced in a loud voice. "Oh, my word! The lines on your palm—you are bound for great fortune, Mrs. Harris!"

A few nearby bar patrons turned towards us, curious.

I studied the creases of her hands, tracing my finger across the deeper lines. "Yes, indeed! I see a voyage in your future, and soon, and it will lead you to vast riches." I glanced around at the handful of interested spectators; a couple of them leaving their table to watch the palm reading. I continued. "Now, this line. This line tells me you're going to live a long life. And this line—" I flashed a charming smile to the small crowd at our booth "—tells me about your love life."

Someone in the group of spectators whooped. Just then, a tall handsome man with graying hair and whiskers spoke up from behind our small audience.

"What's Mrs. Harris' love line say, miss?" It was the barman who had taken our orders earlier when we'd arrived at the pub. He had winked at Mrs. Harris and I wondered how often she frequented his establishment.

Mrs. Harris looked at the barkeep like she wanted to take his shirt off with her teeth.

"Well, sir, her love line is solid, strong, and true," I said.

A few people cheered and Mrs. Harris clapped her hands together and held her palm up. She slid out from behind the booth. "The lines don't lie," she announced, moving around the crowd to get closer to the barman. She flung her arms around his neck and gave him a big kiss on his cheek. "Solid, strong, and true, like she said!"

The barkeep put his arm around her waist and pulled her in tight for a passionate kiss on the mouth and again our little audience cheered. He slapped her on the bottom before returning to his post behind the counter.

"I thought he was going to tell me to stop," I said to her quietly. "Friend of yours?"

"Aye, ya daft girl," she said with a chuckle. "That's *Mr.* Harris!"

"Pardon me, would you do mine too?" A man shoved his open hand in front of me, palm up.

The woman next to him added, "Mine too?"

"My girl here will read both o' your palms for a pint. How's that for a good deal?"

The two exchanged uncertain looks.

I excitedly grabbed the woman's hand. "Oh, my word!" I ran my fingertip down one line. "You will…" I paused. "No, I mustn't."

"What? What does it say?" she demanded.

While the man got me a drink, I told her about the handsome man she would meet in a year or so and he would whisk her away and it would be the great romance of her life.

She stared at her palm. "You can see all that on my hand?"

"Of course she can!" Mrs. Harris added. "This is the great and magical Madame Pringle. 'Ave you never heard o' Madame Pringle?"

I forced myself not to giggle.

"I like the sounds of this gentleman I'm to meet. He won't like it though." She nodded to her male acquaintance who had returned with my beer. Thankfully, he hadn't heard her comment. "What else does it say?"

I studied her palm again. "Hmm. This line here, see how it has multiple breaks in it? That means your life will be steady and calm for a while and then change suddenly and then be steady again."

She nodded, her eyes growing wide. "That *does* sound like my life, miss!"

Since my tolerance for drink had reached its peak, Mrs. Harris began collecting payment on my behalf while I read palms for a small lineup of bar patrons, all of them happy to part with a couple shillings to know what the future held for them.

Just as I was about to read my twelfth palm for the night—or was it my thirteenth?—the front door of the pub swung open and Everett stormed over to our booth, his eyes hard and his jaw clenched.

He waved away the few other people in line. "Be gone, please. Cora, we're going home."

The man sitting across from us, his palm still in my hand, would not be so easily moved. "Wait your turn!"

Everett shot him a furious glare. I placed his payment back in his palm and softly curled his fingers around it. "Next time. My apologies, sir."

Glancing at the coins and then at me, Everett watched and waited as the man grumbled and slid out of the booth. I had hoped Everett would sit down but he stayed planted in place.

"*Sister*," he said. "We need to go."

The edges around his face and form went a little fuzzy all of a sudden and I very much wanted to curl up in the corner of the booth and have a little nap.

"But can we not stay here?" I looked up at him through my thick eyelashes. "Please, sir?"

"No, we may not." He lowered his voice. "This is no place for a lady."

Biting my lip again and grinning, I looked at Mrs. Harris. "Why did you bring me here? You have tricked me!"

Her lips puckered as she tried not to burst before snorting with loud laughter along with me.

"Fine," I said, "but only because I am quite tired."

Mrs. Harris stayed to assist Mr. Harris, and I assume that meant to drink more, while Everett and I went upstairs to his flat, me clinging to his arm to steady myself.

Burying my face in his arm and breathing in his scent, I looked up at him.

He is so devastatingly beautiful.

"Is it true you're a teetotaler?" I asked, somehow adding a few extra t's into the word.

"Yes," he said, helping me right my posture as we climbed the steps to his flat.

"Why?"

"I have seen too many people lose themselves at the bottom of a bottle." He fished in his pocket for his key as I leaned against the wall next to his front door. "Other people can do as they like, but it is just not for me."

He pushed the door open and I stumbled inside.

"Oh, look. Home again. How I *adore* this place." I fell into the armchair by the window and watched the little people outside on the street, free to go as they pleased. I never thought I would envy poor people so much.

"If you dislike my home, you are free to leave at any time," Everett said, his tone exhausted and burdened. He stripped off his coat and threw it over the back of the other chair. "I did not realize you loathed it so much."

"It is not the place I mind. It is the company."

"Oh, well, that is much better."

"Not you, fool." I turned my heavy head to look at him. "I am alone here all day. You are away all afternoon and late into the night and sleeping in the morning. Why must you be gone so often?"

Everett's face and voice softened. "You would be happier if I were here more?"

"Of course," I said, rising from my chair and heading to the bedroom.

I was so tired. Closing the door seemed like too much work at the time. As I began undressing, Everett's eyes widened and he quickly turned around.

"So, you don't despise me then?" he asked.

"Do you know how to unlace a corset?"

There was a long pause.

"Pardon?"

I had managed to get my skirt, bustle, and petticoats off. I had learned how to deal with the corset myself but my intoxicated and sleepy state had made this specific task challenging.

"I just want to go to sleep and I can't get the laces untied," I moaned, my semi-numb fingers fumbling with what suddenly felt like a snarl in the ribbons. "I've got a knot."

My corset, stockings and chemise remained on, tied in place.

"Please," I said softly.

I heard him clear his throat as he slowly turned around and approached me. Carefully, he pulled the laces loose without untying them all the way. I suddenly became very aware of his warm breath tickling the tiny hairs on the back of my neck. His familiar manly, woodsy, entirely lovely smell made my stomach flutter. My heart was beating so fast, I thought he must be able to hear it.

"I could never despise you, Everett," I said quietly.

After loosening the final lace, his fingertips grazed my lower back through the thin cotton of my chemise and I nearly shuddered from the shock running down my spine.

"Will that do?" he whispered.

I slowly turned to face him. He was even closer to me than I had originally thought.

"Yes, thank you," I said.

I watched his eyes to see if they would dart down even for a second to admire me in my delicates. I wanted him to look. I wanted him to touch me. I wanted his hands to cup and caress the curves and valleys of my form. I wanted to feel his skin against mine.

But no. His gaze was only on my lips. It remained there as he spoke again. "You should go to bed, Cora."

I stared at him for a moment, my mind wrapping itself around what he had said.

I disappeared behind the bedroom door and tugged the corset over my head, throwing it to the floor. I slid into bed, furious with myself and at him.

Perhaps he despises me. If not, perhaps he should.

TEN

Cora

Friday, August 10, 1888

"Why would you think for even a moment that drinking in a pub was a responsible, intelligent thing to do?"

Pressing two fingers to my temple, I glared up at Everett from my seat at the table, watching as he paced. "To be fair, Mrs. Harris and I were both intoxicated when we made that decision."

He let out a loud, fake laugh. "Oh, don't worry. I will certainly be having a talk with Mrs. Harris about her conduct."

"Perhaps you should have that talk with her now so I may go back to bed," I said, thinking longingly of sleep and a spot of laudanum for my headache.

He ignored my suggestion. "You obviously don't look and act like people around here. You specifically brought attention to yourself. Did you *want* to get hurt?"

"Nothing bad happened. On the contrary, I *made* money." I lazily gestured to the few coins scattered across the table. I tried to smile smugly but moving the muscles in my face made my head hurt more.

Everett stopped for a moment, eyeing the coins with suspicion. "Folks around here will fall for anything."

"Will they? Good to know," I said. "I can try other methods next time." I slowly stood, blinking a few times as the dizzies struck. "Now, if you are quite finished scolding me like a child, I will return to bed."

"Wait." Still scowling, he grabbed the wrapped parcel from the seat of the other chair and slid it across the table to me. "I was going to give this to you last night." He did not have the excited, anticipatory smile of someone giving a gift so I became hesitant.

I pulled the twine from around the brown paper wrapping and unrolled it. Tucked neatly inside was a gray cotton dress, the entire thing dotted with tiny white flowers. It was simple, plain as can be, and a far cry from the dresses I had in my trunks. Looking at it made my heart ache.

Is this what I have been reduced to?

"It's been in the theater costume room for ages. I don't even think it has ever been worn," he added quietly. "I believe it will fit."

I looked up at Everett, smiling weakly as my head throbbed. It was a sweet gesture, truly, and he took a huge risk by stealing it for me, but it would take me some time to get used to this new life and the lack of frills, flourishes, and ribbons that came with it.

"Thank you," I said. "You did not need to do that."

"But now you can leave the flat and not attract so much attention. You will be much safer. You and Mrs. Harris can take walks now."

Right into the Thames, I should think.

I traced my finger over one of the flowers, touching each of the tiny bumps of embroidery thread that made up its petals. "It's lovely."

"I think you'll look lovely in it, too."

It was that comment that jarred the fuzzy memories from the night before and, recalling our intimate moment, I wanted to disappear. I wondered if the front window was locked—perhaps I could leap out and escape my discomfort and humiliation with a dramatic leap onto a moving omnibus.

"I believe I will return to bed now. I am really not feeling well," I said finally after staring glumly at the dress for a moment. "Please excuse me."

It was not a complete lie. However, the pain in my head was nothing compared to the stinging humiliation I felt. I simply could not bear to face him again so soon after the uncomfortable exchange from the night before.

Everett and I shared a supper of mutton, bread and potatoes. The dress remained, still half-wrapped in its brown paper, laying limp on the windowsill. My headache had subsided but I still felt a bit weary. I had only seen Mrs. Harris for a moment earlier that day. The woman, cheery as usual, apparently dealt with drink far better than I.

Finally, I ventured a few words. "I apologize that you came home to an empty flat and did not know where I was. I imagine that caused some worry and I do apologize for not leaving a note."

Everett had evidently given up on some of his anger, his expression gradually softening and his jaw slowly unclenching. His eyes, lifting from his plate to my face, were still hard and serious.

He has gone from loving me to loathing me.

"Well, that's more of an apology than I expected," he mumbled before taking a bite of his supper. He opened his mouth to say something but the tidy stack of coins on the table caught his attention and he stopped. "How do you know how to read palms? Is that a fashionable hobby for ladies these days?"

"Oh," I said with a laugh. "I do not know how to read palms. I made it all up."

His eyebrows perked up. "Really?"

"Of course. They are just lines." I took a bite of meat. "My aunt Charlotte taught me how to read people and tell what they want most. Every human being is driven by their desires and our desires really only come down to a couple of things—money, security, power, or love."

Everett chewed slowly as he considered this. "And what do you desire?"

Before I could answer, there was a knock at the door. Everett got up and wiped his mouth with his palm as he opened the door, coming face-to-face with Tom Lindsey. Mr. Lindsey immediately glowered at Everett and then looked at me and then back at Everett.

"Mr. Lindsey, so nice to see you." I quickly rose from my chair. "Can I offer you some tea?"

"What is the meaning of this?" Mr. Lindsey's face grew redder by the second, his pudgy fingers curling into fists at his side. "What is this unseemly living arrangement you have chosen, Mrs. Pringle?"

I tried to keep my voice calm as the large, tall man pushed Everett out of the way and advanced towards me.

"I do not know of what you speak, Mr. Lindsey." I gave a light, dainty chuckle. "Mr. Rigby is a friend who offered his assistance to me when I needed to move out of my home."

Mr. Lindsey cast a sideways glance into the bedroom. I regretted not closing the door or making the bed. This left Mr. Lindsey to see a twisted pile of blankets on the one bed in the flat.

"Oh, I am sure he has offered his assistance to you, Mrs. Pringle." He scowled at Everett. "This is preposterous. You rejected me for this gutter rat." His eyes narrowed. "This damn mongrel."

"There is no need of that," I snapped. "How did you find out where I—"

"Mr. Lindsey," Everett said, "I realize this must look unorthodox but I assure you—"

"Do not speak to me, you filth," Mr. Lindsey hissed at him

before looking back at me. "You did not respond to any letters I sent and when I went to your home, you weren't there. Mr. Jennings provided your new address. I did not expect to find *him* here with you in this … place." His eyes roamed the room as his lip curled in disgust. "Gather your things. You are leaving with me. Now. You deserve better than to be his whore."

"I am no one's whore and I am not going anywhere with you. You need to leave." I pointed at the door. "Please go or we will call the police."

The corners of Everett's eyes pinched for a moment. There was something reluctant in his manner.

Mr. Lindsey stomped to the doorway before looking back at me. "I knew of your dalliance before but I was prepared to forgive it if you married me. But you really are his harlot."

Tom Lindsey knows everyone worth knowing. He is going to destroy me. And quite possibly Everett as well.

"Mr. Rigby and I are wed." The words were like an unstoppable train, careening off a track over a high ravine. I felt myself falling, the wreckage tumbling all around me.

Mr. Lindsey's lips curled and Everett slowly turned to face me, his eyes wide and his jaw set.

"You married him instead of me." His mouth twitched as he clenched his teeth. "You stupid woman."

Everett frowned. "Perhaps you should leave, Mr. Lindsey."

He gave one final snarl before storming down the hall, his heavy footsteps pounding on the rickety stairs. Everett slowly moved to the door, closing it. His eyes darted as he thought, his hand squeezing a fistful of hair at the back of his head.

"I… I had to say something." I swallowed. "I'm sorry. I should not have said that. Surely it is better if people think we are married than living in sin."

He glanced at me quickly but didn't say anything. Leaning against the door, he rubbed his jaw, his eyes still moving in frantic concentration.

"What is it?" I sat across from him. "Please say something."

"I have to go." He whipped the door open. "I will explain when I get back. Keep the door locked."

He disappeared down the hall before I could reply. I whipped the door back open and called after him. "Everett!"

Movement from nearby caught my eye and I jerked my head to see Mrs. Harris staring at me, bewildered, from her doorway.

"You and Mr. Rigby are *married*?"

ELEVEN

Cora

Friday, August 10, 1888

Mrs. Harris stayed with me while I waited for Everett to return. I explained everything to Mrs. Harris, even including the complicated situation with Everett's charade and such.

She stayed quiet until I was finished. After a moment to take in all that I'd said, she commented, "I have to admit, I'm relieved he's not your brother."

Only half listening to her, I drummed my fingers on the tabletop. "Hmm? Why is that?"

"Because of the way he looks at you."

Just as I was about to ask what she meant, someone knocked on the door loudly. "It's me," Everett said from the other side.

Unlocking the door, I let him in. "Where did you go in such a hurry?"

Everett leaned his back against the wall. He just looked at me, his eyes heavy with concern, as he rubbed the back of his neck. "I went to the theater to beg for my job."

"Whatever for?"

"Tom Lindsey is a theatrical investor. Half the shows the Princess Royal puts on are because of *his* money," he explained. "I wanted to get to the theater before Lindsey did and persuade the manager to keep me, to explain why you are here and explain that you and I are *not* married *or* living sinfully, and that the whole situation is a misunderstanding." He closed his eyes and slid down to the floor. "Lindsey got there first."

I quickly took a seat, my legs feeling weak underneath me. "Oh, no. Everett."

A crease formed between Mrs. Harris' eyes as she watched him. "What happened?"

"I got sacked, that's what happened." He thumped the back of his head against the wall. "The bloody bastard threatened to pull his funding if they didn't get rid of me. He gave them no choice."

She put a hand on her chest. "You poor dear. You'll land on your feet, surely."

"I don't know if I will," Everett said, a glint of a tear in the corner of his right eye. "Lindsey knows everyone in London theater so he'll make sure nobody hires me. I'm finished."

Mrs. Harris stood. "I'll tell you what. I'll go talk to Mr. Harris right now and get him to keep an ear out for anybody looking for a capable pair of hands."

Frowning, Everett nodded up at her as she left. "Thank you, Mrs. Harris. I appreciate that."

The flat went silent after Mrs. Harris closed the door. I didn't know what to say to comfort Everett. He eventually spoke up but his eyes stayed planted on the floor. His words were quiet and slow. "You should go to Lindsey as soon as possible and tell him we are not married and swear to him that our conduct was never unseemly."

"Do you think he would get you your job back if I did?"

"No, but he would consider taking you as his wife."

"I am not marrying that ogre," I said. "Why would you think I would?"

He finally looked up to meet my gaze. "I can't afford to take care of you anymore. Mr. Lindsey can provide a home for you. Security, influence. The finest gowns and jewels you could ever want. He can give you those things." Everett ran a hand through his hair. "Waiting for a letter from your aunt may no longer be an option."

Sickened by the notion, I shook my head. "No. Everett, no. I will not marry him."

"Cora, you must—"

"I must do no such thing and I will ask you to never suggest it again." I rose and stepped to the window, watching the busy street below. "What happens now?"

He took a moment to consider. "If I can find work doing odd jobs, perhaps we can keep the flat for another month. I expect we will need to relocate."

"I can sell two of my dresses," I said, turning back to him. "I hate wearing black anyway."

He frowned at me. "You should keep your mourning dresses."

"I will mourn not having a roof over my head," I said. "The dresses will fetch a few pounds."

"Fine," he said. "Do you have any skills we can make use of? Do you sew or cook or bake? Can you make anything?"

I thought about my life back in Molesey, before everything was done for me. Even back then, we had a cook and a housekeeper. "I am afraid I am useless with a needle and thread."

"Perhaps you could find work as a governess."

I scoffed. "No, thank you." Thinking of my childhood aspirations, I tapped my lip. "What if I auditioned for a play?"

Everett's mouth tightened as he considered this. "Surely you are not serious."

"I assure you, I am quite serious."

"You have no experience," he said. "If Lindsey can get me banned from working at theaters across London, he will certainly make sure you won't be an actress."

"He cannot possibly have *that* much sway all over London."

"You might be surprised," he said, his knowing and

condescending look burrowing into me. "Besides, you must know how many actresses support themselves when they're off stage."

I winced at his vulgar reference. "Well, yes, but—"

"I know that world far better than you do. Yes, a few actresses succeed but many, *many* do not and it is not a road I would recommend you try."

"I only need a temporary solution," I reminded him. "Give me one good reason why I should not at least try—"

"You are too old."

His face stiffened as soon as the words left his lips and he winced so subtly that his lids barely moved—but I noticed.

I glowered at him. "Too old? I am only two and twenty." I turned away from him, white hot rage snaking up my body like vines. "How dare you."

"Most actresses start when they are much, much younger—"

My eyes darted back to him. "Everett, I quite understand you. I am far too old and withered to be an actress. I am an ancient witch, too hideous to even be considered for a part. You need *not* go on."

"You know that is not what I meant."

Sitting at the table, I crossed my arms over my chest. It was rather presumptive to think I could not make it as an actress. It was true, I had no formal experience. However, much of my adult life had been spent acting—acting as if I came from a wealthy and well-connected family to impress my social circle, acting like I enjoyed the company of influential people in order to win their approval even when they disgusted me, acting like a woman who loved her husband when I had come to feel numb to his presence.

I had certainly never stepped foot onto a playhouse stage but I knew myself to be exemplary at playing a role.

I bit my lip, searching for solutions, my eyes landing on one of the coins on the table. I slowly slid it closer to myself and picked it up, moving it smoothly between my fingers, watching as the sunlight from the window glinted off its metallic contours.

"I am going back to the pub tonight to make a little money." I glanced at him. "It was easy when I was intoxicated. Think of how effective I could be reading palms sober."

I expected Everett to protest but the day had beaten him down too much to bother. In any case, he knew there was no point in trying to persuade me once I had made up my mind.

Everett came with me to the pub that night, taking my fee for me as I traced the lines of calloused hands and the wrinkles of aged fingers. Mrs. Harris spoke to her husband on our account to make sure we would not be evicted from our makeshift in-house business. He agreed to keep us indoors and off the street in exchange for fifteen percent of our takings.

I did my best to vary the imprecise predictions I gave to my patrons, especially since many of them watched as I palm read for others before handing over their own four shillings.

"This line here," I said to a middle-aged woman, likely my twenty-fifth customer of the night, "this tells me you are soon to have a bout of good luck."

"What, like wiv money?"

"It is unclear, madame." I inspected her dry hand closer. "Oh, wait. This line. This shows me that you have lost something important to you. Yes, yes! That must mean you will get lucky and find something you have misplaced." I smiled sweetly at her.

Her captivated eyes widened further. "But what have I lost?"

"Your marbles," hollered someone from behind her, sloshing a bit of beer onto the wooden plank floor.

"Your five minutes are over, ma'am," Everett said, nodding to the man behind her in line.

She reluctantly slid out from the booth, looking confused, muttering something about not knowing what she misplaced.

My next customer was a burly gent with round shoulders, sausage-like fingers, and arms the size of tree trunks. He tossed a coin at Everett, who deftly snatched it out of the air, and squeezed into the booth, his size making it a struggle. He plopped his massive hand out in front of me.

"What say you, missy?" He grinned, his gaze lingering on my bosom.

Between the gloom of the pub and the layer of dirt on his hands, it was hard to tell where the lines on his palm actually were. Forcing back my urge to cringe, I raised his hand and peered at it closely.

"Oh. Oh, dear," I said. "This line says not of your future, but of your past. How interesting."

The man looked down at his hand and then back up at me. "What?"

I looked into his eyes. "You did something bad many years ago. I cannot say for certain what happened but this line here—this line tells me you got away with it."

A few of the spectators whispered among themselves.

His face stiffened as he glanced at our audience. "I ain't done nothin."

They immediately went quiet but I continued.

"This small line here, do you see it? It forks in the middle. *This* one is about your future. It's a cautionary line. You can either keep a low profile, watching yourself, and live a long life. See how this line is long? Or you can go the other away," I pointed to a shorter broken line, "and meet an untimely end."

He blinked a few times and raised to his feet, his still face failing to hide his worry. "Alright."

As he returned to his table across the room, Everett glanced at me and gave me a subtle nod. Earlier that evening when he had seen the brute come in, Everett had whispered to me.

"Everyone knows he roughs up his wife. If he comes over here, you put the fear of God into him, but don't mention his wife specifically."

A few customers later, a young woman joined us at our booth. She slid her coins over to Everett and shyly stretched her open palm out to me. Before I could take her hand in mine, she pulled back.

"God won't be cross with me for this, will 'e?" Her voice was high and quiet.

"Well," I said, quickly searching for a response, "I cannot speak for God, of course, but I see far more sins occurring in this very room and just outside. Perhaps God should focus on those more and less on a bit of fortune-telling that does not hurt anyone."

Biting her lip, the young woman slowly brought her hand forward again and I surveyed the creases in her delicate palm.

"This line here tells me of a great romance—a true and boundless love." I looked at her. Her eyes were fixed on her palm, her eyes soft, her pink lips curving into a weak smile. "This line shows that you and your true love will have happy times together. It will not be perfect all the time, but it will be a strong marriage and this line means a happy family."

Of course, all of the contours on her tiny palm were just random lines that meant nothing. But I had apparently struck a meaningful chord, as the young woman suddenly burst into tears.

Between heavy sobs, she eventually squeaked out the words, "How did you know?"

Everett and I exchanged glances, not knowing what on earth we should do.

"My husband—he died in an accident last month," she continued. "I am carrying his child." She moved her palm forward a bit more, closer to me. "Please, is there anything else you can tell me?"

She was dressed simply but well enough for the neighborhood. Her round cheeks and the amount of flesh on her arms were encouraging signs.

"All I can tell you is that the family line, right here, is a good one. Your family or perhaps your late husband's family will care for you."

"That's not what I…" She stopped herself and shook her head, lowering it.

I cupped her hand. "I am sorry for your loss."

She raised her head again, her big brown eyes flooded with tears. "Thank you."

As she slid out from behind the booth and headed for the door, wiping tears off her pale cheeks, Everett leapt up from his seat. I watched through the thick glass of the pub window as he caught up with her on the street. He spoke to her briefly before putting her shillings back into her hand. She went on her way and Everett's eyes met mine through the window. I quickly looked away and busied myself with my next prospect.

It was after two in the morning when Everett and I returned to his flat upstairs, a healthy little collection of coins to show for our work.

Everett sat at the table, counting our take for the night. He made a separate pile to give to Mrs. Harris in the morning.

"Not bad," he said, sitting back in his chair. "Perhaps we should see if we can read palms near a theater at intermission. Maybe even near an opera house."

"What is this 'we' you speak of? I believe *I* was the only one of us doing the palm reading."

Everett rolled his eyes.

I yawned. "People who have been drinking are far easier with their money than patrons of a theater or opera."

"Yes, but those people *have* more money to spend on a palm reading."

I shook my head. "No, I think we are better off staying at the pub for now."

"We made some money this evening but it's not going to be enough to keep a roof over our heads and food on the table. Besides, that pub has the same customers almost every night. Eventually, we will run out."

"We can find other pubs—"

"We will likely have to scrape more than fifteen percent off the top for them—"

"Is that with or without the money you give back to pretty

young widows?" I snapped, raising from my chair.

"You just don't want to go to the theaters because you might see your society friends."

I glared at him and turned to watch out the window, the glow of the streetlight keeping the sidewalk bright. It was so late and yet the street was still busy with pedestrians and vendors. London never slept, even in the witching hour.

"Do you believe in ghosts?"

"Hmm?"

Crossing my arms, I turned around. "Ghosts. Spirits. The afterlife."

"I never really thought about it." He had returned to busying himself with counting our take for the night.

"You were never told ghost stories as a child?"

"On occasion, yes."

"And never once did you consider their existence?"

"I'm sure I believed they were real at the time." His eyes were still focused on the coins in front of him.

I joined him at the table again, finally getting his full attention. "That young widow," I said, "I think she wanted to know more about her husband's existence, not her own future."

"Her husband doesn't exist anymore," he said. "You think she wanted to know … about his spirit?"

"Why shouldn't she wonder if her husband is watching her? If his spirit is still haunting her?" My eyes landed on our little stack of coins and the wheels in my head began to turn. "If you could pay someone to talk to a loved one who had passed away, wouldn't you?"

His eyes narrowed. "You are speaking of spiritualism."

"I am." I smiled and leaned closer to him. "I saw an ad in the newspaper a few months ago for a spiritualist who charged a pound for a one-hour session with her. She performs séances out of her home and lets her customers talk to their deceased relatives *through* her."

"We don't know how to do that—"

"We can figure it out, it cannot possibly be that hard. Surely we can put together a few clever tricks—"

"Oh, can *we*?"

"Yes, of course we can! And I can act—"

"Oh, can you?"

I slapped my palms down on the table. "I promise you, I can." I folded my arms across my chest. "You are not the only actor around here."

Everett sighed, shaking his head. "This is absurd."

"Exactly what is so absurd about it?"

"You should not have to lower yourself to such indelicate acts. What of your social standing?" He hesitated. "I dare say, *if* we do this, you will not be accepted by the same class of people as you once knew."

I felt my brows knitting together as I thought about this very real consequence. I waved the thought away with a small shrug.

"Although your concern for my reputation is appreciated, it is unnecessary. I only need enough money to stay alive long enough to hear from my aunt. Once I am in America, I will be in good company once more."

Well, good-ish company. I do not expect my aunt and her husband rub shoulders with high society on a regular occasion. No matter. I will get there and marry up, just like before.

Biting my lip, I prepared for Everett's further protests. Instead, he drummed his fingers on the tabletop, deep in thought. "I know a pawnbroker who has a spirit board for sale." He slid his chair back and grabbed his coat and an empty sack. "I'll return in an hour or so. You get some rest."

"Wait, where are you going *this* time? The pawnbroker's shop is surely closed at this hour."

He smiled and pulled a shiny brass key from his pocket. "I need to go get you a costume."

TWELVE

Cora

Monday, August 20, 1888

I inhaled deeply, my eyes shut tight. "There's someone here with us."

"Who? Who is it?"

I angled my head slightly. "I see … the most beautiful green eyes. Such a gentle, kind face."

"That sounds like my mother!"

"Yes, I believe you are right," I whispered, my palms flat on the table in front of me. "She says she misses you very much and that she is so proud of the woman you have become."

"Oh, my word. Is my father there too?"

Moving my eyes beneath lowered lids, I paused. "I see many faces with her. You have lost several family members but they are all there together on the other side." I gave a quick nod. "Wait. I see a tall man. He is smiling."

"My father was rather stout."

"Mm," I continued. "This man is younger. Maybe a brother

or a cousin?"

"I… I don't know—"

"A friend from your childhood?"

Everett released an audible sigh.

My eyes flashed open so I could glare at him. "What?"

"If it's a friend from childhood, the customer won't remember them as a tall man, will they?" He frowned, his hand roughly rubbing the back of his neck. "They won't care about someone they don't know or remember. You need to pay attention to what the customer says and what breadcrumbs you're offering in return."

Smiling sweetly, Mrs. Harris patted my hand. "You're doing a fine job, dear."

"You should probably keep your eyes open," Everett added. "You need to watch their body language, not just listen to their responses."

I looked up at Everett again. "Can we stop for the night? We have been doing this for two hours."

Mrs. Harris, kindly acting as our customer, looked relieved. "Mr. Harris will be looking for me so I best head out. I can come tomorrow to practice again if you like."

Everett nodded and crossed his arms over his chest as Mrs. Harris made her escape.

I was about to get up when Everett sat across from me. "Again."

"Everett, please. No more for tonight."

"You need more practice. You have to get this right." I closed my eyes. "Mmm. How interesting. No spirits are coming to me. I guess the gate is closed for the night." Smirking, I opened my eyes again.

"Cora. Don't be difficult."

"*You* are the one who is being difficult. I will do fine tomorrow." I gave a light shrug. "I have always been a natural performer with excellent improvisational instincts."

"Indeed," Everett sniped. "When was the last time you acted a part, your wedding day?"

I scowled at him. "Perhaps you of all people should not jest about pretending to be someone else." I raised from my chair. "I am going to bed."

"Cora, please sit down." He stretched his arms over the tabletop, palms up.

I slowly lowered myself again and slid my hands onto his, taking note of every rough deviation and crease on his fingers. My neck warmed at the subtle caress of his thumb.

I closed my eyes and started my act again, fighting off the shakiness in my voice. "Oh, great spirit realm, we ask to enter. We seek the guidance of souls beyond our world." I opened my eyes again. "I forgot to ask who you want to talk to."

Everett smiled warily. "You have to remember to ask before you start your whole speech. It diminishes the moment."

"I know." I winced. "Sorry."

"My mother," he said, his smile fading.

He had never spoken of his parents before. Well, he had previously told me his family were successful merchants and traders based in the West Indies, but by the solemn look on his face just then, I knew that was part of his lie.

"How did she die?"

He frowned at me. "Vague questions and comments, remember?"

I felt uncomfortable bringing his family into our act, just as I would feel uncomfortable bringing my late parents into it. It seemed far too personal. Too painful.

"What was her name?"

He let out a long breath before speaking. "Vaishnavi."

"That is a lovely name."

I closed my eyes again and clasped his hands a little tighter. "We seek to speak with Vaishnavi. We seek…" I opened my eyes again. "I cannot do this with you. It does not feel right."

"It is going to feel personal with everyone who comes to you."

"Yes, but I do not know *them*." I slowly pulled my hands from his and folded them in my lap. "How long ago did she die?"

"Cora, I don't want to talk about—"

"You brought her up."

"You don't really care about my real life, remember?"

"Yet here I am, asking you."

Everett sank down a little into his chair, his gaze focused on the flickering flame of the candle on the table. "I was born in Bombay. My father was a soldier based in India. He married my mother. Shortly after I was born, the three of us boarded a ship back to England." He let out a long exhale. "During the long voyage, illness made the rounds from passenger to passenger and both my parents died." He finally lifted his eyes to meet mine. "But I lived." He gave a little shrug. "Somehow."

"It's a miracle," I said.

"Or a curse."

Silence hung in the air, occasionally broken up by sounds from nearby flats or the street outside.

"My mother died when I was two," I said. "Childbirth is an arduous business."

Sometimes I wished the baby boy had lived so I could resent him for taking my mother from me. He did not. Aunt Charlotte moved in with us soon after. She told me Papa was catatonic for months after my mother's death.

"Ah," Everett said after a long pause. "We are both orphans then."

"How do you know about your parents?"

He hesitated before speaking and lowered his gaze to his hands, still resting on the tabletop. "I was raised by my father's brother. He would kindly remind me how generous he was to take me in, how philanthropic he was to take pity on a boy who happened to have darker skin than his own sons." His jaw tightened.

"He sounds like a bloody bastard," I said with a scoff.

Everett studied me, a surprised and amused grin spreading across his mouth. "Profanity, Mrs. Pringle. I am shocked."

I had not seen that glimmer in his eyes since before I moved out of my home and into his.

As I lay in bed that night, staring into the darkness, I

went over all the tactics Everett and I had been practicing as we prepared for my first ever performance as a spiritualist. I thought about the little plays I performed in as a young girl and how much I had enjoyed them. This was quite different though. I thought about Aunt Charlotte and her tarot and palm readings and how Papa turned his nose up at us, calling our little games "nonsense" and then smiling to himself as he went back to his evening tea.

What would he say if he could see me now?

I heard the scratching of Everett's pencil on paper, and I wondered if he was still writing plays. He and I had been snapping at one another regularly since that night I drank too much and acted like a fool, giving birth to an uncomfortable tension between us. The warmth I saw in his eyes earlier in the evening was only the first hint of that uneasiness subsiding.

I should have just married Mr. Lindsey.

By not marrying Mr. Lindsey, I had given up my last chance at a comfortable existence and sabotaged Everett's life in the process. As a young woman, all I wanted was a life of friends and parties in London but when the opportunity had shown itself, I had rejected it. And why? All because Mr. Lindsey was not my ideal partner. Dr. Marshall Pringle had been far from my ideal partner but that certainly hadn't stopped me from marrying him.

The squeaks and whines of the aged easy chair from the other room told me Everett was settling in for the night. His hushed snores usually started up minutes after those familiar sounds, but not that night. He shifted in his chair a few times, but still sleep did not come. I wondered if he was thinking about our eventual financial demise or perhaps regretting ever meeting me in the first place. Either way, I would not blame him.

The next afternoon, Mrs. Harris came by the flat, her hands folded neatly in front of her.

"Mrs. Harris, you are so kind. I do not require your assistance today as I feel quite prepared—"

"Never mind that," Everett said. "Take a bit more practice while you still can—"

"That's not why I'm here," Mrs. Harris cut in, biting the corner of her lip. "I'm afraid there's a hitch in the plan."

Everett and I exchanged glances.

"Mr. Harris don't want you doing your, uh, performance in the pub tonight." She winced. "He saw your ad in the paper and he don't like it."

Everett took a seat at the table and closed his eyes, running a hand through his hair. He sighed, glaring at the cobwebs on the ceiling of his home.

"Certainly Mr. Harris will be reasonable," I said. "He knows we cannot change venues now that the ad is published. What if we give him twenty-five percent of our taking for the night?"

"I'm afraid that won't do," she said. "He said what you're doing isn't Christian."

"And what exactly does the Bible say about drunkenness? He doesn't seem to mind that so much," Everett said matter-of-factly.

Mrs. Harris frowned at that comment. "I done you a great number of favors these past few weeks so I'll be taking none of that, Mr. Rigby."

Everett crossed his arms over his chest, sliding down slightly in his chair.

I looked around the flat. "We will have to do it here then."

"Here?" Everett repeated. "What do you mean 'here'?"

"Here, in this room."

He laughed. "Absolutely not. I'm not going to have a bunch of strangers in my *home*."

"We paid good money for that ad so people *will* come here." I looked at Mrs. Harris. "Is your boy available this evening to man the door downstairs? We can offer him ten percent—"

Everett sat up straighter. "What if some brute comes in that door and tries to kill us?"

"I would like to think young Mr. Harris would not direct a

murderer to come upstairs," I said coolly.

"I'll do it!" Frank appeared in the doorway, obviously overhearing our conversation. "I'll keep the ruffians out."

I looked at Everett for confirmation of my plan, one eyebrow cocked in a I-told-you-so manner.

"I suppose we have no choice," he said, his eyes settling on the wall behind me. His face softened slightly as he looked about the room a bit. "I'll light some candles. It'll add to the atmosphere." He paused thoughtfully. "This could be better, actually."

The focus in his eyes somehow heightened their color as he went to work shifting his belongings around to create something of a set for my performance. He must have sensed me watching him as he glanced at me over his shoulder, a shy smile playing on his lips. I quickly lowered my eyes.

"Do me a favor, boy," Mrs. Harris said to her son from their flat, the door still open. "Don't tell your father about this."

I hadn't expected a reason to make use of my enormous ostrich feathers. As I tucked them into my bonnet and pinned them in place, I was grateful I had chosen not to sell them off so hastily. They certainly added a level of drama to my spiritualist ensemble. My crimson gown included a bit of sparkle which would give an ethereal effect while I sat among candlelight, its lace sleeves hanging loose off the shoulder. Half of my curls were tucked into a neat bun under my bonnet while thick, round, orange coils lay upon my neck and shoulders. I loved an excuse to let my bountiful hair down as it was one of my most favored features.

Thanks to some help from Mrs. Harris, my corset and bodice were tied more snug than usual and my neckline glittered with the faux diamonds Everett had taken from the theater's prop room. A red stain made my full lips more prominent and I added just a touch of charcoal around the eyes to make them more intense, even in the dim light of the flat. As for my décolletage, more of that was left unconcealed than I was used to. It seemed to be the way of entertainers of the fairer sex.

I slowly opened the bedroom door and revealed my completed look to Everett. He was busy gathering his things to move into the bedroom while a couple of chairs had been brought over from Mrs. Harris' flat. His eyes grew wide as he took in every detail from hat to hem.

"What do you think, Mr. Rigby?" I said in a breathy, sultry voice.

He did not reply right away. "I think … I think you look…" he finally tore his eyes away from me, "the part."

While he and Frank moved some things into the bedroom to make more room for guests, I placed other props around the area: a bouquet of dead roses we got for cheap from a nearby flower shop, a window curtain made of dark damask we borrowed from Mrs. Harris, and the skull stolen from the theater that was used for a production of *Hamlet*. Everett told me he did not think the skull was real, but I was not fully convinced. I positioned several candles around the room and Everett trailed after me, lighting each with a match.

Looking at me, he blew out the match. "Are you ready?"

A wave of anxiety struck my abdomen. Ignoring it, I lifted my head high. "Of course."

The advertisement we purchased invited patrons to the pub beginning at half-seven in the evening. Frank would just have to guess which customers coming and going into the pub were actually looking for me. Five minutes before our performance was to begin, Frank left us to start his job as doorman downstairs as I clasped my black lace gloved hands together tightly, squeezing my thumb to try to make my hands stop shaking.

"Should… should I stand or should I be sitting when they come in?"

Everett hesitated. "Uh … I think either is fine."

"Right." I nodded. "Perhaps I will just stand."

I stood. And I stood. And I stood a bit longer. After twenty minutes, I took a seat and drummed my fingers on the wooden tabletop.

Everett leaned against the wall, his arms crossed in front of his chest. "What a waste of money that advertisement was."

I frowned. "Maybe *The Gazette Weekly* just has the wrong audience."

"We couldn't afford an advertisement in any of the larger publications," he grumbled. "I better go downstairs and make sure Frank is—Oh. Good evening. Come in."

My eyes flashed to the doorway as a young woman smiled at me. She looked nervously into the room. "Good evening. Are you the spiritualist I read about in the paper?"

Her voice was more refined than I had expected for this part of town. Perhaps the ad would draw people from all over the city!

"I am Madame Pringle," I said, sliding into the elegant, slow and deliberate voice I had chosen for the act, slightly lower than my natural register. "It is a pleasure to make your acquaintance, my dear."

Everett smiled graciously at her. "Sessions with Madame Pringle are ten shillings."

"Oh, yes, of course." She fished the fee from her reticule, handed it to Everett, and he directed her to sit in the chair opposite me.

"What is your name?" I said, suddenly aware that Everett and I had not discussed where he would be during all of this.

Is he going to sit with us? Is he just going to stand there lurking?

"Mary," the young woman said, worry still present in her brown eyes. "I would like to try to contact my best friend from childhood, Helen."

I nodded. "Of course. We will certainly try, my dear."

I glanced up at Everett and gave him a quick nod to sit down. His mouth tightened and he lowered himself into the chair immediately—taking the seat to the left of me—and quite stiffly, as if he had forgotten how to bend like a human. Mary sat on my right.

"Now," I began, "let us place our palms down on the table with our fingertips overlapped at the edges so that we create a portal so the spirits can come and find us." Hesitantly, three sets of hands moved into position on the table. Everett and I exchanged a quick glance as my pinky finger touched his.

I took a deep breath and fixed my gaze on one of the candles across the room, careful to look at no one. "Oh, divine spirits. We call to you and ask you to join us here this night. Awake from your everlasting slumber now. We seek your guidance." I lowered my voice to a whisper. "Come to us, restless spirits. We beg you to join us here tonight. We seek our friend, Helen."

I was silent for a moment, feeling nothing but the measured rise and fall of my chest. I slowly raised my eyelids and let my gaze crawl about the room as if I was seeing it for the very first time.

"Here again," I said in a slightly deeper voice. "You dare disrupt my sleep again to serve your purposes." I turned to Mary in a smooth, fluid motion. "You seek your little friend, yes?"

Mary gave a subtle nod, the glimmer of the flickering candles dancing on her round cheeks.

"Very well." I closed my eyes for a moment and then reopened them, forcing my voice to go higher, imitating the tone of a girl. "Mary, I am here."

"Helen, is that you?"

"Yes," I said. "I have missed you so."

"I miss you too, my friend."

"I never thought I would see you again," I squeaked.

I could feel Everett watching me carefully and suddenly I felt very self-conscious acting in front of him. Now that I had a paying customer sitting in front of me, I put in much more effort than during the hours he and I had practiced. The voices and the twitching eyes—none of it seemed very refined, I had to imagine.

"I am sorry I did not get to say goodbye," Mary said.

I tried to remember to keep all my responses unspecific, to draw more information from my client, and to not come forward with my replies too quickly, stretching out the length of the session.

"It is not your fault," I said. "It happened so fast." Smiling, I gave her hand a gentle squeeze. "I felt no pain."

Mary raised an eyebrow. "Truly? But you were in a house fire."

Blast. I assumed it was an illness.

"The smoke overtook me before the flames," I said.

"Is your family with you? Peter and your parents?"

I nodded. "Of course. They are all here." *Keep it ambiguous.* "I hope you are well."

"Oh, Helen, I am. I am recently wed," Mary added. "I wish you could have been there."

"I wish I could have been there too. I am sure you were a beautiful bride." I let my eyelids gradually close and my head fell limp onto my shoulder.

The window whipped open just then, sending a rush of wind into the room, making the candles hiss their indignation. The timing could not have been more perfect.

I breathed in suddenly, my eyes flashing open. Startled and blinking frantically, my gaze bounced around the room.

"Helen has left us," I said, using my original voice. "The Other has left us as well."

Everett glanced at Mary, his face looking as alarmed as hers. Mary gave a little nod, sliding her hands off the table and into her lap.

"She was really here in this room with us, wasn't she?"

I nodded, my face as still as stone. Placing a hand to my chest, I released a long breath, feigning fatigue.

Mary rose and made a shy goodbye to us. Everett walked with her down the stairs until Frank could hail a hansom for her. Everett jogged back up the stairs, his smile wide and his arms outstretched.

"What in the world was that?" he exclaimed. "That was magnificent!"

I smiled, pursing my lips a bit. "I told you I could act."

He grabbed my hands and pulled me up from my seat,

wrapping his arms around me and twirling me around the darkened room. I giggled as my toes lifted off the floor.

"And the bit with the window was brilliant!" I grabbed onto his firm forearms. "How did you end up making it work?"

"I attached a thread to my wrist and to the window frame and just kept it unlatched. It worked even better than I expected."

It was perfect," I added.

The glee in his eyes filled my heart. As he held me close in the candlelit room, my blood quickened. Everett's gaze lowered to my bottom lip for a moment.

"Sorry to disrupt," Frank said from the doorway. "Should I send the next one up?"

Everett's arms dropped from my waist and we both took a step backwards, away from one another. Everett closed the window while I took my seat again.

"Yes," I said. "We are ready for the next one."

THIRTEEN

Amelia

Tuesday, August 21, 1888

"You should have seen it. You would have been delighted by my acting mastery." I feigned a swoon, the back of my hand held to my forehead as I used a breathy voice, my body falling back limply against my chair. "Please, kind lady, help me speak to the ghost of my beloved friend!" I dropped my hand. "The whole display was preposterous."

Simon smirked first at me and then at Mr. Woodacre across from him. Wright Woodacre, a regular guest at our breakfast table, smiled behind his teacup before taking a sip.

"I am sure your performance was nothing less than brilliant, my darling girl. I look forward to your West End debut," Simon mused, one eyebrow cocked. "What about this Madame Cora character? Do you think she suspected you were not sincere?"

"She was far too enraptured with her own performance to notice any flaws in mine," I said while buttering some toast. "Oh, and then the window *happened* to fly open during the session.

What ridiculous rubbish."

Mr. Woodacre set his tea down and folded his arms over his chest. "Am I to presume you do not believe beings from the spirit world ever try to contact their loved ones who still reside in the land of the living?"

I glanced over at Simon before arching an eyebrow at Mr. Woodacre. "I think I have discovered why the men who govern Britain never seem to accomplish anything quickly. Their heads are too full of nonsense like ghosts and ghouls to actually oversee our realm efficiently."

Mr. Woodacre, the personal secretary to a preeminent MP, had only worked in Parliament for two years but already his bevy of political connections was most impressive. I teased him at every opportunity but knew that once he gained real influence there, a relationship with someone in government would be necessary if we were ever to achieve our goal of women's suffrage.

I just needed Mr. Woodacre and Simon to continue sleeping together until then.

Mr. Woodacre chuckled. "I will have you know, Mrs. Baxter, that ghosts and ghouls only enter into parliamentary matters once or twice per debate at the very most."

I laughed loudly as Simon peered at Mr. Woodacre intently, his eyes so soft and warm. Mr. Woodacre did not catch it as he was scanning the headlines of the newspaper folded on the table nearby.

"No, I do not believe the wakeful spirits of our loved ones try to communicate with us," I clarified, brushing a toast crumb from the skirt of my sensible, plain brown dress. "Mainly because I do not believe in spirits at all. This quack makes an income from the grief of vulnerable, desperate individuals and it is most shameful."

Simon sat back in his chair. "What Mrs. Baxter failed to mention is that this spiritualist bought an ad in *The Gazette Weekly* and that is how she discovered this ambitious woman in the first place."

The corner of Mr. Woodacre's handsome mouth perked up. "And do you unmask the unwholesome business practices of everyone who advertises in your publication or just ones you do not approve of?"

I chewed my toast, pretending to mull over my reply. "I will have to let you know if and when any of your MP acquaintances are up for reelection and want to run advertisements in our paper." I let my lips curl into a wide, mischievous grin. "Just imagine all the destruction I could do there."

Soon after Mr. Woodacre made his departure, finding it prudent to leave our home separately from Simon at all costs and, as always, using the door out to the garden when leaving. He was exceptionally private about their longtime relationship, constantly fearing it might jeopardize his political ambitions. Hee was right to feel so. Mr. Woodacre's nerves had only recently eased enough for him to give Simon a quick peck on the cheek in front of me before leaving in the morning.

I wondered if our neighbors suspected anything of his overnight visits.

"Perhaps I shall go visit this spiritualist sometime." Simon slid further down in his chair and crossed his ankles under the table, his hands folded on his flat stomach. "It could be fun."

I rolled my eyes. "Save your coin for the opera."

"You are working on *what*?"

Mr. Granville stared at me, his bulging eyes blinking aggressively and his dominant nostrils flaring, as he stood over my narrow desk. He had been looking over my shoulder as I typed out the first paragraph of my article about going to see Madame Pringle.

I let my eyes slowly rise to meet his. "This article will be in tomorrow's edition. I told you to leave a space for a thousand words—"

"And I did because you said you were working on something good, but you just left out the part about the subject being one of our advertisers." He gesticulated wildly as he spoke, perspiration beading at his temples. "Let me guess—it wasn't a positive experience."

"How did you ever guess?"

"Mrs. Baxter, how do you think we keep the lights on in this place? How do you think we keep our families fed and our wages paid? Our advertisers! We have to keep them happy. This should not be a new concept to you."

I crossed my arms over my chest as he lectured, my lips pursed in irritation. I let him go on for a bit, letting my mind wander to more important topics as he ranted before cutting in while he took a breath.

"Has she purchased a second advertisement for tomorrow's edition?" I already knew the answer.

"No, I do not believe so."

"Ah. What a shame. What shall I write about instead?" I slid my spectacles off and inspected the lenses for dust before resting them on the bridge of my nose once more. "By that, I mean what should I write about that would get half as much attention as an undercover exposé on a swindler? You know how our readers hate those types of stories."

The fact was that our readers *loved* those types of stories. If anything, *The Gazette Weekly* was famous for those types of stories—or infamous, at the very least.

A shadow on Mr. Granville's jaw shifted as he clenched.

"Shall I just continue working on this story then?" I smiled up at him sweetly, my hands folded in my lap.

"Very well," he grumbled as he stalked off to his office, slamming the door behind him.

My fingers returned to the keys of my typewriter, pounding the letters faster and harder than usual to make sure Mr. Granville could hear my progress.

"You play that man like a fiddle," Mr. Turner said from his desk.

"Not well enough evidently," I said, not bothering to hide the glumness from my tone.

"Are you still moping about the Tabram story?"

"Of course I am." I glanced at him before skimming over what I had just typed. "It is not *just* that story. It is that story as well as lots of other stories that make a journalist's name." I sighed. "It is bad enough I have to use a pseudonym for many of my stories in the first place."

My pen name, Ambrose Spellman, was used for any article deemed "inappropriate" for a woman journalist to cover. I rarely knew what byline would be displayed on a story until I saw the newspaper in print.

"Still," Mr. Turner added, "I think you have persuaded him to let you write a lot more serious stories than he ever expected to give you." He turned in his seat to face me. "You were supposed to write housekeeping tips, remember?"

I gave a little shrug as I continued to type, occasionally glancing at my little notebook for reference. "He is the most predictable man alive. Predict what he is going to say, have your reply at the ready, and you are likely to get your way." I smiled wide at Mr. Turner. "Like most men."

He swung his legs back under his desk and got back to his typewriter. "I'm glad *I'm* not predictable."

I smiled smugly. "I knew you would say that."

It was about four o'clock the following day when the bell above the office door jingled. Our sweet receptionist Mrs. Davies greeted the visitor before getting barked at by a very angry woman.

"I want to speak to the owner of this rag this instant," she bellowed. "I have never been so disrespected by a business in my entire life."

My eyes widened as her familiar voice rang in my ears. *It's her.*

I silently slid my chair out and eased myself under my desk, tucking in every bit of my dress and dragging my chair as close to me as possible. Mr. Turner leaned over in his seat and raised an eyebrow at me. I put my finger to my lips and he sat up straight again, shaking his head slightly at my bewildering behavior.

Having heard the furious yelling from the front room, Mr. Granville appeared in the doorway of his office. "I'm Thaddeus Granville, the editor here. What can I do for you?"

I heard the angry flutter of a newspaper being waved about. "I purchased an advertisement and then one of your reporters wrote a scathing review. What is the meaning of such indecorous treatment?"

I rolled my eyes at her use of the word "review," like it had been a major theatrical production and not a fraudulent act at a kitchen table.

"Is Mr. Spellman here? I would like a few words with *him* perhaps," Madame Pringle continued.

Mr. Granville stood two feet from my desk as he spoke to her. "I'm afraid Mr. Spellman is not here at the moment. Perhaps we can discuss this matter in my office. Would you like some tea?"

Madame Pringle's shoes stomped by my desk and into Mr. Granville's office, followed by Mr. Granville. I let out a long breath and, as quietly as possible, slid my chair out and rose to my feet. I brushed a few specks of debris from my skirt as Mr. Turner watched me, amused.

I quickly made my escape out of the office and up the staircase. From the corner on the landing one flight up from our office, I could watch who came and went from the office entrance. After about ten minutes, I saw Madame Pringle leave and get into a hansom cab.

It was not the first time an angry story subject had barged into the office looking for Ambrose Spellman and it would certainly not be the last.

FOURTEEN

Cora

Thursday, August 30, 1888

Tapping my fingertips on the table, I frowned at Everett. He leaned against the wall nearby, watching out the window for potential customers. Only one young lady had come round earlier in the evening and the session had gone reasonably well. However, no other patrons had come by since.

"We had more customers from our first advertisement," Everett said. "Maybe we should—"

"Do not even think of it," I snapped. "I am never spending a penny at that newspaper ever again. Our customers have dried *up* because of that stupid article." I sat back, my arms crossed tight. "I have never been so insulted."

The editor would not even offer a partial refund for my advertisement. Instead, I had been offered a discount on a subscription. He had laughed and requested I leave when I demanded a retraction. The nerve!

Everett stayed quiet, his eyes moving between each pedestrian passing by. He had been unnervingly quiet since my visit to *The Gazette Weekly* and it was wearing on my nerves. Finally, his silence forced me to make conversation.

"Do you think our session earlier this evening went well?" I ran my thumb over the nail on my opposite thumb.

Everett glanced at me before looking back at the window. "Yes, it was fine."

"Fine?"

He looked back at me again, one eyebrow slightly arched. "It was good."

"Was it fine or was it good?"

His mouth tightened as he looked from me to the window again. "It was good."

I straightened my back and tipped my nose up. "I was. It comes very naturally to me."

A tiny glimpse of a smile flickered at the corner of his lips. "Indeed." He stiffened. "Oh, we've got someone."

Everett gave Frank—once again acting as our doorman—a quick nod and smiled wide at the thin man who entered the flat, his eyes slowly roaming every surface of the small room. He was an older man, possibly over sixty, and likely over six feet tall, even with his slightly hunched shoulders. His top hat was scuffed at the edges and his cheeks were so sunken that they formed a hollow dip in each side of his face. He leaned his cane against the table and he and Everett took their seats at the table with me.

"Are you the Madame Pringle I've heard so much about?" the man queried in an exceptionally deep voice—a much stronger sound than I had been expecting from such a withered man.

"I am," I said.

"My name is Jasper Hill. It is a pleasure to make your acquaintance, Madame Pringle."

From the corner of my eye, I could see Everett's eyes widen and his friendly smile disappear.

"Who are you looking to communicate with this evening, Mr. Hill?"

"My late wife, Edith."

I nodded and closed my eyes, my hands outstretched on both sides of me, Mr. Hill and Everett each hesitantly taking one. I breathed deep and began my routine.

"Voices of the spirit realm," I began, "come to us this night, we beseech you. We ask you to bring forward our friend Edith, wife of Mr. Hill, from the other side. Oh, wise and mysterious spirits, please bring her to us."

Everett gave my hand a squeeze. Something was wrong.

My breaths grew shallow and I let my head fall, rolling to one side. When the moment felt right, my eyelids slowly slid open.

"You seek Edith," I said in my special voice reserved for The Other, the character I had created to act as a conduit between myself and the spirit realm. "She's a pretty one." I looked at Mr. Hill, my eyes narrowed. "She's feeling shy. What do you want to ask her?"

Everett's fingers tightened in my hand again. I wanted to kick him under the table, but I did not dare. Even if something was amiss with Mr. Hill, there was nothing to be done for it now.

"I wish to ask her if our children are there with her in Heaven," Mr. Hill said somberly. "And I wish to know if she approves of my second wife."
"Alright, sir. Seems simple enough. I will find your Edith, sir," I said, my tone gritty. I closed my eyes again and, after a moment, I summoned a sweet voice with some maturity to it. "Jasper. You have come."

"Edith?"

"Yes, my dear. I am here, and so are the children. We are all here together."

Mr. Hill nodded, his face grave. "You know of my new wife?"

"I do."

I lifted my eyelids just enough to see Mr. Hill through my eyelashes. His posture was rigid, his jaw tight, but his eyes had remained closed as I had directed.

"And?"

"She is kind of heart," I said, "and she will be a fine companion for you."

Mr. Hill scoffed and let go of my hand, yanking his palm away roughly. "That is quite enough. You can stop the charade, Mrs. Pringle. I have what I came for."

Everett let out a sigh and let go of my other hand. I stayed in character, desperate to win back Mr. Hill's trust.

"My dear, why do you—"

"Hold your tongue, you witch," Mr. Hill snapped. "You are nothing but a fraud and a trickster—and a bad one at that. There is no Edith, all of my children are living, and I have no second wife."

"I see." My voice was barely above a whisper.

"I read an article in the paper about you and had to come see for myself," he continued. "I was especially surprised when I saw that Madame Pringle operated her schemes from *my* property."

Everett, wincing, tried to cut in. "Mr. Hill—"

Mr. Hill rose to his feet. "I am a Christian man, Mrs. Pringle, and your practices are nothing less than the devil's work. The pair of you will be out of this flat by the end of the month."

He grabbed his cane and started for the door, Everett following after him.

"Please, Mr. Hill," he said. "We are in a desperate situation. We will cease our act, we promise, if we can remain in your building. I have paid my rent on time for five years. Please do not turn us out, I beg you."

Mr. Hill just glared at Everett. "My decision is final, Mr. Rigby. Good day to you." He slammed the door behind him.

Neither of us moved as we absorbed what had just happened in what seemed like an instant.

"This is my fault," I whispered. "This is all my doing. I am so sorry, Everett."

He shook his head. "It is my doing just as much as yours."

My lower lip quivering, I felt a tear slide down my cheek. "You would be much better off if you had not met me. You would have a home and a job."

Everett smiled wearily. "Please don't cry."

"What will we do?" I sobbed. "That article has ruined everything. *I* have ruined everything."

Just then, Frank burst through the door, his chest heaving. "What has happened? Mr. Hill—"

"Has evicted us," Everett finished for him, running a hand through his thick dark tresses.

"Oh, no, Mr. Rigby," he said, his long, lanky arms dropping to his sides. "That's awful." His face contorted as he struggled for a reply. "I'll tell my pa to keep an ear out at the pub, to see if anyone has a room to let for the pair o' ya." He glanced between us. "I mean, I assume you two will be stickin' together."

I looked up and met Everett's gaze, his image blurry through my tears. "I would not blame you if you abandoned me after all the suffering I have caused you."

His mouth tightened. "I am not going to abandon you." He looked back at Frank. "Yes, please do tell your father for us."

Before rushing off, Frank stopped short. "Oh, I almost forgot. The lady that came by earlier this evening. She came back with a letter for you, Mrs. Pringle."

He delivered it to my quaking hand before scuttling off and I hastily opened the note. As the words swam upon the page, I wiped my eyes furiously and attempted to read it again.

"This," I said, "is our salvation."

FIFTEEN

Cora

Friday, August 31, 1888

"I cannot believe you made me take an omnibus," I said to Everett, moments after we arrived in Spitalfields on that hot and sticky afternoon. I let my shoulders sag slightly. "It just feels so … common."

Everett arched a brow at me, the hint of a smirk playing at the corner of his mouth. "Shall I call a carriage next time for your royal highness?"

Pursing my lips in annoyance, I strode on ahead of him, tilting my chin up.

"We are quickly running out of money," he added, catching up to me with quick strides. "We cannot afford to take hansoms everywhere."

"Everywhere," I repeated, glaring up at him. "Because we are constantly on the go. My social calendar is terribly full."

"Cora—"

"The theater, the opera, a party or two," I continued. "There is always something on the go and we are paying drivers several times a day." I stopped and glared at him. "Do you want to make a positive impression on these people or not? What will it say if my hem is filthy and I smell of whatever I happen to step in on our way there?"

"They live in Spitalfields," he reminded me in a hushed tone.

I understood what he meant. One of the poorest areas of London, the streets were crammed with merchants, immigrants, and evidence of severe poverty. The most noticeable thing about the area was the stark contrast of grim destitution so close to busy and prosperous shops, bright silks draped in their store windows.

After a few minutes of following Everett down this street and that, I spoke up. "Do you know your way around all of London or just the poorer parts?"

He shot me a look over his shoulder.

"I mean it," I said. "Your sense of direction is quite remarkable."

"I've lived in many different areas of London," he said. "All over."

We navigated through the busy streets of Spitalfields and a few other pedestrians got between us, my wide skirts hindering my path, and Everett rushing on ahead without me. When he realized I was not at his side he stopped, and a lady nearly bumped into the back of him.

He smiled weakly back at me. "Apologies. I am not used to getting around with another person." Everett offered me his arm, I took it, and we navigated the busy street together.

A few minutes later, we stopped at a dark and narrow house, looming over the corner where two busy streets met. Four stories high and not especially well-maintained, the house was heavy with windows, each one somehow a slightly different shape and size from the one next to it. Its exterior of weathered gray stone made it look as if the house itself was coated in dust. A small wooden plaque hung by the door, reading *The Hemlock*, its letters tall and thin like a drooping branch from a dead tree.

Everett kept glancing at me, probably to see if I would let cowardice overtake me. I put my shoulders back and approached the front door. A glimpse of movement from an upstairs window caught my eye as I lifted the heavy knocker on the door, the handle embellished with the iron head of a demon baring his angry fangs.

I looked up at Everett for reassurance. He folded his hands in front of him and gave me a nod and a calm smile, holding my gaze for a moment. I took a deep breath and waited. After a moment, a middle-aged woman greeted us by opening the door by about an inch and looking at us through suspicious, narrowed eye slits.

"Yes?" she spat in a cockney accent. "Who are ya?"

"Good morning," Everett said, his tone friendly, as he pulled the letter from his pocket. "We were asked to come to this address to speak with Miss Baudelaire."

The woman's face softened slightly at the reference, but she still snatched the letter from Everett's hand. She gave it a quick skim and looked us over once more. "Alrigh' then." She opened the door wider. "Come in. I'm Mrs. Jones, her housekeeper. 'Ave a seat an' I'll go fetch 'er for ya."

I followed Everett into the great room, the heavy front door thundering as she shut it behind us before disappearing down a hallway. The floors creaked underfoot, and I found myself holding onto Everett's arm again. He led me to the purple velvet chaise in the middle of the room and I exhaled slowly as I sat, my eyes gradually adjusting to the dim lighting.

Everett leaned his head closer to me. "Are you having second thoughts?" His breath was sweet, and his lips were so close to my cheek that I felt the heat rise in my neck.

"No," I said, counting the number of cobwebs between each spoke of the staircase bannister nearby. "Why do you ask?"

"Because you are squeezing my arm so tightly I am concerned it may fall off."

I looked at him and then quickly pulled my hands free, clasping them together in my lap so I might stop them from shaking.

"Mrs. Jones could have at least offered us some kind of refreshment," I said quietly, desperate to appear unmoved.

"You must forgive Mrs. Jones' rudeness," a smoky voice said from the darkened hallway. "She is a barbarian."

Everett and I bolted to our feet as a figure stepped out of the shadows, the spiraling smoke from her cigarette visible before the rest of her. Minerva Baudelaire swept into the room, a long cigarette holder held tight within her bright red lips. The train of her lavish, glittering red and black sequined gown dragged behind her as she walked towards us.

I had never seen a woman under three feet tall look so elegant and powerful.

She plucked the cigarette holder from her mouth and effortlessly blew a smoke ring. "Oh, do sit down," she said with an eye roll under her thick black eyelashes. "I'm not the queen." She grinned. "Not yet, anyway."

We both sat immediately, like a pair of well-trained hounds.

"It is an honor to meet you, Miss Baudelaire," Everett said, beaming at the sight of her. "I saw you perform many times growing up."

She studied him for a moment and used her cigarette holder to point at him. "You look familiar. What is your name, young man?"

He gave me a quick glance. "Everett Rigby, ma'am. I've done props and lighting at most of the small theaters and music halls in London. I believe we have crossed paths a few times over the years. You have a remarkable memory to recognize me."

I did not even know he worked at any music halls.

She stepped onto a little stool before sitting in an armchair across from us and took a long, thoughtful inhale on her cigarette. "Any relation to Henry Rigby?"

"Yes." Everett glanced at me again as he spoke. "He was my uncle."

The corner of her painted lips curled up. "He was quite the rotter, wasn't he?"

He laughed. "Yes. Yes, he was."

She knows more about Everett than I do.

Mrs. Jones appeared out of nowhere to trade Miss Baudelaire's cigarette holder for a glass of sherry. She placed two glasses on a nearby table for Everett and me.

Perhaps not a barbarian after all.

Miss Baudelaire slowly moved her eyes from Everett to me. "Madame Pringle."

I smiled and gave a single nod. "Yes, ma'am."

She pointed at me and wiggled her finger. "Do a turn for me?"

Rising to my feet, I did a slow spin as directed. Miss Baudelaire nodded and I took my seat again.

"Bella said you were a beauty. She was right to think so."

Miss Baudelaire's letter had explained that one of her troupe's members, Bella, had come to the flat for a reading as a sort of blind audition. Miss Baudelaire could not come herself as she was too easily identifiable.

I beamed. "That is very kind of you to say."

"She also said your act is horrendous and needs a tremendous amount of work."

My shoulders fell a bit. "Oh."

"But she is obviously good enough to garner your attention," Everett added, "or you would not have invited us to talk about potential opportunities."

Miss Baudelaire's lips pursed slightly. "Our act has been wanting since the unfortunate departure of our former spiritualist. The fool met a rich American and went to New York. She was quite a good performer. You will need to either be comparable to her or exceed her in popularity. We will work on your act and provide costumes."

I nodded again. "Yes, ma'am."

"We will also provide you a new name since Madame Pringle is a little uninspired as well as tarnished, thanks to that article about you in the *Gazette Weekly*."

I winced. I had hoped she had not read it. It seemed not

much escaped Miss Baudelaire.

"We can also provide you with lodgings here," she continued, "but, naturally, rent and meals will come out of your weekly pay. You have potential, Mrs. Pringle, and we will see where we are in a month's time. Stay for lunch. We can discuss business after."

I beamed. "Thank you, Miss Baudelaire."

"Yes, thank you so much," Everett added.

Miss Baudelaire's mouth tightened as she looked back at him. "Apologies, Mr. Rigby. I can only provide lodgings for the talent."

I had not even considered that Miss Baudelaire might not want Everett as part of the arrangement.

"He is my manager," I said quickly.

"No, *I* am your manager now," she corrected, her eyes still on him.

I panicked. I did not want to venture into this strange new world without Everett.

"You must know, he has a lot of experience working with performers and stage props and costumes. Perhaps you would consider bringing him on as well?"

She took a long drag on her cigarette, looking Everett over for a moment.

"Fine," she eventually said, the words mingling in the cloud of smoke between us. "It just so happens that our prop master is having some back trouble and could use the help at the moment."

Everett's face lit up. "Thank you, Miss Baudelaire."

Miss Baudelaire waved a dismissive hand before setting her eyes on me. "We will begin your retraining as soon as possible."

"Yes, of course." I nodded.

"Welcome to Minerva's Marvels," she said. "Do not make me regret this."

It had been a while since I had eaten a meal at a long table surrounded by new acquaintances. Mealtimes had become quiet affairs with just Everett and I, or occasionally with Mrs. Harris.

The meal on offer at The Hemlock smelled delicious and the scent nearly overtook me as Everett and I made our first appearance in the dining room. Despite the formal setup, two people at the far end of the table were eating and chatting away, not bothering to wait for anyone else. Steam curled from the edges of the hot meat pies they speared with their forks, juice drizzling out and onto their plates. Nothing had ever looked so appetizing to me in my entire life. My stomach let out a soft grumble in response and I placed my hand over my middle to smother the sound.

Mrs. Jones moved swiftly around us and slid a bowl of potatoes onto the table next to several other large serving dishes full of assorted meats, breads, and vegetables. I had become so accustomed to meager meals that seeing such a buffet before me was something of a spiritual awakening.

Mr. Jones gave his wife a little pat on the bottom as she glided out of the room. She let out a surprised, "Oh, sir!" and grinned as she disappeared from view.

As Mr. Jones left to assist her, Everett took the opportunity to lean over to me.

"We know that one," he whispered, nodding to the petite woman at the end of the table.

I did not recognize her underneath the dark makeup around her eyes. As I tried to remember who she was, she turned to us, one eyebrow raised.

"Oh," she said, leaning back in her chair. "You two. Joining the troupe, are you?"

Her voice was high like a young girl's and I suddenly realized she was the woman who had come to see my act under false pretenses. If I recalled correctly, she wanted to make contact with her late parents. She had not been terribly complimentary when describing my act to Miss Baudelaire but I had apparently been good enough for a recommendation all the same.

"Yes," I said. "I believe you had a part in that, so I thank you."

"Don't mention it, love. The name is Jezebella, or just Bella if you like," she said, her parlance rougher around the edges than when we had met her previously. Her voice suddenly went silky smooth as her gaze landed on Everett, looking as if she wanted to devour him. "Nice to see you both."

The tiny hairs on my neck prickled.

Bella has no way of knowing if Everett and I are romantically involved or not. How dare she presume we are not. Or, perhaps, she does not care.

Mr. Jones joined us, bringing in yet another serving dish before picking up a pair of plates and handing one to each of us. "Help yourselves. We don't stand on ceremony here."

As Everett and I greedily piled our plates, Mr. Jones introduced us.

"Friends, this is our new spiritualist, Cora, formerly known as Madame Pringle." Mr. Jones began filling a plate for himself. "We'll come up with a better name for you."

I smiled and nodded, forcing the shock I felt away from my face. We barely knew this man and yet he was calling me by my first name. The impropriety was alarming.

"Who is this fellow?" The man sitting across from Bella pointed at Everett with his fork. "Does he also speak to ghosts?" His words sounded so lovely, cradled by a Spanish accent in a deep, husky voice.

"This is my companion, Mr. Rigby," I said. "He is joining the team as well, to help with some of the backstage matters."

Bella's shoulders squared and an eyebrow perked up as soon as I said "companion." The woman really was tremendously shameless.

"And no," Everett added, "I don't speak with ghosts."

"Nice to meet the pair of you," the Spanish man said warmly. "I'm Diego."

Everett took the seat next to me but paused for a moment, struck by a thought. "You throw knives, right?"

Since Diego had just taken a bite off a thick chunk of bread, Mr. Jones cut in.

"Throws knives, juggles blades, and swallows swords." Mr. Jones sat next to Diego with his plate. "That last one is a fool's errand, my friend."

He gave a shrug. "The people, they love it."

"They'd love it more if you cut your throat open," Bella said, dragging a finger across her neck.

Swallowing hard I winced, a bloody image forming in my mind. The thought of dining did not appeal to me suddenly.

"Have you ever had any accidents with a blade?" Everett's eyes were wide with fascination.

Diego shrugged again. "A few."

I was thankful Everett did not get the chance to ask him for details as we were soon joined by Miss Baudelaire and Mrs. Jones. Miss Baudelaire took a seat at the most ornate chair at the head of the table, a small set of stairs beside it. Mrs. Jones poured a glass of sherry for Miss Baudelaire and served her a plate before sitting beside her husband. I found it rather unorthodox that the housekeeper ate with us.

But not many things were orthodox in that house.

I could feel Miss Baudelaire's eyes lingering on me as she sipped her drink. I did not know how informal I should be with her, so I stayed silent. I felt like a lowly courtier waiting for the monarch to speak to me first.

"Mrs. Jones showed you your rooms?" She looked at the two of us from under heavy eyelids. "I hope they will suffice."

"Our rooms are lovely, thank you."

My bedroom was plain—a narrow bed, a dresser, a small writing desk, and a simple vanity—but Everett's bedroom was no more than a hammock hanging in an attic closet.

"Thank you for inviting us to dinner," Everett added. "This food is splendid."

Bella leaned across me to grab an apple from a basket. "Minerva likes to keep us well fed. It's a wonder we're not all round as these here apples."

Mr. Jones patted his round belly. "Speak for yourself, lass."

I turned to Bella. "I apologize. I did not ask what your act is."

She took a big bite of her apple and crunched loudly, wiping the juice from her lips with the back of her hand. "I'm an acrobat."

"Oh, how exciting!"

"And I make things," Mr. Jones added. "We have a little taxidermy display called the Zoo of Wonders—I make all of those. I also make drawings, potions, charms, things to sell during intermission and the like."

Mrs. Jones frowned at him. "You *make* things." She shook her head and looked at me. "My Basil is a proper artist, 'e is. He acts like it's nothin' but he's a real talent."

Smiling sweetly at his wife, Mr. Jones looked at her with such love that it warmed my heart.

"Do you all live here at The Hemlock?" I asked.

"All of us except Diego. He's got a wife and little ones," Bella said. "How many children you got now anyway?"

Diego shrugged. "I don't know, maybe six or seven."

"The only one of us missing this evening is Magni," Miss Baudelaire said with a roll of her eyes. "He lives here but does not spend much time here." She sighed. "It is for the best."

Everyone at the table snickered and scoffed, except for Everett and I.

I glanced at Everett. He was reflecting on this comment carefully.

"Magni?" He looked from Mr. Jones to Miss Baudelaire, his eyes wide. "You're not talking about Magni the Magnificent, are you?"

"This was a mistake," Everett said moments after we got into the hansom cab and directed the driver to his flat. "We still have a little bit of time—we can still find another place to live—"

"Who is this Magni person and why are you acting like this?"

"Magni the Magnificent is a magician," he explained. "I knew him when he was just starting out and he was a horrible man. Arrogant and vain and—"

"Talented?"

Everett threw me a look. "Yes, unfortunately." He clenched his jaw. "If it was just the arrogance I was concerned about, it would not be a problem. He is a rake."

"Ah," I said. "You think I will fall in love with him, is that it?"

He sat back in his seat and considered this for a long moment. "No. I would hope you would be a better judge of character than the many, *many* women he has wooed." He was quick to change the subject. "I'm surprised Miss Baudelaire would have him as part of the Marvels. He has double-crossed his assistants, other illusionists, craftsmen who create his props, everyone. If he thought it would bring him an inch of publicity or money, he would do anything."

I pondered what I could do to latch onto some of Magni's publicity. After all, publicity was half the battle.

"I would at least like to meet Magni before we flee," I offered softly. "It sounds as if you knew him years ago. It is possible he has become a better person since then." I gave a little shrug. "I plan to continue with moving into The Hemlock tomorrow as planned. We have a place to live, we have food to eat, and we have a bed to sleep in—"

"*You* have a bed to sleep in."

"A hammock is a *type* of bed." I smiled at him and batted my eyelashes.

That maneuver no longer worked on Everett. He knew me too well by then.

"You are free to take your chances in a vermin-ridden common house if you prefer," I said, my words clipped, before softening my tone again. "I feel safer at The Hemlock than out there." I looked at the window, the streets of London at night flying by. "We have been given a chance. A real chance. I would rather not just give it up so quickly." I placed my hand on his and looked at him. "Please."

Everett stared down at our hands, transfixed. His gaze drifted up my wrist, along the length of my arm and over my neck, pausing at my lips before flicking up to my eyes. His thumb brushed the edge of my wrist ever so delicately and the feeling of such a subtle gesture made my stomach tighten.

Finally, Everett nodded his agreement and slid his hand away from mine.

SIXTEEN

Cora

Saturday, September 1, 1888

A devilishly handsome and well-dressed man of about thirty years of age greeted us in the dining room the next morning. The way he looked at Bella from across the table made me wonder if they had ever had a relationship, or perhaps he just looked at all young and pretty women that way. However, as soon as Everett and I walked in, the man's eyes darted directly to me and he sprang to his feet, immediately forgetting his previous flirtation.

"Good morning, new friends. Welcome, welcome!" he exclaimed. "It is very nice to make your acquaintance. I am Magni, the resident magician here at The Hemlock. You must be the Madame Pringle Bella told us about."

I found it rather telling that he would welcome me to a house that was certainly not his own.

"Unfortunately, the name Madame Pringle is to be retired," I said. "For the time being, it is just Mrs. Pringle. This is my partner, Mr. Rigby."

Completely ignoring Everett's presence, Magni lifted my hand to his lips and laid a gentle kiss on my knuckles. "Our acts are quite similar, you know. We both use themes relating to the occult." He grinned. "People come to us to feel a little bit scared. It excites them."

Although he was laying it on a little thick, Magni oozed charisma. It was hard to not be a little captivated by him.

He finally dropped my hand and offered Everett an extra firm handshake. "Mr. Ridley."

Everett faked a smile. "Rigby."

"Yes, yes, of course." Magni turned his attention back to me. "Perhaps once you have found your footing within our little troupe, we can do some kind of act together. Audiences love that sort of thing."

I could practically hear the steam rolling out of Everett's ears next to me.

"Perhaps." I smiled up at him through my eyelashes. "However, are you not afraid that I would steal some attention from you?"

I glanced at Everett just long enough to see him grinning smugly.

Magni gave an uncomfortable chuckle. "We are on the same team, Mrs. Pringle. No need for us to be competitors. I think a few of my many, *many* adoring fans would find your presence in my act enthralling." He smirked. "I do not mind sharing a few of them."

I faked a smile and made my voice flat. "How generous."

"What about your act is completely unique to you compared with all the other women out there claiming to speak to beings of the other side?" Minerva tented her fingers. "We need something to make your act stand out and catch attention."

"The difference between them and I," I began confidently, "is that I really *can* speak to spirits and they only pretend."

Miss Baudelaire narrowed her eyes. She did this a lot. It was her way of showing displeasure while trying to be kind.

"Yes, of course. And Magni really levitates." She raised an eyebrow at me. "You're going to need to come up with something better than that, my dear."

I frowned and remained silent, embarrassed that that was the best thing I could come up with.

My training had begun right after breakfast. Miss Baudelaire had summoned me to follow her up to the fourth floor of The Hemlock. Mostly used for storage it was a dimly lit, warm, chaotic, and dusty mess. Several large magic props lined the back walls, boxes and crates of related pieces piled in front of them. Three crates of poorly made taxidermy animals were placed closest to the door. I hoped that was not the Zoo of Wonders I had heard about the evening before. Various pieces of furniture, some broken and some not, were stacked in the corner. A long wooden table lined one wall while all sorts of tools hung above it in—almost certainly Mr. Jones' workspace.

I sat on an old, weathered chaise as I listened carefully to every word Miss Baudelaire had to offer me.

"Right," she continued, "you're young, alluring, charming, and beautiful. These are all things that work in our favor."

I smiled brightly.

"However, most of the spiritualists attracting audiences are *also* young, alluring, charming, and beautiful."

My shoulders and my smile fell.

"However, most do not come from the upper classes as you do. That part is unique to your act. We can use that."

I smiled again and gave a single nod, folding my hands in my lap, feeling smug that she couldn't tell I had been raised a middle-class clerk's daughter before rising in status upon my marriage.

"You'll need to have a firm grasp of several methods for communicating with the other side. We'll start with séances here at the house with individuals and then bring in groups. Eventually, you'll be performing on stage for audiences. That is where the money is. I will see if Basil can whip up a few props for you. Perhaps Mr. Rigby knows a few lighting tricks we can use."

I nodded enthusiastically. "I am sure he does."

"Perfect." Miss Baudelaire gave a single affirmative nod. "That reminds me, you're not sleeping with him, are you?"

My eyes bulged. "Of course not! Miss Baudelaire, I—"

"I have seen the way you two look at one another," she explained in a detached tone. "I can't have one of my girls becoming pregnant."

"I promise you, that will not be an issue for me." I lowered my eyes. "He and I are friends."

After a pause, she said, "Mr. Rigby is Indian, right?"

"His mother was Indian," I said. "He was born in Bombay but raised in London."

"Perhaps we can use that." She tapped her cheek with her finger as the wheels turned. "The English love all things foreign and exotic." She glanced at me and frowned. "Well, all but the people themselves, of course."

She was not wrong. For a city so full of different cultures and races, I had seen countless curious looks thrown in Everett's direction in the streets and I was not sure if it was because of his Indian heritage or because of the inherent mystery attached to a person of mixed race. It was clear Everett was used to it, but I certainly was not.

"India," Miss Baudelaire repeated to herself, pacing in front of me again. "India could work."

"For what?"

"Your father was a merchant who traveled around India. He brought you on one of his many journeys there." Her voice took on an air of melodrama and she gestured with her hands as she pulled the story out of thin air. "It was there, at the edge of the Ganges, that you had your first experience with speaking to the dead."

I raised my eyebrows at her. "Pardon?"

"You tried to push the voices away but the more of India you saw, the more the spirits rushed to you because they could tell that *you* and you alone could hear their cries for help." She pointed at me as she spoke. "The legend of your otherworldly gifts spread between every village and every city until you, at last, decided to embrace your true calling. You were given a name by the Indians which translates to—" she finally looked right at me "—the Mystic of the Taj Mahal." She smiled proudly, clearly waiting for my enthusiastic praise.

My eyes widened, and I let out a startled chuckle. "I know nothing of Indian culture—"

"Do you really think our audiences are the world-traveling type?" She tilted her head at me. "Audiences come to see us because they want an escape from their everyday lives. By creating this persona for you, you have preexisting fame from your time in India—"

"A place I have never been—"

"—and people will come to see your act just to say they saw someone famous." Her dark eyes narrowed. "The poster is going to be marvelous."

SEVENTEEN

Cora

Saturday, September 22, 1888

"Seems a little unfair that we had to pay full price to see our *own* troupe perform," Everett said as we grabbed a table a few rows back from the audience. Just as he spoke, a man with a glass of beer in each hand bumped into the back of Everett's chair, a bit of froth sloshing over the rims.

"Not to worry," I said, my pursed lips curling into a coquettish smile. "We will have plenty of money soon. Think of this as an investment."

Everett quickly wiped at the bit of beer foam on his shoulder, frowning at the man as he carried on to his table.

The drumroll began, announcing the presence of the first act of the evening.

"The biggest voice in London from the tiniest woman in England," the announcer roared, "Miss Minerrrrrrrvaaa Bauuuudelaaaaaire."

The curtains whipped open, revealing Miss Baudelaire in a

glittering costume, an oversized collar of emerald and sapphire-hued peacock feathers around her neck and shoulders, a matching fan clutched in one of her small, delicate hands.

A piano that sounded like it desperately needed a touch of maintenance sang out from the side of the stage as Miss Baudelaire launched into her first song—a bawdy tune about a rather buxom pirate woman who, well, enjoyed herself at every port in the West Indies. The audience joyfully sang along, not letting a small thing like not knowing all the lyrics stop them. They went wild as her enormous voice filled the packed room. Her vocal range was truly impressive—vast with a fruity sweetness to it. I would never have guessed that sound would come from her as she spoke quite differently off stage—always even, firm, and authoritative.

As the cheering from the audience calmed slightly, Miss Baudelaire placed her hand on her chest. "Thank you, everyone. We're going to have so much fun tonight!" The cheers exploded once more, reaching up high into the rafters. "We've got your favorite Spaniard and some of his shiny and very, very sharp friends." A woman a few tables over wolf whistled. "We've got the dazzling Jezebella, the most *flexible* woman this side of Paris." With her hand on her hip, she winked as she said 'flexible,' and strutted the front of the stage, encouraging the audience to take that as innuendo. "And, of course, we've got some fantastic new tricks from Magni the Magnificent!"

As the crowd cheered, Miss Baudelaire hurled herself into another go at the chorus of the song she had just finished. By the time she skipped backstage, my ears were ringing from the volume.

My eyes suddenly felt dry as I had forgotten to blink.

I wanted that. I wanted *that.* I wanted that sound, that excitement, that exaltation, that joy, that admiration. I wanted all of it. I wanted people to love me as much as they loved Minerva Baudelaire and her risqué songs. I wanted people to know my name. I wanted people to be jealous of my immortality.

I looked at Everett, my face warm with the rush of the realization. As Diego and Bella took the stage together, a man slid a glass of wine onto our table, a note tucked neatly underneath.

I held up the note. "Care of Magni the Magnificent," I whispered, the hall around us having gone very quiet suddenly.

Everett rolled his eyes. "He's likely never tried wooing a woman without the assistance of liquor."

On stage, Bella stood against a wooden board in various poses while Diego, his back turned to her, flung knives at her, using only a small mirror to aim and, hopefully, not injure or kill her. He took his time between throws to build the audience's anticipation, and each time he threw the crowd gasped and then cheered as the knife whipped by Bella's limbs, striking the board with a sickening thud. She seemed so comfortable up on that stage, not even flinching as knives flew by her bare arms.

Bella took a bow and disappeared backstage as Diego began juggling three knives, then four, then five, the gas lights of the music hall glinting off the smooth metal blades. I had never seen Diego shirtless before, so I had no idea his torso was almost completely covered with tattoos, even some poking out from over the top of his striped trousers. As he wrapped up his act a large hoop lowered from the ceiling, and Bella returned to the stage in her acrobat costume. Before the hoop reached the floor, whoops and excited shouts began, soon joined by a brisk melody on the nearby piano.

Her blonde curls were pinned in a tight bun behind her head, and white stockings covered her strong, defined legs. Her costume was a formfitting frilly thing that only covered her torso, shimmery silver fringe framing the curve of her hips and waist. Although she was petite and young-looking in everyday dress, the costume especially accentuated her perfect hourglass figure. Sheathed in silk slippers, her tiny feet skipped lightly across the stage as she flung herself through the hoop, somersaulting to the edge of the stage before walking on her hands, her dainty toes pointed in the air above her. The audience loved that. She hurled herself onto the hoop, climbing up it and hanging from it using only the muscles in her thighs. She crossed her arms while hanging in the air like that and yawned, making the audience laugh. She hung from it, swung from it, and climbed over it in every possible way. When no one was expecting it, the hoop raised higher off the stage and Bella dangled from it by only her ankles. Finally, she flung herself off the hoop, cartwheeled across the stage and posed on the floor—her big finish. She bowed low as the hoop disappeared into the rafters.

Magni made his grand entrance onto the stage next, his eyes looking like balls of ice framed by dark makeup. He plucked his tall top hat off and pulled several silk scarves from within it, ending with a colorful pile of them on the floor of the stage. Finally, at the bottom of the hat, he located a deck of cards, and put his top hat back on.

"You there, the lovely lady in the blue dress," he said to a woman at a table near the front. "Would you care to pick a card from the deck? You can shuffle them first if you wish before you pick one, doesn't matter. Memorize the card, show it to anyone around you, and then put it back in the deck."

She did as he asked, and he made a show of shuffling the cards between his hands, sending the cards in a high arc between his hands. He did a few more card shuffling tricks before sitting at the edge of the stage, his legs dangling off the side. He lifted his top hat from his head and plucked a single card from inside his hat, holding it up for the woman in the blue dress.

"That's my card!" she shrieked.

The audience cheered and Magni hopped to his feet again, performing several more card tricks in quick succession and a few sleight of hand illusions.

I did not manage to see all of these because I was too busy watching Everett. His eyes were locked onto the face of a man sitting at a nearby table. I could only see him from profile—a thick-necked, broad-shouldered laborer type. His beefy torso hardly fit inside his shirt. He and his friends at his table cheered and pointed as Magni continued his act.

The man must have felt himself being watched and he eventually turned to see Everett. He blinked a few times, wincing, before he smiled wide. He immediately left his seat and advanced on our table, ignoring the calls from behind us for him to get out of the way of the stage. Not only was he well-muscled, he was also especially tall.

He grabbed Everett's hand, pulling him up out of his chair and embracing him heartily. "Everett! How are you? It's been too long!"

Everett looked far less thrilled about seeing this behemoth of a man. "Hi, it's nice to see you."

Finally noticing the persistent and vexed yells from around us, he crouched down by our table.

"I never thought I'd see you in a music hall again," he said. "I thought you had left England, old boy."

Everett shrugged. "Didn't quite make it." He looked at me. "Mrs. Pringle, this is my cousin, Neil. We grew up together. Neil, this is my—" he hesitated "—friend, Mrs. Pringle." He gestured to the stage. "We've recently joined Minerva's Marvels. Mrs. Pringle is a spiritualist."

"Well, it's nice to meet you, missus." He looked back at Everett with a knowing smirk before turning back to me. "Are you performin' tonight?"

I had only been allowed to perform two séances at The Hemlock so far. Miss Baudelaire had not given any hints at when I may be allowed on a stage, but I was getting anxious.

"Not this evening," I said.

As the two of them chatted quietly together, I looked back to the stage as Magni performed what was likely his final trick of the evening: displaying an empty box to the audience, saying a few specially chosen phrases, and then opening the box to reveal Miss Baudelaire inside. Miss Baudelaire's final song was just as indelicate as her first but this one was about a man from Bethnal Green who finds out his wife made him a cuckold and gave him a most unfortunate rash. The lyrics were full of innuendo and Miss Baudelaire played up every pun with a wink and a jut of the hip. The audience laughed like they had never heard anything so hilarious. She gave a deep curtsy and the crowd were on their feet, shouting and asking for an encore. Like the professional she was, Miss Baudelaire gave her fans what they begged for, retaking the stage with a smile.

As we walked back to The Hemlock after the performance, the cool night air felt refreshing on my skin and the subtle breeze reminded me that autumn would be arriving soon. Minerva, Bella, Magni, and Diego had taken advantage of the free drinks provided by the music hall and were singing a jolly tune on their way to a pub.

I looked up at Everett, strolling beside me. "Did you say Neil is your cousin?"

"Yes."

"Were you close growing up?"

"Like brothers."

"Really? You have never mentioned him."

"You never asked."

He was right. Still, I did not like being reminded of what a useless friend I was to him.

"I suppose I haven't," I said.

I heard Everett let out a quiet, tired sigh. "His father was my father's brother."

"Oh," I said. "The cruel one?"

"Yes, that one."

"Was he kind to Neil?"

"The only person Henry Rigby was ever kind to was a barkeep or perhaps the proprietor of a gin palace or anyone who handed him a bottle, really."

When I was silent for a moment, Everett went on.

"He managed a couple music halls and small theaters. I grew up learning how all the pieces fit together, how to repair costumes and do lighting tricks and mend props. A few performers taught me how to do different speaking styles and it turned out I had a knack for mimicry."

"I am quite familiar with your talent for voices."

"Indeed."

"You still use that voice though, for the most part," I said. "You know you do not have to anymore—"

"I do have to," he cut in. "I feel powerless without it."

We were both silent for a moment.

"How long ago did your uncle die?"

"He lived by the bottle," he said, staring straight ahead as he walked, "and then died by the bottle when I was fourteen."

I caught myself staring at his sad eyes, unable to look away from them. The life he had lived was so different from mine and yet, there we were, thrown together by the fates. He looked down at me and his stern gaze softened. I wanted to take his hand in mine, slip my fingers between his, and tell him he would never again be under the thumb of another unkind man.

Before I could, Magni yelled over his shoulder, "Mrs. Pringle, you are coming with us, right?"

I could not help but notice the invite was only directed at me and not for both Everett and I.

"Oh," I said, startled by the invitation. "No, that is a generous offer—"

Miss Baudelaire, her cheeks rosy, stopped and turned around. "Minerva's Marvels are going to a pub tonight. Are you or are you not one of Minerva's Marvels?"

I exchanged a look with Everett. He gave an encouraging nod. I had hoped he would not want me to go. I did not wish to part from him just then.

"Yes, I *am* one of Minerva's Marvels," I said brightly, skipping ahead to take Diego's arm.

The five of us turned and I looked back at Everett, his hands in his pockets, walking alone back to The Hemlock.

EIGHTEEN

Amelia

Friday, September 28, 1888

With no one but Simon and my mother to keep her company, Simon's young stepmother and her growing belly graced our parlor chaise on a regular basis, at least three times per week. Simon and I joined Beth and my mother for dinner at her home once a week, but Beth was usually silent in front of her. When with Simon and I, she was significantly different.

"I like the name 'Frederick' or perhaps 'John', but 'John' is so common but then 'Frederick' is not terribly uncommon either," she prattled quickly. "Maybe something from the classics could be unique—something like 'Ulysses' or 'Apollo' or 'Atlas.' Of course, those are just names for boys. It could be a girl. I suppose I have no way of knowing until the day of." Beth looked at Simon with large, concerned eyes. "Do you think your father would agree to a name like 'Athena' or 'Iris' for a girl?"

Simon blinked at her and then looked at me with pleading eyes. I could tell he had not been listening and had no idea what

Beth had just asked.

"Perhaps, if the baby is a girl, you could consider naming the baby after Joseph's mother. I believe he would appreciate that," I said, stirring my tea.

Simon crossed his long legs, sliding down a little into his armchair. "Oh, please do not consider naming that poor child 'Dorcas.' She was a wretched woman and my father loathed her."

"Oh." Beth sipped her tea. "Well, it does not matter. I think it will be a boy. Do you think your father would be happier if it is a boy?"

This poor girl.

She obviously did not know Joseph very well before they married. Then he just left her in Britain, away from her family, while pregnant. It seemed exceptionally heartless to me.

"I think he will be happy no matter what, as long as the child is healthy," Simon said with an encouraging nod.

"Of course." She bit the corner of her lip. "I hope I will be a good mother."

"You certainly will be," I said. "You are sweet and-and-and—"

Naïve. Dim. Child-like.

"—you will be wonderful," Simon added. "What you cannot handle, Ivy can assist with and there will always be servants around, and a governess when the child is old enough, of course."

Beth nodded. "I just wish I could ask my mother for advice."

"Perhaps you could invite her to stay for a while so she can attend the birth," I suggested, beaming. "My mother, I am sure, would love to meet her and wouldn't mind another guest. There is more than enough room—"

"I do not believe so. Rather, I know so," Beth remarked quietly. "She is dead."

"Oh."

"I am sorry to hear that," Simon added with a knowing and somber nod.

Simon's own mother had understood him far better than his father ever would and her death had sent him to a very dark place for quite some time.

"Consumption." Beth smiled wearily. "I was twelve." She took a moment to stare out the nearby window before looking back at me. "I read that article you wrote in the newspaper about Madame Pringle, the spiritualist. You are such a terrific writer."

I smiled.

"But," she continued, biting her lip again, "I think you may have been a little harsh."

I frowned.

"You wrote the article as if you knew for certain that Madame Pringle had no abilities at all."

"I did so because she does not," I said firmly.

"You only went to a single session with her and you mislead her. No wonder the reading was not accurate—you lied to her. It probably caused the lines of communication to get muddled."

"The lines of communication?" I winced, my whole face tensing. "You believe Madame Pringle and people like her can actually speak with spirits from the other side?"

Simon looked from me to Beth, drank his tea, and stayed silent.

"I do," Beth said. "In fact, I plan to meet Madame Pringle and see if she can contact my mother."

"Oh, I do not know if that is such a good idea," Simon said. "Not in your delicate condition."

"My sources have actually told me that she is no longer offering her unique services," I said, doing my best to hide my triumph.

The last time I had been in that area, I had checked in with a nearby barkeep and he told me she had been evicted for offering her unique services out of their flat. The barkeep had not seen her around there since then. It was a promising bit of news and I was pleased to hear it.

Beth sipped her tea. "Oh, I know. I wrote to her. My letter was received by a neighbor who gave me her new address. I have an appointment to see her next week."

I stared at her.

"Oh, and she does not go by 'Madame Pringle' anymore,"

she added. "She calls herself 'Lady Selene' now."

"'Lady Selene,'" I repeated flatly, nodding slowly. "Lovely."

My thoughts raced.

Perhaps I need to do a follow-up article. Seeing her again myself would be too risky though—I would have to get detailed notes from Simon in my stead, or maybe from Beth herself if she would agree to such a thing.

I put aside my ambitions for a moment. "I do not think that is a good idea, Beth."

"I know you think she is a fraud—"

"I *know* she is a fraud," I said. "She cons vulnerable people for financial gain."

"You have no proof that she is *not* speaking to spirits—"

"She has no proof that she *is*!" My voice had raised suddenly. "I find behavior like hers abhorrent. I do not want to see someone in my family hurt by her lies and trickery."

"How can you believe spiritualism is just lies and trickery when so many intelligent people have found comfort from it?" She paused to consider her argument. "Arthur Conan Doyle—he's a spiritualist and one of the most clever men in Britain."

I rolled my eyes and shook my head at her. "I really must insist you not see that imposter."

Beth glowered, and she was quiet for a long while. "I was not asking for permission. I *am* going to see her."

"What a foolish waste of time and money," I blurted.

"Amelia," Simon snapped, glaring at me.

I squared my shoulders. "My apologies, Beth. I went too far."

She lowered her eyes. "You do not know as much as you think you do." She stood, avoiding eye contact with me. "I feel tired very suddenly. I think I will return—" she hesitated "—home."

Simon bolted to his feet. "I will get a hansom for you and travel with—"

"That is quite alright, Simon. I am fine to travel alone," she said, one hand resting protectively on her belly. Her eyes met mine for a second. "I am not a child."

Simon saw her to the door. Once she had left he returned to

the parlor doorway. "Was that entirely necessary?"

I sipped my tea, staring straight ahead at the spotless mantle above the fireplace. "She is a guileless little girl who has accidentally stumbled into adulthood."

"She is not just some young cousin you can tease," he clarified. "She is my stepmother and your mother-in-law. You ought to remember that and you ought to know better."

Guilt stung me all over like a swarm of jellyfish. Before I could apologize for speaking out of turn Simon stormed off, leaving me alone in the parlor to wallow in my remorse.

I did not have time to indulge in my self-pity for long. The following night the Whitechapel killer struck again, and the news spread through London like the Great Fire.

I knew Mr. Granville would likely run a special edition ahead of our usual Wednesday print run and I needed to get a story together and show up for work on Sunday to show him I was a better and more determined reporter than Mr. Turner would ever be. Our newspapers featuring stories about Martha Tabram, Mary Ann Nichols, and Annie Chapman had all sold out. I needed this one.

"Please come with me," I begged Simon early on Sunday morning from my perch at the foot of his bed.

He blinked at me and propped himself up on his elbows. "Woman, what are you on about?"

"He killed two women last night. If we are quick, we can get to Whitechapel and beat the rush before every other reporter in London gets there."

"Why do you need me?" His voice was hoarse and one of his eyes had fallen shut.

I hesitated. "Because Mr. Granville will be angry with me if I go alone."

Mr. Woodacre finally rolled over and looked up at me. "Did you say *two*?"

Simon sighed. "Won't he be angry that you went to Whitechapel with or without your big, tough man to protect you?"

Mr. Woodacre gave Simon a curious smile. "Wait, are you supposed to be the big, tough man?"

"Obviously."

Mr. Woodacre wiped at his eyes. "If what you are saying is true, then the entire city is about to start panicking." He slid out from under the sheet and grabbed his pants from the nearby armchair.

"At least stay for breakfast, Wright," Simon pleaded.

I added, "Unless *you* would like to escort a lady to—"

"No, no, no, no thank you. Although going to the scene of a horrible double murder sounds like a lovely way to spend a Sunday morning—"

"Two separate scenes. Not even that close by," I corrected, pausing to think. "Depending on the times they were found, the killer must have had access to a carriage." I looked up at Mr. Woodacre as he buttoned up his shirt. "This is no East End tradesman."

Mr. Woodacre's fingers stopped mid-button. "I believe you have your headline, Mrs. Baxter."

I leapt off the bed and rushed to get ready to leave. As I scurried out of the room I heard Simon add, "Wait, what is happening?"

I arrived at the *Weekly Gazette* office at lunchtime. Both crime scenes were overflowing with reporters, as I feared they would be, but I managed to get a couple of quotes from some local residents as well as a short quote from a police officer who was able to confirm my suspicion about the distance between the two murders. Simon, anxious to get back to familiar territory, hovered behind me as I gathered my notes and cursed myself for not owning a camera.

I was already typing madly at my desk when Mr. Granville arrived. He stopped in place beside me and watched as the letters combined into words before his eyes. He sighed loudly.

"Mrs. Baxter—"

"Not to worry, sir, Mr. Baxter came with me. I was entirely

safe." I gestured to the page. "I am on to something here though, don't you think? The killer must have had some kind of transportation. It is not like he could have hailed a hansom in the middle of the night. One of the constables I spoke to this morning said the first murder may have been interrupted and so he just hopped in his carriage and found another unsuspecting victim a few minutes away."

"A man with a carriage? A man of wealth?" Mr. Granville considered this, a subtle smile creeping onto the corner of his mouth. "That would surely sell some papers." He drummed his fingertips on my desk as he thought. "Keep going with that. Good work, Mrs. Baxter."

This is it. This is my chance. Finally!

"I have it on good authority that Scotland Yard has received a letter from the killer," he said.

My eyes widened. "Really? What does it say?"

"My source would only say the details made him shudder," he said. "And believe me, he is not the shuddering type under most circumstances. Hopefully we'll know its contents in a day or two."

A letter from the killer sent *to* Scotland Yard with gruesome details was an enormous story. This murderer was truly a monster.

We both looked up as the office door opened and Mr. Turner arrived, slightly out of breath, his notebook under his arm.

"Oh. Mrs. Baxter," Mr. Turner said. "I didn't know you would be in today."

"Well, I am. I almost have a story about the two new victims complete."

Mr. Turner glanced at Mr. Granville. "You have a story?"

"Yes. I do."

Mr. Granville gave a single nod. "One of the on-duty constables is on record saying the killer might have money or, at the very least, ready access to a carriage."

"Killer?" Mr. Turner repeated. "As in singular?" He sat at his desk and flipped to his page of freshly taken notes. "I just spoke with a constable who told me he expects two killers are working together. One person couldn't have murdered all these women alone."

I blinked at him. "What? No. Your source must be mistaken."

"It is quite possible neither constable is right and both are just trying to get their name in the paper," Mr. Granville mused. "However, given the area of London where these murders are occurring and given the social status of the victims and given that a man of wealth would never do anything so ghastly, Mr. Turner's source is likely right." He sauntered toward his office. "You can have that done before two?"

Mr. Turner nodded as I bolted to my feet. "You are not serious."

The two men turned to me, puzzled.

"What makes you think a man wealthy enough to have a carriage could not carry out these murders? Rich or poor, they are the actions of an individual who is quite disturbed. Income has nothing to do with it." The words spilled out of me, fast and without hesitation. "All of the details we have show a very distinct pattern with each victim and no evidence that it was more than one person." I blinked at Mr. Granville, not quite believing what was happening. I had been so close. "You just said it was a good angle, that I should keep going."

Mr. Granville gave me a pitying look. "The constable you spoke to was likely just trying to impress a lady. A man is more likely to tell the truth to another man."

Mr. Turner nodded in agreement and said, "Mm," as he loaded his typewriter.

"He was quite sincere, I assure you," I said, my words clipped. "And what about this letter from the killer? Was it written by one person or two? Do we know what kind of education level the killer might be from this letter?"

Mr. Turner glanced up at our editor, barely interested in what I had just blurted out. "Hmm? What letter?"

"Never mind the letter, Mrs. Baxter," Mr. Granville said with a shrug. "It's probably a hoax anyway."

I stared at him, my jaw clenched. "Unbelievable." I made a show of ripping my story from my typewriter, crumpling it up and throwing it in the nearby bin. I pointed to Mr. Turner's typewriter. "We are going to look like bloody blind fools."

I grabbed my coat and stormed out. In the back of the hansom I took home, I finally let my angry and frustrated tears out.

I had been so close.

NINETEEN

Cora

Monday, October 8, 1888

"I believe I am ready to join the rest of the Marvels on stage for a live performance."

Miss Baudelaire looked up from the newspaper she was reading in her private study. "Oh, you do, do you?" She inhaled from her cigarette and released a ring of smoke from her lips.

Squaring my shoulders, I folded my hands in front of myself and gave a single nod. "I do indeed."

"And why do you believe you are ready?" She put her eyes back to the newspaper. "And don't say 'Because I *feel* ready.'"

I took a step forward. "My act is based on improvisation, a skill I have always done well with. I have practiced for countless hours, I have been doing private séances, and I've spent some time improving my onstage persona with Magni. I *am* prepared, Miss Baudelaire."

Magni had impressed me at the pub that night after I watched them perform and had offered to coach me on stagecraft.

Obviously, I had enthusiastically accepted his kind offer and we had been hard at work, perfecting my act and adding flourishes and tricks that I would not have thought of myself. I owed him a debt of gratitude.

Considering this, Miss Baudelaire looked up at me again. "I suppose we could add you to the program on Saturday." She lowered her eyes to her newspaper again. "I'll have Mrs. Jones whip up a stage costume for you. Let Mr. Rigby know if you need any props made."

I gave a gracious nod. "Thank you, Miss Baudelaire."

Closing the study doors, I practically skipped up to the attic to find Everett. I made sure to keep my face as still as stone as I reached the top of the steps.

Perched on a stool and painting some kind of potion bottle, Everett beamed when he saw me. His face immediately tightened as he saw my serious expression.

"No?" He put his paintbrush aside, his shoulders lowering slightly.

My smile spread wide across my face and I squealed, my fingers curled into tight fists. "I am in this Saturday's show!"

I flung my arms around his neck and he pulled me in tight. He somehow smelled of cinnamon that day, or at least his neck did as I nuzzled my face against his shoulder. I felt so small in his arms.

We held onto one another longer than a hug between friends warranted but I did not mind. I was too happy at that moment to think of impropriety.

Sliding out of his embrace I said, "I should go find Magni and tell him the good news."

The glitter in Everett's eyes dulled.

"In addition to the rest of the Marvels, obviously," I added quickly.

He gave a nod. "Of course."

As I made my way through the winding hallways of The Hemlock, I found Magni in the billiards room, his usual haunt.

Leaning forward over the pool table, his cue in position, he looked at me over his shoulder, flashing me his flawless grin. The top couple of buttons on his shirt were undone and a few curls of chest hair peaked out.

"Lovely Mrs. Pringle," he said, looking back to the top of the table. "You are positively glowing about something." The balls cracked as he took his shot, sinking several of them. Turning to face me, he took a long drag from his cigarette and stubbed it out in a nearby ashtray.

"I have some excellent news," I said. "I will be joining the Marvels on stage for the performance on Saturday."

Magni put his pool cue on the table, took both of my hands in his and squeezed them. "That is excellent news indeed. We should celebrate."

He glided over to the liquor cabinet and rifled through a few crystal decanters, locating a bottle of whiskey. He poured two small glasses and handed one to me.

"To Lady Selene, the Mystic of the Taj Mahal, and her blossoming career." He held his glass up before tossing its contents down his throat.

It burned as it hit my tongue and I winced. "I think I prefer champagne."

He poured me a second tumbler. "I will buy us a bottle on Saturday night after your first show."

Us?

The second drink made my head feel heavy and my body warm. I silently scolded myself for accepting a drink before noon.

What would Everett say?

Pushing the thought from my mind, I smiled at Magni. "You have helped me so much. I feel much more confident in my performance than I did previously. I owe you a debt of gratitude."

He shrugged. "The pleasure was all mine, my dear. Just try to remember me when you are headlining your own show."

"Oh, stop," I gushed. "What about you? Have you ever done your own act?"

Magni looked awkwardly into his whiskey glass and leaned against the bar. "I had my own show for a while, but I am a wretched businessman. Being under Minerva Baudelaire's thumb keeps me in line." He flashed his wicked smile. "Under her roof, I am forced to be a good boy."

"And when you are *not* under her roof?" I raised an eyebrow at him.

His eyes turned hungry as they trailed from my eyes to my neck to my bosom and back up again. "Well, Cora, sometimes I misbehave."

Before I could respond, Magni pressed himself against me, pinning me to the bar, his mouth crushing mine, the smell of whiskey and tobacco smoke filling my nostrils. I turned my head away, guilt wrapping around my stomach like a spiderweb.

"I mustn't," I said quietly.

Magni's brows knit together, he stepped back from me and cleared his throat. "My apologies, Mrs. Pringle. I misunderstood." His lip curled into a subtle snarl and I immediately realized he was less remorseful and far more annoyed. He had not shared his stagecraft procedures with me out of the goodness of his heart. He had a motive all along.

How could I have been so blind?

Magni helped himself to more whiskey as I fled the billiards room, wiping the taste of his mouth from mine. I shut myself up in my room and sat on the bed.

It was then that I noticed an envelope resting on the little bedside table. Going by the address on it, the letter would have been delivered to Mrs. Harris before reaching me here at The Hemlock. Everett must have brought it over from her flat and left it for me.

I recognized the handwriting immediately. Sitting up quickly, I snatched it up and tore it open in a hurry.

Dear Cora,

I am so sorry to hear of Dr. Pringle's passing. The loss you must feel must be overwhelming—first your father and now your husband. Please try to remember that God only gives us the challenges he knows we can endure. You will make it through this trying time.

Yes, of course, you can stay with us in North Carolina. America is different but very exciting. I think you will fit in well with my new friends here as many of them have daughters your age.

Please write back as soon as possible and let me know when we can expect your arrival. I miss you, my darling girl.

All my love,
Aunt Charlotte

Charlotte's letter had finally come. Finally, after all these months. I reread it over and over again—probably ten times at least. I eventually folded it closed along the creases, tucked it back into its envelope and slid it into the little draw in the side table.

Living with Charlotte meant security. It meant dropping myself into a pre-built life with pre-chosen acquaintances, and, knowing Charlotte, pre-planned suitors lined up for me once I arrived on America's shores.

Would I want that?

My gaze stayed on the envelope laying limply in the drawer. Going to America was the obvious choice; the responsible choice. I had turned to spiritualism in order to survive until I could afford passage to North Carolina. If I sold my belongings that day, I would nearly have enough for the journey as private séances paid well.

I recalled the feeling of utter and undeniable *want* that I had felt at the sounds of the enthusiastic cheers while watching the Marvels perform. They were adored and admired by so many. What an incredible way to live!

And, of course, there was Everett. He had saved me when I had no one else to turn to. The idea of not having him in my life was … daunting.

I was different from the woman who had written to Aunt Charlotte, begging for rescue. Like the girl in *Alice's Adventures in Wonderland*, I had tumbled down the rabbit hole. And I wanted to see what was at the other end.

I slid the drawer closed.

TWENTY

Amelia

Saturday, October 13, 1888

"I cannot even believe you are dragging me all the way to Shadwell for *this*." I glared at Simon as the hansom rolled along, navigating the streets of East London. "This is not a good idea."

"It will be so much fun," Beth said cheerfully, taking my gloved hand in hers. "I promise!"

I shook my head. "If Madame Pringle sees me—"

"She won't," Simon cut in. "We will sit in the back and have a jolly time. Relax."

Mr. Woodacre peered uneasily out the window, a deep crease forming between his eyebrows. He had been my one and only ally in my argument against going to that evening's performance of Minerva's Marvels at the Four Georges Theatre. Alas, Beth insisted since she had enjoyed her recent private séance so much. Not only had the spirit of her late mother been summoned successfully, but that of her grandmother, too. It was a big night for chicanery, to be certain.

"In two months, I will be housebound," she had whined, patting her rounded belly. "I want to do things while I still have the chance."

Mr. Woodacre, like myself, had been talked into this little outing. He was reluctant because he felt Shadwell, the opium capital of London and home to some of the city's poorest residents, was not safe for any of us to visit, let alone a young and pregnant woman.

Beth had lied to my mother about where we were going so late. She would have fainted if she had known our actual destination. To Beth's credit, my mother actually believed it.

Perhaps my mother is losing her gift for sensing falsehoods in her advancing age.

I had only agreed because I felt like I needed to make amends with Beth after my recent rudeness.

Also, because Simon demanded.

"Wait," Mr. Woodacre said, "I thought her name was Lady Selene or something to that effect."

"It is," I said with a quick eye roll. "She changed it."

"She probably felt like she had to since a vile woman at a newspaper tried to decimate her reputation," Simon said, grinning at me.

"Vile woman," I echoed. "I should put that on my stationery."

Our cab shuddered to a stop in front of a shabby theater that looked as old as London itself. We hustled out as Simon paid the driver and we joined the queue to get inside. The large poster advertised the main event of the night: *Minerva's Marvels, introducing Lady Selene, the Mystic of the Taj Mahal.* Mrs. Pringle's likeness featured heavily, a crystal ball floating above her two open hands, the Taj Mahal visible in the crystal ball. Her large, intense eyes gazed into the ball while her red curls fell upon bare shoulders. It was scandalous. The men in the line kept staring at it and making lewd comments about the woman now known as Lady Selene.

Well, almost all the men in line, anyway.

"What other acts do you suppose will be featured?" Mr. Woodacre asked, squinting at the small print along the bottom of the poster. "I cannot quite read it from here."

"I think Magni the Magnificent is one of the opening acts," Simon said. "I saw him in Covent Garden last year. He is quite good, actually."

I knew what magician he was speaking of. I recalled Simon's comment about the performance: "More like Magni the Magnificently Attractive." Of course, that had been uttered quietly between two friends in private and not outside on a street surrounded by laborers, dock workers, and tradesmen.

Beth's grip on my arm was causing a cramp. I looked down at her little hand and then back at her. "Are you having second thoughts? We can leave right now if you—"

"No, no," she blurted. "Just excited. Look, the doors are opening."

As planned, we found seats at the back. I was silly to be nervous about Lady Selene seeing me from the stage—no chance of that with us so far away. The seats surrounding us were full, as was the loft that overlooked the stage from above. The curtains drawn across the stage, faded with age, looked as if they had been a moth's meal. Friends shouted over to friends from across the room and the laughter and chatter grew louder as the show's beginning drew nearer.

Minerva, a singing dwarf, began the show, followed by brief performances from an acrobat and then Magni the Magnificent. At the end of his act, he stepped to the front of the stage.

"Ladies and gentlemen. It is a truly special night. Tonight we present the debut performance of Lady Selene, the Mystic of the Taj Mahal." The crowd clapped and whistled. "My friends, she has gifts that go beyond explanation. After traveling the vast domain of India, she was blessed with talents that will make the hairs on the back of your neck stand up." He gave an exaggerated wink and grinned mischievously. "And I'm not just talking about the spiritualism."

The crowd loved it, cheering louder than before. Mr.

Woodacre's eyes widened and he glanced at Beth, probably to check if the poor dear looked faint from such a remark. She was just as amused as everyone else in the audience, laughing and clapping at the jest.

"Please give a warm welcome to the woman who speaks to the spirits from the other side, Lady Selene, the Mystic of the Taj Mahal!"

The stage lighting lowered as Lady Selene stepped out of the darkness, a lit candle held in each hand. The cheers from the crowd lowered at the sight of her. Despite my distaste of her skullduggery, she certainly did look ethereal on that stage that night.

Her large eyes were lined with black makeup, giving her a Sphinx-like appearance. A sapphire-colored silk scarf held some of her coppery curls from her face while the rest were free to cascade over her shoulders. Delicate gold chains were intertwined throughout her ginger locks, matching the gold bangles dangling from her slender wrists. Her gold sheath dress was simple, draping perfectly over her ample curves. Intricate deep blue lace lined the edges at the bottom hem and along the seam that ran up the side of one leg. Nipped in at the waist and cut low in the front, the dress showed off Lady Selene's décolletage, glittering stones and gold chains covering her upper chest. The strings of a sitar were plucked by a musician offstage, adding an element of exotic mystery and divinity to her very presence. In time with the music, she moved her bare arms slowly through the air and her whole form shimmered in the flickering candlelight. She slowed to a statuesque pose and the music came to an end.

The room was silent as a cemetery.

She said in a breathy voice, "My dear friends. Are we ready to connect with the other side?"

The crowd erupted into cheers. Beth smiled at me, clapping her hands and practically jumping up and down in her seat. Simon gave me a "Well, *I'm* impressed!" expression and Mr.

Woodacre looked stunned at the display on stage.

"My goodness," he said, blinking a few times.

"Isn't she beautiful?" Beth exclaimed, leaning over to him. "So lovely and charming in person as well."

Mr. Woodacre, unsure of how to respond, just replied with a thoughtful, "Mm."

"Tonight, on this very stage, I will contact spirits from another dimension, right before your eyes," Lady Selene announced. "If you are prone to fainting or have sensitive nerves, I recommend you exit the theater now."

As she spoke, a round wooden table was carried on stage, followed by two ornate, high-backed chairs. Placed in the middle of the table was a small chest.

"Magni mentioned my travels across India," she said, standing at the front of the stage, her syrupy voice carrying throughout the room. "As I stood at the edge of the Ganges River, the holiest place in India, all I could hear were whispers of hundreds of restless spirits. I was terrified. I tried to block them out but as I traveled from village to village, they became louder." The sitar player once again plucked the strings of his instrument, summoning a gentle melody to enhance her story. "One day, I met an old woman who knew instantly that I had been given a gift. She sensed it in me, just as someone had sensed it in her many years before. She trained me to focus on one voice at a time and I was soon able to choose which spirit to communicate with."

I raised an eyebrow at Simon. He just shrugged, his face practically glowing with delight.

Listening to her speaking, I found it interesting that her diction sounded like that of a woman from the upper classes. I had noticed it before when I visited her flat for the séance and had continued to wonder if that was part of her act, too, or if she really was an educated woman from a family of status.

Lady Selene scanned the congregation. "Who among you here tonight would like to make contact with the spirits that dwell beyond our plane, just out of reach? Who misses a loved one or a friend who has passed? Raise your hand if you…" She hesitated, wincing. "…if you…" Placing two fingers to her temple, she clutched the edge of the table.

"I apologize, dear friends. Sometimes a spirit communicates with me, knowing I can reach someone that they were close to, and they are rather persistent."

A few in the audience gasped and whispered.

"This spirit is named … John," she announced, wincing and looking as if she was struggling to focus. "He was young when he died tragically." She opened her eyes wide. "Who among you had a loved one named John who died young?"

I sat back in my chair and shook my head.

What absolute balderdash.

Two women from opposite sides of the audience spoke up.

"The John who is trying to get through was somewhere between fifteen and thirty years old when his life was lost," she went on.

Wow. The spirits are a little vague, aren't they?

"That's my boy!" one of the women cried out, standing up in her chair.

She was invited on stage to speak further with "John" through Lady Selene.

"His death was quite sudden, wasn't it?" she asked the woman once they were both seated at the table.

"Yes." The poor woman was in tears at this point. "Yes, 'twas."

Lady Selene took her hands in hers. She closed her eyes and raised her face to the rafters. "He says he wishes more than anything he had had a chance to say goodbye."

That is usually how sudden deaths work.

The woman let out a sob. "Oh, my sweet boy," she whimpered.

"John wants you to know that he misses his mother so very much." Her voice went saccharine sweet. "He also wants you to know that you should not blame yourself or judge yourself too harshly." Selene's face turned puzzled. "I am not sure what that means. Do you know what that means?"

The woman held a hand to her chest. "Yes. I know exactly what he means by that." She bit down on her lower lip, stifling another sob.

Selene nodded and closed her eyes again, feigning listening to a far-off voice. "He says he is also glad to know you are well taken care of."

My hands curled into fists in my lap. *The woman is well-dressed and well-fed. She is obviously living well without her son. You do not need to talk to ghosts to figure that one out.*

Selene's flock cooed and gasped in response to every comment made onstage. They were eating it up. I considered if I might just go home without my party before I lost my temper right there and then.

Her following onstage feat involved automatic writing: using a pen and paper, she carried messages over from the other side by closing her eyes and writing their words as they came to her. Once again, my friends were astounded and impressed. Once again, I glared at the stage, my arms crossed over my chest.

For her big finish, she invited three volunteers to join her at the table on stage. They held a séance together, using a spirit board to contact the dead. All four participants held their fingers to a wooden planchette and, as if possessed by a spirit, it guided them to letters across a board, slowly spelling out messages and words. Via this spirit board, the group was contacted by someone called Oscar who drowned in the Thames "not so long ago."

"What do you mean, Oscar? How many years ago?" Lady Selene asked the board.

Ten silent seconds later, one of the others at the table gasped, "It's going to the number two."

"It's spelling out 'days,'" another added. "Oscar is saying he died two days ago?"

Lady Selene nodded solemnly. "We have been joined by a recently deceased spirit, my friends. This is a rare event indeed."

Just then, a large shadow passed over the stage and something thundered from underneath the stage floor. Members of the audience screamed in surprise; one woman even fainted, slumping over in her seat—either that or she had enjoyed too much of the theater's best gin.

Lady Selene looked up and around, her eyes wide. "Oscar! Are you here in this theater right now?"

The four at the séance table looked to the planchette as it slid across the board.

"Oscar, you *are* here with us!" she yelled. "You are welcome here, Oscar! Please give us another sign that you are here as a friend and are not here to haunt or frighten."

The planchette made a quiet scraping sound as it slid across the board.

"No," one of the participants said quietly. "He says no!"

Another shadow swept over them again, plunging the stage into darkness for a sliver of a moment. The lights went dim and a gauzy white shape was visible on stage for a split second, causing shrieks to erupt from both crowd and stage.

Beth gripped Mr. Woodacre's arm, her eyes big around as saucers. "Oh my goodness!" Her other hand moved to her stomach and her brow suddenly pinched. She winced suddenly and looked down to her stomach.

Our eyes met in the dim. "Beth, are you alright?"

She ran her palm over the curve of her belly. "Yes, I think so." Her cheeks were flushed. "Well, I am not certain—" She winced again, inhaling sharply.

"Take some deep breaths," I said, nudging Simon. "We are leaving."

I thought Simon might make a fuss, but once he saw Beth's hand clasped to her stomach he knew I was serious. Beth leaned on me as we made our way out of the theater and over to one of the waiting hansom cabs on the street.

I glanced at Beth. "Perhaps we should call for a doctor from here—"

"No, you mustn't," Beth pleaded, grabbing my hand. "What

if your mother finds out we came here?"

"Beth, dearest, you could be ill—"

"No," she said firmly. "No, I want to go home. We will call my physician from there."

Although the streets had cleared a little since our earlier trip, that journey felt like it took hours. We all sat in silence, watching Beth occasionally wince and rub her belly as she soothed the baby inside.

TWENTY-ONE

Cora

Saturday, October 13, 1888

As soon as I stepped backstage after the performance, I found a chair to collapse into and inhaled deeply the smell of dust, wax, wood shavings, and wine. I put my head back on the ripped and faded upholstery and looked up into the rafters, listening as the thrilled crowd filed out of their rows and went back to their real lives. I thought about the sound of their applause, holding it in my memory. I wanted to reach out with my palms and capture every clap like a firefly and keep it safe in a jar for always. I wanted to preserve every single one forever.

I closed my eyes as a tear slowly rolled down my cheek. It clung to my jaw for a moment before slipping off.

Miss Baudelaire found me, her cigarette holder between two fingers. "Good God. Are you alright?"

Smiling, I brushed at the tear trail and admired the smudge of black makeup that had transferred to my fingers. "I have honestly never been better."

"Glad to hear it. You did very well, my girl." She took a puff from her cigarette and forced a stream of smoke out of her painted lips. "You better get changed and clean yourself up. I've got some people who want to meet you."

Before I could enquire what she was talking about, Mrs. Jones appeared with a dress hanging over one arm. I ran my hand over the heap of red taffeta, admiring its sheen.

"Where did this come from?"

"I found it in the same gutter Minerva pulled you out of." She frowned at me. "I made it, you daft cow. Now let's get this on you." She nodded to a backstage dressing area. "Then fix your face. You look a fright."

In any other situation, I would have glared at the woman for not knowing her place but I was too intoxicated on success even for that.

Once Mrs. Jones had me all laced in and looking presentable and I had removed my stage makeup, Miss Baudelaire was distracted by an acquaintance and they were chatting about the good old days. I slipped out of the backstage to go find Everett. Since the first clap from the audience had first echoed in my ears, I had wanted to tell Everett how blissfully happy performing had made me. I wanted to share my joy with him. I wanted him to know that him being in my life had led me here and that that meant something to me and I wanted him to know it.

The first thing I saw were Bella's legs wrapped around Everett's waist.

He stood in front of the stage, facing it, while Bella had been sitting on its edge. Her hands cradled his face, their lips pressed together, Everett's fingertips brushing her bare knees.

I let out a quiet gasp and whipped around, trying to escape back to the safety of backstage before either of them spotted me but it was too late. I had seen them, and they had seen me seeing them.

"Cora?" I could hear Everett jump up on the stage. "Cora?"

I tucked away one of my curls in front of the mirror and his eyes met mine in the reflection. His guilty, guilty eyes.

"Sorry, were you looking for me?" I said to his reflection as I absentmindedly adjusted my necklace.

He lowered his eyes. "It's not what you think."

I blinked at him in the mirror. "You can do whatever you like."

His face tightened. "Bella kissed *me.* I didn't kiss her."

"She *is* beautiful." I smiled sweetly at him, ignoring the stinging sensation at the back of my eyes.

He opened his mouth but Miss Baudelaire appeared at my side before he could respond.

"Time to go, Lady Selene."

Everett looked at my gown as if he had not noticed it before that moment. The pleading look in his eyes weakened my resolve, and I was close to forgetting what I had just witnessed.

A theater employee dropping something nearby startled me out of my haze and I fled to the hansom cab waiting outside. Once the cab pulled away, I took several deep breaths and placed my hand over my stomach, hoping to ease my nerves.

I had my chance. I have had a thousand and one chances. Surely he has had enough of me. I have no right to be possessive of him.

"Are you alright? You look terribly flushed," Miss Baudelaire said.

"Yes, I am quite well." I nodded frantically. "Just a lot of excitement for one evening." I pretended my stomach was not still heaving beneath my corset. "So, who is this mystery person we are going to meet?"

"You are absolutely ravishing," the tall man said, lifting my gloved hand to his lips. "It is a pleasure to make your acquaintance. I am Royal K. Wyndham." A sly and handsome smile spread across his lips. "And, my dear, I would like to take you on an adventure."

Royal K. Wyndham smelled of mint and money. Probably in his early forties, every piece of clothing on his person looked tailored to perfection. With hair the color of lemonade, Mr.

Wyndham's hairline had retreated into an aggressive widow's peak and his understated moustache was neatly groomed. His smile and manner of speaking dripped with confidence without sneaking into arrogance. I liked him straight away.

"Well," I said, "I have always wanted to go on an adventure with royalty."

He let out a laugh. "Oh, I think you and I are going to get along very well."

Mr. Wyndham offered me his arm and the three of us took a table at one of London's most lavish eateries. Ordering a bottle of champagne for the table, he was unlike many of England's wealthiest class in that he was generous with his laughter and smiles.

As the waiter filled my flute, Mr. Wyndham glanced at Minerva. "Miss Baudelaire, where have you been hiding this gem of a girl?"

Her subtle smile appeared. "Well, tonight *was* her first stage appearance."

"Oh, yes, that's right," Mr. Wyndham smirked. "You are a natural on stage, Mrs. Pringle, if I do say so myself. I believe I have an eye for these things."

"That is very kind of you to say, Mr. Wyndham." I smiled at him through my thick eyelashes and reached for my champagne. "Tell me about yourself. Miss Baudelaire tells me you work with entertainers, but she would not provide specifics."

"Well, I am an investor. I invest my time, money, and connections and take emerging and established acts—" He paused for dramatic effect, glancing at Miss Baudelaire. "—on tour."

I let out a startled chuckle. I was lucky I did not drop my glass that very second. "On tour?"

"Yes, my dear," Mr. Wyndham said with a sanguine smile, sitting back in his chair. "Have you been to Scotland?"

"No, sir."

"Northern England?"

I gave a shy shrug. "I went to Sheffield once as a child."

Mr. Wyndham nodded. "I think a tour around Britain will be just the thing for your career."

"Are you sure?" I looked at Miss Baudelaire for confirmation. "My career has only just begun."

Miss Baudelaire and Mr. Wyndham exchanged glances.

"The thing is," she said, "we find that if an act has some name recognition outside of London, the act can bring in more money." She paused. "However, we already have a tour scheduled for another act, but we want you to replace him."

I looked back and forth between the two of them.

How long had these two been planning this before mentioning it to me?

"What act?"

Mr. Wyndham's mouth twisted into a sideways frown. "Let's just say that Magni the Magnificent is less than a magnificent draw these days. More like Magni the Menace. He's more trouble on tour than he's worth."

Miss Baudelaire plucked up her champagne glass. "He was a good moneymaker a few years ago but a magician can only perform the same tricks so many times before the audience gets tired of them."

I thought of my own act and took a sip of my drink.

What if I *run out of ideas? What if* my *act becomes stale? Will Miss Baudelaire throw me to the wolves too?*

"He is going to be furious," I said to Miss Baudelaire, genuinely concerned. "Do you expect he will make trouble for me?"

"If he does, he can expect to be swiftly evicted from the Marvels *and* The Hemlock," she replied.

"Well, of course I am thrilled you would consider me for the tour," I said. "When would this be?"

"Next month." He beamed.

"So soon? My goodness."

"Strike while the iron is hot, my dear," Mr. Wyndham said, finishing off his flute of champagne.

I was sitting on the edge of my bed, doing some mending, when there was a soft knock on my door.

"It's me. Can I come in? I need your desk," Everett said from the other side.

The image of Bella's athletic limbs wrapped around him and their lips together flashed into my mind and I recoiled.

"Yes, come in."

"Thank you," he mumbled, coming in and leaving the door open a couple inches. He dropped some pages onto the desk and set to work.

After a few minutes of uncomfortable silence, save for the scratches of his pen and the sound of thread feeding through cotton, I decided to speak to him.

"What are you writing?"

"I am working on my play." He glanced back at me quickly before putting pen back to paper.

"Ah. The muse finally returned, has it?"

He shrugged. "Perhaps."

I tied a little knot and snipped the thread. "You did not say much after I told you about the tour."

"And you didn't say much when I told you," he hesitated, "that Bella kissed me."

Before I could respond, my attention was stolen by an argument from downstairs.

"You miserable hag," Magni yelled. "You can't do this to me, I need this tour!"

"It was Mr. Wyndham's decision, not mine," Miss Baudelaire said calmly. "Try not to take it so personally. It's just business."

"Oh, yes. I am sure that's it."

"It's the truth. Your last tour did not do as well as expected. We're all in this to make money. A tour is not worth doing if we *lose* our investment."

I was impressed that Minerva's tone was so calm in response to Magni's thunderous and threatening shouts. She must have dealt with it before, I realized.

Everett and I glanced at one another as the argument continued. I listened keenly as he went back to scribbling.

"The tour *will* make money, Minerva! That's what I do and that is what I have always done—make money." He scoffed. "Well, I make money for you and Mr. Wyndham. I can't say I see much of that cash myself."

Miss Baudelaire did not take the bait on that one. "Now is probably a good time to tell you I'm making Cora the headliner for Friday's show."

I winced, preparing for the impact of Magni's head exploding.

"Five years, I have been a member of this family. Five years," he said quietly, almost so quietly that I could barely hear him. "That whore walks into this house and suddenly *she* is your star?"

Everett snapped his head up at that comment. I waved a hand at him and he reluctantly went back to his task. Not that I appreciated being insulted but I knew Magni would certainly best Everett if it came to fisticuffs between them.

"Why don't you go take a walk? You need to calm down," Miss Baudelaire said. "Go have a drink somewhere, find a pretty lady to spend your coin on."

"This is preposterous," he said, his feet heavy on his way to the door. "Unbelievable."

He was likely still muttering to himself as he walked down the street to, I assume, his favorite brothel. I set my sewing things aside and closed the door as gently as I could before returning to my spot on the edge of the bed.

"You found my performance satisfactory then?" I forced a sweet smile.

Everett's pen halted. He turned in his chair to look at me, his eyes soft and serious. "Of course. You were wonderful. I knew you would be."

"Really?" My heart felt so full I thought it might burst.

"You were invited on a national tour after a single performance," Everett said. "How do you *think* it went?"

"I suppose it went well." I sighed. "Oh, Everett. It felt

incredible up there." I bit my lip. "Perhaps I will speak to Miss Baudelaire and Mr. Wyndham about you joining me on the tour."

"You will do no such thing." He took my hands in his, surprising both of us I think. "This is an incredible opportunity and I don't want you to risk it so you can bring a friend along. Besides, we'll make more money with me here helping with the Marvels than on the road with you."

"Do you not *want* to come?"

"Of course I do, but not if it means making less money." As Everett said this, his thumb brushed over mine, but he did not realize he was doing it right away.

Our eyes met and we both sat motionless. I wanted him to kiss me so much my stomach ached. He slowly lifted my hand to his lips and laid the most gentle of kisses on my knuckles. The breath left my lungs as he kissed my hand again, this time further down on my finger and then again, so carefully, on my fingertips. My heart seized in my chest as he slowly lifted his gaze to meet mine. The agonizing yearning in my abdomen drummed fiercely.

A knock at the door nearly startled me half to death. Everett immediately dropped my hands, gave a groan, whirled around in his chair, and went back to his messy pile of papers on the desk.

"Sorry to disturb," Mrs. Jones said from the other side of the door. "Mr. Wyndham is here to discuss the tour."

"Thank you. I will be right down straight away."

Curse you, Mr. Wyndham. Why did you have to come here now*?*

Everett looked at me over his shoulder, his full lips curving into a weak smile. "Forgive me. I don't know what came over me."

I shook my head quickly, eager to ease the new awkwardness between us but all useful words evaporated. I adjusted my hair quickly in the mirror, smoothed my skirts, and left the bedroom.

Mr. Wyndham stood by the front door, smiling up at me as I came down the curved staircase. "Good afternoon, Mrs. Pringle."

"Good afternoon, Mr. Wyndham. How lovely to see you."

Mrs. Jones brought tea in for Miss Baudelaire, Mr. Wyndham,

and I. Afternoon faded into evening as we discussed dates, venues, and a few local performers who might act as openers during our various stops.

"Right now we've got you booked for Brighton, Birmingham, Manchester, and Glasgow," Mr. Wyndham said, reading from a ledger while thinking out loud. "I'm still working on a few dates for Scotland. Perhaps we could squeeze a show in at Bristol…"

"This is all so exciting," I said.

Miss Baudelaire smiled demurely. "Hopefully your next tour will include Paris. I will certainly be joining you for that one."

I blinked. "You are not coming with us on this tour?"

"No, my girl. Do you expect these animals to manage themselves without me?"

Mr. Wyndham checked his gold pocket watch and gave a sideways frown before looking back up at me. "I have a table waiting for me at this lovely new place in Marylebone. Would you care to join me?"

If I had been dazzled by the dining establishment Mr. Wyndham had taken me the previous night, I was entirely overwhelmed by that evening's destination. The golden chandeliers sparkled high above us as we were led to a table for two. Tall marble pillars inlaid with carved flowers lined the walls. The wait staff wove around the tables, the patrons and one another with precision, like dancers performing their choreography to perfection.

Going to dinner with Mr. Wyndham alone could easily have been uncomfortable, but strangely it was not. Mr. Wyndham was an excellent conversationalist and knew how to put one at ease. He was friendly and pleasant and seemed genuinely happy to be assisting in my career.

As we sat, I could not help but look around at the elegant eatery. When I looked back at Mr. Wyndham after a moment of shameless gawking, I was surprised to see him watching me. I immediately looked down at the row of glimmering silverware.

"Forgive me, I should not be staring," I said. "It has been too long since I have been in a restaurant like this."

"No need to apologize. Half the people in here come in to people watch anyway," Mr. Wyndham said. "Besides, with so many patrons looking at you, why shouldn't you look back at them?"

I tittered.

"I am quite serious," he said. "It is difficult to keep one's eyes off of you."

"Mr. Wyndham—"

"Please, call me 'Roy,'" he said, smiling with his eyes. "I have a question for you, my dear. Are you and Mr. Rigby romantically involved?"

Before I could answer, our waiter came by with two menus. My mind raced, barely thinking about my dinner.

"The salmon here is quite good," Mr. Wyndham said casually as if he had not just asked me anything at all.

"Is it? Excellent." I nodded and continued to hide behind my menu.

Eventually the waiter returned, and I had to give my hiding spot back to him. Mr. Wyndham raised an eyebrow at me as the waiter left us alone again. He was waiting for an answer.

"Well," I said, "why do you ask?"

His face was awash with guilt.

"Well," he chuckled, "I do not want to step on anyone's toes."

"I am afraid I do not understand."

A grin tugged at the corner of his lips. "Well, if you do not object, I would like to get to know you better. I would like to … court you, as it were."

"Oh," I said. "Mr. Wyndham, I—"

"If you are not interested, I assure you, I am content with keeping our relationship professional," he added quickly.

He is lovely. He is a gentleman. He has money and influence and he can make you famous.

"I, uh—"

Do not throw away this chance. What kind of life could Everett Rigby ever provide for the two of you?

"Cora?"

It was not Mr. Wyndham who had said my name, startling me. My head jerked up to see Viola Lockhart walked towards our table, her eyes wide in surprise.

I stood up, immediately realizing I did not know how to greet her now. We had not been friends for quite some time. To my surprise, she took my hands and kissed my cheek, like we were close acquaintances.

"It is lovely to see you, Cora. How *are* you?"

I snapped out of my stunned silence and smiled at her. "I am quite well, thank you. How are you?"

Across the room, Dr. Lockhart and another couple from my old social circle craned their necks to see me.

"I am well." Viola touched my arm again. Her fake friendliness repulsed me.

Smelling the money on him, Viola glanced at Mr. Wyndham, obviously looking for an introduction.

"Viola, this is Mr. Wyndham. Mr. Wyndham, this is my friend Mrs. Lockhart." I plastered a sweet smile on my face, the same one I used to wear so often. "I have not seen her in several months."

Viola ignored that remark and gave an annoyingly placid smirk. "It is nice to make your acquaintance, Mr. Wyndham. How do you know Cora?"

You just had to ask, you wretched witch.

"I am organizing her tour," he said coolly. "It's going to make Lady Selene a household name."

I gulped and slowly looked back at Viola.

"Lady Selene?" She looked at me. "What—"

"A lot has happened since we last spoke," I blurted. "Perhaps we can discuss everything over tea sometime?"

"Of course." Viola reluctantly nodded. "We are still living at the same house in Mayfair, I trust you remember the address. Send me a note next week and we will arrange something." She gave me another quick peck on the cheek and scurried back to her table to fill them in on our uncomfortable little rendezvous.

I took my seat again and let out a breath.

Mr. Wyndham bit the corner of his lip, trying to restrain his amusement. "You two seem close."

I laughed louder than I meant to. His shoulders shook as he laughed along with me.

That night when I returned to The Hemlock, Miss Baudelaire was waiting for me in the front parlor, smoking alone in the dark on the chaise.

"Did you mean to startle me, Miss Baudelaire?"

Mrs. Jones took my coat as I shrugged it off into her arms.

A stream of smoke filtered out of Minerva's nostrils. "How was dinner?"

"It was fine," I said, letting my inflection linger on the last word. "Mr. Wyndham seems a good man to do business with."

"Mmm." Her eyes narrowed in that very specific manner of hers as she sucked on her cigarette holder. "Did he bring you home in his carriage?"

"Of course."

"Did he suggest the two of you have a relationship outside of the business?"

"'Suggest' is likely a weak word for it, but yes."

"And how would you feel about that?"

I sat on the chaise across from her. "Have I been sold into an arranged marriage? If I have, I would like to at least be aware of it."

One corner of her bow-shaped lips curled up. "My girl, I want you to tread carefully with Mr. Wyndham. He is important to my business and I must keep him happy." The area between her eyes pinched. "He has never shown an attraction for any of my girls before, so this must be dealt with delicately."

I crossed my arms over my chest. "What specifically are you asking of me?"

Miss Baudelaire's lips tightened and she let out a small sigh.

"This may seem sudden, but I need to know if you could potentially see yourself in Mr. Wyndham's bed."

My eyebrows popped up. "Well, that *is* sudden."

"If not, you need to speak up now before he becomes emotionally invested," she said. "You need to keep him happy."

"He is a charming man who could provide a woman with a good life," I said. "I would be a fool to not encourage his attention, so why wouldn't I?"

"Why?" she repeated. "Perhaps the fellow we have staying in the attic?"

I dropped my eyes from hers for only a moment. "What does Everett have to do with this?"

Minerva rolled her eyes.

"The poor boy deserves better than to be strung along by you forever. I do not know how the pair of you ended up together but it's clear you are not a good match." She shook her head at me. "Mr. Wyndham would be ideal for you *and* your career."

I looked at her.

She went on. "He has *connections*, my girl. If you ever wanted to, say, explore a career as an actress, well, Mr. Wyndham could do that for you."

My heart fluttered. "Really?"

Cora Wyndham, Leading Lady of the London Stage?

TWENTY-TWO

Amelia

Sunday, October 14, 1888

"I should never have said anything about my discomfort," Beth whined, struggling to sit up against a stack of pillows. "I am entirely fine."

The doctor had recommended Beth keep to her bed for a few days after our little fright at the theater. It had been a few days and Beth's boredom and restlessness were getting to her—and every person who visited her.

"The doctor said you can resume your routine after a week of bed rest," I said before lowering my voice. "No more trips to see the spiritualist until you evict that child."

Beth giggled. "Thank you again for not telling your mother about that."

"Are you quite serious? She would be far angrier with me than she would be with you."

As if she had heard us speaking of her, Ivy Spencer whirled into the room like a windstorm of lace, frills, and chiffon.

"Beth, dear, do not be shy about telling Amelia to go away if you are tired," she said coolly as if I were the family dog pestering her for scraps under the table. "Remember, you must think of the baby now."

Beth laughed. "I am far from tired, Mrs. Spencer." She smiled at me sweetly. "Amelia makes me laugh and my mother believed a mother who laughs will have a happy baby."

"What utter nonsense," my mother said, chuckling.

Beth's tiny frame sunk into the enormous bed, her brow pinching and her lips tight.

"Ma*ma*," I hissed.

Mama's eyes widened for a sliver of a moment, remembering Beth had been close with her deceased mother.

"Actually, now that you mention it," my mother said, "I believe Mrs. Beeton says something to that effect."

I smiled weakly at her. At least she was making an effort.

But within the pages of your worn copy of Mrs Beeton's Book of Household Management, *does she say anything about not being such a thoughtless cow?*

"Only a few more days and you will be up and around again," I said. "Here, I brought you something to keep your mind occupied." I pulled a book from my bag and held it up.

"*The Strange Case of Dr. Jekyll and Mr. Hyde*," she read out loud.

Mama stopped puffing up pillows for a moment to glare at me. "Your taste in reading material is appalling. An expectant mother should not be reading frightening stories."

Beth snatched it from me like it was a slice of bread and she was starving. "Thank you *so* much."

Since she looked eager to dig into the novel Mama and I excused ourselves. She had tea brought in for both of us without asking, forcing me to stay for at least a few minutes. We sat in her parlor, the clinking of our cups and saucers the only sounds in the room.

"How is Simon?"

"He is well."

Clink.

"How is Papa?"

"He is well."

Clink.

I looked at her. "When are they returning?"

Mama winced. "I am sure they are trying their best and we should try to be patient—"

"You know I am not asking for myself," I said. "The baby is coming in a month and a half. Joseph should be here. Joseph *needs* to be here."

Mama frowned. "Babies are a woman's responsibility, not the—"

"He married that poor girl and then left her here alone. The very least he can do is be here for the birth," I shot back.

"Oh, you know those two and their work." She rolled her eyes and sipped her tea.

I slid my cup, still half full, onto the nearby table. "Joe did not even set her up with a household of her own. He just left her here with you so he could avoid the responsibility of having a wife again. Do not tell me you are fine with his lack of consideration."

"Perhaps he thought she would be lonely in his house by herself." Mama gave a feminine little shrug of one shoulder. "She is a lovely girl. I enjoy having her here. It has been nice to have the company."

I lowered my eyes for a moment. "Did Papa ever take a long work trip when you were expecting?"

She replied hesitantly, "No. He was always here for that."

I nodded. "Papa was not around much when we were growing up, but he would never have just left you with people you did not know when you were pregnant."

"What am I supposed to do about it, Amelia?" Her voice was so hushed, I could barely make out what she said. "I cannot just order Joseph to come home."

"Write to Papa and ask that he do it. Joe will listen to him."

Mama sipped her tea again and sighed. "Very well."

My gaze landed on the newspaper sitting folded on a nearby

chair, its front page screaming about the Whitechapel murders. Since his letter to Scotland Yard had been published, the media had come to call him Jack the Ripper. Jack had continued to sell copies for us and every other newspaper in the country, but Mr. Granville persisted in denying me the chance to write anything related to the matter. A few other newspapers had also eventually written stories about the Ripper possibly being a wealthy and educated man, just as I had wanted to.

Every newspaper I saw with headlines about the murders was a not-so-gentle reminder of what I was not *allowed* to do.

"I certainly hope they don't have you writing about those horrendous murders," Mama said.

"No," I sighed, picking up my tea again. "They do not."

"Thank goodness." She shook her head at the nearby paper and tutted. "Absolutely dreadful. I am so relieved they are not sending you over there to write about that unpleasantness."

"Yes," I mumbled. "That would be a shame."

"When are you going back to writing household tips? I loved those." Mama beamed, her face switching from somber to gleeful in a flash. It was a bit unnerving.

"They did not sell newspapers," I lied. "Mr. Granville decided to cut them when our readership dropped off."

"Oh, that's too bad." She pouted and then eyed my abdomen over the rim of her cup. "Any signs of a stork coming for a visit?"

"No, Mama. My monthlies are quite consistent, thank you."

She scoffed. "Amelia, must you always be so distasteful?"

I grinned. "Yes."

TWENTY-THREE

Cora

Wednesday, October 17, 1888

Everett was quiet during breakfast the next morning—even quieter than usual. I kept glancing at him across the table but he would not meet my eyes, instead choosing to look at me only when I was chatting with Miss Baudelaire or Mr. Jones. Bella glanced at Everett constantly, trying desperately to get his attention.

"Is it true you're Mr. Wyndham's newest pet?" Bella grinned at me while crunching on a pear, its juice running down the side of her thumb and wrist.

Everett met my eyes before looking down at the table.

"Yes, Mr. Wyndham and I have become friends," I said, skirting around what she was really asking. "I expect we will have many mutually successful business opportunities together."

"Business opportunities?" She gave a meaningful look to Mrs. Jones across the table. "Is that what they're calling it these days?"

Mrs. Jones' mouth puckered as she hid her smirk, Mr. Jones

chuckling beside her.

"Mr. Wyndham has shown himself to be a true gentleman," I added. "I do not know why you are all suggesting otherwise."

Minerva shook her head at Bella, silencing the table immediately.

When I excused myself after breakfast, Everett silently followed me out. Miss Baudelaire glanced at me, a warning look in her eyes.

Everett waited until we were in the front parlor before putting himself at my side.

"Good morning, Everett," I said quietly, continuing my pace across the room. "Pleasant weather we are having."

He frowned at me. "When are you going to tell me what is happening here?" His dark curls were growing long, dangling over his eyes.

I could not bear to meet his gaze. "Well, I am about to ascend the staircase. Now I am ascending the staircase—"

"Cora, stop."

He took my hand and I halted. Since I was a step further up than Everett, our heights were closer than usual. With his face just above mine, avoiding eye contact became much more difficult.

Everett caressed my hand with his thumb as he considered his words. "You had dinner with Mr. Wyndham last night?"

I swallowed. "Yes."

Everett moved a bit closer. "Miss Baudelaire wants me out of the way so Mr. Wyndham will not be jealous. Is that correct?"

"Yes," I whispered, my voice faltering.

"Does he have a reason to be jealous?" His voice was soft. More timid than usual.

I looked up at him but I failed to find the right words. "It is complicated."

Everett's gaze burned into mine, searching hard to find the truth in my eyes. "No, it's not."

I swallowed, my throat suddenly very dry. "What are you asking?"

He stepped closer, as close as he could be without touching me. Like a raindrop, his eyes slid down from my eyelashes, over the apples of my cheeks and down to the curves of my lips. "You know what I'm asking."

If Everett had lowered his lips to mine in that moment, I would not have pulled away.

But he did not touch me.

"Should I leave you?" The words were faint, like a suggestion of a question.

No, you should absolutely not.

I hesitated, knowing how much better off he would be without me. Surely the stress I brought into his life was not worth the effort.

He would be so much better off without me.

"You can do what you like," I said weakly. My tone sounded far more timid than I had intended. "You are not bound to me."

"Am I not?"

My stomach felt uneasy with guilt and want and confusion. I could not meet Everett's longing gaze, no matter how much I wanted to.

"Do you want to leave? You have meals and a bed—"

"I have a hammock," he reminded me.

"What if this is my only chance to stop this Lady Selene nonsense and be taken seriously as a performer? Miss Baudelaire said Mr. Wyndham has the connections to make that happen."

Everett crossed his arms over his chest and looked at me for a moment, his eyes narrowed. "Would you marry him if it meant becoming an actress?"

I hesitated. "Probably."

"You would manipulate the man and pretend to love him for that?"

"I have married a man before for much less."

"Yes, and look how successful that union was," he snapped.

I glared at him. "Who I marry is none of your business—"

"Of *course* it's my business, Cora," he shot back, his voice tipped with vitriol. "By a series of strange incidents, I *am* bound to you and, despite your self-absorbed arrogance, I love you."

His jaw twitched as those final three words were tagged on at the end. He looked away, his eyes fixed on the polished staircase railing. I had a feeling he hadn't meant those words to escape. But they were out, hanging in the air between us—that unspoken thing that hid behind every exchanged glance and every word we spoke to one another. I knew he cared for me and certainly felt an attraction to me, but those three little words answered so many questions that hummed in my heart every time he looked at me.

Well, not *every* time. For instance, as we stood together on the staircase, he looked more irritated with me than enamored.

Ignoring the weakness in my legs and the rising heat on my neck and in my stomach, I studied the contours of his face. His perfect full lips that curved into a smile when I needed it the most; his eyes that were the most exceptional shade of light blue I had ever seen; his skin an exquisite bronze.

When he looked back at me, I immediately lowered my eyes to the floor.

"Everett, I—"

Magni's bedroom door swung open, the door rattling on its hinges from the force. Shirtless and carrying a half-empty bottle of cheap wine, he swaggered in our direction.

"A lover's quarrel?" he slurred. "So early in the morning?"

"Piss off," Everett grumbled.

Magni shuffled onto the staircase, relying heavily on the railing to stay upright. "Oh, do stay silent." A slimy grin slithered across his unshaven face. "Doesn't feel very good being replaced, does it?"

Everett squared his shoulders as Magni took a big gulp straight from the bottle.

"A little bird told me you and Wyndham are getting friendly," Magni went on. "Is that how you stole my tour? You just spread your legs and suddenly it's your name on the posters?"

I glanced at Everett. His nostrils flared and his hands were curled into fists, but just as I thought, Everett was not the type to raise a hand to another person.

Unlike me, apparently.

Before I even knew what I was doing, my palm struck Magni's face, a loud crack echoing through the parlor. Despite falling back onto the previous step, he still held tight to the neck of his bottle.

"You are pathetic," I spat.

Mr. Jones had appeared in the parlor. "Oy. No fightin' in the house please. Save it for the stage where we can charge people to watch."

My palm burned from the impact. Magni stayed put on the stairs for the moment, cursing and putting the bottle back to his lips.

Everett's eyes gleamed as he grinned at me. "Well done."

The moment between us had evaporated but we could not take back what we had said.

I winced. "Everett, I—"

"Everett, I need some help with something," Mr. Jones called.

"Yes, sir," he replied before looking back at me, smiling warily.

He joined Mr. Jones without another word and I shut myself up in my room.

Cora Pringle: Fraud and Indecisive Fool.

TWENTY-FOUR

Amelia

Thursday, October 25, 1888

"Since the Christmas season is just around the corner," Mrs. Carrigan said at that evening's L.A.E.W. meeting, her authoritative voice carrying over the low rumble of chatter in the room, "we need to start thinking about our annual Christmas fundraiser. I challenge you to come up with something new and innovative and we will discuss further next week." She smiled at the hushed audience. "Does anyone else have anything to add before we take a little break?"

I was out of my seat before I fully realized I had stood up. I had considered bringing my idea to the group, but I was not sure if I would have the courage to actually go through with it. Dozens of pairs of eyes landed on me curiously and my cheeks went red.

"Yes, Mrs. Baxter?" Mrs. Carrigan smiled sweetly at me.

I moved to the end of my row so I could face everyone at once. Clearing my throat and swallowing, I caught an encouraging nod from Esther.

"As I am sure you are all aware, many women of the East End are in a particularly difficult situation right now. So many of them are unable to work because it could be a matter of life or death. A woman must be in desperate circumstances to turn to that sort of work in the first place, and now they are in danger every time they are in the street at night." I cleared my throat again and continued. "What if we prepared next month's charity baskets for—" I considered my phrasing carefully. "—a select group of women in Whitechapel?"

Every woman in that room knew what type of woman I meant—the fallen kind.

Esther beamed at me, but even Esther being proud of me did not make up for the vast array of meaningful glances exchanged among the other League members just then.

After a dreadfully long and uncomfortable silence, Mrs. Carrigan was the first to speak. "My dear, those women are in that … predicament … because of their own sinful choices." She looked at the other ladies. "Our charity can be better spent elsewhere."

The rest of the women nodded in agreement, adding an "Indeed" here and a "Quite right" there.

I persisted. "I only make this suggestion because if a handful of these women do not have to go out at night to work, they might not be—" *Killed. Violently murdered. Slaughtered in the street.* "—harmed."

I was met by a room of blank expressions.

"And-and-and there is evidence that suggests not all of the victims are, in fact, prostitutes," I sputtered. "Not that it matters either way, as they are still human beings and in need of our assistance."

"We understand your concern for these poor wretches," Mrs. Armstrong, another society member, said gently. "However, these women have turned their backs on God with their trade, numbing themselves with liquor. Any food we give them would just be traded for liquor."

I fought hard not to roll my eyes at her. Mrs. Armstrong had, on several occasions, tried to persuade the rest of us to add temperance to the society's mandate. I told Simon about it later that night over a glass of sherry and we both had a good laugh about it.

"Your heart is in the right place, Mrs. Baxter," Mrs. Carrigan added, keeping her voice soft so not to hurt my feelings. "However, if we provide charity for women who live unlawfully, it sends the wrong message about our society." She looked back at the rest of the ladies and I was greeted by several somber nods of agreement. "Now, unless anyone else has anything else to add, let's break for tea and some of my delicious cucumber sandwiches."

Smiling weakly and feeling utterly defeated, I retook my seat.

I know exactly what you should do with your cucumber sandwiches, Mrs. Carrigan.

After the meeting, Esther suggested we take a walk in Hyde Park.

"So, do you legitimately fancy a chat, or do I just look like I need to complain to someone?" I sighed as we promenaded. "I was fairly certain the idea would be rejected but I knew I had to at least try."

She sighed. "It was a good idea and I am glad you brought it up. Even if it gets one other woman in that room thinking about the dire situation, perhaps some good will come of it."

The air was crisp, and the grass had yellowed with the changing seasons.

"I keep having nightmares about Jack the Ripper," I admitted. "I suppose that comes from thinking about it all the time. I have tried to stop picturing it all in my head, but the details keep creeping in."

"Those women are not just names in a newspaper. They were people with friends and families," Esther said, her eyes fixing on a patch of bare trees nearby, their twisted fingers reaching for the sky. "A lot of people do not understand that."

"Imagine how different the murders would be treated if they were women from Mayfair or Belgravia or Marylebone." My long sigh escaped as a cloud from my lips into the brisk fresh air.

Esther paused for a moment. "I thought I would have seen another article from you concerning spiritualism by now."

I shrugged and watched as Esther retrieved something from her reticule. She unfolded a clipped newspaper article and handed it to me.

I read the headline aloud. "'Famous spiritualist Miss Margaret Fox admits hoax.'"

Esther nodded, urging me on.

Having always been a fast reader, my eyes flew over the words. Margaret and Katie Fox were famous for hearing rapping sounds in their New York home when they were young ladies. The noises were said to be communications from ghosts who haunted their house and they began holding séances and going on speaking tours, becoming rather famous from it all. Although their fame had dwindled in the forty years that had passed, the sisters were credited for starting the spiritualist religion and inspiring many others to try their own hand at communicating with the "other side."

It was all complete hokum, of course.

"She admitted to making the noises … with her ankles?" I looked at Esther again.

"Then she goes and demonstrates how she made the cracking sounds in front of an audience," she said with a laugh. "I suppose that's one way of getting your name in the press again."

"It might be time I write a follow-up to my article about Madame Pringle," I said.

"I believe so." She grinned and nodded to a nearby hansom cab. "Go and write something good."

TWENTY-FIVE

Cora

Wednesday, October 31, 1888

"Will you really be gone from The Hemlock once we return to London?"

Everett seemed surprised by the question. Surrounded by a river of train passengers and noise, he leaned closer to me as steam rolled through the air around us, both of us sheltered from the cool rain under his umbrella.

"Yes, I'm afraid so," he said, just loud enough for me to hear.

I wanted to embrace him. I wanted to tell him to sneak onto the train and come with Mr. Wyndham and I on this tour of Britain but I knew that would be unwise: I did not want Everett seeing me trying to charm and impress Mr. Wyndham and I did not want Mr. Wyndham seeing, well, Everett look at me the way he did.

"Where will you go?"

"I found a room to rent in St. Luke's, not far away. You will still see me almost every day."

Before I could insist he find some place in Spitalfields, Mr. Wyndham appeared among the crowd, joining us at the platform. "All the luggage is on board and ready to go." His smile and polite nod at Everett were kind enough but lacked sincerity. "Mr. Rigby."

The two were similar in height but Mr. Wyndham was a little softer around the middle, his hair a little thinner than Everett's head of thick dark locks. Everett's smile was shy but intensely gorgeous when shared with its lucky recipient while Mr. Wyndham, generally more jolly, laughed and smiled much more freely.

"I know you will take care with my dear friend," Everett said. "I have the utmost faith in you." I wondered if he had meant that as a threat.

"Of course," Mr. Wyndham said, shaking Everett's hand in a firm grasp before turning to me. "You and I had best be off."

I nodded and gave Everett a weak smile. I did not know what to say. He and I had not been parted for more than a few hours over the last few months and now I was leaving for several weeks. Before I could struggle anymore, Mr. Wyndham offered me his arm and we moved through the crowd and onto the train. As I followed Mr. Wyndham down the aisle to our seats, I looked for Everett's face among the crowd, catching only glimpses of him among the throng of travelers. All too soon he vanished, and regret stung my throat.

The trip to Brighton was fairly short and quiet. Mr. Wyndham mostly just read his newspaper while I stared out the window, glancing at him occasionally. I tried to hide my frequent yawns behind my gloved hand.

Mr. Wyndham noticed and chuckled to himself. "Do trains make you tired, my dear?"

"Forgive me." I lowered my eyes in faux shyness. He liked me best that way. "My nerves have disrupted my sleep a little."

"You're nervous about the tour?"

Fear of failure had left me staring at the ceiling for hours on many nights leading up to our tour departure. When I was not struggling to sleep, I was dreaming of my failure, and sometimes of Everett running off with Bella.

I nodded. "Yes. What if audiences outside of London respond differently?"

"They will adore you," he said. "Almost as much as I do."

I smiled. "You have been so kind to me, Mr. Wyndham."

He leaned forward a bit, sliding his hand under mine and bringing it up close to his face. "And I will continue doing so." Closing his eyes, he left a soft kiss on my hand, letting his mouth linger for a moment.

The way he looked at me just then was all too familiar. It was how half the men in the audience usually looked at me during my performances. A hollow feeling grew and spread within my stomach.

He should not say such intimate things to me.

The thought startled me. In turn, my sudden reluctance to his advances confused me.

Why do I suddenly want to throw myself off of this train?

"I love Brighton, don't you?" I blurted.

I had only been there once before with Papa when I was a child, but Mr. Wyndham did not need to know that.

Mr. Wyndham sat up. "Of course." He gave a small shrug. "Perhaps our next visit will be during the summer months."

I laughed. "Are you already planning our next tour?"

Folding his hands in his lap, he replied casually, "Perhaps our next visit will not be work-related."

I swallowed. "Oh."

The hollow feeling in my abdomen deepened.

Our Brighton hotel was even more spectacular than I could have imagined. I went right to the balcony overlooking the shore, inhaling deeply the scent of the salty ocean air. Even though England was quickly dipping into late autumn coolness, couples and families dotted the beach boardwalk below. The cold air felt refreshing on my skin as I wrapped my arms around myself.

Mr. Wyndham joined me on the balcony, his steps slow and quiet. "Beautiful."

I rested a hand on the balcony railing. "It is marvelous."

"Yes," he said, looking directly at me. "Truly magnificent."

I avoided his intense gaze by looking back out to the waves.

"I have to go sort out some details with the venue, but I will return for dinner," he said, his voice returning to its usual friendly tone. "My suite, six o'clock?" He was already on his way out the door.

"Not in the dining room?"

What was the point of being seen at an exclusive hotel in Brighton if you were going to just eat in your room?

"Six o'clock!" he called back over his shoulder, shutting the door behind him.

Rolling my eyes, I went to the door and slid the chain across the lock. I leaned against it and crossed my arms over my chest.

Thank goodness I have my own room—

My eyes narrowed as they landed on the door beside the water closet door. Mr. Wyndham had booked us adjoining rooms at the hotel. That could not have been an accident.

I slid the chain across the lock on that door too and went back to the balcony, now glaring at the couples and families on the beach.

It is almost November. What are you fools even doing on the beach?

I took a seat on the edge of the queen-size bed. Thinking over all of the things Mr. Wyndham had said since boarding the train in London, I knew there was a strong possibility he might propose during the tour. We had certainly been spending a lot of time together, dining together regularly in fabulous restaurants or with Minerva at The Hemlock. I had yet to see his home in Fitzrovia but expected an invite there soon. He was a lovely and clever businessman, certainly.

A woman could do worse.

My eyes landed on the adjoining door between our rooms.

If he knocks on that door this evening and requests to see me, should I agree? If I refuse, is the tour over? Is he the type of man to expect to share a bed with a woman before marriage?

Marriage. The word struck me, resting uneasily in the pit in my stomach that had formed and not quite gone away.

My fingertip traced a fine trail of stitches on the ornate duvet and my eyes slowly traveled from the end of the bed where I sat and up to the pillows. I tried to imagine what sharing a bed with Mr. Wyndham might be like. My experience was limited to dispassionate and dutiful episodes with Marshall so imagining bedding Mr. Wyndham in any other way was challenging.

In my mind and without any intentional input on my part, Mr. Wyndham was suddenly replaced by Everett—the two of us wrapping ourselves around one another. His lips on mine, bare skin on bare skin, fingertips brushing the most sensitive of places. My abdomen ached again, throbbing just above both my hips. My breath ran short as my heartbeat quickened and the heat rose in my cheeks.

I blinked hard and returned to the coolness of the balcony, taking big gulps of the salty sea air.

When dinnertime came, I excused myself from dining with a disappointed Mr. Wyndham, citing weariness and a headache. I ate alone in my room instead, a fork in one hand and a novel in the other. I made sure to avoid the balcony in case Mr. Wyndham ventured out to his and saw that I was well enough.

I had avoided his advances for one day. Only several weeks more to go.

Thankfully, I overcame my "illness" shortly before my performance and it all went as planned. The audience hung on my every word, enraptured by my charms and tricks.

After I waved my farewell to the appreciative public, my heart hammering in my chest, I pulled myself away from their hungry cheers, slipping into the little room that served as the venue's backstage area. Immediately met by Mr. Wyndham, he grabbed my hand and brought it to his lips.

"You were sensational," he exclaimed before kissing my knuckles again. "You were spectacular!"

"Mr. Wyndham, please do not act so surprised by my talents." I smiled up at him coyly.

His bright eyes settled on my mouth for a moment and my insides immediately twisted, and not in a pleasant way. Mr. Wyndham met my eyes once again, his grin spreading even wider than before. I was grateful he was too much of a gentleman to embrace me just then, but it was clearly what he wanted to do.

Something caught his notice from behind me and he dropped my hand, his smile relaxing a bit.

"Mrs. Pringle, I'd like you to meet one of the investors in our tour," he said, extending his hand to one side.

Looking over my shoulder, I gulped. My lips tightened as I forced a polite smile.

"Mrs. Pringle, this is Mr. Lindsey, an old friend and partner of mine."

Tom Lindsey, looking not the least bit surprised to see me, cracked a crooked, amused smile. "Mrs—" He paused for effect. "—*Pringle.*" He gave the smallest of nods.

I glanced at Mr. Wyndham. He must have been used to Mr. Lindsey's lack of decorum because he didn't notice his friend's cold greeting to me.

"Good evening, Mr. Lindsey," I replied, forcing a casual tone. "I hope you enjoyed the performance."

"Mm. Quite."

Oh no. What is he going to tell Mr. Wyndham?

"Mr. Lindsey and I actually have met before," I added quickly.

"Truly? What a small world we live in," Mr. Wyndham said, his face still lit up. "I think tonight's successful performance calls for a drink. Shall I get some champagne sent up to my suite for the three of us? It'll be a lovely time."

No one has ever had a lovely time with Tom Lindsey. I refuse to believe such a thing.

"The performance has left me so weary," I said, slipping into a simpering voice. "I think I will just excuse myself for the night."

"Oh, come now, Cora," Mr. Lindsey said. "Have a drink with Wyndham and I."

Mr. Wyndham glanced at him when he called me by my first name but did not speak up against his partner's impropriety. I wondered exactly how much financial backing Mr. Lindsey was providing to our little venture. Mr. Wyndham smiled at me, giving an encouraging nod.

I sighed. "One drink."

Our get-together in Mr. Wyndham's suite was delayed because several audience members had waited for me, requesting my autograph. One man asked if I could keep an eye out for the ghost of his dead mother. I said I would, of course, although I thought asking personal favors of a stranger was a bit much.

While Mr. Wyndham dealt with some business with the hotel manager, Mr. Lindsey escorted me up to Mr. Wyndham's suite, me still in my stage costume and makeup and him stinking of alcohol. We were silent as we made our way to the third floor and neither of us spoke as he unlocked Mr. Wyndham's suite with his friend's keys.

I went right for the champagne bucket, already in the room waiting for us.

Pretending I knew something about champagne, I lifted the bottle and read the label. "How long have you known I was Mr. Wyndham's new project?"

"Only since this evening." He grabbed the bottle from me and expertly popped the cork. "Your name never came up. All he said was 'beautiful,' 'wonderful performer' and 'charming.'" He glanced at my décolletage and curves. "He left out a few other details that would have given you away."

He poured two glasses and handed one to me. I sipped my glass gingerly, the bubbles playing on my lips and tongue.

"You should know that I do plan to tell him the truth about you." He downed his glass of champagne in a single swig and poured himself another half glass.

"And what truth is that?"

Mr. Lindsey glared. "You're married."

"I am not."

"What, did the mutt die? How tragic." Pulling a flask from inside his jacket pocket, he poured its brown contents into his champagne, the two liquids swirling together in the glass.

"Do not call him that," I snapped. "He is ten times the man you will ever be." I took a seat in the armchair by the window, putting some space between him and I. "Mr. Rigby and I were never married."

Mr. Lindsey's pursed his mouth. "You're lying."

"I am not lying."

Taking the chair across the room, he took a gulp of his cocktail. "You were living with him though, in that hovel."

"Yes, but my relationship with Mr. Rigby has always been strictly professional. He offered his home to me when I needed one so I accepted his offer."

"His offer was better than mine?" The irritation in his eyes as he spoke was stinging.

"Mr. Rigby's offer did not require an agreement of matrimony," I said. "As a woman recently widowed, that was appealing to me."

Mr. Lindsey snorted and emptied his glass again. I wondered how many glasses he could drink before it would even affect him in the least.

"You don't expect me to believe—"

The door opened, and Mr. Wyndham let himself in. Mr. Lindsey and I quickly plastered on jovial expressions to keep the room's mood cheerful.

"Friends!" Mr. Wyndham lifted the champagne bottle from the ice bucket. "I see you started without me."

I brought him two glasses, he poured for us and we clinked them together.

"A toast to Lady Selene," he said, his smile warm and genuine.

I slipped into my sultry voice. "To us."

His smile spread wider across his face and his cheeks pinked.

I eventually excused myself to my room next door, eager to get away from Mr. Lindsey. I was in bed when the quarrelling began. Mr. Lindsey's voice was always loud anyway but Mr. Wyndham's voice gradually grew to reach the same volume. I stepped lightly to the door between our rooms and slid silently to the floor, pressing my ear to the gap between door and wall.

"That cannot be true," I heard Mr. Wyndham exclaim. "I do not believe it."

"Why would I lie to you?" Mr. Lindsey replied, sounding more than a little drunk.

"Because you're jealous," he snapped back. "She hurt your pride by turning you down so you don't want me to have her either. Is that it?"

Mr. Lindsey mumbled something I could not hear, likely from the other side of the room.

"I… I know," Mr. Wyndham shouted back, his tone dripping with defeat. "But I care for her. She is so beautiful, just the type of woman I would want to be with."

Mr. Lindsey said something else, but I could not hear. This was followed by the sound of the door opening and closing hard, causing the chandelier above me to quake from the impact. I returned to bed, uneasy about what the following morning might bring.

It was worse than I imagined.

Mr. Wyndham had slipped a note under my door, ordering me to join him for breakfast downstairs at nine o'clock. He seemed like more of an early riser than a man who breakfasts at nine, but we had both had a late night.

He did not even rise from his chair to greet me when I approached his table. He was too busy glaring at a newspaper, his coffee drained but his toast left untouched.

"Good morning," I said sweetly before sitting in the empty

chair across from him.

"Is it?" The newspaper stayed put in front of his face.

"Perhaps I will just return to my room if I'm to share breakfast with *The Gazette Weekly* instead of you," I snapped.

Wait. How did he get a copy of that newspaper in Brighton?

"Mr. Lindsey brought this newspaper from London yesterday," Mr. Wyndham said, as if hearing my thoughts. "He said I might be interested in reading this."

He turned the newspaper around so I could read the large, bold headline: *American Spiritualist Sisters Revealed to be Charlatans.* The subheading was even more damning: *Spiritualist con artists plentiful in Britain.*

My eyes widened and I snatched the newspaper from his grip. "No, no, no, *no*."

"You are mentioned by name specifically." Mr. Wyndham's face tightened as he shook his head. "Our remaining shows in Brighton have been cancelled as it seems like several other papers across Britain have picked up the story of this Fox woman."

"What? But about the contract?" The words came out at nearly the volume of a yell.

A few other restaurant patrons looked up from their breakfasts, disturbed by my outburst.

"We should not discuss this here," Mr. Wyndham pulled the newspaper back from me. "I need to go deal with this now and get in touch with some other venues before the entire tour is cut."

As he tucked the newspaper under his arm, I caught a glimpse of the author's name, and it was just the name I had expected to see.

Ambrose Spellman.

TWENTY-SIX

Amelia

Friday, November 2, 1888

"Your article has caused quite the scandal," Mr. Granville said, sipping his tea and grinning mischievously, fat raindrops hitting the thick glass of his office window. "The spiritualists have condemned poor Ambrose Spellman as a closed-minded buffoon. They are demanding his resignation immediately."

"Of course they are." I rolled my eyes. "Funny how they condemn the writer but not the Fox sisters for their decades of manipulation. Or, at the very least, Maggie Fox for telling an audience about how they tricked people all that time."

"The spiritualists are claiming Miss Fox was forced to lie on stage for money or fame or the like." He slid his tea onto his tidy desk. "No matter. Mr. Spellman's job is secure for the time being."

I snickered. "I will certainly let him know. I am sure he will be most grateful."

As I returned to my desk, my smug satisfaction quickly faded at the sight of Mr. Turner hammering on his typewriter. I knew he was working on yet *another* story on the Whitechapel murders. I was determined to pretend I had moved beyond my frustration, but the envy still stung with every letter pressed.

I did not have time to dwell on my jealousy, however, because it was in that moment that the office door whipped open, thrown wide so roughly that teacups jingled against their saucers and the glass in the nearby windows shook.

"Ambrose Spellman," roared the fire-haired woman in the doorway, storming right by Mrs. Davies' desk. "Where the devil are you, Mr. Spellman?"

Her angry eyes darted around the quiet office before landing first on Mr. Turner. "Are you Mr. Spellman?"

Before he could answer, her gaze flicked over to me and then widened with realization.

Madame Pringle had found me out at last.

The tips of her nostrils flared as she approached my desk, her eyes narrowing, her full lips puckering.

"You."

I swallowed and rose from my desk. "Amelia Baxter." I glanced at Mr. Turner. "Lovely to see you again, Mrs. Pringle. How do you do?"

Mr. Granville appeared in the doorway of his office and winced when he saw who was glaring directly into my face.

"My tour was cancelled because of you," she hissed. "I have gone from admired to despised … because of you."

"All I did was reveal the truth," I said, straightening my back. "If people despise you because of your manipulation and subterfuge, well, that is no concern of mine."

"You know nothing of what I do for people." Flames flickered in her pupils as they bore into me. "And you have no idea who you are dealing with."

"Oh, I know exactly what kind of person you are, Mrs. Pringle. You use your wiles to fool susceptible people into believing your tricks." I smirked. "You are not the first person to play this game and I am sure you will not be the last."

She opened her mouth to respond but Mr. Granville cut her off.

"Mrs. Pringle, please leave this office or I will have the police remove you," he said, sounding bored. "Do you wish for even *more* bad press?"

I could have hugged Mr. Granville just then.

Mrs. Pringle shot a look at him and then continued glaring at me. "You will regret this."

She marched back the same way she came, her heels loud on the scuffed wooden floor.

"Oh, dear," said Mrs. Davies as Mrs. Pringle slammed the door shut behind her. "Oh dear, oh dear, oh dear."

Mr. Turner rose, sliding his arms into his jacket and grabbing his notebook. "Do you expect she will seek retaliation? Does she seem the type to you?"

Absolutely.

I waved my hand at him. "No, I should not expect so."

My eyes flashed open as Simon flung my bedroom door open. I winced at him in the dark, my head heavy with confusion, before glancing out my window. Going by the quiet outside and the sky's particular shade of dark gray, I guessed it to be at least two or three in the morning.

"What is it?" I croaked, my mouth dry.

"Someone just threw something through the front window downstairs," Mr. Woodacre said, appearing behind Simon, his hands fumbling with his shirt. "Matilda has already sent someone to fetch the police. I have to go." He disappeared into the darkness of the hallway.

"Please, you must stay," Simon said over his shoulder before chasing after him.

I could hear their argument as I slid out of my bed and Matilda appeared out of the darkness to help me into my dressing gown.

Mr. Woodacre seemed very determined to leave.

"You know perfectly well why I have to leave," I heard him say. "What am I supposed to tell the police, that I am your wife's..." He struggled to choose the appropriate word. "...companion?"

I looked at Matilda, her eyes lowered. She was paid extra to keep Simon's relationship with Mr. Woodacre a private matter. I just hoped she had kept her promise to stay silent about it.

After Matilda helped me into a pair of boots, the upstairs gas lamps were lit and I made my way downstairs to inspect the damage. The rug in the sitting room glimmered with shards of glass, sparkling like an early winter frost. Stepping down from the stairs, glass crunched and cracked under my boot.

Mr. Woodacre, now fully dressed, jogged down the stairs and stopped at the bottom step. "Do be careful, Amelia."

"Thank you for your concern but I am quite well. If you are going to go, you best do so now."

He tipped his head to me and made his escape out the back garden like usual. Simon, now wearing pants, joined me at the bottom of the stairs, Matilda close behind him.

Matilda advanced to go light the gas in the sitting room, but I put my arm out to stop her.

"Wait," I said. "Do you hear that?"

The noise from the street was naturally louder because of the large hole in the front window, but I thought I heard something else coming from that direction.

I squinted with tired eyes, trying to focus in the darkened room. Suddenly, a flash of movement by the curtain caught my attention. I grabbed Simon's arm and Matilda grabbed mine and we all let out three different levels of a shriek.

"What was that?" Simon whispered.

I leaned closer to him. "Why are we whispering?"

"I don't know," he hissed back. "It seemed like the proper thing—"

As the bottom of the curtain fluttered, we all shrieked again.

"What is that on the floor over there?" Matilda pointed over to the darkest part of the room that lay in shadow.

I squinted. "A wooden crate perhaps? Is that how they broke the window?"

Feeling the crunching and cracking of the glass shards under my boots, I stepped slowly and carefully towards the crate, wishing my eyes would adjust to the darkness more efficiently.

Simon and Matilda edged away from the stairs, following me into shadow. The wooden crate was perhaps two feet long, a brick tied to each side of it with twine.

Just as I tipped the crate over to inspect the inside, Matilda lit the gas in the sitting room, and everything went from bad to worse.

Gasping, my eyes bulged as a rat screeched at me from inside the wooden box and tumbled out as I tossed the crate over, flinging it in absolute shock and terror. The scream that escaped my lips was like no other sound I had ever made before.

The sudden illumination of the room must have startled the other uninvited guests, as they scurried out from their hiding places—out from the curtains, out from under the armchair and sofa, and out from the fireplace. I am certain there were other hiding places involved but I was too preoccupied dashing to the staircase to notice. I was later told by Simon that I shoved him out of the way and nearly knocked Matilda over, but I did not recall doing such a thing. Simon's scream was just as loud as mine. Matilda got close enough to one of the rats to kick it away. She climbed up onto the easy chair and burst into tears, erupting into whiney sobs as the furry fiends scampered around the legs of the chair.

A loud knock on the door startled all of us.

"Scotland Yard," they announced from the other side of the door.

The three of us inside all looked at one another.

"Matilda," I said, nodding at the door, and pulling my dressing gown tighter around myself.

"Please, Mrs. Baxter," Matilda said with a pathetic sniff. "*Please* don't make me." She gave another sorrowful squeal as one of the rats stopped and stared up at her.

I looked at Simon but he just shook his head firmly. "Oh, I am not leaving these stairs. Perhaps never again as long as I live."

With a tiny reluctant whimper, I stepped down from my place on the stairs and quickly unlocked and opened the door. I immediately returned to the stairs, trying my best to fake a pleasant smile at the police officer, puzzled as he was.

"Evening," he said, raising his eyebrow at me. "We were notified of a disturbance. May I come—"

Seeing the opportunity, one of the rats made a dash for the open door, running over the officer's foot on its way out.

"Bleedin' Christ," he blurted, lifting his foot and stumbling sideways. He looked back at us, his disgust quite clear on his ruddy face. "My apologies." He craned his neck to peer into the sitting room. "What on earth…?"

"Someone threw a crate of rats in through the window!" Simon blurted.

The officer frowned at Simon. "Yes, I gathered that." He inched into the sitting room, watching the floor, towards Matilda. "Miss, can you get down from there?"

Another rat streaked across the carpet, making its escape from our home on tiny pink feet. Matilda shook her head frantically.

As the policeman coaxed Matilda down from her perch, Simon glanced at me and then looked back at the sitting room floor, his eyes darting whenever a rodent came into view.

"So, who did you anger *this* time?"

TWENTY-SEVEN

Cora

Saturday, November 3, 1888

"You look familiar," said the man beside me, sliding closer to me on the wooden bench. "I never forget a face."

Not able to restrain myself from wincing at his odor, I leaned slightly away from him and looked in the opposite direction. No matter where I looked though, the police station was full of drunkards and vagrants, harlots and bullies. I felt several sets of eyes on me.

"I've got it. You're that lady who talks to ghosts," he said, sounding pleased with himself. "I saw you a few weeks back."

"You must be mistaking me for someone else," I snapped, my knuckles going white as I clung to my reticule.

While staring at the bit of dirty floor directly in front of my feet, I thought about Mr. Wyndham—the look in his eyes as he told me the tour was off and that he did not think my career was salvageable. He had not even taken the train back to London with me.

Now that I could not make him any money, our courtship was evidently off as well.

Perhaps Mr. Wyndham is not a good man after all.

An inspector in a respectable brown suit looked down at a clipboard before raising an eyebrow at me. "Mrs. Pringle?"

I nodded.

"I'm Inspector Fitzpatrick. Please come with me."

I stood immediately, glad to be getting away from the piss-sodden pants of my companion on the bench. I followed the inspector down a narrow hallway and into a small, dimly lit office.

"What, no interrogation room, inspector?" I cast my eyes about the shelves and files and books, many of which could have done with a dusting, and took a seat. "I have to say I am a little disappointed."

"Our interrogation rooms are a little full at the moment." He sat behind the small desk and folded his hands together on top of it. "In case you hadn't heard, we've got a murderer on the loose."

"Why waste your time on me then?" I smiled sweetly. "Unless you believe I'm the one killing those poor women. Why even bring me in?"

Inspector Fitzpatrick glared. "You threatened Mrs. Amelia Baxter yesterday at her place of employment and then, hours later, her house was vandalized. Do you *really* expect anyone to believe you *weren't* involved?"

"Vandalized?" I repeated. "In what way?"

He narrowed his eyes, his mouth twisting into a sideways frown. "As if you don't know."

"I don't!" I pinched the inside of my gloved hand to summon tears. "How could you think I could be capable of such a thing?" I sniffed and looked away.

"Someone smashed the front window of her home and sent a care package into her front room," he said. "A crate of rats."

I put a hand to my mouth. "Oh, my good god!"

"Yeah. Someone was trying to send her a message."

Minerva. It must have been.

"I do not even know where she lives," I exclaimed. "I would never degrade myself to do such a repulsive act!"

"Obviously we don't think you pitched a box of rodents in yourself, but we think you know who did it."

"I do not, I swear."

Inspector Fitzpatrick sat back in his chair, the light shifting on his face to reveal dark shadows under his small, beady eyes. I imagined many in Scotland Yard were putting in a lot of extra hours at that time. After a short pause, he continued his questioning.

"Did you or did you not threaten Mrs. Baxter yesterday?"

"I simply wanted to discuss her latest article about spiritualism and correct a few of the many errors she made concerning my specific talents. I only wanted a retraction."

He glanced at his clipboard. "'You will regret this,'" he read. "That doesn't sound very genial to me."

"I never said that," I said with a quiet chuckle. "Is Mrs. Baxter claiming I said that?"

"Several other employees at *The Gazette Weekly* claim you uttered those words, yes."

"Absolutely preposterous," I said, laughing. "They are attempting to frame me. Do I look like someone capable of tossing out threats?"

Hopefully he was the type of man who assumed a respectable woman was more like a wilting calla lily and less like a thorny rose.

"I would not presume anything of you, Mrs. Pringle. After all," he said with a small grin, "you talk to ghosts. I can't imagine all of the other things you can do."

"I have an alibi, Inspector."

"No need. I know *you* didn't personally toss a crate through a window. You would never dirty your own hands," he said, eyeing my delicate gloves. "A man was spotted leaving the scene after the incident. You don't happen to know who that man was, do you?"

"No, I do not." I paused. "Mrs. Baxter was not hurt, was she?"

"No. Would you care if she had been hurt?"

Tipping my nose up, I squared my shoulders. "It would be well-deserved."

Fitzpatrick raised his eyebrows.

I smiled. "A joke, inspector. Calm yourself."

"I promise there is nothing funny about intentional property damage, Mrs. Pringle. You would be wise to remember that."

"Absolutely," I said. "May I go?"

He glared at me. "You will let me know if you remember anything, won't you?" He handed me a card.

"Yes, inspector." I rose. "You have my word."

I let myself out of the cramped little office and, once outside on the street, dropped his card and watched as the wind carried it away.

Once safe and sound in a hansom on my way back to The Hemlock, I let out the slow sigh and let my shoulders slump. I was brought up to be a respectable lady and had somehow fallen far enough to be mingling with the criminal element.

How had things gone so terribly wrong?

As the cab jostled along crowded streets from Belgravia to Spitalfields, I watched as the quality of the people, businesses and houses gradually descended. Top hats were replaced by bowlers and parasols were replaced by faded and stained skirts. Young children selling flowers on street corners were replaced by thin orphans holding their desperate palms out for charity. Ladies shopping for lace and gloves became tired mothers trying to manage their unruly broods before finally turning to women of loose morals, their faces bright with gaudy makeup, using their eyes to sell their bodies to any man who passed by. I dared not think about how desperate I would have to be before turning to that life.

Are these women not scared of the Ripper?

I closed my eyes and shook my head. I had few cards left to play but I still had my name and the ability to draw a crowd. I needed to use that while it was still an option.

Pounding the ceiling of the cab, I yelled, "Driver, onto Whitechapel if you please."

Spitalfields was a diverse area of London, some streets burdened by poverty and crime while other streets were comfortable homes and flourishing businesses.

Nearby Whitechapel, however, was a different story altogether. I had heard stories of the grim lives of the people there and read articles in the newspaper detailing the despicable state of it, but I suppose I had never imagined it being as abysmal as it really was.

I paid the driver. "Can you wait for me? I promise I will not be long, and I will pay you for your time."

I was not actually sure if I had enough money in my reticule to pay for that promise, but he reluctantly agreed to wait as I stuffed my small purse into a hidden pocket in my skirts.

A barefoot urchin rushed to my side. "Spare change, kind lady?"

He was quickly joined by four other children, their hands tiny and speckled with filth. My eyes darted left and right and gently moved in between the children, trying to ignore their disappointed whines.

The neighborhood was swarmed with reporters, each one trying to get some ghastly detail about the butcher haunting the alleyways of Whitechapel. A constable strolled by a few streets down, inspecting the rough types that littered the lanes and doorways. A few men broke away from the busy street and rushed the officer, peppering him with questions.

"Any more clues you want to tell us about?"

"Any signs of the Ripper's return?"

"When is Scotland Yard going to catch 'im?"

"How are the good folks of this city supposed to feel safe when there's a monster on the loose?"

"It's been a month. Is it possible the Ripper's reign of terror is over?"

The constable shooed them away like flies and continued his patrol of the area, ignoring every single inquiry.

Before the band of reporters could disperse, I spotted a nearby wooden crate on the side of the street and climbed atop it, a few of the locals watching me curiously. One of the reporters looked my way and narrowed his eyes as I made myself as tall as I could, using a nearby lamp post for balance.

"I am Lady Selene, the Mystic of the Taj Mahal," I cried at the top of my lungs, "and I have had a vision!"

Several more heads turned to me, children stopped begging for change and a man selling bruised and browned apples halted his rickety cart to survey the spectacle.

Slowly raising my hands up, my palms to the sky, I made my declaration. "The Ripper came to me in a dream. He told me he is not finished with his dark deeds just yet." I closed my eyes for emphasis. "Long Liz and Kate Eddowes will not be his last victims."

Several women gasped and shrieked in the gathering crowd below me. From the end of the street the constable was advancing towards me, trying to squeeze through the unwashed deluge between us. The reporters who had been haranguing him moments before were all watching me with keen interest, their pencils flying over the open pages of their notebooks.

"When will he strike again?" one man yelled.

"Soon," I lamented. "Jack the Ripper will return to Whitechapel soon and the streets will run red with the blood of an Englishwoman once again. He will never be satisfied—"

A large hand gripped my slender wrist, yanking me down from my makeshift podium. I stumbled into the constable as I tumbled off the crate and he roughly shoved me into the upset crowd.

"Begone, woman!" he ordered. "Everyone, please go about your business. Rest assured, there is no sign of the Ripper returning—"

"But 'ow do you know?" an angry woman hollered back at him. "Scotland Yard ain't done nothin' about it."

A man stood tall at her side, pointing his thick finger right in the constable's face. "You coppers ain't got a clue, no more than any of us."

"Yeah!"

The constable held up his hands. "Everyone needs to remain calm—"

"How are we supposed to be calm when there's a killer on his way to rip us apart?"

I wriggled my way out of the crowd before things got out of hand. At once, one of the reporters approached me.

"Lady Selene, can you tell me more about this vision you had?" he asked. "Did the Ripper tell you anything else? Who the next victim might be?"

I surveyed his features. "Do I know you?"

A whisper of a wince flickered across his eyes. "No, miss, I don't believe so—"

"You work at *The Gazette Weekly*," I said, letting out a laugh. "Good day to you, sir."

I took a few steps towards my waiting hansom before a second reporter rushed to my side. "Lady Selene, would you care to talk about your vision? Our readers would love to hear what you have to say."

I smiled sweetly at him, glancing at *The Gazette Weekly* reporter over my shoulder. I fluttered my thick eyelashes at the second reporter and lifted one of my shoulders up slightly, feigning shyness. "Of course. I only want to help if I can."

Just as planned.

TWENTY-EIGHT

Cora

Monday, November 5, 1888

I was playing Old Maid with Miss Baudelaire and Bella when Everett stormed into the front parlor of The Hemlock. Smiling, my stomach turning pleasantly at the sight of him—his curls as dark as a countryside night sky and eyes as deep as the Atlantic, his jacket dotted with a few scattered raindrops.

When he did not smile back, my own grin faded.

"Good morning, Everett," I said hesitantly. "Lovely to see—"

"What is this?" He held up that day's newspaper, angry creases in the corners where he clasped the pages between tight fingertips.

I gazed up at him through my eyelashes. "That appears to be what the English call 'a newspaper.'"

Minerva glanced at the both of us before lowering her eyes in disinterest. Bella giggled silently, hiding her smirk behind her cards.

His face was like a stone. "Cora." His voice had an essence of warning to it.

Knowing exactly what it was, I did not need to survey the page again.

"I did an interview," I said coolly. "I need to regain my reputation after—"

"And you thought *this* was the way to do that?" Everett exclaimed, lifting the paper up to read a quote. "'The streets will run red with the blood of an Englishwoman once again.' Have you gone mad?"

"*The Gazette Weekly* article about me made me look like a fraud—"

"You are, though, love," Bella remarked quietly.

"I am not willing to go down without a fight. Getting my name in the papers was a solid move." I looked at Minerva. "Do I have a performance booked for Thursday or do I not?"

"Indeed," she said.

Everett glanced at her and then back to me. "Can we speak privately?"

Rising, I placed my cards on the table. "Apologies, ladies."

Everett stomped into the empty dining room and closed the door behind us. I crossed my arms over my chest, preparing myself for my scolding. For a moment, he just looked at me, his eyes hard. Finally, he folded his arms, just as I had done, and leaned his back against the opposite wall.

"Did you know I lived in Whitechapel for a time when I was a boy?"

I fought the urge to cringe. "No, you never told me that."

"The people there have nothing. If they're lucky, they have their friends, they have their families. Most drown in liquor because it's cheaper than a bed to sleep in or a hot meal to eat and it numbs the pain of a hard life. And right now, those people are terrified."

I swallowed and lowered my eyes to the floor.

"Those poor wretches were just going about their day, trying to survive, and a lady in a fine dress who is obviously educated comes in and announces that someone they know and love is going to die a horrible death soon. You traumatized that lot to get your name in the paper." Everett shook his head. "Those butchered women were real flesh and blood people and you took advantage of them," he continued, his voice going quiet. "I know taking advantage is part of the performance, but I never guessed you would act so thoughtlessly."

I lowered my eyes as an ache rose in my throat, begging to let loose a string of sobs, but I forced them back.

"You are angry with me," I whispered, a tiny creak escaping along with the words. I dragged my eyes up to meet his, taking a deep breath to maintain my composure.

"I am in shock at your lack of shame."

A tear slid down my cheek. "You are right, Everett. I should not have done it. I was not thinking."

His face softened slightly. "Are you acting now or—"

"No, Everett, I regret my actions." I snapped with a glare. "Satisfied?"

"Good," he said, pushing the dining room door open again.

Wiping the tears from my cheek, I followed him back out to the parlor.

"What of the smashed window and the box of rats?" Everett asked Miss Baudelaire. "Who was behind that?"

Bella ran her eyes up and down Everett, letting her gaze linger shamelessly.

"I have no idea what you are speaking of," Minerva said. "However, for her sake, I do hope that woman has learned her lesson." Her eyes never left her playing cards.

Ah. Minerva *had* been behind the vandalism at Mrs. Baxter's home. I had guessed as much but she had never mentioned it before now.

Everett nodded. "I see. What will it be next time, Miss Baudelaire? Will you just have the woman killed?"

"You can let yourself out, Mr. Rigby," Minerva said flatly. "Good day."

He only glanced back at me with cold, hard eyes before he left.

Mrs. Ash gripped my left hand tightly as Miss Ash, her adult daughter, held my right hand much looser.

"Oh, divine spirits," I called out into the sitting room, the light around us quivering gently as my breath tickled the flames of the nearby candles. "It is I, Lady Selene. I have come to you once again to ask for your guidance. We seek a good man who left this realm far too soon. We seek—" *Oh, no. What was his name again? Oh, yes. Right.* "—Harold Ash."

Mrs. Ash gave a sharp intake of breath at the name of her late husband.

"Harold Ash," I repeated. "Come and find us. We long to speak with you."

"Please," Mrs. Ash whispered.

I let my head lull to one side, eyes closed. Since I had traveled to Mrs. Ash's Fulham home alone, I had to depend on my acting abilities entirely, rather than tricks with props or lights. I would have asked Everett to join me but he was still furious with me. I still did not trust Bella entirely and none of the others were available.

So, I was on my own.

"Elizabeth?" I croaked in a low voice. "I am here."

Mrs. Ash choked on a little, surprised sob. "Oh, my word. Harold, is that really you?"

"Yes, my dear."

Miss Ash stayed quiet. I had sensed earlier that she found me repulsive but was going along with her mother's wishes by welcoming me into their home for the evening.

"I miss you," Mrs. Ash gushed. "We both miss you so very much, my darling."

"And I miss you, my dear. Caroline grows more beautiful every day."

Miss Caroline Ash was far from beautiful, all sharp angles and points. In her gaudy yellow gown, she looked like a pineapple.

"Are your parents there?" Mrs. Ash's eyes brimmed with tears. "Is my brother there?"

"Yes," I whispered roughly. "They are all here."

"Do you eat or drink?" Miss Ash's voice was flat as she spoke.

"Only for pleasure," I replied. "There is no hunger here, in the spirit realm, but there is always the most delicious food to enjoy."

"Harold" answered a few more questions, always giving dubious answers meant to soothe Mrs. Ash more than anything.

"I must leave you now," I said, speaking low. "Goodbye, my dear."

Mrs. Ash sniffed. "Goodbye, my darling."

My head slumped down, my chin resting on my chest. I counted to ten.

I let out a sharp gasp and raised my head suddenly, whipping my hands from the palms of the Ash women. "Where am I?"

With our séance over, Mrs. Ash, her daughter, and I had a lovely late dinner and Mrs. Ash peppered me with questions about my abilities.

During our delicious dessert of custard, Mrs. Ash told me more about her departed husband, describing him as the most handsome man she had ever laid eyes on, despite what I had seen of his portrait hanging in the drawing room.

"He was very kind," Miss Ash added.

"Yes, he was, wasn't he?" Mrs. Ash's lower lip quivered. She stood. "Excuse me for a moment, ladies."

The moment she stepped out of the dining room, Miss Ash made her move.

"Papa *never* called my mother 'Elizabeth,'" Miss Ash said, avoiding eye contact with me.

I carved into the custard, my spoon gliding smoothly. "What do you mean? Did I miss something during the séance when I was in a trance?"

"Oh, stop it," she said. "You know exactly what I am speaking of. You called Mama 'Elizabeth' while pretending to be Papa but he *never* called her that."

"Perhaps he did in private."

"Never," she said casually. "He always called her 'Lizzie.'"

She looked directly at me for emphasis. "Always."

"Sometimes people change once they—"

Before I could finish, she slid a piece of paper from her sleeve; the article from *The Gazette Weekly* that she had cut out of the paper and saved.

I only glanced at it. "Do you believe everything you read?"

"I tried to persuade my mother not to invite you here, but she insisted," she hissed. "Papa would be so angry that she was spending our money this way, let alone having you stay the night."

When Mrs. Ash wrote to request a séance with me originally, she asked me to spend the night afterwards. She had been hearing an assortment of strange sounds in the house and thought I might be able to tell if it was her "darling Harold" or not. Perhaps she thought he was trying to sneak in through a fireplace or some silliness, I am not sure. I, of course, had agreed, always preferring to stay in a grand house, rather than trying to find an inn so late in the evening.

Shortly after our late supper, the three of us turned in for the night. I was curious about the sounds Mrs. Ash could be hearing so I stayed awake as long as I could, reading my old hardbound copy of Shakespeare's comedies and keeping an ear out for curious noises.

Just after midnight, the scratching began. I shot up in bed, snapping my book shut. The scratches stopped, soon replaced by a series of creaks. The wind had picked up, causing the whole house to whine, nearly masking the squeaks.

The noises were definitely real, I could assure Mrs. Ash of that. But those specific sounds were not unknown to me. I opened my bedroom door as slowly as possible, turning the knob ever so carefully and pulling the door a tiny bit at a time. My bare feet moved along the cold floor, silent as can be, the wind concealing my movements perfectly.

Finally outside Miss Ash's bedroom, I grinned. Whispers from inside her room, followed by quiet gasps and sighs, confirmed my suspicions. Caroline Ash was a bad, naughty pineapple.

I quickly skipped back to my room and listened for Miss Ash's window opening and closing and the scratching sounds caused by her visitor climbing back down from her room.

At breakfast the next morning, Mrs. Ash asked me if I had heard the noises. "Is it Harold's restless spirit or not?"

"Our loved ones communicate with us from the other side in all sorts of ways," I said. "I see no reason that your dear husband could not be trying to speak to you through sounds in the house at night."

Miss Ash gave a derisive sniff and buttered her toast while her mother sipped her tea, her eyes welling with tears again.

"Oh, I owe you some money," she said, rising from her chair. "Let me go get that for you." She whisked away from the breakfast table.

"I am not going to let her give you a penny," Miss Ash snapped. "You are a charlatan."

"Perhaps," I replied, smiling at her over the gilded rim of my teacup. "But you may want to discuss the matter with your secret lover first."

It is a good thing Miss Ash's teacup was almost empty because she immediately dropped it back onto the saucer, causing both to crack. All the while, Miss Ash's eyes were as wide as the damaged saucer in front of her.

A couple of hours later, I stepped out of the hansom that had carried me from the train station, back to Spitalfields, smug satisfaction still coursing through my veins.

A constable eyed me as the cab pulled away from The Hemlock's front step.

"Good morning, miss," he said in a thick cockney accent. "Are you the one who talks to ghosts and all that?"

"I am Lady Selene, yes," I said, resting my suitcase on the curb. "Would you like an autograph?"

Another constable appeared out of nowhere, grabbing my wrists roughly from behind. "Ma'am, you are under arrest for the murder of Mary Jane Kelly."

TWENTY-NINE

Cora

Friday, November 9, 1888

"Mrs. Pringle, we meet again."

Turning away from Inspector Fitzpatrick, I faced the grimy, mold-speckled stone wall of my jail cell.

"Mrs. Pringle, are you angry with me?" His tone was mocking. It is a wonder he wasn't just standing there, openly laughing at me.

I shot him a glare. "I have been waiting for someone to come speak to me for four hours."

"Oh, come now," he said. "It's only been two."

"How could I possibly know that?" I huffed.

Inspector Fitzpatrick nodded to a nearby guard. "I hope she hasn't been giving you any trouble, my good man."

"No, sir," he said gruffly. "Just kept askin' me if I knew who she were."

I huffed again and turned back to the wall.

"Of course she did. You can unlock the door now."

I heard the jingling of keys and the whine of the door.

"Mrs. Pringle, please come with me."

Raising to my feet, I extended my delicate wrists together in his direction, awaiting handcuffs. "I am a dangerous criminal, Inspector Fitzpatrick. Don't you think you should take every precaution?"

He rolled his eyes. "No, I don't think that's necessary in this instance. Now, come with me or I'll leave you in here until tomorrow."

I kept my head lowered as we walked, trying my best to ignore the hollers and snide comments of the delinquents in the other cells. The walk from the jail seemed to stretch on and on, people gawking at me as I was, once again, brought to his office for questioning.

"Please have a seat, Mrs. Pringle," Inspector Fitzpatrick said, closing the door behind us.

I sat, squaring my shoulders and tipping my nose up. "Did you just have me arrested for your own amusement? Or were you just so desperate to see me again?"

His glare was stern. "On the same day we last spoke, you went to Whitechapel and announced that Jack the Ripper would kill again soon and that it would be an especially bloody affair." He tented his fingers together. "How could we *not* suspect your involvement?"

Oh. He is serious.

"I do not know—or, rather, did not know the woman—or-or even her name," I stammered. "I do not even know what happened. The guard would not tell me."

Inspector Fitzpatrick sighed, wincing slightly. "The body of a prostitute named Mary Jane Kelly was found this morning. I didn't see it meself but…" He glanced at me, the color draining from his face, the dark shadows under his eyes becoming more prominent. "It's not like the others."

Ah. My "vision" had been a little too well-timed.

"She was found in a rented room instead of in the street," he continued. "He didn't just cut her up. He obliterated her. Blood all over the place." His unfocused gaze drifted to the newspaper on his desk. "Just horrible."

"You really think I could do something so sickening? So barbaric?"

"We have to follow every lead, Mrs. Pringle," he said, dragging his eyes up to meet mine. "Scotland Yard is already under enough scrutiny as it is. You predicted a bloody murder and, well, now you've got one."

"You must know I was arrested soon after getting out of a hansom cab," I said. "I took a train from Fulham this morning where I was all night. I have two women who can attest to that."

Inspector Fitzpatrick took out his notebook and scribbled that detail down. "What were you doing in Fulham?"

I hesitated. "A séance, sir." I provided Mrs. and Miss Ash's names and address.

"I'll have an officer look into this," he said, tucking his notebook back into his waistcoat pocket. "In the meantime, I'm releasing you on the condition that you don't go predicting any more bloody murders. We've got enough to deal with right now."

I nodded and clasped my hands together to stop them from visibly shaking.

Inspector Fitzpatrick tapped a finger on his desk, pausing. "Did you *really* have a vision of a murder in Whitechapel?"

I lowered my eyes demurely before lifting my gaze again. "My abilities are both a curse and a blessing, Inspector."

He chuckled. "Of course they are." He stood and opened his office door for me. "Do tell us if you have any more premonitions, Mrs. Pringle, particularly if they can identify this monster. This needs to end."

I made my way out of the police station but before I could get a cab, a reporter blocked my path.

"There she is!" someone else yelled from somewhere as a few other reporters crowded around me.

"Lady Selene, did your recent vision include Mary Kelly?"

"Are you still a suspect in the Jack the Ripper murders?"

"Is it true Scotland Yard is using your abilities to help track down the Ripper?"

The press were hungry for details, whatever juicy tidbit would help them sell more papers. They were just as guilty of using these murders to their advantage as I was.

It seemed selfish to just leave them hanging, starving for a morsel.

"Scotland Yard *is* taking my vision seriously and have asked for my cooperation since my abilities could aid their investigation," I said clearly. "This murderer, whoever he is, is a depraved villain and he must be caught. None of us are safe until then."

A hand slipped around my arm and pulled me out of the huddled mass of men. I looked up to see Everett, his hand sliding to my lower back, moving me away, the reporters throwing additional questions at me as Everett hustled me into a nearby hansom.

I smoothed my skirts. "Oh. Hello."

"You are using the Whitechapel murders to your advantage *again*."

"No, I wasn't!" I exclaimed. "I may have used my arrest to my advantage but not the murders. It is completely different. I *told* you I would never do it again. I had the press under my thumb back there—"

"I figured I better pull you out before you announced another incriminating vision." He sat beside me.

"I have an alibi—"

"But what if you hadn't?"

A jolt of fear ran through me. *Would Scotland Yard ever* really *consider me a suspect? Surely not.*

"Scotland Yard is desperate to point their finger at someone, I grant you, but they are not *that* desperate to blame someone like me."

"You don't know that," he said quietly.

I looked out the window. "Where are we going?"

"Miss Baudelaire asked me to fetch you home."

"And here I thought you had found me at the police station because you were concerned about me."

Everett looked at me for a moment, his eyes so serious. "I am always concerned about you, Cora. I always will be." He turned to watch out the window.

"Are you still angry with me?"

"I was never angry with you."

"You *seemed* angry the other day."

"Disappointed," he said after some thought.

I squared my shoulders. "I think I would rather you were angry with me than disappointed."

He turned to me and a tiny, amused smile played on his lips. "Oh, there is always time for both."

When we arrived back at The Hemlock, a rather enthusiastic clergyman halted our entrance, a worn copy of the Bible clenched tightly within his boney grasp.

"You!" he exclaimed when he saw us approach. "The devil has claimed you as his servant, tricking you with his evil ways!" He gestured to The Hemlock's front facade behind him. "This house is the portal to Hell and everyone who lives there is damned to burn in the fires for all eternity!"

I frowned at him. "That is terribly rude of you, sir."

He grabbed my hand. "I will pray for your soul."

Whipping my hand away from him, I spat, "My soul is just fine, thank you."

"Begone, old man," Everett warned, knocking on the front door to The Hemlock, guiding me away from the angry preacher.

"The blood of Mary Kelly is on your hands, woman," the clergyman growled. "Just as her wicked life and vile sins damned her, so shall yours."

I turned on my heel and thrust my pointed finger in his face. "You know nothing of her life or of mine. We women do what we need to survive while men do what they like, casting their accusations and judgements because they can instead of helping the poor wretches because that actually takes effort and compassion." I looked at the Bible in his hand. "Have you ever actually read that book? I think not." I glared hard at him. "My hands are clean, sir, and so were hers."

The preacher scowled and stalked off while Everett guided me into the house. He looked down at me with his soft eyes and was about to say something but the two figures in the front parlor stole our attention. Miss Baudelaire and a well-dressed gentleman of means were having tea together and both of them smiled at us as we entered, particularly at me.

"There you are, my darling girl," Miss Baudelaire said warmly, sliding off her chair to greet me, her arms open. "I was so worried about you. If those bullies harmed a hair on your head, you must tell me."

Minerva was almost as good as I was when it came to acting innocent.

I hid my disbelief and smiled sweetly, letting her take my hand in hers. "I am quite well, thank you."

I caught a glimpse of Everett's stunned expression as he looked at the gentleman sitting in the easy chair before us but neither of us spoke.

"Lady Selene," Minerva said, "I would like to introduce you to Mr. McCormack."

Mr. McCormack stood. I gave him my hand and he kissed the top of it. "It is lovely to meet you, Lady Selene."

I tipped my head, not sure what level of performer I should be displaying at that moment; feminine demurity, flattering flirt, or mysterious oracle.

"Is it true you were questioned by police this morning about the latest Ripper murders?"

I glanced at Miss Baudelaire who gave a tiny, subtle nod.

"Yes, sir. They are hoping to use my visions to assist in tracking down the killer."

"Are they now?" He took a seat again and gestured for me to sit in Minerva's chair across from him. I hesitantly took it, knowing she detested anyone else sitting in her chair. "That is very interesting."

"I intend to assist them in any way I can, of course." I pursed my lips ever so slightly.

"Naturally." He crossed his legs, his gaze lingering on my face. "Lady Selene, I book talent for the Princess Royal Theatre and I would like you to grace our stage, showcasing your unique talents."

That's why Everett recognized him!

"The Princess Royal?" I glanced at Miss Baudelaire. "Me, sir, truly?"

"Truly. The sooner, the better," he said.

News of my fulfilled "prophecy" and subsequent arrest had spread all over London much faster than I had expected. He wanted to use the press around my name to sell tickets and I was happy to oblige.

"I would be honored and delighted, Mr. McCormack."

Everett and I excused ourselves to the dining room while Miss Baudelaire and Mr. McCormack talked business. As soon as we were out of sight and sound, I threw my arms around Everett's neck and squealed.

"Congratulations," he said into my neck, hugging me tight to his chest. "This is what you've worked so hard for."

Pulling away slightly, I could look up at him. "What *we* have worked for."

He smiled, and I buried my face in his shoulder, letting myself drown in the smell and warmth of him. I could feel the rapid beat of his heart under my cheek. Slowly, I looked up at him again, my gaze lingering on his full lips.

"Everett," I whispered, our eyes meeting in the tight space between our faces.

I closed my eyes and parted my lips slightly, preparing for the kiss I had wanted for so, so long.

"Oh, am I interrupting?"

Everett slid his arms from my person and I stepped away sheepishly. Magni lifted a flask to his smirking lips.

"We just got some good news, that's all," I said quickly—too quickly, perhaps.

"Mrs. Pringle has been invited to perform at the Princess Royal," Everett added.

Magni's jaw clenched. "The Princess Royal?"

"Indeed," I said. "Miss Baudelaire is discussing the details in the parlor right this moment."

Magni's eyes drifted to the door in the direction of that room. He stared at his flask before pitching it across the room into a cabinet, shattering the glass pane of its door. "You don't say."

Dear Mrs. Pringle,

As you are likely aware, The Maidenhill Club has been a prestigious and highly respected London women's club for nearly twenty years.

We would like to extend an invitation to you to visit our club on November 15th at 1pm. We request that you kindly RSVP by November 12th if you are available to join us on that date.

Mrs. Theodosia Taylor
President

Dear Mrs. Taylor,

I gratefully accept the invitation. I am honored and look forward to meeting on November 15th at 1pm.

Mrs. Cora Pringle

THIRTY

Cora

Thursday, November 15, 1888

I was meant for this.

That was the only thing I could think as I glided into The Maidenhill Club on that sunny, cool afternoon. A domestic took my jacket and showed me inside straight away—I was obviously not only expected, but a highly anticipated guest.

After months of living under the cobwebs at The Hemlock and within the dingy walls of Everett's flat before that, the glittering luxury of everything and everyone at The Maidenhill Club was like walking from the browns and grays of autumn to the crisp whiteness of winter in the country.

Sparkles and light danced among the crystals in the multitier chandeliers. The walls of the main hallway were decorated with an assortment of Rococo period paintings and portraits of prominent club members, adding to the soft, feminine atmosphere. Somehow, the air itself smelled of vanilla. Women wearing nothing less than the most timely fashions glanced my way curiously, nodding graciously as I strolled by.

The trick is to take everything in while appearing like this level of opulence is what you were born into. You deserve the finest of the finer things and nothing less will do.

I caught sight of my reflection in a mirror with an ornate, gilded frame. Knowing I would be judged on my appearance as well as my character and acquaintances, I avoided any of the deep, dark, and dramatic colors I wore when performing and went for a softer palette—a gown of cream with a teal flower pattern, a tight-laced corset, and a full, voluminous bustle trimmed with dozens of tiny teal ribbons. My curls were pinned away neatly into a high bun, fixed carefully into place and accented with a large but respectable peacock feather.

One of the women broke off her conversation to approach me. "Pardon me. Can I help you?"

"Good afternoon," I said. "I received an invitation from Mrs. Taylor. I am Mrs. Pringle."

Briefly, confusion washed over her face. "Yes, of course. Mrs. Taylor is in the music room. Please follow me."

As we walked, my heels clicked on the marble floors. One woman near the music room door, upon making eye contact with me, immediately looked away and whispered to her friend nearby. Her companion took a sly glance in my direction, less than subtly, before the two of them exchanged meaningful looks.

Ignore them. They are just curious about the new blood, that is all.

"Please wait here," the woman said, leaving me by the music room door.

The young lady at the piano finished her impressive performance and the audience of about thirty clapped their appreciation. She stood and curtsied, her shy smile barely visible on her young face. It took me a moment to recognize Miss Polly Foster, somehow looking more grown-up since I had last seen her. It felt like years ago.

Her eyes met mine from the back of the room and I gave a polite nod. Her eyes, meanwhile, grew large at the sight of me and she quickly looked away.

She returned to the piano bench after someone nearby encouraged her to play again and her fingers went to work with another light and cheerful melody.

A statuesque woman of about forty sidled up to me, gesturing to Polly with her fan.

"Miss Foster is rather accomplished, isn't she?"

"Indeed she is," I said. "Although she has improved since I last heard her play."

"Oh. I did not know you two were acquainted," she said with a slight inflection. "Do you play?"

We sold our piano when Papa became ill and Marshall preferred silence to music in our home, despite there being a perfectly good piano in the parlor.

"Very poorly," I admitted.

Her face betrayed her disappointment. "Shame." Her eyes narrowed in thought for a moment. "Do you know any other club members?"

"Yes," I said. "Mrs. Lockhart and I are … acquainted."

The elegant woman arched a perfectly groomed eyebrow. "You seem uncertain."

"We were good friends for several years when our husbands were colleagues. However, our paths—" I hesitated again. "—diverted."

"I see." She paused to watch Polly for a moment before turning to me again. "I am Mrs. Taylor. I am glad you could join us this afternoon, Mrs. Pringle."

"It is lovely to meet you."

I had guessed as much, especially when she began asking me questions. I knew to expect several more before I would be accepted into the exclusive club; questions about my parents, education, background, and social connections.

Polly completed another song and shyly curtsied one more time.

Mrs. Taylor smiled sweetly at me. "Please, come with me."

She could have asked me to stand on my head and I would have tried my best to do it. She had that kind of quiet authority about her.

Mrs. Taylor, to my surprise, proceeded around the small audience of ladies. I had not expected an introduction to the whole group. I pushed my worry aside and smiled prettily instead.

"Thank you Miss Foster for that delightful performance," Mrs. Taylor said, addressing the group. "Now, as promised, we have with us the infamous Lady Selene, the Mystic of the Taj Mahal."

My eyes widened and I looked sideways at her. I forced my mouth into a smile again, but my heart was not in it. I was too distracted by the ringing in my ears.

The ladies before me whispered to their friends nearby. I made direct eye contact with one woman in the front row—none other than Viola Lockhart herself. I tore my eyes away, back to Mrs. Taylor.

"Tell us, Lady Selene, about how you found your special abilities," she said before taking a seat in the front row.

This was obviously no longer a club membership interview. It had never *been* a membership interview. I had been brought to entertain them, not to be one of them. I would never be one of them.

I will never be good enough for them.

Fighting the ache in my throat, I swallowed. "I, uh, traveled all over India and I, um, met with several spiritual people there and the, uh, voices began."

I had given the speech so many times on stage and yet now, the words just clumsily tumbled out of my mouth. It did not help that Viola was smiling smugly right in front of me.

"Have you ever been possessed by an evil spirit?" a lady from the audience asked.

"No."

"How did you know there would be another murder in Whitechapel?"

"I had a vision about it," I said dryly. "I am sure you all read the stories in the paper about it."

Polly raised her gloved hand. "I was wondering if you have

… always had special abilities?" The look on her face was of genuine concern, I wanted to hug her.

"No, Miss Foster," I said. "Not always."

Someone else spoke up. "Why do you think you were chosen to have these abilities?"

After what felt like two hundred more stupid questions, Mrs. Taylor stood again. "Thank you for speaking with us today. It has been most interesting. Would you be willing to give us a demonstration of your abilities?"

Over the course of the hour that I had stood before them all, being poked and prodded with their curiosities, I had hardened. I had been a fool. I saw no reason to give them free entertainment any longer.

Looking directly at Mrs. Taylor, I said, "No. No, I would not." I smiled sweetly at the rest of the ladies. "If you care to see my unique capabilities, please do see my upcoming performance at the Princess Royal Theatre later this month."

Mrs. Taylor's lips pursed ever so slightly before spreading into a fake smile. "Very good." She clapped, signaling to the other ladies that they should clap for me as well, and they did as their leader ordered.

As Mrs. Taylor and the rest of the ladies filed into the adjoining room for refreshments, a woman from the audience tried to ask me a question.

"I am so sorry," I said, receiving my coat from the servant. "I am expected elsewhere."

"Are you?" Viola said, appearing beside me. "Or are you making that up as well?"

"Oh, Viola," I said. "Have you always been so cynical?"

I walked away from her, but she followed me outside.

"You are a fraud," she hissed from behind me. "You have never even been to India. You are taking advantage of people. How do you sleep at night?"

I slowly turned to face her. "In a pile of money."

Her eyes narrowed, and the edges of her nostrils flared. "I do not think I ever knew you at all. The Cora I used to know would never degrade herself in this repugnant manner."

"The Cora you knew?" I repeated. "The Cora you chose to ignore entirely when she needed help? When she needed her friends the most? When she was a desperate widow?"

Viola stiffened. "Your husband's grave was barely cold before Tom Lindsey was seen sniffing around—"

"I rejected his proposal," I blurted. "Besides, I was days away from being homeless. I had to at least consider it. What was I supposed to—"

"Then I hear that you married that half-breed and the two of you moved into a slum?"

I wanted to slap her. If we weren't surrounded by people on the side of the street, I may have seriously considered it.

"Mr. Rigby gave me a home when even my closest friends abandoned me." I shot her with an accusing glare. "We are not married," I admitted, "but he has shown himself to be nothing less than the truest friend I have ever had."

"Well." She crossed her arms in front of her chest. "You have finally proven you are more than just a country clerk's daughter, haven't you? Is there nothing you won't do for a little name recognition?" She scoffed. "Well, now you have it. You just have to manipulate grieving families to do it." She lifted her skirts and headed back inside before stopping in the doorway to look back at me. "What if someone told you that you could speak to your father again and it was all just tricks?"

How dare you, you disgusting shrew.

I had learned plenty of new and interesting profanities since joining the world of music halls and theater, and every single one of those words came flooding to my mind as she turned and disappeared back into the club.

I stared at the door as it swung closed, but another woman pushed it back open before slowly approaching me, her large green eyes cold and her cupid bow lips pursed tight like she had just tasted a lemon.

"Mrs. Pringle, may I have a word with you?"

"I am sorry, I have an appointment I need to—"

"This will only take a moment, I promise." She stepped closer to me and tugged on the lace of her fine gloves, her eyes studying my face.

"Of course," I said, nearly grumbling.

"I was wondering if you had spoken to Mr. Wyndham recently." Her eyes were quite calm but the tension in her jaw gave her discomfort away. "Sometimes I get apprehensive when Royal stops talking about his little side projects, as I know what that usually means." She glanced at my abdomen area before returning her gaze to my face.

I raised an eyebrow at her. "Mr. Wyndham and I have ended our business partnership."

It was only then I noticed the orangey red curls poking out from under her hat.

She looks a bit like me. Mr. Wyndham has a type.

My stomach twisted with the realization of what this conversation really was.

"How do you know Mr. Wyndham?" My throat had suddenly gone quite dry so the words came out with a slight creak at the end.

"Mr. Wyndham is my husband." She tilted her head slightly, still smiling calmly. "Let me guess. He never mentioned me?"

I winced. *That bastard.*

"He never does," she said, tugging at her gloves again before folding her hands in front of her. "Am I to believe you are not in the family way then?"

"No, ma'am," I said quietly. "Our relationship did not stray so far."

"Ah. Well," she said with a nod. "You are one of the lucky ones then."

My neck burned as I thought about the way he gazed at me those many times and the way I thought he wanted to marry me. Even upon learning of his wife, I was still irritated that I was not even the only woman he wanted to bed outside of marriage!

How many others were there?

I very much wanted to know but I dared not ask.

Minerva must have known he was married and just chose *not to tell me.*

I was such a fool!

"If I had known he was married, I would not have—"

"Oh, I know, I know. It is not your fault." She rolled her eyes and then casually watched a pair of children playing down the street. "Now I know why he has been in such a foul mood as of late." She looked back at me. "Mr. Wyndham loves the hunt, you see. Losing out on a prize doe like you would certainly vex him."

I did not know if I should take that as a compliment or not.

"How dare Viola speak to me like that? I should get Minerva's goons to throw a crate of rats into a window of *her* house and then maybe one at the club too."

Everett winced and glanced around at the few pedestrians around us. "Perhaps you ought to not say that too loudly."

As planned, he and I had met up at nearby Hyde Park after my "interview." It had turned cold and damp, so we had the park to ourselves for the most part. I slid my hand under his arm and nestled closer to him, shielding myself from the wind.

"And the whole scene with Mrs. Wyndham," I exclaimed, having already told Everett about learning of her existence and our little exchange. "I have never been so humiliated and uncomfortable in my life."

"I could kill him for not telling you he was married," he said. "I obviously didn't care for the man, but I didn't take him for a scoundrel."

"She asked if I was with child." I winced. "Apparently he has abandoned multiple mistresses when they are in a delicate condition."

Everett halted.

"Do not give me that look, please. I am more of a lady

than that."

His shoulders relaxed just as a pretty woman strolled nearby, pulling his attention away. At first I thought he was simply admiring her pleasant face and pleasing figure. No. Instead, he was observing the small boy that trailed after her.

As Everett watched the child, I watched Everett; a tiny smile tugged at the corner of his mouth and his eyes softened. The toddler picked a yellow leaf from the grass and excitedly showed it to his mother.

My stomach tightened as the realization struck me.

He wants to be a father. And I cannot give him that.

I pushed the thought away and tried to remember what we had been speaking of. I clung tighter to Everett's arm, the wind picking up around us.

"I thought I may have been worthy of membership at The Maidenhill Club," I said. "How could I have been so blindsided?"

"It's just a silly club," he said, trying to calm my anger.

"It is *not* just a silly club," I persisted. "It is prestige. It is society. It is success. Being a member of that club means you are an individual of esteem." I sighed. "I have money. People *know* who I am. I dress fashionably." I looked up at him. "What more do they want from me?"

"They apparently wanted you to perform for them for free." He rolled his eyes. "The nerve."

"Viola thinks I am some sort of monster," I said quietly, casting my gaze at the naked trees, yellow leaves piled at their feet. "Perhaps she is right. Perhaps what I am doing is horrendous."

A silent pause passed between us. Eventually, Everett spoke up.

"Do you remember that fellow who came to us when we first moved to The Hemlock? We did a séance with him so he could speak to his wife and daughter."

"The gentleman who cried when he thanked me?"

"Indeed," he said. "And there was that one elderly couple who were so grateful when you were able to connect them with their son one last time?"

"They offered to pay me an additional fee." I smiled weakly. "I had forgotten about that."

"And there was that—"

"Excuse me. I am so sorry to bother you," said a young woman also on an afternoon walk. "Are you Lady Selene?"

I smiled at her. "Yes, you are correct."

"Oh, my word!" she exclaimed. "Would you sign my autograph book?" Before I could respond, she was searching in her beaded reticule.

She thrust a small notebook at me and then her companion gave me a pen. I scribbled in her little book and handed it back to her.

"We both have tickets to see you at the Princess Royal," her friend added. "We are so looking forward to it."

"Thank you." My throat hurt from emotion for the second time that day. "That is very kind of you. Truly."

When I finished playing celebrity Everett continued, his brow furrowed.

"That reminds me," he said, "on my way here I went by the Princess Royal to check to make sure they had the right sort of lights for your performance. I was surprised to see someone amending the Lady Selene poster outside."

I stopped walking mid-step. "What do you mean 'amending'?"

"They were adding something over it," he said, a deep crease forming between his eyes. "A big red stripe."

I looked up into his handsome face as he bit his lower lip, fighting to hide his truly devastating smile. My heart quickening in my chest, I was afraid to speak the words in case I cursed myself.

"Sold out?" I whispered.

Everett nodded slowly, his tiny grin spreading across his face.

"Ha!" I blurted, practically yelling, ignoring the annoyed looks nearby.

Closing my eyes and putting my face to the clear blue sky, I inhaled the fresh park air deeply, filling my lungs like they had never truly breathed before.

THIRTY-ONE

Amelia

Thursday, November 15, 1888

Simon had never been the contemplative type. Thus, I knew something was amiss when I came across his stick insect-like form by the fireplace, his eyes focused on the orange embers in the hearth. He was sunk low in his easy chair; so low that his chin rested on his chest and his long legs stretched out straight before him.

"Simon, darling, are you quite well?"

"Not in the least," he said, reaching for his empty brandy glass. Picking it up, he frowned and turned it sideways in his hand, inspecting it carefully and sorrowfully.

A knock at the door interrupted our exchange and Matilda opened the door. Simon glanced up lazily to see who had arrived but could not be bothered to raise from his chair when Beth came in, handing her bonnet and coat over to Matilda. She took one look at Simon before giving me a worried look.

"Goodness, Simon. What is the matter?" Her voice was like a

perfectly tuned piano key—one of the high note ones, specifically.

Simon waved his empty glass at Matilda before she could disappear, and she nodded in understanding.

"I am heartbroken," he said, rolling his head over to his right shoulder, his neck entirely limp under the weight of it. "I may never smile again."

Beth folded her delicate hands together, resting them against her pregnant belly. "What has happened?" She looked at me, but I could only shrug.

"Wright has decided to—" He glanced at Beth. "—end our companionship."

"Oh, no," she said, whisking to Simon's side and kneeling by his chair, taking his hand in hers. "That cannot be. He cares for you, I know it."

I winced, suddenly imagining Beth not being able to stand upright again, her round middle sending her spiraling across the parlor carpet like a toy top.

"Of course he does," I added. "He loves you. What could he possibly be thinking of?"

"He's a politician," Simon mumbled, accepting another tumbler of brandy from Matilda. "He said he cannot risk someone finding out and using it against him. He said it would destroy his career."

"Nonsense," I said. "The two of you have always been discreet. You are a married man for goodness sake."

"Perhaps the stress of Mr. Woodacre's job is making him think unclearly," Beth suggested. "I know he is always so busy."

"Not this time, I'm afraid," Simon said, turning his face back to the fireplace, its weak little flames curling and dancing among the bits of blackened wood.

"What can we do to soothe your mind, dear Simon?" Beth glanced at me. "Shall we sit with you, or should I return home so you can have peace and quiet?"

I offered both my hands to her and she smiled gratefully as I raised her to her feet.

Simon waved a hand. "Heavens, no. I need some enjoyment to take my mind off my dark thoughts." He rose and took a rather large gulp from his glass. "Not another word will be said of that man."

After another glass and one game of cards, Simon had changed his mind.

"Wright thinks he is always right." His left eye was partially closed. "Even if it *is* his name, he's not. Sometimes he is wrong. Well, most of the time he is right. I mean, all of the time he is technically 'Wright' because it's his name but sometimes he is both 'Wright' *and* not right, at the same time."

Beth and I exchanged glances over our cards.

"Incorrect," he eventually added. "That is what I meant."

"You seem like you want to discuss what happened with Mr. Woodacre," I said, trying my best to keep my tone soft.

"I do not. For one, he is dreadfully dull sometimes. Parliamentary reform this and House of Commons that. He wants to be prime minister someday." He gave a loud snort into his glass as he took another drink. "What a bloody fool."

I looked at Beth and mouthed "I'm sorry." She smiled sympathetically.

"Simon, dearest, perhaps you should go to bed," I said, smiling sweetly at him. "You will feel better in the morning."

"Will Wright be back in the morning?" he snapped. "No, he won't."

"Perhaps I should call it a night as well," Beth said, giving her belly a pat.

She did not seem weary to me, her eyes sparkling as usual, her skin glowing with the freshness of youth. However, I did not blame her for wanting to leave the discomfort of my heartbroken and intoxicated husband.

"Certainly," I said. "I'll get you settled upstairs."

As we rose from our chairs, Simon continued.

"Speaking of which," Simon gestured to Beth's stomach, "is my father ever coming home?"

I shot him a glare. "That is quite enough. Go to bed."

Simon shrugged, sliding his glass onto the table. "Maybe Wright was right. Of course he was right. It's his bloody name."

"Go to bed, Simon."

"He said you would put him in danger with your articles and we would be found out because of you," he said to his empty glass.

I squared my shoulders. "What?"

Simon lazily dragged his gaze up to me. "When I told Wright that the rats were a message from that bloody spiritualist woman, he became worried that Lady Selene would get back at you again by revealing our secret to the world. If not her, then someone else surely." He looked away and shook his head. "I shouldn't have told him."

"Simon." I swallowed. "I did not know."

He rolled his eyes. "Politicians. They spend more time thinking of their reputations than anything else." He chuckled to himself. "Doesn't matter. He is a coward."

I cringed. It hadn't been some little quarrel as I had predicted. Wright was correct to be afraid for his reputation, given his career path, and *my* career could have put *his* career in jeopardy. Or, worse, his very life. He was absolutely right to worry. I had no idea what Mrs. Pringle would do to get back at me as I had no way of knowing what anyone might do for revenge.

I had chosen a dangerous path and Simon had chosen to marry me anyway. Mr. Woodacre, however, had made no such choice.

"I am so sorry, my darling." My stomach tied itself in a knot as I looked across the table at my dearest best friend. "It was never my intention to put you in such a position. What can I do?"

Simon shook his head. "I don't know." Beth and I watched as he uneasily slid his chair back and made his way upstairs.

Beth, who had not spoken for a few minutes, looked at me, her eyes large and concerned. "What did he mean by 'the rats'?"

Beth and I shared a quiet breakfast the next morning. Simon was still snoring away in his bedroom, sleeping off what I would expect to be a grievous headache later on. My young mother-in-law and I parted ways after breakfast, she in a hansom cab back to my childhood home and I to work.

An attractive man in a very fashionable hat and coat leaned against the beam near Mrs. Davies' desk, showing off a trick involving floating a pen across his knuckles. I recognized him immediately. With one smooth twist of his wrist, the pen vanished. I gave a quiet clap from behind him and Mrs. Davies' mouth broke into a wide smile.

"That is extraordinary," she said. "But where did my pen go?"

"Have you checked your pencil cup, miss?" the man asked, gesturing to the little cup of writing instruments on the other side of her desk.

"No," she whispered, plucking the same pen from the cup. "Impossible."

"Very impressive indeed," I added. "What can we do for you, sir?"

"I am waiting for a Mr. Spellman. I have rather enjoyed his articles about Lady Selene," he explained. "I was hoping to discuss—" He paused. "—an arrangement with him."

"I will certainly pass on your compliments to Mr. Spellman," I said. "What kind of arrangement?"

He gave a slight wince. "I would rather speak directly to Mr. Spellman if possible—"

"Sir, you already *are* speaking to Mr. Spellman," I snapped. "What is it that you want?"

"Ah. My apologies, ma'am," he said. "Would it be possible to speak with you in private? It is a matter of a delicate nature."

I led him to a small room, usually reserved for tea breaks, across from Mr. Granville's office. Closing the door behind us, I gestured to one of the chairs and took one myself.

"Now," I said, wanting to get this over with, "what can I do for you?"

"I would like to make you an offer," he said. "I happen to know you have one hell of a grudge against Lady Selene. I don't know why, and I frankly don't care why. However, I have quite a lot of information on Mrs. Pringle that I think you would like to obtain."

"What kind of information?"

"I know how she does every single one of her stage tricks," he said, crossing his arms over his chest. "I taught her about half of them myself."

"Why would Magni the Magnificent just give away tricks to another performer?"

"Probably because Magni the Magnificent thought he and Lady Selene would make a good double act someday." He frowned. "It would appear that is not likely to happen anytime soon. So, I've come here."

"What are you looking for in return?"

"I would like to get off this godforsaken island and go to America. I figure a hundred and fifty pounds will get me across the sea and settled in comfortably."

I laughed out loud. "You are joking. Your information is not worth *fifty* pounds, let alone one hundred and fifty." I lowered my voice. "Besides, we do not pay our sources."

"Come now. We are both professionals. We both know how this works."

"They are not my rules, sir."

Magni sighed, his mouth twisting into a frown. "Fine. I'll go to some other newspaper and have *them* take down Mrs. Pringle's duplicitous and manipulative act instead."

He roughly slid back his chair.

"Wait," I said, holding up a hand. "Please give me a moment."

I left him alone and went to Mr. Granville's office.

"Who is that fellow?" He lowered his copy of *The Daily Telegraph*. "Friend of yours?"

"Magni the Magnificent, a magician who has worked closely with Lady Selene," I explained, speaking as fast as I could. "He wants financial compensation in exchange for an explanation of how she does her stage tricks. Our next issue comes out the day of her performance at the Princess Royal Theatre. The timing could not be better. I think we should consider the offer."

Mr. Granville furrowed his thick eyebrows. "I think not."

"You did not even ask how much money he wants."

"No matter the cost, it's still too much. We do not pay our sources, you know that."

"Our readers have come to expect these stories from us. It would be the final story in my series about Madame Pringle," I said. "It would be quite the finale."

Mr. Granville raised an eyebrow at me. "You really seem to despise that woman."

I had been denied my chance to write about the women killed by the Ripper, but I had been given free rein on bringing Cora Pringle down. Even if I could not stop one bad person from harming the people of London, at least I could perhaps stop another.

I nodded.

"Remind me to stay on your good side." He paused, tenting his fingers in front of him. "How much?"

"One hundred pounds," I said, knowing fully that Mr. Granville would never, ever agree to a hundred and fifty pounds.

"Ridiculous!" He laughed. "Offer him fifty."

Back in the tearoom with Magni, I offered him a hundred pounds.

Simon does not pay attention to our accounts anyway. He will never notice fifty pounds missing from our finances.

"Fine," he grumbled. "But you should know this is highway robbery."

"Absolutely." I flipped my notebook open to its first blank page. "Now. What have you got for me?"

THIRTY-TWO

Cora

Wednesday, November 21, 1888

Yes, I believe this will do quite nicely.

I stood in the center of the stage at the Princess Royal Theatre, basking in the glow of the newly installed electric lights flooding the boards beneath me.

"How does it look from over there?" Minerva smiled at me from the shadows of stage left.

"Wonderful," I said. "I will never be able to go back to a normal life after this day."

She joined me on stage. "Mrs. Jones needs you backstage to do a final fitting of the new costume." She looked out into the empty audience, a subtle smile appearing on her painted lips.

"Have you ever performed on this stage, Miss Baudelaire?"

"No, I haven't," she said quietly, her eyes still fixed on the hundreds of seats. "My act is far too salacious for this audience." She looked back to me, the dreamy look disappearing from her gaze. "Keep that in mind tonight. This is a different audience than you are used to. Now, go."

She gestured to stage right and I nodded obediently, practically floating back to the dressing room area. None of this felt real.

Mrs. Jones helped me change into my elaborate costume, a glittering creation she had been working on for two weeks straight. My skin looked like milk against the sheen of the red silk. Hundreds of tiny sequins sparkled like magical fairy dust whenever the fabric swayed. The snug bodice pushed my full breasts up higher on my chest than I ever thought possible. Delicate black lace gloves reached my elbows while my upper arms were left bare. With the exception of a few tendrils that hung down by my neck, my curls were piled high atop my head and decorated with gold chains, small faux gems, and an enormous white ostrich feather. I am sure that if Mrs. Jones could have made it happen, she would have somehow embedded a wooden ship among my locks to make them appear even more like Marie Antoinette's.

I gave a little half twirl in front of the mirror to check my angles. Just as I predicted, my waist had never looked so small and my hips so round.

"It is perfect, Mrs. Jones," I said. "Your skill with a sewing needle is incomparable."

"I know," she said, sounding rather bored. "He seems to fink so as well."

My stomach fluttered as Everett stepped into the reflection of the mirror.

Everett Rigby had looked at me adoringly many times before. However, those gazes were wide-eyed combinations of love and attraction. This expression was different. His mouth was a perfectly straight line. His eyes were wide as he took in every detail of my appearance, but his brow was slightly pinched in the middle. His usual looks of longing ended when he realized I had seen him staring, but not this time. Instead, he studied my face, hair, and costume for a long time. Even when our eyes met in the mirror, he continued to hold my gaze.

Mrs. Jones saw this exchange, cleared her throat, and made up some excuse to leave for the room. When the door closed behind her, Everett took a few steps closer to me before placing his hands into his pockets.

"So?" I said with a wicked grin, desperate to lighten the atmosphere between us. "Do I look presentable?"

"You are a work of art, Cora Pringle," he said.

My smile softened as my cheeks warmed. I rarely took compliments on my appearance so much to heart but the sincerity in his voice and eyes told me I should.

"Then why do you look so serious?"

His gaze hit the floor like a stone. He closed his eyes and released a sigh through his nose before pulling a document from the inside of his coat. It was a folded-up page of a newspaper.

"Oh, is that one of my interviews?" I clapped my hands together. "How delightful. Thank you for saving it for me."

I had done a few interviews over the previous days to promote the event. Not that we needed to, what with all seat already sold out. Every newspaper reporter I had spoken to about my upcoming performance had hung on every word, laughed at my quips, and had gushed about my beauty and charm.

"No, Cora, it's not your interview."

I raised an eyebrow at him just before Minerva burst into the room.

"That bloody ingrate," she raged, her voice deep and furious, a rolled newspaper in hand. "I will destroy the bastard, I swear it."

"What has happened—"

Before I could even finish the question, Everett handed me the newspaper article and I frantically unfolded it. My eyes ran over the length of it, the pace of my heart becoming more frantic, the sound of my blood boiling pulsing in my ears. I curled my fingers into a ball around the article, the satisfying crunch of the paper within my palm. It fell from my quivering fingers.

A lump formed in my throat. "Why would Magni do this?" The words came out in a thin whisper, my throat closing in around them.

"Jealousy," Everett said simply.

"He gave away many of his own tricks, not just mine. Has he gone mad?" I looked at Minerva. "What would make Magni do such a foolish thing?"

Miss Baudelaire clenched her jaw. "Many of your early stage dates were originally his. He felt you were stealing his act, stealing his fame."

Upon hearing Minerva's shouts, Bella—my opening act—joined us in the dressing room. Her makeup was about half done and a few strings from her costume had yet to be tied.

"What's happened?"

Everett gave her a quick explanation of the crisis.

Bella's face fell and she paused, thinking. "Do you think the newspaper would have paid for something like that?"

"Why do you ask?" Minerva looked up at her.

"Three days ago I caught him leaving The Hemlock with a suitcase. He told me not to say anything." She winced. "He said he had a ticket for a ship to America for that afternoon."

We stood in silence, trying to process everything.

Bella added quietly, "Perhaps no one has read it."

Even with Bella there to warm up the crowd before my performance, stepping out onto that stage felt like dropping down into my own empty casket, laid open in my damp grave.

My entrance music began. The plucking of those divine sitar strings had never sounded so miserable with only a few people clapping. Bella announced my entrance in a voice loud enough to reach the back of the theater, even though such effort was not worth the trouble. The night was already lost to us.

Taking a deep breath, I strode onto the stage, summoning every speck of confidence in my being. The theater lights blinded me for a moment, and I thought perhaps that the seats were filled.

But no. Once my eyes adjusted, I could clearly see that the fifty or so people that had bothered to come had all been moved closer to the stage, leaving most of the theater seats empty. My gaze danced between the empty rows in the stalls and then up into the balcony.

I cleared my throat and struggled to gain control of my quivering legs.

"Good evening everyone!" I cried out. "I am Lady Selene, the Mystic of the Taj Mahal."

One single pair of hands clapped for me.

"Do you feel the chill in the theater tonight? I certainly do. That means the spirits are among us tonight!"

No response. The silence walloped me, smacking me hard in the stomach.

"I trust you feel that too. Let's start this evening's journey, shall we?" I strode the length of the stage. "Will someone join me on stage so that we may contact the spirit realm together? I do not have the strength to reach the other side alone."

"You're a bloody fraud!" someone yelled.

My teeth chattered, every click and crack deafening inside my head.

"I do not know what you have been told," I said aloud, the wavering in my voice clear for all to hear—all who even bothered to show up anyway, "but the spirits are disappointed that you have turned your backs on them."

"Trickery!" someone responded from one of the seats close to the front right of the stage.

"We want our money back!" someone else yelled, their words thrown at me from the left.

"That article is full of terrible lies, written out of hatred and jealousy for my gifts!" I screamed, watching as two audience member silhouettes made their way down the aisle to the lobby. "Please, do not leave. Come up on stage and we will summon the spirits together!"

A few more onlookers left their seats. As they scoffed among themselves, I felt a hot tear escape down my cheek and slide down my neck.

One of those spectators came back, a dark figure among the sparse little audience, and approached the stage. I did not recognize her, even as she glared up at me from right in front of the stage, but it soon became evident we had met before. She was perhaps in her fifties, shocks of gray woven through her tight bun, and her dress was plain but clean and well-kept.

"You told me, right to my face, that my three children had reached out to you, to speak through you in order to communicate with me." She shook her head at me. "I am ashamed for taking your lies as you took my money. I am ashamed, but *you* should be more ashamed."

My dry throat ached as I recalled the séance performed in Everett's old flat. She had told me of having three babies in quick succession and then losing them all at once to smallpox. I remembered the strain on her face and pain in her eyes as she described the ache she had lived with since then.

"You lied to me," she said. "You lied to all of us."

The words were like a fearsome vice, clamping down on my heart with reckless abandon. I did not even try to stop her as she turned and left, following some others down the aisle and out of the theater. All I could was watch them go.

"Cora."

I slowly turned my head to the left. Everett stood just beyond where the stream of the theater lights illuminated the stage.

My chest heaved as I looked into his pitying face. I loathed being pitied. I would rather have been hated than pitied. Another tear rolled down my face and I swiped at it, leaving a smudge of makeup on my middle and ring finger.

I took one last look into the empty void of the audience before fleeing backstage. From that point on, everything was a blur.

I am Cora Pringle, damn it. I am better than them. I am better than every single one of them out there.

I went straight for the dressing room, locking the door behind me. I leaned my head against it and felt Everett's palms slapping it.

"Cora!" His fraught whacks turned to pounding fists. "Cora, let me in!"

Sitting on the nearby dressing table, likely left by some other entertainer or maybe even Bella, was an abandoned bottle of gin.

Beneath the sound of Everett's pleading words, I could hear Miss Baudelaire and a theater manager of some kind arguing about money.

"Can I please come in? It'll be alright, just let me come in."

They despise me. My fingers curled around the smooth glass neck. *They all hate me so, so much.*

Something heavy hit the door, and it bulged slightly from the impact. The manager yelled about property damage. Something hit the door again, and this time the door made a cracking sound in response.

The rim of the bottle found my thirsty lips and I gulped greedily.

I do not deserve to be hated.

I beckoned the abyss with every drop on my tongue and embraced oblivion.

THIRTY-THREE

Cora

Thursday, November 22, 1888

The moment I woke up, I instantly regretted it. Daylight streamed in from the window, hitting my eyes and plunging me into a deep pit of agony. I buried my face back into my pillow and drew the blanket over my head, a deep moan spilling from my dry lips.

To emerge from bed was to move, and to move was to ache.

Pulling my knees up to my chest, I winced and curled up into myself, hiding from the world that existed outside my blanket sanctum. Dizziness washed over me, and I felt like I was drowning in a giant vat of molasses. Whipping the blanket down, I took heavy breaths to stave off nausea.

There was a soft knock at the door and I yanked the blanket back up, covering everything but my eyes and above.

Mrs. Jones opened the door a crack. "Are you awake, Mrs. Pringle? Do we need to summon a doctor?"

I swallowed, my throat a collection of barbs. "No. Thank you."

"Miss Baudelaire would like to speak with you when you're able. Shall I get you some tea?"

"Yes, please," I croaked. "Thank you."

A few minutes later a tea tray appeared just inside my door, and I crawled from my bed to cradle its warmth in my palms. The house sounded lively in the rooms neighboring mine and also below in the front parlor. The grandfather clock chimed just once as I finished my tea and began the long and arduous process of getting dressed and fixing my tangled hair. Gloomy circles resided beneath my bloodshot eyes, highlighted by lines that I swear were not there the day before.

Is that what a collapsed life does to a person? Does it age them by ten years overnight?

Just as I closed my bedroom door behind me, Everett stopped on the stairs.

"I was just coming to check on you," he said. "You look well."

Still feeling faint, I took his arm so he could assist me down the stairs. "You are a terrible liar."

"Well," he said, considering, "better than I expected."

I winced.

"Thank you for getting me home and into bed last night," I said quietly.

"How do you know it was me?"

I looked at him and I couldn't help but smile a little. "It is always you who takes care of me."

His eyes warmed.

"However," I said, raising an eyebrow at him, "I should like to know who put me into my nightgown before putting me to bed."

His mouth twisted into a smirk. "Perhaps it is better if you do not know."

"Good lord." I stared at him. "You didn't—"

"Mrs. Jones took care of you this time," he said. "Calm yourself."

I maneuvered around Miss Baudelaire's chair and took a seat on the chaise with Everett next to me while Bella drank tea in the adjacent easy chair next to Minerva.

"Good afternoon, Miss Baudelaire." I lowered my eyes demurely.

Miss Baudelaire tapped her long cigarette holder into a glass tray and put it to her lips, inspecting me silently through narrowed eyes. "Afternoon, Mrs. Pringle."

"I must apologize for my reprehensible behavior last night," I said, softening my voice. "What happened was an unfortunate setback and my response was entirely unacceptable. I hope, in time, you can forgive me for my regrettable decisions."

Bella snickered.

"It does not matter, Cora," Minerva said. "The damage had been done before your little episode in the dressing room."

I nodded solemnly. "I understand."

She took another long drag from her cigarette holder. "Several venues have already contacted me about your upcoming performances. They no longer want you on their stages."

I glanced at Everett. He looked as worried as I felt.

"I have no choice but to evict you from this house and from my employ," she said, her tone cold, her expression blank. "You have until Wednesday to have all of your things removed from your rooms."

I stared at her. "What?"

"You're out o' here, missy," Bella quipped in her high, girlish timbre.

I shot her a glare before looking back at Minerva. "Please, Miss Baudelaire. I beg you. Please give me another chance."

"Another chance?" Miss Baudelaire repeated. "After Mr. Wyndham ended your tour, I gave you another chance. That *was* your second chance." She shook her head and gave a small shrug. "You are no good to me. I do not run a charity, Mrs. Pringle. How could I possibly make use of you now?"

At this remark I burst into tears, no acting required on my part. I had not expected this response. I thought perhaps she would keep me from the stage for a while and then reintroduce my act once audiences had forgotten about that stupid article. I thought, perhaps, I could change up my performance and take on a new identity, leaving both Lady Selene and Madame Pringle far behind me.

But no. Lady Selene and Madame Pringle were both long dead now, and there was nothing for it. Cora Pringle, on the other hand, wanted to join them in their shallow grave.

"Please, Miss Baudelaire," I repeated, "please do not abandon me."

My head pounded. My vision was obscured from tears. My stomach, again, swayed with nausea.

"You will have the remainder of your wages by the end of the day," she said, sliding off her chair and stool. "I have nothing further to say on the matter." She left us there, the smoke from her cigarette leaving a trail in her wake.

My chest quivered as I sobbed into Everett's chest, my fingers clutching the front of his shirt. He leaned his cheek on top of my head.

Bella remained seated across from us, loudly slurping from her teacup like my wretched life had not just been further devastated.

"Did you know," she said brightly, "you're actually hideous when you cry?"

I had hidden away in my bedroom for the rest of the day, taking my meals and my tea from the comfort of my bed. I still felt unwell all afternoon, so I read a book, slept, and stared out my little window, watching all the carriages and pedestrians pass by.

Around nine o'clock, a creak outside my door alerted me to someone's presence.

"Cora," Everett said. "Are you awake?"

I let him in and sat with him on the edge of my bed, offering him the rest of my cup of tea. Despite it being nearly cold, he smiled wearily and accepted it.

"Any luck?" I bit the corner of my lip.

He took a long sip and stared silently into the cup.

"Not to worry," I said, squaring my shoulders. "We have a few more days to find other employment. Plenty of time."

It was, by far, my worst acting performance to date.

"You know you're welcome to share my home again," he said quietly, returning the empty teacup. "It's smaller than my old flat but it's got four walls and a ceiling." He gave a little shrug. "I don't mind going back to sleeping in a chair."

This lovely man would offer me his last bite of bread of it was all he had in the world.

"I have leaned on your goodwill enough for a lifetime already," I said, my eyes lowering from his adoring gaze.

As I slid the cup back onto the small side table, my fingertips lingered on the top edge of its drawer. I pulled it open, lazily navigating through a pile of papers inside. When I found the folded letter at the bottom, I took it out, stared at it, and turned it over in my hands.

"It might be time to consider other options," I said, directing my words at the letter. "If you did not feel compelled to take care of me—"

"Cora, what—"

"Your life *and* mine would be easier if I just went to America and lived with my aunt like we planned," I blurted, my words lacking sincerity. "I need security. I am no longer in a position to have that in London. America is my only option."

Everett focused on the floor so hard I thought he might burn a hole right through it. He stood and crossed his arms over his chest, a deep crease forming between his eyes as he considered my words. His deep thoughts eventually took him over to the other side of my bed, where he sat back down and stared out the window, his eyes on the dark London street on the other side of the glass.

"Please tell me what you are thinking," I whispered.

Everett's shoulders sagged as he let out a long sigh. "You should go to America."

I stared at the back of his head, a few of his long dark curls escaping over the collar of his jacket. I longed to wrap my finger around one of those thick locks and slide it under my thumb.

"Should I?" I managed faintly, my throat suddenly smarting.

Tell me to stay.

He continued staring directly ahead. "Yes."

"Would you ever consider leaving England?"

Say you will come with me.

He looked at me and blinked a few times. "And go to America?" He smiled weakly and went back to avoiding eye contact. "I am not sure I would—" He paused a moment to consider his words. "—fit in."

White Britons, generally, were not terribly warm or embracing of those with darker skin but white Americans, from what I had read, were much worse.

"Oh. Right." I bit my lip. "Of course."

"But you need to go." His tone was firm, like he was giving me an order.

I stared at him for a moment, daring him to look me in the eye. He would not.

"Then I will go alone," I said, my voice barely above a whisper.

"Good."

"Good."

We sat in silence for a moment, not looking at one another. Finally, he stood and went to the door, looking at me for a moment before he left the room.

"Goodnight, Mrs. Pringle."

"Goodnight, Mr. Rigby."

After he closed the door again, I continued staring at the space where he had stood moments before.

What exactly just happened?

THIRTY-FOUR

Amelia

Sunday, November 25, 1888

I bolted up in bed, woken up by someone banging furiously on the door downstairs. Unsure what time or day it was, I stumbled from my blankets and into my dressing gown and hobbled to the doorway.

If it's rats again, I swear I am moving out of this house.

The living room lightened softly as Matilda and her candle approached the door before peering out the narrow little window beside it. She gave a little gasp and I scurried to the top of the staircase.

"Who is it?" I, for some reason, whispered loudly, like I might not want the person on my own step to hear me.

"It's Mr. Woodacre," she exclaimed, "and he's hurt!"

"Bring him inside for goodness sake," I said, hurrying to greet him after she opened the door.

She ushered him inside and took a worried glance out into the street, either to see if he was alone or to see if anyone nearby might gossip about a handsome eligible bachelor showing up at my door in the middle of the night. He was without his hat and coat—right away, not a good sign.

"Mr. Woodacre, come in," I grabbed his hand and pulled him to an easy chair in the parlor.

"I dare not sit," he said, already seated. "I might get blood on the furniture—"

"Do you seriously think I give a fig about…"

Matilda had turned on the gas lights as I spoke, and his appearance had startled me so that I immediately forgot my words. A crimson streak marked a cut on his lower lip, black and red crust lined the edges of one nostril, and one eye looked significantly puffier than the other. The bottom of his trousers were caked with muck and his hair was wet, flat, and streaked with rain.

"What on earth—"

"I have upset you," he said, giving a little wince as he moved his sore arm. "I should not have come here but I was not sure where else to go that was nearby. I should go—"

"You would not dare," I snapped.

Matilda returned with some soap and water and began dabbing at Wright's face with a cloth while he tried his best not to pull away or grimace.

"Tell me what happened." I sat on the little footstool nearby and stared up at him.

"I was visiting some friends in a private gathering above an inn." He lowered his eyes. "I believe you know the inn that I speak of."

My eyes widened. "Oh, Mr. Woodacre."

I knew exactly what inn he was speaking of. Simon, Wright, and a group of their friends with, well, similar interests sometimes met to socialize at that very specific inn. Some of the gentlemen there, like Wright and Simon, wore men's clothing during these occasions while some wore dresses, wigs, and makeup. They did nothing nefarious during these social events: a bit of gossiping but mostly card playing and drinking. I had begged Simon a few times to let me come with him, but he always refused. It was meant to be kept as quiet as possible because such a gathering would not be approved of by most. Keeping it exclusive was a safety measure.

"I had only meant to stay for one drink but ended up lingering. There were quite a lot of us and perhaps some of us had a little too much to drink or we were too loud." He touched a fingertip to his mouth to check if it was still bleeding. It was. "Whatever the reason, several police officers broke the door down and, well, showed us what they thought of our little affair. I managed to get away through a window at the back." He looked away from me. "I think they arrested Simon."

"Oh, god." I put my hand to my mouth. "Oh, no."

"I tried to make him come with me, but he was trying to help one of our friends who was being beaten." Wright's eyes went glassy. "I fled like a coward."

"You did nothing wrong," I said the words, but I was not sure I actually meant them.

Of course Simon got arrested trying to help someone. Of course he did.

I stood. "What jail would they be held in?"

"You will not be able to go see him until tomorrow morning, if at all. They might not let—"

"I am Simon's *wife*," I reminded him. "They will let me see him."

They really did not want to let me see him.

"Mr. Baxter is your husband, eh?" The tall prison guard laughed and looked me over from head to toe, pausing briefly at the level of my chest. "You know what 'e done?"

"You must allow me to see him," I said very slowly and clearly as I suspected his comprehension capability might be limited. "Or must I summon our family's lawyer?"

"Oh, keep your hair on, miss." He scoffed. "Follow me."

The smell of the jail was almost overwhelming. I tried to be subtle, lifting my wrist to my nose to block the mix of mold, damp, and waste.

The guard looked back at me and snickered again. "Change your mind yet?"

"Please continue," I snapped.

We arrived at a row of cells at the end of a dimly lit, musty hallway and the guard wordlessly left me alone. Simon, sitting with his back against the stone wall, looked up at me and smiled weakly, his messy hair hanging over his forehead, nearly covering his blackened right eye. His jawline was a mix of purple and yellow bruising while a multitude of angry red scratches lined his hands.

"Good morning, wife," he said, resting his arms on his bent knees. "You are looking lovely this morning."

I wrapped my fingers around the bars of the cell. "Are you alright?"

"Never better."

The man in the cell to the left of Simon's approached the bars, leering at me. "Fancy a go, love? I'm sure your man won't mind so much." He grinned, baring his putrid gums and rotten teeth at me.

"No, thank you," I said, not looking away from Simon, watching him struggle to his feet.

He grimaced as he stood and hobbled a bit as he moved closer to the bars. He put his hand over my fingers and leaned his forehead against mine.

"I take it Wright told you I was here."

"He came to our house last night directly from the raid," I said in a hushed tone.

"Is he injured?"

"He's a little roughed up but he will be fine. He is still at our house as far as I know. Hopefully, he does not sneak out while I am here." I looked up into his sad, unfocused eyes. "His injuries will heal, I promise."

He gave a short nod. "Good."

"He seemed rather guilty that he left you there."

Simon looked down at me, one eyebrow perking up slightly. "Did he?"

I lowered my voice to a whisper. "He still loves you, I know it."

Someone stirred in the cell to the right. The prisoner's nose was a mess of dried blood and one eye was swollen completely shut. One of his shirt sleeves was just gone, a ragged edge left at the shoulder where the fabric had been torn.

Simon frowned at him. "You alright, Peter?"

Peter nodded and immediately winced, putting a hand to the back of his head and then inspecting the bit of dried blood on his fingers. "Oh, I suspect I'll live."

"How did the police find out?" I whispered. "Your friends are always so careful."

"Someone snitched on us," Peter said. "I heard the guards talking."

"Who would do such a thing?" As soon as the words left my lips, I looked at Simon. "It couldn't be … could it?"

He rolled his eyes, his lips in a tight frown. "You do not seriously think Lady Selene would tell the police about our gatherings."

"Why not? My last story destroyed her reputation." I reminded him, "I was at her performance at the Princess Royal. It was a catastrophe."

"How would she possibly even know? You should not assume she was involved—"

"She had someone toss a box of rats through our window, Simon. I do not know what else she is capable of."

Peter shuddered. Simon shot him a look, and Peter took a seat on the floor of his cell again.

"Amelia, do not seek revenge, I beg you." Simon shook his head. "I know you are already considering how best to get her back. I implore you, consider no further."

"You cannot expect me to just accept this kind of treatment from her—"

"You do not know it was her! Just like you do not know the rats were her either!"

I backed up from the cell, dropping my hands to my sides. "You could have been killed. What, do you expect me to do nothing about this?"

"Yes." He sighed. "Yes, that is exactly what I want you to do."

I just blinked at him, not knowing what to say. After a long silence between us, Simon spoke up.

"Does anyone know I am here besides you?"

By *anyone*, he meant *anyone from the family*.

"No."

"Good."

I hesitated. "What if I contact Papa's lawyer, Mr. Stafford? He could advise you—"

"No. He will tell my father."

"What if he finds out some other way?"

"Then you will be a widow," he said darkly, crossing his slender arms over his chest and leaning his shoulder against the bars. "Perhaps we can bribe a guard to release me. We can get my name off any lists they may have. Then we can hire a different lawyer not affiliated with the family. We can use the money in the safe at the house."

Oh, no.

I swallowed, my chest suddenly feeling hard and hollow.

"I believe, I mean, I think much of the money in the safe … has been used."

"What do you mean? What did you spend it on? I know you enjoy your charitable giving but there was quite a lot of money in there—"

"No, not charity." Closing my eyes, I decided to go with the hard-and-fast approach of making Simon furious with me rather than postponing the inevitable. "I gave it to Magni the Magnificent so he would tell me how Madame Pringle does her stage tricks."

Simon backed away from the cell bars, staring at me. "Tell me you are joking."

My throat constricted and my eyes burned. "Simon, I am so

sorry. I was going to tell you—"

"Tell me? You were going to *tell* me? You were not even going to *ask* me, you were just going to tell me?"

I glanced at Peter who was silently watching our exchange from his cell, not even being subtle about it.

"I had to give him—"

"No. No, Amelia, you did not *have* to do it. You did it because you wanted to." He gave a shrug. "You did it because you did not care how your actions might affect me, your husband—"

"You are as much a real husband to me as I am a real wife to you," I snapped.

"That was your idea, I will remind you," he said, jaw clenched. "Whatever the reason, you still should have asked me. My role as your husband may not be traditional but we still share a home and … you are my best friend." His shoulders fell as his entire upper torso relaxed in defeat and exhaustion.

The hurt look on his face pushed me over the edge and I felt a tear slide down my cheek. "I am sorry. You do not know how truly wretched I feel."

Simon studied my face for a moment before moving to the back of the cell, away from me. He leaned his back against the wall and slid down it until he sat on the dirt floor.

"See what you can do about getting me out of here," he said quietly. "Tell Mr. Stafford I was arrested for illegal gambling or something. I don't know, make something up. We will deal with the rest later."

I nodded and made my leave of the jail, taking a hansom cab directly to my mother's house. I was in such a daze the whole way that the driver could have taken me to Dover and back and I do not think I would have even noticed.

A servant greeted me at the door. I waited in the sitting room for Mama but Beth found me first, her pregnant belly looking especially rotund. She waddled over to me, her face alight with joy in seeing me, and took my hand.

"Amelia, how are…" She stopped, her glowing smile

disappearing. "What has happened? Is everything alright?"

I explained the situation, using the illegal gambling story Simon had suggested. I felt like a proper scoundrel, lying to Beth's face. The poor girl had come into our family, had been abandoned by her husband while pregnant, and just wanted to be my friend. And there I was, lying to her.

"Not to worry. I am sure Mr. Stafford will be able to help," Mama said to me, giving my hand a gentle pat a few minutes later. "I will go send for him."

Beth smiled sweetly at me. "See? Everything will be alright. Do not be mad at Simon for his folly. I am sure he did not think he was doing wrong."

I do not know if it was my guilt or the painfully earnest look in her eyes, but either way, a loud, ugly sob leapt from my throat. I am not sure who was startled more by the sound, Beth or I.

THIRTY-FIVE

Amelia

Monday, November 26, 1888

Mr. Woodacre had returned home the day before, but only when I gave him my permission to do so. He did not seem to mind me tending to his wounds so much. He was far too busy worrying about having to take a few days off of work, knowing that he would get questioned by his superiors if he did go in.

I found myself alone at breakfast, my neglected toast growing cold on my plate as I stared at Simon's empty chair, feeling numb.

I had not heard a word from Simon or Mr. Stafford yet, no matter how many times I asked Matilda if there were any messages for me.

Every single time, she lowered her eyes and said, "No, ma'am."

Sipping my tea, I considered my next course of action in regard to Simon's imprisonment. I thought about taking the day off and going to visit him in his cell but then thought better of it. With our weekly publication day landing on a Wednesday, Mondays and Tuesdays were the worst possible days to be missing from the office. Mr. Granville would never let me hear the end of it.

I was still in a fog when I arrived at work. I probably said good morning to Mrs. Davies, I cannot even be sure, but I was sitting at my desk before I even noticed the yelling.

Blinking at Mr. Turner, I looked from him to Mr. Granville's office door. "What on earth—"

"They have been at it since before I got in," he said, his shoulders slumped as he hammered away on his typewriter. "I think I heard Mr. Granville say something about you."

I had always envied his ability to carry on full conversations while still writing.

"Oh, good," I muttered. "Lucky me."

The other loud voice coming from Mr. Granville's office was almost certainly Esther. Suddenly, the door to Mr. Granville's office flew open.

"Mrs. Baxter, do join us, please," he bellowed, spittle flying from his mouth. Despite the polite words, his request was most certainly an order.

I closed the door behind me as I joined the couple, both of them huffing away with arms crossed.

"Good morning." I smiled sweetly. "Did you have a good weekend?"

Mr. Granville tossed me a glare, unamused by my chipper remark, while Esther's lips puckered, keeping her grin at bay.

"Mrs. Baxter, what exactly is our business here?" Mr. Granville looked at his wife as he spoke.

How I adored being used as a prop in a couple's squabble.

"We report the news, sir."

He continued, folding his hands behind his back. "If an event occurred over the weekend and if I decide it is newsworthy, what do we do about that news?"

"We report on it." I glanced at Esther, hoping for a clue of what was happening.

"Thaddeus—"

"You see, Mrs. Baxter, our publisher does not think we should publish anything about this certain event but I disagree—"

"For goodness sake, just tell me what event you are referring to," I spat.

He frowned at me. "Police were tipped off about a party of men above an inn on Saturday night. Several men were arrested."

She exchanged a look with her husband before lowering her eyes.

Bloody hell and also bullocks.

"A party of men? I had no idea that was even a crime." I smirked. "Perhaps we should have stopped men from gathering a long time ago."

"Mrs. Baxter, please," he replied. "This is serious."

"What is so serious about a party of men gathered in a room above an inn?" I crossed my arms over my chest and looked straight at him.

If Mr. Granville was going to force this conversation upon me, I was going to force him to actually say what he meant.

After a long pause, he whispered, "Sodomites."

"Oh, dear. Well, that does sound serious," I said quickly, keeping my tone light. "When the police arrived, what exactly were these men doing?"

His jaw tightened. "Mrs. Baxter—"

"Were they paired off or was it just one colossal bacchanal?"

"Mrs. Baxter!" He sighed at me, his nostrils flaring at the edges.

"From what my sources tell me, there was nothing improper occurring in that room," I snapped, my tone hardening. "They were playing cards and having a jolly time. This was followed by the police bursting in and ruining a perfectly enjoyable evening."

"If it was such an innocent event, a dozen men would not be in prison right now," Mr. Granville said. "I say we cover this event because it is another prime example of our great and glorious realm descending into the gutter."

"You are entirely correct, Mr. Granville," I replied. "It was certainly *not* an innocent event. After the police intruded, they beat several men half to death. Perhaps we should write a story about *that*."

Mr. Granville laughed. "I think not."

I glared at him. It was only then that it occurred to me that Mr. Granville might not realize my own husband was one of the men imprisoned that night. Either that or he was being insulting and cruel on purpose.

"No, Mrs. Baxter has a good point," Esther chimed in. "All the other newspapers will be covering the story about arrests. Perhaps we should consider covering the story from the angle of the abused men."

"Absurd," he said. "We will do no such thing."

"When did you become such an enthusiast for Scotland Yard anyway?" She raised an eyebrow at him.

"And when did *you* get involved in editorial decisions?" he snapped back. "*I* am the editor, *I* choose what we write about and we *will* cover this story as it is meant to be covered. That is my final word on the subject."

Esther stared daggers at Mr. Granville before stomping out of his office. I followed her out, trailing after her until we were on the sidewalk in front of the office door. She nodded at a little alley between our building and the next, a safe distance away from my workplace.

"Thank you for trying," I said, smiling weakly.

"Sometimes he is just so impossible." She shook her head. "Hopefully you will not have to write about it. Were any of Mr. Baxter's friends involved?"

"Mr. Baxter, actually." I winced. "And several of his friends."

"Oh, no, Amelia. I am so sorry." She wrapped an arm around my shoulder and gave me a squeeze. "I hope he is uninjured."

"Uh, well, no, not exactly." I shook my head, forcing the image of his bloodied and bruised face out of my mind. "He will be alright. The family's lawyer is working on getting him out now, but I am still waiting to hear from them—"

"Mr. Baxter is imprisoned?"

I gave a shallow nod.

"Oh, dear." Esther bit the corner of her lip. "Mr. Granville is receiving the list of the arrested men later this morning."

"If he is getting the list, all of the major newspapers will be receiving the same list of names and everyone will know." I swallowed, fighting the ache in my throat that had suddenly returned to torment me. "Well, this week is certainly off to a tremendous start."

"I am so sorry, Amelia." She spoke so softly for a woman I had seen effortlessly command large audiences. "What can I do?"

"I do not know," I said. "I fear it may be too late and our secret is about to be revealed."

Just as I feared, the list of names was slapped on my desk just before noon.

"This is certainly outrageous," Mr. Granville said while standing beside my desk. "This changes everything."

I swallowed, my throat feeling dry very suddenly. "Oh?"

He thrust a finger at the paper. "Look for yourself!"

Using the tip of my index finger, I slid it closer to me, my eyes drifting over the names. A few sounded familiar but none stood out to me. When I reached the bottom of the list, I read it again.

Simon is not here. Simon is not here!

Looking up at him with an innocent smile, I said, "Friends of yours, sir?"

"Of course not," he snapped. "Do you recognize any of those names?"

"I do not."

"Not even the fifth name from the bottom?"

I slid my spectacles up higher on my nose and read it a third time. "Clive Farrell. No, I do not know the name, sir."

Mr. Granville snatched the list back from my desk, grinning from ear to ear. He only looked like that when he had something *really* juicy in the works.

"Young Mr. Farrell is the son of a certain M.P." Smug

satisfaction practically dripped from his round face.

"Ah."

He tapped on his chin, considering our move. "Your recent articles about the spiritualist woman were popular, especially among the more conservative, traditional set."

I scoffed. That had certainly not been my angle on purpose.

He continued, "Good Christians don't like this parlor séance business. Church attendance is down, and they believe alternative systems of belief are at play."

I winced and stayed silent. Mr. Granville need not know I skipped church because of a lack of faith.

"We are going to run an editorial piece on this molly house tomfoolery," he said, "and you are going to write it for me."

I blinked at him. "Oh?"

"How can a man be trusted with the governance of this realm if he cannot even keep his own son in line? We must insist Farrell resigns."

"That hardly seems necessary," I said, rising from my chair. "I think we are much better off writing an article about the beatings those men received—"

"Absolutely not." He waved a hand at me. "We must stand our ground and show politicians that they and their families are not above the laws that they themselves create—"

"Sir, I will write no such thing." The words escaped into the space between us and it took me a moment to realize I had been the one to utter them. "I will not pen an article *or* an editorial that lays undue shame upon those men. They were hurting no one and the way they were treated was abhorrent. I will not do it."

Mr. Turner stopped typing and looked at me and then at Mr. Granville. I wondered if either of them could hear my heart thundering.

Mr. Granville studied me. "You are taking the side of deviants."

I squared my shoulders. "This newspaper once had a goal of pointing out the wrongs of our society. The way our society treats people who are different is disgraceful. I will have no part in it."

"Fair enough." He gave a single nod. "I would never ask you to write something that went against your conscience." He strolled to his office and stopped in the doorway. "Mr. Turner will write the article instead and you, Mrs. Baxter, will finish out the rest of the week and then clean out your desk." He coolly closed the door to his office behind him without another word or a second glance at me.

I am not sure how long I stood staring at the inlay detailing of that door. Mr. Turner stood, startling me out of my daze.

"Mrs. Baxter," he said. "Are you alright? Can I fetch you some tea perhaps?"

"I'm fine," I snapped. "Will you actually write that article?"

He gave a small shrug. "I need this job."

I looked away from him in disgust and let out an irritated sigh. "Why are so many men so very spineless?"

Grabbing my reticule off my desk, I announced my departure for lunch and left as fast as my feet could carry me. Once on the street, I hailed a cab.

"Get me to Fleet Street as quickly as you can, driver," I said. "There will be an extra three shillings in it for you."

The air was thick with the smell of paper and ink as I made my way to Esther's office above the presses. I loved looking over all of it with her, watching as periodicals, catalogues, our newspaper, and other materials appeared before our very eyes. The men working the machines were too busy sliding paper in, keeping plates inked and moving bundles of paper to notice me as I made my way upstairs.

"Amelia? What is it? Is it about Mr. Baxter?"

I told her about Mr. Granville's order for me and my subsequent firing.

"I have made the decision that I will no longer write for *The Gazette Weekly*," I explained. "Or, rather, the decision was made for me since I refused to write negatively about—" I gave a quick glance around me. "—Mr. Baxter's companions. I could not live with myself."

"Do you wish me to speak to Mr. Granville on your behalf?" Esther rose from her chair, looking prepared to rush out the door that very moment. "I will. I hate that he put you in that sort of position."

"Simon's name was not on the list. I do not know why," I said. "I would ask that you interfere in a different manner."

She raised her eyebrow. "I am afraid to ask what you have in mind."

"I know what I am asking is more than likely too much to ask of you, and I feel guilty even bringing it up, but I thought it might be worth a try. Mr. Turner will be submitting the column." I hesitated. "But I would like you to print my version of the column instead," I blurted.

Esther's face tightened as she took a seat behind her desk again, copying her husband's habit of tenting his fingers as he considered his options.

"He would be furious with me for printing something he had not read or approved of."

I gave a shallow nod, my gaze moving to the floor. "I know."

"But it would get attention, certainly," she thought out loud. "It would be provocative."

"Indeed."

She rose to her feet again and watched the presses through the large window at the front of her office. "It would be a serious betrayal of Mr. Granville's trust. The newspaper is his life. He is not just a business partner." She looked over her shoulder at me. "He is also my husband."

For some odd and unknown reason.

I nodded. "I understand. Please do not give it another thought. I should not have—"

"I admire you for wanting to stand up for people who are treated unfairly. That takes courage." Her eyes drifted over the various presses on the floor below. "What if we printed it as an open letter?" She whipped around to face me, her eyes wild with inspiration. "It could be *accidentally* slipped into every issue of *The Gazette*."

I blinked at her. *This is actually happening.*

"It can be anonymous if you prefer," she added, giving me a look of warning.

I had applied for a job at *The Gazette Weekly* because it had a reputation as a publication with a radical streak but during my time there, that progressiveness had faded. If I wanted to be a legend like Nellie Bly, I would have to be just as brave and just as eager to take risks.

I squared my shoulders. "I am taking a stand. It is not much of a stand if it's anonymous, is it?"

THIRTY-SIX

Cora

Wednesday, November 28, 1888

The docks were bustling with humanity from all classes and walks of life. I hired a boy to pull my lone trunk, having pawned most of my belongings in order to afford passage to America, and I led him through the boisterous throng.

The crowd smelled of hopes, dreams, and sweat. Passengers with multiple crates and parcels hugged their loved ones goodbye, while solo travelers with nothing but a sack slung over their shoulder gave one last look at the land that had treated them unkindly. Further down the dock, men with thick arms offloaded cargo of barrels and chests from a moored merchant ship.

Everett and I had made our uncomfortable goodbyes the day before, neither of us saying much of anything. We did not even hug. We shook hands. *We shook hands*, like two businessmen agreeing on the terms of a contract and not like friends who had been through so much together.

I found the ticket office and joined the queue, my stomach

turning, shuddering as a biting autumn wind whipped down the dock.

What would America be like? What if Aunt Charlotte and her husband were no longer at their last address? What if her husband did not allow me to stay?

The night before, I had dreamt I was with Aunt Charlotte in her new home and Everett showed up at the door. He had asked me to come back with him and I had said yes. However, when he pulled me into a hot air balloon with Queen Victoria, I realized it was just a dream and woke up.

I arrived at the front of the line and reached for my reticule. However, when the woman behind the window asked for the total I owed her for my ticket, my hand froze.

It simply would not move.

Standing there with my hand clutching several pound notes, I stared at her and then blinked at the money.

"Ma'am, is something wrong?"

"Yes." The word crept out like the ghost of a reply.

"Pardon me, ma'am?"

The roaring in my ears dulled the impatient shouts from behind me.

"Apologies," I said, my eyes still locked on the fistful of bills between my fingers. "Forgive me." I moved aside and the passenger behind me stepped up, taking the ticket that had previously been meant for me and my new life.

The boy, using my trunk as a seat, raised an eyebrow at me from his waiting spot on the dock. I could feel my pulse thumping in my ears, overpowering the hum of the crowded dock around me. I joined the boy and my trunk. Looking up at the ship that was supposed to be my gateway to salvation, my whole body felt heavy and tired.

"Ma'am?"

"Hmm? Sorry?"

"I asked you if you got your ticket or if they were sold out," the boy repeated.

"No, I forgot to do something," I said. "I require your assistance a little longer until I find a cab." I offered him a coin and he smiled wide, stowing it away in the pocket of his shirt.

A few minutes later, I gave my driver the address to Everett's flat in St. Luke's. We had agreed to write to one another, but I was not sure either of us really meant it. At the time, I thought maybe cutting ties off completely might be the way to go but as the hansom got held up in the street, I reconsidered.

If I never spoke to Everett again, my heart would break.

Eventually, the cab rumbled by St Luke's Hospital for Lunatics, a wide building with a series of tall, narrow arches along the entire façade, giving the building an imposing air—not that the poor wretches contained within its walls could appreciate its architecture.

I knew we were close, as Everett had mentioned his rented room was cheap because of its proximity to the hospital. Just as I expected, the cab stopped nearby in front of a tall Georgian building, five stories high. I paid the driver.

"I can increase your tip significantly if you carry my trunk up to the fourth floor," I said, pursing my lips slightly in a demure little simper.

"Sorry, I got a bad back." He snapped his whip and the cab disappeared around the corner, leaving me on the street with my trunk.

A cold breeze sent dust swirling up from the road and I gave a shudder, glancing up the many windows of the building.

This better be the right address.

And so I dragged my trunk inside and then up three flights of stairs. Up and up and up. Several angry residents shouted at me from inside their homes while a few others whipped their doors open to holler at me in person.

"Do you have to hit every damn step with the bloody thing?" a large bald man bellowed at me.

Wiping a layer of perspiration from my forehead, I let the trunk drop to the floor and stood upright. "Yes, sir, I do."

His eyes bulged as he took in my frame and my dress, realizing I looked to be a lady of gentle birth and society and yet, there I was, struggling to haul my own trunk and sweating, my chest heaving as I endeavored to breathe.

"Oh, uh, sorry, miss. Just try to keep it down." He went back into his flat and left me to my task.

I made a very unladylike face at his closed front door and lifted the handle on my trunk again. The trunk lifted and then immediately hit the floor again, the leather strap handle dangling in my grip. I stared at it, cursed, and thought I might cry right there in the hallway. I had no choice but to then push the trunk up the stairs from the bottom. Slowly. Very, very, *very* slowly.

Once the trunk was flat on the landing of the fourth floor, I let myself collapse onto the stairs, my moist forehead resting on one arm as I tried to catch my breath.

If Everett turns me away after all of that, I will stab him.

And just like that, there he was.

One brow raised and eyes blinking curiously, he peered at me from over my trunk. I could not speak, let alone explain myself or my sorry condition. I knew my hair was probably disheveled and plastered to my forehead and my face red as an apple. Everett, of course, looked like his usual self, except perhaps a little tired as shadows underlined his pale blue eyes.

I could never grow tired of looking at those remarkable eyes, shadows underneath or not.

"Did you move that trunk up three flights of stairs?"

I nodded, my throat still terribly dry.

"Do you have any other trunks with you? Downstairs perhaps?"

I shook my head.

He pulled me to my feet and up the remaining few stairs. Gripping his hand in mine, I let myself lean into him as he helped me into his flat down the hall. He left me to sit on the edge of his bed as he retrieved my trunk from the corridor.

"I'll go get us water for tea," he said, kettle in hand, dashing down the hallway to the shared water closet.

With him out of the room for a moment, I took the opportunity to shed my jacket, gloves, and hat and absorb my surroundings. This flat was smaller than his home above the pub where he lived before. It was one single small room, too small for the various trunks and furniture now residing within it. His trunk, scuffed and crumbling at the corners, was pushed up against one of the four brick walls and his bed was up against the opposite wall. The one window was narrow and covered by a yellow curtain that, I guessed, had once upon a time been white. A small table, littered with papers and writing implements, likely served as both a dining table and workspace.

Everett returned and hung the kettle in the fireplace. He nudged at the coals with the long iron poker, shifting the bits of tinder around in the hearth.

He leaned against the wall behind him, looking at the kettle. "I assume you are here because you wanted to avoid a long sea voyage."

"Yes," I said, still gasping a little. "That is absolutely it."

He sighed, a long pause unfolding between us before he spoke again.

"Cora, why are you here?"

"I do not like how we said our goodbyes." I straightened my posture, setting my shoulders back. "Our parting seemed unfitting to a friendship such as ours."

"A friendship such as ours," he repeated, a tiny smile tugging at his mouth, his eyes lowered. "And what kind of friendship *is* our friendship exactly?"

"Well," I began, "we have been through a lot together, you know. I believe we have much in common, you and I."

"Indeed?"

"Yes."

"And why are your things here?" Everett turned in his chair, eyeing my trunk by the door. "I have the oddest sensation, like we have been here before."

"I could not just leave my trunk at the docks, could I?"

"True enough, I suppose." He retrieved teacups from a cupboard and continued preparing our tea, his back to me.

"I also wanted to ask you…" I hesitated. "…why you encouraged me to go to America."

He stopped stirring and turned his head, looking at the floor instead of at me. "You seemed like you had your mind set on it."

"You have never been shy about sharing your opinion on my actions before."

He turned back to the tea. "You have a chance at security with your aunt and uncle. Perhaps fame and fortune are beyond your grasp but at least they could provide you with a home."

"You really think I should go then? You really want me to leave?"

"Yes."

I leapt to my feet, my exhaustion suddenly very much gone. "Why are you being so cold and unfeeling to me?"

He turned around and folded his arms over his chest, finally meeting my eyes. "Am I?"

"Yes," I said, my words clipped. "You are."

"I want you to be safe, that is all. How is *that* being cold and unfeeling to you?" His voice was firm and slightly louder. "You do not know what it is like to be desperate for a place to live. You do not know what it means to be truly hungry, and I pray you never find out."

I blinked at him, stunned. He had never spoken to me like that before.

He continued. "You would go mad with the want. You have had your challenges, certainly, but you do not *really* understand how bad things might get for you here. You likely cannot even comprehend such a thing because you are a vain and spoiled woman who seems to have run out of luck. And yet, here you are when your greatest chance of survival was on that ship to America!" He pointed to the window for unnecessary emphasis.

"You were more than happy to follow me when I joined the Marvels," I spat, "just waiting for me to find fame so you could latch onto it—"

"You know very well that that is not what I was doing. I had just lost my flat, because of *you*—"

"Oh, certainly, like you had nothing to do with the séances in your kitchen. Sir, you are far too self-righteous for your own good." My voice rose to outdo his. "No, you followed me because—"

"Because I thought, perhaps, you loved me back just a little." Everett stared at me, his brow furrowed.

The same tenseness hung in the space between us, albeit with a layer of relief laid thick on top. Relief that he still loved me, even after all that I had done. I still had questions that needed answers though.

"If you loved me so much, why did you not discourage me from courting Mr. Wyndham?"

"For the same reason I encouraged you to go to America." His voice was only slightly softer now. "Also, I did not exactly *encourage* you either—"

I did not let him finish. "Why did you reject me ... that night?"

I lowered my eyes, recalling the night I offered myself to him and he sent me to bed alone. The embarrassment I had felt in that moment had bruised both my ego and my heart.

"You were drunk. I was not about to..." He hesitated. "... make advances."

"But you wanted to."

He closed the space between us, his gaze going back and forth between my eyes and my lips, the same movement his eyes had made so many times before. His breathing grew shallow and it was the only sound in the room besides the occasional crackle from the fire.

"Of course I did," he said, his words barely above a whisper. "That night and many other nights that came after."

As he lowered his face to meet mine, I put my finger to his lips, dragging my fingertip down over the full curves of his mouth. He raised an eyebrow at me.

"And what about now?" I purred into his mouth, letting the edges of my lips brush his as I spoke.

Everett searched my eyes for my approval and, enveloping me in his arms, pulled me into him. I put my hands on his chest and I felt his heartbeat under my palm, the pace of it quickening as I looked up into his eyes.

To my surprise, he did not kiss me right away. I had assumed he would ravage my mouth with his after the way he wrapped his arms around me, but he did not. He kept looking between my eyes and my lips, his brow slightly furrowed. He looked, I believe, slightly afraid.

He is still uncertain of my feelings for him. Surely he must know that he is the only one I desire.

"You are my dearest friend," I said, fighting the urge to tear up or choke on my words. I smiled. "And I love you … just a little."

It was not until I said the words out loud that I realized that it really was profoundly and achingly true.

His mouth spread into a wide smile and his eyes sparkled. I did not stop him, not even to toy with him, when he tried to kiss me again. I closed my eyes, feeling the gentle caress of his lips on mine, soft and sweet, just like him. My hands slid from his chest and I laced my fingers together behind his neck, my lips tingling. One of his fingertips moved in a slow circle on my lower back as our kisses grew steadily hungrier.

A screeching sound from below broke the spell and we both looked down to see that we had unknowingly wandered, bumping into a chair. Everett grinned and I giggled, burying my face in his chest. Just then, his mouth moved to my neck and a tiny sigh escaped my lips, my toes curling inside my shoes. I took hold of his waistcoat and tugged his lips back to mine as they missed his company dreadfully.

We had certainly kissed before, several months earlier, but this felt quite different. I had fallen for him under false pretenses, then I hated him, and then I had fallen for him all over again. I really *knew* him. Everett Rigby had seen me at my best, my worst, and then somehow at my even-worse-than-that. He had done so much for me and all because he loved me and thought there was a chance that I might love him too. He never gave up on me, despite the many signs that suggested he should.

Perhaps if I had known he could kiss like this, I would have told him I loved him sooner.

Taking a moment to catch our breaths, Everett closed his eyes and leaned his forehead to mine, our chests rising and falling a little more rapidly than normal. A wave of an unfamiliar want rose in my stomach, combined with an intense longing in my heart.

"I feel as if my heart is going to burst," he said with an awkward laugh.

I placed my hand onto his chest again to feel the racing beat. He watched as my finger traced along the edge of his waistcoat, stopping at the top button, running my fingertip over its smoothness. We exchanged a long look. My pulse quickened as my fingers slid the button from its hole, my hands then moving down to the next button, picking up speed as I went. Once my work was done, he shrugged the waistcoat off and tossed it onto the nearby table, never taking his eyes off me for a moment.

Everett knew what we both wanted.

He took my mouth again, this time devouring it greedily. His enthusiasm for me only heightened my own desire for him. He worked the buttons of my bodice while I shed my skirts. One by one, my garments hit the floor, landing in a pile at our feet.

I had considered this moment in my mind so many times but having nothing to compare it to, I was not sure what to do or expect. I of course had shared a bed with Marshall on a regular basis but it had always felt so formal. So clinical. So purpose-driven. I mostly worried I was failing as a wife by not becoming pregnant. Never before or during any of our times together had I felt anything resembling pleasure.

We were only removing our clothing but already, the rush and exhilaration of it was more enjoyable than anything I had felt with Marshall.

Once I was down to my corset, Everett moved behind me

and slowly worked the laces out of their grommets. I wondered if he might burn his fingers when he touched my impossibly hot skin. Finally, the corset was discarded.

Moving even closer to me, he touched the back of my neck with the tip of his nose. The feel of his warm breath at my nape, followed by the sensation of his mouth meeting my flesh, sent a shiver through me. His lips descended, leaving tender kisses down the side of my neck and up along my jawline. It felt utterly divine.

I lifted my chemise over my head. My fingers quivering on the laces of my pantalettes, Everett removed some of the many pins keeping my hair up and in place. He buried his face into my curls, his hands resting on my bare hips.

My stockings, both tied with pale pink ribbons, stayed on.

I would have taken them off but, before I could, Everett spun me around and pulled me tight to him again. He kissed me like he had been waiting for our lips to meet for decades, like my mouth was water and he was dying of thirst. I pulled away from him just enough to roughly tug his shirt from his trousers, letting my palm brush against the bulge nearby. His shirt joined the heap.

Everett's hands cupped my buttocks and he effortlessly scooped me up, my legs wrapped around his waist, our lips never pausing for more than a brief moment. We had to stop to giggle when his feet got tripped up in the pile of garments we had left on the floor.

I loved Everett's laugh, so open and joyful, and I adored the way his eyes sparkled when something amused him. If given the chance, I intended to try my best to amuse him, if only to see that smile.

As I bit my lip to stifle my laughter, I moved a ginger curl out of my face, gently tucking it behind my ear. Everett's silly grin faded as he looked at me for a long moment.

"You are so incredibly beautiful."

I cupped his face with one hand, my other arm wrapped

around his neck, and kissed him softly and tenderly. He lowered me onto the bed, his lips returning to my neck before beginning their southward descent.

I raised my head from the pillow, inspecting his actions. "What are you…" My lips parted as I inhaled sharply. I fell back into the pillow, deciding it was better to let him continue.

Everett Rigby was a most excellent and thorough explorer, making pilgrimages to the various curves and corners of the realm, not hastening his journey too quickly, nor taking too long. The new territories he claimed left my breath shallow and shuddering. I gripped the blanket in my fist, my toes curling again, and my back arching. I needed him to come home from his travels immediately. I needed him to come home to me.

"Everett," I whispered.

I disliked how desperate my voice sounded, but I had never felt such a need like that before. His mouth was back on mine in a flash.

As he hovered above me, his eyes fixed on mine, the image of Marshall and our unpleasant nights together flickered in my mind. Everett must have seen me wince at the bad memory.

"What is wrong? Did I hurt you?"

"No, quite the contrary." I let out a long breath and a giggle.

I gently pushed him onto his back and positioned myself on top of him, kissing his chest, his firm stomach, and then the gentle curve of his hipbone.

I needed to be in control, just like I had imagined it. I had never been in control with Marshall. I needed it to be this way with Everett. For now, at least.

My lips found his delicious mouth once again and he kissed me slow and gingerly, his firmness pressing against me. Reaching in between us, I guided him in and I gasped from the sensation.

Just before my eyes clamped shut, Everett's went unfocused and he let his head fall back against the pillow. With his hands on my waist, Everett guided my hips as we took this expedition together, creating a new civilization built just for two.

I pressed my forehead against his, the pattern of our breaths creating a frantic melody between us. When the intensity became nearly overwhelming, I buried my face against his shoulder, moaning into his warm skin. I had no map to follow for this adventure, but the experience was spectacular.

Everett's head hit the pillow again, his chest heaving under me. Smiling, he kissed my forehead and wrapped his arms around me, holding me to him.

I had never before felt so blissfully happy and content.

"My offer of marriage still stands, by the way," Everett said a few minutes later, my head on his chest.

I lifted my head to look at him. "I certainly hope that was not a proposal."

"I asked once already and was rejected quite soundly," he reminded me. "I am in no hurry to be rejected a second time."

"To be fair, sir, your first proposal was not terribly romantic either."

"You do not seem the romantic type."

"A woman can be both romantic and practical." I traced my finger around a patch of dark chest hair.

"You are suggesting you would have accepted my proposal if I had been more romantic. I feel like that is entirely untrue."

It was.

"Perhaps," I said. "Are you or are you not proposing a second time?"

He gave a little shrug. "No, Mrs. Pringle, I am not proposing a second time. I am simply stating that my original offer of marriage is still available, despite your previous refusal."

I put my head back down, too exhausted to dance around the subject any further. "I will keep that in mind."

Smiling into the warmth of his chest, my heart skipped a beat.

THIRTY-SEVEN

Amelia

Thursday, November 29, 1888

Simon had only been in jail for a few days, but his high cheekbones seemed slightly more prominent, his face somewhat more sunken in, as I ushered him into the hansom cab. As he looked to the left and right of him before getting in, I noticed yet another yellowed bruise. His hair seemed flatter and limper than usual, but at least most of his injuries were healing by then.

I raised an eyebrow at him. "I would not worry about being spotted by someone we know if that is what you are concerned about."

He gave me a look and climbed up to sit beside me. I clutched his hand, bringing it to my lips. He put his head back on the seat and released a long breath as we rumbled away from the prison.

"You can have a hot bath when we get home," I said, using my best everything-is-fine voice. I forced myself not to shudder as I realized my own mother has the same voice. "Cook is preparing a goose for supper and we shall have a few drinks to celebrate your release."

Simon smiled, his eyelids appearing heavy. "Thank you. That sounds lovely."

I put my arm around his shoulder and he soon fell asleep with his head against my meager bosom, the various shades of London gray passing by our windows.

Once back at home, Matilda opened the door for us, giving a little gasp at the sight of Simon's injuries.

"You have a visitor waiting for you in the parlor," she said quietly while taking our coats, a tone of warning in her voice. "I told him it would be better if he came back later but he insisted on staying."

Simon and I exchanged glances and I poked my head around the corner first. I swallowed and pasted a pleasant smile to my lips. Sitting in one of the easy chairs, his legs crossed, the newest issue of the *Women's Suffrage Journal* open in front of him, was Jospeh Baxter, my father-in-law, an empty teacup on the table beside him. I wondered how long he had been sitting there. I also wondered what other reading material he may have discovered in our collection.

"Joseph," I said. "We did not realize you were back in London." I folded my hands in front of me, swiftly moving into prim-and-proper mode. "Would you like some more tea?"

"No, thank you, Amelia." He folded up the periodical and set it aside. "Is my son with you?"

For a second, I considered telling Simon to make a run for it, rather than force him to face his father when he was looking less than his best. However, I would never hear the end of it from my parents so I did not dare.

"Yes," I croaked. "Simon, your father is here."

Simon moved into the doorway of the parlor and gave a quick nod. "Good afternoon."

Joseph rose to his feet. Although Simon was tall, his father was still about an inch taller and certainly broader about the chest, particularly for a man in his fifties. Except for their similar heights, there were no two men more dissimilar in all of the United Kingdom. Simon was friendly to everyone while Joseph was cold and seething. Simon was stylish while Joseph paid no attention to what he wore or how he looked.

Simon took time to show affection to those he cared for while Joseph left his pregnant wife alone in England with complete strangers. At least he had come back for the birth.

Joseph slowly advanced towards us, inspecting the remnants of his son's wounds. "You look abhorrent."

"You should see the other fellow," Simon quipped.

Joseph did not respond, not in the slightest. He looked at the various scuffs on Simon's garments, his eyes narrowing slightly.

"You smell like a gutter," he finally added.

He knows.

I did not know how he knew about the arrests, and I did not know how I knew he knew, but he knew.

"Do I?" Simon glanced at me. "I think it might be my new coat. I got it from a fishmonger. Nice chap but a *terrible* gambler—"

The back of Joseph's hand hit Simon's face with a loud crack. I let out a shriek and slapped my hand over my open mouth as Simon whirled on impact, stumbling backwards until his back hit the wall behind him with a thump and he slid to the floor.

Simon glared up at his father, his cheek bright red, his eyes watering from the sting.

"Nice to see you too, Papa," Simon mused from the floor. "How I *do* miss our talks while you are away."

I helped him to his feet, throwing Joseph a scowl over my shoulder. "You should leave, sir."

Joseph ignored me. Instead, he just stood there glowering.

This was not the first time Joseph had struck Simon. The first time was when we were eight years old and Simon had taken one of my dolls home with him. Joseph had seen Simon playing with it and he figured roughing Simon up would make him want to play with toy soldiers and the like instead of dolls. When Simon knew his father was getting suspicious about his son's attraction to men and my mother was getting suspicious about my lack of attraction to, well, *anyone*, Simon and I decided we could get married to throw our parents off the scent.

As they say, the rest is history.

"Amelia is right," Simon added, rubbing the edge of his jaw. "Perhaps you should leave."

"Who do you think paid for this house? It certainly was not you," Joseph said, his face relaxing. "You have never worked a day in your life. You were always too busy being a dandy." He paused, his lip curling into a snarl. "And a god damn deviant."

Simon dabbed at the edge of his nose as a thin trail of blood had appeared. "Blast. Not again."

"Did you hear what I said?"

"Oh, I heard you," Simon snapped. "You do not know what you are talking about—"

Joseph cut him off. "I know about the molly house arrests, you damn fool. Who do you think paid to keep your name out of the papers?"

Simon tipped his head back and put a handkerchief to his nose. "That was appreciated but not necessary. It is all a misunderstanding. I was simply having drinks with a few of my friends." His voice was calmer than expected.

Shaking his head, Joseph finally looked at me. "Your father would like you to petition for divorce, given the circumstances. We have discussed the matter. It should not affect the partnership between our two families if you part ways." His face was completely calm as he spoke. "Perhaps you could marry Simon's brother instead."

"I am not divorcing my husband," I said, loudly and slowly so Joseph could fully comprehend my words.

Also, I would never in a million years marry Simon's brother. The man has the personality of lukewarm porridge.

"You may want to reconsider," Joseph said. "Simon will not be receiving financial support from now on. Your father will cut you off as well if you do not petition for divorce."

I blinked at Joseph. "He told you that?"

"Indeed. He would like to see you settled with a man who will actually give him grandchildren. He heard about your little opinion piece about the arrests in the newspaper and he is very disappointed."

I rolled my eyes. "Oh, I am *so* glad my father has my best interests at heart."

Joseph checked his pocket watch. "I am late for a meeting." He did not even say goodbye, he just left, the door crashing shut behind him.

Simon, his nosebleed having stopped, looked down at me. "What opinion piece about the arrests?"

I shook my head. "Not important."

I chose a really unfortunate time to get fired from my job.

That evening, Esther and I took our usual seats as we waited for the rest of the L.A.E.W. members to arrive and the meeting to start. I leaned over to her, shielding my words with the back of my hand.

"I suppose Mr. Granville is not terribly pleased with either of us at the moment."

"He will get over it." She smiled weakly, her eyes lowering slightly. "Eventually."

Since I was not flush with funds the last time I saw her, Esther had kindly agreed to cover the cost of publishing my periodical with the promise that I would pay her back in full at a later date. Of course, that was before the Baxters and the Spencers had both decided to disown Simon and I, cutting off their support. Without any income at all, I was not even sure how we would afford to live, let alone pay for a pamphlet that had already been distributed within thousands of copies of *The Gazette Weekly*.

It was a conversation I was certainly not looking forward to. Although it weighed heavily on my mind, the whispers that grew louder around us were a considerable distraction.

Mrs. Carrigan smiled sweetly when she saw Esther and I.

"Good afternoon, ladies. Would you be so kind as to assist me with some of the refreshments?"

"Of course," Esther said, quickly sending me a subtle look as we rose from our chairs.

We followed Mrs. Carrigan down the hall and into a study. No refreshments in sight. Not even a single wretched cucumber sandwich.

"Several club members have spoken to me, raising their concerns that recent actions from the two of you in relation to a pamphlet you wrote and you published." She nodded to me and Esther. "I agree with their concerns. Your unseemly, radical opinions could give the League a disreputable appearance."

"Unseemly and radical?" I repeated. "What exactly is unseemly and radical about what I wrote?"

"Mrs. Baxter, please do not make this more uncomfortable than—"

I took a step towards Mrs. Carrigan. "No, no, I want to know—"

Esther raised a hand to interject. "What are you proposing we do about these concerns?"

Mrs. Carrigan seemed reluctant to just come out with it. "I must ask the both of you to resign."

"I see." Esther's lips tightened and the edges of her nostrils flared ever so slightly. "How many women came to you with these concerns?"

Mrs. Carrigan frowned and leaned closer to Esther. "You must know I would not ask you to resign if it were only a few of our more conservative members."

I wanted to march back into that room and scream at them for their cowardice, backwards ways, and hateful spirits. These women wanted to be understood and taken seriously, but when it came to another group of disadvantaged people, well, that was going too far.

Hypocrites and cowards. All of them.

"Perhaps we will just leave now and you can tell the group we have resigned. That will be fine." There was a slight crack to

Esther's voice as she spoke.

"Of course," Mrs. Carrigan said. "Thank you for understanding."

Oh, we understand perfectly.

Shortly after our League evictions, Esther and I reconvened at a nearby tea house.

"Mrs. Carrigan does not give a fig about women's rights," Esther said, spearing her fruit tartlet with her fork. "She has always been one of these women who wants to *seem* like she is forward-thinking but really is not at *all*."

"I would say many of the League members were similar in their mindset."

"Exactly." She popped some pastry in her mouth and chewed quickly. "That silly club was a waste of our time. I am sure our efforts would be appreciated much more at another suffrage society."

I barely touched my lemon cake. It had looked delicious on the tea room display counter but as soon as the plate was placed before me, eating seemed beyond my abilities.

Esther sighed. "My offer is still open, just so you know."

I looked up from the pastry. "Hmm?"

"I am willing to tell Mr. Granville that he needs to rehire you," she said, "if that is what you want."

My lips parted and an enthusiastic plea for help nearly escaped, but I closed my mouth just in time. Biting my lower lip and staring at the table, I shook my head.

"Are you sure?"

I slowly nodded and finally looked up at her. "I lost my job, was forced to resign from the League and I have been disowned by my parents." I paused, a blanket of calm settling over me suddenly. "I think, perhaps, I need a change."

THIRTY-EIGHT

Cora

Monday, December 3, 1888

I tossed my novel to the foot of the bed, my eyes roaming the silent flat, sighing aloud to myself. Once again, I was left at home to wait for Everett while he traveled up and down the streets of St. Luke's, Hoxton, Hackney, and Clerkenwell looking for work. Between the two of us, we had a little bit of money to survive on but it would not last for long.

The blankets beneath me were a bit tangled, in part due to that morning's escapade. Once we had discovered our knack for pleasing one another, we had found it a little tricky to stop. I smiled sleepily, recalling the delicious sensations that flooded my entire body each and every time we united. We had lost track of time on multiple occasions. Mealtimes became more of a theory than a regularly scheduled event.

I poked at the fire. I swept the floors. I dusted the shelves. I mended a pair of trousers. I did all the things a proper wife was meant to do.

Staring out the window, I people-watched from my little perch. Looking around the flat again, I noticed a stack of paper under the bed that I had not noticed before. I left my chair and knelt by the bed, sliding the bundle out. Dust had collected on the edges of the pages and on the fibers of the twine that held it together.

My chest tightened as I read the title on the cover page: *The Rise and Fall of Lady Selene* by Everett Rigby.

I ripped the string off in a hurry and sat on the bed with the pages in a heap on my lap, reading faster than I ever had before. Everett had taken *my* story and turned it into a play. He had taken something that was not his to take and used it for his own benefit.

That manipulative little snake.

The edge of the first page wrinkled as my fingers curled around it. I thought about tearing the pages up into tiny pieces and tossing them one by one out the window, letting the wind carry them away. I considered feeding them into the fireplace. Or perhaps I could ask Everett for a walk along the Thames and then I could toss the pages into the river right in front of him. Then, perhaps, I would push him in, too.

My fist gradually loosened as I read to the bottom of the first page, then to the end of the second, and then the third and fourth. The play was not exactly an accurate depiction of my life but it was … charming. The dialogue was delightfully playful and comedic. There were many moments where the character of Cora poked fun at herself but it was never in a hurtful way. Depicted as clever and charismatic, I used my feminine wiles to trick silly fools out of their money. I was suddenly a lovable scamp and not a villain loathed by all of London.

Rushing to finish the play, I frantically flipped the pages to see how it ended. The reporter meant to be Amelia Baxter, depicted as a jealous and miserable hag with a personal vendetta against me, is confronted by a *real* ghost at the end and begs Lady Selene to ask the ghost to leave her alone, realizing she has made a terrible mistake and needs Lady Selene's help to banish the ghost from her home. I imagined the character of Cora winking at the audience.

I raised my head suddenly, struck with a most magnificent idea.

I hope he still lives here.

Shivering as I lifted the door knocker, I gazed up at the impressive Mayfair home, its white stone façade gleaming against the gray autumn skies above. I gripped my parcel of pages under one arm so tightly the script was now bent in the middle.

A housemaid answered the door, appearing peevish when I said I did not, in fact, have an appointment to meet with the gentleman of the house but that it was most imperative that I speak with him immediately. She reluctantly allowed me to step inside, bidding me wait in front of the door while she went to fetch the master. She did not even show me to the sitting room or take my coat. I had worn my best dress on this outing, knowing it is what her employer would expect, but leaving me by the door like a salesman seemed unnecessary.

Of course I *had* just arrived entirely unannounced, so I suppose I too was at fault.

I inched further inside, surveying the elegant, richly-decorated interior. I had only ever seen the home while full of party guests and with the lights lowered. I saw nothing of the man I was looking for in this decor.

Then I saw the two marble sculptures further down the hallway; one statue of a bare-breasted Greek goddess and one bust of the man himself.

Ah. There he is.

"Mrs. Pringle," Mr. Tom Lindsey appeared at the end of that hallway and sauntered towards me, the buttons of his ill-fitting waistcoat under tremendous pressure from his pronounced gut. "You *are* still Mrs. Pringle, aren't you?"

"Indeed." I smiled sweetly, shoving my distaste out of my mind. "How are you, Mr. Lindsey?"

Mr. Lindsey spotted a nearby servant. "Will you please take Mrs. Pringle's coat and get us some tea? Heavens." He rolled his eyes.

Once we were settled in the sitting room at last, Mr. Lindsey answered my question.

"Did you hear the news? I have married." He chuckled. "You missed your chance and now I've been snatched up by the most beautiful woman in London."

"That is wonderful news indeed. I am very happy for you."

"She was a chorus girl at the opera but she's done with all that now." He raised an eyebrow and smirked. "She's sixteen."

He said "beautiful woman" when he should have said "girl." The poor thing.

"Ah," I said, trying not to sound disgusted. "Well done. Congratulations."

He hesitated before speaking again, glancing at me and then into his teacup. He wasn't usually timid about saying anything.

He cleared his throat. "Did Mr. Wyndham tell you about Mrs. Wyndham?"

"No," I said, my jaw tightening. "She never came up in our many, *many* conversations. I only found out of her existence when she introduced herself to me at The Maidenhill Club last month."

He winced. "Roy is a man of many talents but loyalty is not one of his strong suits. I told him he should be ashamed of himself for treating you so poorly." Mr. Lindsey frowned and shook his head. "I told him you deserve much better than to be his-his-his … distraction."

I felt a tiny smile tugging at my lips. Mr. Lindsey had never been a perfect gentleman but perhaps he was not the monster I thought he was. A little uncouth at times, maybe, but well-intentioned.

He glanced at the parcel I had brought. "Did you bring me a present?"

"In a manner of speaking, yes." I slid the pages out of their protective brown wrapping. "I believe that you and Mr. Rigby once had an agreement that he would write a play and you would produce it." I held it up so he could read the cover. "Well, he has done it. He has written you a play—a very good one, I dare say."

"The Rise and Fall of Lady Selene," he read aloud and then peered at me. "You're his muse, eh?"

"I suppose I am, yes." I tidied the pages and set them on my lap. "However, the Cora in this play is much more clever than I am. It is a comedy, you see. Very light and witty and jolly throughout. Audiences love a comedy. Rich or poor, comedies really bring the people together and help them forget their troubles for a while."

"A comedy, eh?" His face brightened. "I love a comedy."

Our tea arrived. Mr. Lindsey poured a little brown liquid from his flask into his cup before taking a sip. He relaxed in his chair, eyeing the script, eyeing his tea, and then eyeing me.

"Why are you pitching his script to me instead of Mr. Rigby? Did he send you on his behalf? He can't face me like a man?"

"He does not know I am here," I said, casually sliding into my sultry tone of voice. "He does not know I have seen this script."

He raised an eyebrow. "Indeed?"

"I just could not wait to bring it to you," I said. "I know you are a wise businessman who would never consider turning down an opportunity like this, so I came to you directly."

Mr. Lindsey's lip curled into a small smile. "Is that so?"

"I know you see so many scripts. I assure you this one is different."

"How so?"

I paused to give a casual eyelash bat and brush away a stray tendril of hair. Mr. Lindsey was a fool for the most obvious of gestures.

"No matter who produces this play, one thing is for certain," I said slowly. "Audiences will pay good money to see a satirical version of Cora Pringle portrayed by the real Cora Pringle."

THIRTY-NINE

Amelia

Monday, December 3, 1888

"Simon, please come out so we can talk," I said to his bedroom door. "You cannot just stay in your room forever."

"*Au contraire*," he replied from inside. "If I keep the door locked, my own father cannot cruelly evict me from my own home."

"He did not specifically say we would be evicted." I winced. "Can I at least come in please?"

I heard him sigh and advance upon the door. "Why should I let you in?"

"Because I am your wife."

He scoffed.

I leaned my forehead against the door. "I need to make sure the person who means the most to me in this entire world is alright."

After a long pause the door lock clicked, and I let myself in. Simon, a glass of liquor in hand, unshaven and wearing only trousers, returned to his armchair by the fireplace and let himself sink down low.

I sat in the other armchair while trying to ignore the scent of the room's stale air. Neither of us spoke for a moment, letting the crackling fireplace fill the silence between us.

"Wright has left London," he said quietly, lifting his drink to his lips and downing the rest of the contents of the glass. "He is staying with his brother's family in Plymouth or Exeter or some other godforsaken place."

"When is he coming back?"

Simon shrugged.

I took his empty glass and refilled it for him at the nearby drink cart. He smiled weakly as I gave it back to him and returned to my chair.

"I got a letter from Mr. Turner," I said. "It appears the police were tipped off about your friends by a jilted lover."

When I had heard this news, I was relieved. The thought that Mrs. Pringle might have done such a wicked act had weighed heavily on my mind and I had nearly succumbed to my lust for revenge on several occasions since that fateful day.

Staring into his drink thoughtfully, Simon said, "Ah." He looked over at me. "What do you think, shall we burn this house down so my father cannot come and claim it?"

"I would rather not."

"Fair enough." His eyes lazily roamed the walls and the floors. "Perhaps we could sell a few things. Do you think the pawnbrokers would want that portrait of my parents that we have downstairs?"

"Darling, *nobody* wants that cursed portrait."

He laughed loudly, the sound giving me a spark of hope.

"Perhaps just the frame then," he added with a grin.

I hesitated. "That typewriter is likely worth—"

"If you sell that typewriter, I will petition for divorce."

We smiled at one another.

"I suppose I may be forced to do something with my life now," he said after a while, his eyelids heavy. "Besides being a gentleman of leisure, I mean."

"What will you do?"

He puffed out his cheeks, sighing loudly as he thought. "Chimney sweep."

I smirked. "Graverobber."

"Rat catcher."

I burst out laughing. "Oh, yes. I have seen how skilled you would be doing *that*."

After a long pause, he spoke again.

"I never thanked you for what you did." He lowered his eyes back down into his glass. "I know you loved that job. You took a massive risk, publishing that piece and defending us. It was very kind of you and very brave."

My throat caught as I looked at his handsome, sad face. "I loved that job, yes, but I love *you* more."

He reached out, offering his hand to me, and I slid my fingers into it. He lifted them to his lips and kissed softly.

"Besides, there are other newspapers I could write for," I said. "Or perhaps I could write articles for magazines. I used to enjoy that."

"Yes, that is an option, I suppose." Simon sipped his drink. "Or you could get downstairs and make use of that shiny new typewriter I got you and write a damn book."

I slipped my hand from his and turned quickly to look at him. "What?"

"How many articles have you written about spiritualists at this point?" He raised an eyebrow at me. "And how many article ideas do you have written down in your notebook?"

A lot.

"A few."

"Liar."

I had wanted to write a book for a long time, it was certainly true, but a book about spiritualism? I had not considered it before.

All very suddenly, those article ideas appeared in my mind as an interconnected web of one single narrative. Related topics I had not even thought of before appeared out of thin air, fitting neatly into the expansive tapestry of the concept forming in my head.

"Amelia?"

I snapped my face over to Simon. "Sorry, what?"

He chuckled. "Are you alright? You have just been staring blankly for ten minutes."

"Have I?" I rose from my chair before he could utter another word. "I need to go do something."

"Oh. Alright," I heard him say as I ran out of the room.

I practically leapt down the stairs, my feet slipping slightly on the polished wood floors as I took the turn at the bottom of the staircase. Matilda stared at me as I ran by her in the hall downstairs.

"Mrs. Baxter, are you—"

"Sorry, can't stop!" I shouted, flinging the office door open and plopping myself in front of the typewriter.

And then, I began to type.

I had always been a reasonably fast typist but never *that* fast before. The letters were pounded onto the paper so frantically that it was a constant hammering drone, drowned out only by my running interior monologue.

Occasionally I had to stop and retrieve my notes from the articles I had written already, rifling through pages and pages of quotes and details. Matilda brought me supper on a tray, although I do not even know if I realized what I was actually eating, food in one hand while my other hand continued to type, struggling to keep up with the thoughts flowing through my mind.

I knew I had something good.

FORTY

Cora

Monday, December 3, 1888

When I returned to the flat later that afternoon, Everett was already back home, his eyes wide with worry and his jaw clenched in frustration.

"Where were you? You could have left a note!"

I smiled sweetly at him. "Hush now, my love."

"Don't mock me, woman. I was about to go out looking for you." He shook his head. "I was scared someone had broken in and kidnapped you or—"

"You are right, I should have left a note. My most sincere apologies." I calmly took off my coat and gloves.

As I put my things away, I noticed a bloody cloth in the waste bin. I looked back at Everett. He had a yellow bruise around his eye and a spot of dried blood around one nostril.

"My god, what happened?" I rushed up to him, placing a gentle hand on his chest.

"It's nothing."

"It is most certainly not nothing," I snapped. "Tell me."

"I was at Mr. Harris's pub, seeing if they needed an extra hand or knew of any jobs, and one of your early customers recognized me." He frowned. "It seems like there are a few folks who are still feeling a bit upset by our harmless little act."

"They attacked you?"

"Really, I'm fine. A bobby happened by and hauled the bastard off." His tight mouth curved into a small smile. "I'm just happy you're safe."

He wrapped his arms around me, kissed my forehead, and then rested his cheek against the same spot.

"I found your play about me," I said.

His body immediately tensed against mine. He paused. "Oh?"

"Indeed."

He swallowed audibly. "Are you angry with me?"

"I was," I admitted, pulling away slightly so I could look up at him. "But then I read it."

He winced. "What did you think of it?"

"I found it very witty and amusing," I said plainly. "As did Mr. Lindsey."

Everett's arms dropped and he moved away from me slightly. "What?"

"He suggested a few tweaks here and there but they were quite minor, really—"

"You pitched *my* play to Tom Lindsey without speaking to me about it first?"

"You wrote about me without speaking to me about it first," I snapped. "That play is as much mine as it is yours so I believe we are now even."

He laughed sarcastically. "Oh, certainly. Exactly how many pages of it did you write?"

"The story is about *me*. The main character has *my* name—"

"Wait," Everett said, his face relaxing. "Tweaks?"

I fetched my reticule and pulled out a folded contract, handing it to him. "Sign this and *The Rise and Fall of Lady Selene* will be produced in the spring."

He stared at me, unblinking. "Are you serious?"

I nodded slowly. Everett snatched the contract from my hand, his eyes flying over the words.

"Mr. Lindsey even agreed to my … conditions," I added.

He did not look up from the contract and I could tell he was barely listening. "Oh?"

I took a second paper from my reticule. "I have a contract as well." I unfolded it and held it up for him to see, my signature already scrawled at the bottom next to Mr. Lindsey's.

Reluctant to take his eyes off his own contract, he finally took a glance at mine. "What is this?"

"I will be playing the lead in the production." I squared my shoulders and let my lips curl into a coy grin. "You always wanted to be a playwright and I have always wanted to be an actress and now—"

I squealed as Everett grabbed me about the waist and swung me around, sending both contracts fluttering to the floor. He kissed me so hard that my lips were actually a bit sore after. My heart began to race as he kissed my neck and nibbled at my earlobe, pulling me against him. I found myself pawing at the various fastenings of his clothes for the hundredth time. Only the most necessary of garments were removed, tossed aside in haste. The bed, apparently, seemed too far away for the passion rising up between us and suddenly my back was up against a nearby wall, my legs hooked around his waist.

After we collapsed onto the floor, my chest heaving against his, I nuzzled my nose into his neck, deeply inhaling the scent of him. I laid a gentle kiss on his cheek, letting my moist lips drag across the rough stubble on his jawline and back up to his ear.

Directly into his ear, I whispered, "Will you marry me?"

Dear Simon and Amelia,

Joseph and I are pleased to announce the birth of a healthy and happy baby boy. He will be christened Joseph Daniel Baxter (after Joseph and after my father) but called 'Joe.' He looks so much like his father but also reminded me of you too, Simon.

The christening is this Sunday. I hope both of you will be able to attend, although you are both welcome to come and meet him before then if you can.

Simon, I know your relationship with your father has always been complicated. It was not my intention to interfere but when he told me about the argument and the disinheritance, I knew I had to speak up. I told him of my uncle in Canada who is like you and lives a happy and quiet life and would not hurt a fly. I know you would not either. I may have become emotional because I just found it so unfair of him to treat you in such a way. Of course, I may have been angry with him previous to that argument because he almost missed the birth of our son.

The doctor <u>had</u> mentioned that I should avoid upsetting situations, but it was soon after that my labor pains began. Not to worry, everything is fine with Little Joe. Joseph was so relieved that the baby was a healthy boy that he has reversed his decision about disinheriting you. You may also still remain in your house and keep your household as is.

Amelia, I believe Joseph is going to speak with your father about the divorce matter. I reminded him that a divorce would cause any existing gossip concerning Simon to get worse, not better, so he might want to encourage his friend to reverse his decision. Hopefully this will resolve matters.

I just want us to be a happy family, especially since Joseph must away back to Canada soon after the christening. The two of you mean so much to me. It would break my heart if anything happened to you.

Take care and I hope to see you both very soon.

Beth

FORTY-ONE

Saturday, May 4, 1889

Cora

Maggie is trying to kill me.

I gripped the edge of the vanity as she yanked and pulled on the corset laces, tighter than what was necessary, I was sure, as I took shallow breaths.

Everett, seated on a bench nearby, gave a sideways frown at my reflection in the mirror before raising a concerned eyebrow at Maggie. "You do realize she'll have to be able to breathe up there, right?"

She gave another yank at this remark and muttered under her breath.

"I don't remember the corset needing to be so tight during dress rehearsals," I added, placing my palm flat on my abdomen.

"Just because Mr. Lindsey sends you congratulatory chocolates before opening night, that doesn't mean you have to eat them all," Maggie said, backing away from me to admire her handiwork. "It'll have to do."

I glared at her. "Hugo ate them, not me."

Hearing his name, our adopted son looked up from his chair in the corner, his enormous brown eyes bright and intelligent, a smear of chocolate still visible on his bottom lip. "Mama, you look pretty."

Everett beamed at him and then smiled wide at me. He picked Hugo up and the toddler squealed with delight. "She isn't even dressed yet, silly boy." My handsome husband looked at my reflection again. "He is right though."

Watching the two of them bond over the past couple of months had been an unexpected joy. Motherhood had not come as naturally to me as fatherhood had for Everett but I had expected as much. Hugo and I were slowly warming to one another, finding a shared love of stories, so I had begun reading Shakespeare to him in front of the fireplace at our new home in Fitzrovia while Everett worked on his next play at his desk nearby.

When Everett had described the young Indian orphan boy in the temporary care of Mrs. Harris, the look on his face had told me everything: we were about to become parents. I was hesitant about bringing a young child into our lives during such a busy, hectic time but Everett, Louise—yes, my old housekeeper was back under my employ—and I had made it work.

With Hugo cradled in one arm, Everett stepped closer and looked down at me. "Are you nervous?"

I considered for a moment. "No, I am not."

"Liar," he said with a smile. "We better go grab our seats." He gave me a quick peck on the cheek. "Do you have a kiss for Mama?"

Hugo nodded shyly and touched his tiny mouth to my chin, leaving a little smudge of chocolate on it. "A kiss for Mama," he repeated.

My heart swelled. I couldn't help it.

After they left my dressing room, I looked back at myself and took a long, deep breath—or at least as much as my corset would allow me.

While Maggie laced me into my first costume, a deep crimson gown with white lace trim, Fannie Dixon rushed into the dressing room and took a seat at the vanity next to mine.

"You are *late*," Maggie grumbled.

My talented co-star raised an eyebrow at Maggie and pursed her full lips. "I always arrive exactly when I intend to." She smiled smugly at me before leaning over and speaking softly.

"I saw Mr. Lindsey's wife in the lobby. The poor girl looks like she's carrying an elephant."

"I know," I said. "I had tea with them on Saturday and she seems miserable. She is not even due for another two months."

She laughed and scurried to change into her costume.

Fannie and I had become fast friends when rehearsals began, and we played off one another so effortlessly. I thought she might be jealous that I was the lead and she the antagonist of the play but if she was envious, she never expressed it.

I should invite Polly and Fannie over for tea sometime. Polly would be ecstatic.

Amelia

During intermission, Simon turned to me, a devilish grin spread across his face.

"I really like that Agatha Badger character," he said. "She seems quite ambitious."

I rolled my eyes. "The witchy nose is a bit much if you ask me."

He shook his head. "Oh, no, I think it really gives the part something special."

"Personally, I prefer the mischievous cackling." I tapped my fingertips together, conspiratorially.

Simon giggled, biting his lip, shoulders quivering.

"I am glad you are not taking that personally," he added.

"If I had not been tipped off that there was a horrible character based on me, I would have been a little put out." I surveyed the theater stalls, every seat taken. "People seem to be enjoying it though."

"Are you *sure* you need my help setting up downstairs? I would really rather not have to miss the last fifteen minutes of the play," Simon moaned.

"You already promised to help me. Besides, I know you have tickets for next week."

He smirked. "How do you know that?"

"Mr. Woodacre told me."

"Cheeky blighter," Simon mused. "He takes one trip to London in the span of three months and he spills all my secrets."

My book had only come out a week before. A few stores had actually sold out and the publisher was already planning a second run. I, of course, was fascinated by the subject matter but I had not expected readers of Britain to be so enthusiastic about spiritualism within the United Kingdom and America or its connection to the women's suffrage movement.

"I feel obligated to write her a thank-you note," I said, my eyes drifting over the packed theater, filled with Cora Pringle fans.

"I am sure the play helped book sales," Simon replied. "But your book likely helped ticket sales in return."

After all the articles I had written about Cora Pringle, that is how my name had become known within London literary circles—*because* of Cora Pringle.

Of course, the women's suffrage newspaper I had recently started with Esther could have had something to do with that as well.

"It's ironic. You despised what Mrs. Pringle did, but because of her you are a bestselling author," Simon mused. "It is all a bit funny, isn't it?"

"It is not like she wrote my book." I sighed. "But yes. I suppose it is uncanny."

I had spent a lot of time thinking about how my life had changed because of that woman, and how her life had changed because of my articles—that woman I had barely spoken to but had spent so much time writing and thinking about, and dissecting.

"Do you still loathe her?"

I paused for a long time. "No. No, I do not believe so. I loathe what she did, but I suppose I understand why she did it. She had few alternatives, really."

"Well, well, well," he said, bearing his teeth in a smile. "Are the two of you going to go hat shopping together now or what?"

"Oh, hush," I said, anxious to divert the conversation. "How are the upgrades coming along?"

"Very well indeed." Simon perked up. "Tenants should be able to start moving in around mid-June I should think."

I smiled, adoring the look on Simon's face at that moment. So satisfied and proud. Since he was now living part-time in Plymouth while Wright established himself as a politician there, Simon had purchased and renovated an abandoned building. And he had done this with a bank loan and not with assistance from his father.

"Are you going to be able to come and see it before the tenants move in?" he asked. "I am told most of them dislike when their landlord goes strolling through to show off his exquisite choices in wallpaper and fixtures while they are living there."

"I have no idea," I admitted. "My publisher is hoping to see the first few chapters of my next book by then." I laughed. "I am still researching the bloody thing."

"You always write about such cheerful topics," Simon said with a grin. "Police brutality and corruption in Britain? Yes, please."

Cora

As I stepped out at the end of the show for the final applause, my eyes first landed on my fellow actors, all smiling and clapping for me. I felt faint with overwhelm as I moved to the middle of the stage to curtsy before the appreciative audience.

I wiped tears from my eyes as the thunder of their applause took root in my heart, spreading like wild vines down my veins and through my blood. I blew them a kiss and swore to remember that feeling for the rest of my life.

I tried to spot Everett up in the private box with Mr. Lindsey, but a wall of tears blurred my vision. Before I knew it, Fannie was pulling me backstage and the curtain dropped, jolting me back into the real world.

The audience had laughed in all the right places. I had made a real connection with them. It felt more meaningful and more real than anything I had done or felt while pretending to talk to ghosts. It was so different but it all felt so wonderful.

In a rushed blur of activity, Maggie stripped me down as I struggled to remove my gaudy stage makeup.

"Mr. Lindsey needs me down in the lobby in fifteen minutes," I blurted over to Maggie as she disappeared with my costume. "Can you help me—"

Fannie, like the angel she was, appeared with my clothes. "Here you go, love."

I smiled widely at her, feeling the prick of tears once again at the corners of my eyes. "Thank you."

"What is happening in the lobby?"

"Some promotional thing," I waved a hand. "Perhaps a photo for the newspaper or something."

"You and Everett are going to Mr. Lindsey's party tonight, right? You said you were coming," Fannie said while fiddling with the laces in the back of my dress.

"Oh, we are definitely going to that party," I said, grinning at her reflection in the vanity mirror.

A few minutes later, Everett found me backstage and ferried me from the dressing room to the elegant lobby.

"Louise picked Hugo up at intermission," he said, his hand on my back as we scurried through the winding passageways of the Princess Royal Theatre.

"Oh," I said. "I did not get to say goodnight—"

My disappointment immediately evaporated as I laid eyes on the crowd in the theater lobby, my ears ringing as the volume doubled when I made my grand entrance.

I lifted my hand high into the air and waved at everyone, smiling wide.

I knew these new silk gloves were worth every penny. I told Everett they were a worthwhile investment.

The air thinned as twenty people all asked for my autograph at once. A pen made it into my hand from somewhere and I quickly scrawled my name on whatever was offered to me—ticket stubs, programs, and paper scraps. Everett helped me navigate through the crowd, apologizing for stealing me away, so we could reach Mr. Lindsey on a raised platform on the far end of the room.

I did not see who was at his side until I was right in front of her. My eyes widened and my hands went numb.

Amelia Baxter, that horrible witch, was seated at a wide table, signing damn copies of her stupid book at *my* debut. On *my* night. She was just *sitting* there, smiling at readers and chatting pleasantly to *my* fans.

I wanted to scream. My mind conjured the image of me lunging across the table, pulling her hair, breaking her glasses and then stabbing her with the shards of glass. Then I would hit her with her own book to complete my violent and worthwhile feat.

For the second time that evening, I put on one hell of a performance.

"Good evening, Mrs. Baxter," I said coolly. "I did not know you were doing book promotion here tonight." I paused. "Tonight, of all nights."

Mrs. Baxter winced. "My publisher only told me about coming here to sign books yesterday. I just go where they tell me to go."

While all the women around her wore their most fashionable at the theater, that horrid little shrew seemed content to show up to the Princess Royal Theatre in a plain, dark gray dress, not a frill or flounce in sight.

What could she possibly be trying to prove by wearing such a dull thing?

A handsome and well-dressed young man popped out of nowhere. "Simon Baxter," he said, his words coming out in quick spurts. "Her husband. Big fan. Loved the play. Adore you."

"Lovely to meet you, Mr. Baxter." I raised my hand and he kissed the top of my gloved hand. "Tell me, what do *you* think of your wife's little book?"

Mr. Lindsey turned to watch this exchange.

Mrs. Baxter threw a warning glance at Mr. Baxter. Subtlety was not her strong suit.

After a moment of hesitation, he declared, "I think the writing is excellent."

Mr. Lindsey laughed aloud. Even this crowd was no match for his deep, booming voice. A newspaper photographer appeared at his side and Mr. Lindsey began directing me with his hands, waving the spouses and fans away from the table.

"Ladies, this fellow is from *The Telegraph*. Here, let's get these two ladies standing together. Big smiles now." He grabbed one of the books from the table and shoved it at me to hold as a prop and pulled a ticket stub from his pocket, offering it to Mrs. Baxter as she stood, looking as uncertain as I felt.

At least I had the confidence and good sense to hide my nervousness.

"Promotional gold!" Putting his hand on Mrs. Baxter's shoulder blade, he led her around the table so she and I were back to back, me holding her book and she holding a ticket to my play.

We both smiled as the flashbulb blinded us.

"I have no idea what is happening. Do you?" I asked quietly through gritted teeth, still smiling at the camera and the fans.

"Mr. Lindsey was a major investor in the publishing of my book," she whispered back. "I just found out this evening when I came down here to sign books."

I paused, the truth hitting me like a brick. "He orchestrated the whole thing. He knew one would help the launch of the other."

"It would appear so."

After the photo op, we both gave a couple quotes for the news article and I ended up signing a few copies of Mrs. Baxter's book, adding my ornate, loopy signature beside her tight, narrow, flourish-free name.

It was a relief to finally get into a hansom cab and away from the crowd and away from the woman who had tormented me for months.

"Just so you know," Everett said, as if reading my thoughts, "Mr. Lindsey invited Mrs. Baxter to his party."

My shoulders dropped, and I slumped back against the seat a little. "Well. Perhaps we should just go home then." I pounded on the roof. "Driver—"

"Ignore her, drive on," he yelled, grabbing my hand.

I frowned at him and pulled my wrist away. "Why would I want to be in the same room as that woman?"

"I had a chance to speak with her earlier. She seemed perfectly friendly. Besides," he said, raising his eyebrow in that knowing way of his, "without her, there might not be a play."

"And without me, she would not be a famous authoress," I snapped.

Everett snickered. "I know you read half of her book yesterday, despite trying to hide it behind a magazine."

I tipped my nose up as a smile slipped onto my lips. "You saw nothing."

The truth was that I was thinking how much I would prefer to be at home just then, devouring the rest of the book by candlelight and having a quiet drink in front of the fireplace.

However, that was not to be. The hansom pulled up to Mr. Lindsey's home in Mayfair and Everett helped me step down.

"You will have a wonderful time," he said, smiling down at me. "It is your night, after all."

"Promise me one thing," I said as we reached the front door.

"Hmm? What's that?"

I grinned. "You and I should spend a few minutes alone together in the garden."

Everett's eyes sparkled at the suggestion.

Thank you so much for reading *The Spirited Mrs. Pringle.*

If you enjoyed this book, I would appreciate it if you could take a few minutes and leave a review on Amazon, Goodreads, Kobo, or Apple Books.

Reviews are the easiest way to show support for an author as they help other readers find the book.

If you would like to get notified when my next book is released, make sure to subscribe to my newsletter:
www.jilly.ca/subscribe

You can also follow me on social media:
facebook.com/JillianneHamilton
goodreads.com/JillianneHamilton
twitter.com/JillianneWrites
tiktok.com/@jilliannewrites

AUTHOR'S NOTE

The spiritualism movement began in 1848 when Maggie (age 14) and Kate Fox (age 11) pulled pranks on their family. By cracking their ankles, they fooled their parents—and, later, massive audiences—into believing the "rapping" sounds were communications from ghosts.

They soon became national celebrities and traveled extensively, giving séances and demonstrations of their messages with spirits. Maggie really did come clean about their act in 1888 but recanted her confession the following year. No matter, spiritualism had already taken hold, particularly in the United States.

Spiritualism crossed the Atlantic to become popular in Britain as well. Considering how obsessed the Victorians were with death and death-related traditions, it makes sense that they would take an interest in the movement. Sherlock Holmes author Arthur Conan Doyle and his wife were avid spiritualists. There is an interesting story about Queen Victoria seeking the services of a medium in order to speak to her beloved husband Albert but this is likely an urban myth.

Two other major events overlapped in the 19th century that helped the spiritualism movement become a success: the women's suffrage movement and the American Civil War.

Many women who made their living as spiritualists also supported women's voting rights. Victoria Woodhull, the first woman to run for president in the United States, was a spiritualist. Although obviously done for different reasons, women's suffrage rallies and spiritualism spectacles were both opportunities for women to speak publicly in front of large crowds and gain notoriety—for many women, this would have previously been unheard of.

As for the Civil War, thousands of young men were killed and bereaved relatives were desperate to speak to their lost sons, brothers, and husbands. Spiritualism provided that opportunity for communication and closure.

The buzz around spiritualism died down for a while but then spiked in popularity again directly after the First World War.

Thank you to Jennifer Quinlan and Colleen McKie for whipping this book into shape.

Thank you to Peter Rukavina for showing me his printing press. Although this book didn't end up including much about the publishing process, seeing the press did give me an understanding of the time and skill it would take to create a publication.

Thank you to my family for their support and my darling husband for his endless patience.